MEN'S LIBERATION

Jack Nichols organized and led groups promoting sex-role freedom as early as 1961, when he was twenty-three. A job as Assistant to the Washington Bureau Chief of the New York Post brought him his first contact with writing. Since then he has coauthored two previous books on topics of concern to males and has been editor, managing editor, and consulting editor of several magazines and newspapers. He speaks Persian and is happily unmarried except to his many friends.

MEN'S LIBERATION

A New Definition of Masculinity

by JACK NICHOLS

PENGUIN BOOKS

Penguin Books Inc, 72 Fifth Avenue,
New York, New York 10011, U.S.A.
Penguin Books Inc, 7110 Ambassador Road,
Baltimore, Maryland 21207, U.S.A.
Penguin Books Ltd, Harmondsworth,
Middlesex, England
Penguin Books Australia Ltd, Ringwood,
Victoria, Australia
Penguin Books Canada Limited, 41 Steelcase Road West,
Markham, Ontario, Canada L3R 1B4
Penguin Books (N.Z.) Ltd, 182–190 Wairau Road,
Auckland 10, New Zealand

First published 1975

Library of Congress Catalog Card Number: 74-21509

Printed in the United States of America

To Elijah Hadynn Clarke,
*who taught me that a man can learn to bend
like the willow*

ACKNOWLEDGMENTS

I am indebted to the following people for their encouragement and assistance and for the interest they have shown in the progress of this book.

I would like to thank my mother, Mary Finlayson Southwick, who discussed my ideas with me at length and who proofed the manuscript before it was sent to the publisher.

I am grateful to Edward Iwanicki, managing editor at Penguin Books, for his conscientiousness and for thoughtful editorial suggestions.

To Joseph Pleck and Nora Jones, let me express appreciation for the materials they provided about the growth of the fledgling men's liberation movement.

Finally, I am thankful for the forbearance and enthusiasm shown by those who were kind enough, while I was writing, to listen to portions of the manuscript: Laurent Nicastro, Steve Yates, Norman Rathweg, Larry Fain, and Randy Butterworth. The discussions I enjoyed with these people were invaluable.

J. N.
New York

INTRODUCTION

The shackled male can free himself only if he allows himself to be somewhat imaginative. Men lacking imagination cannot conceive of a life better than the one they know. When discomforts overwhelm them, they will realize they are suffering bondage, but most men born in cultural captivity walk their cells weighted by invisible chains.

"From what do we need to be liberated?" ask such men, assuming that talk about men's liberation is a media fad. Certainly dominant men are firmly in control, they think, failing to see that no one is minding society's store.

The perspectives criticized in these pages are not only those of the old-fashioned stereotypical male. Although stereotypes still swagger in our midst, masculinism has been refined by today's American male. His role as provider and his tendencies to dominance, competition, control, rational structuring, and toughness have assumed new dimensions. The modern male hopes to show that his own brand of clobber power is of a much higher order than that of cave men wielding their clubs.

He gives the impression of complexity and intellectual force. He reads and "proves" his knowledge by taking tests. He can construct rational arguments that are unique and potent. He tries to speak in a dominating tone of voice. He is not given to emotional displays, and he prides himself as realistic, having come to grips with the "tough facts" of existence.

At the same time, he is often at odds with members of the opposite sex. Women, once docile and undemanding, seem to be asking for the moon. Some are actually aggressive! Although he does not discuss the intimate aspects of such problems with other men, the modern male is not easily satisfied by conventional romantic commitments.

As it now stands, he is somewhat antidomestic. He

11

would like to travel. He would also like to be closer to his children, but he may wish that the responsibility for their "nourishment" did not keep him chained tightly to one location. He believes, though, that it is his duty—his primary function—to support his family. The laws of the state insist that he do so. Once married, he is usually cut off from old buddies, from friends of the opposite sex, and from passionate attachments to other men which might suggest that he is peculiar. In the midst of such alienation, he struggles with romantic jealousy, his own and that of his partners.

His salary buys less, but his pride begs him to say, "The woman in my life doesn't have to work, and I like it that way." What he really may mean is that although his harem has only one occupant at a time, he does not want her wandering about too freely without the veil that the home provides. He is not nearly as secure in his masculine role as he would have others believe, and he allows his mate's growing independence to threaten him emotionally.

The first four chapters of this book are the most complex. It is necessary to see how our culture teaches men to use their minds. These culturally induced modes of thinking affect all the aspects of living examined throughout the rest of the book. "As a man thinketh," we are told, "so is he"; although it seems more difficult for men to turn their critical faculties inward rather than toward externals, the first four chapters, by criticizing reliance on the intellect, demonstrate the influence that structured mental constructs have over daily matters. These chapters suggest that men incorporate the lengthy route they take over theoretical scaffolding into a shorter one: intuitive perception, which cultivates and utilizes feelings as primary instruments of perception.

The concerns of men have been tied to appearances of achievement. Since appearances are deceiving (men confuse symbols with reality), there is usually a painful schizophrenia shining between the way a man looks to others and his self-image. The conflict is most painful to men who try to appear confident but are not. The modern world abounds with such men. They use symbols and follow rites to give the illusion of being whatever masculinist values teach them is worthy. Their attempts at convincing others that these illusions are real cause havoc in present-day relationships.

I hope the following pages will open thoughtful men to the kind of self-examination that brings new insight into their roles, their leisure, their work, their emotions, their sexuality, and their relationships with children, friends, parents, and their own bodies. I hope too that these pages will suggest new values for political activity, optimism for relationships between the sexes, and visionary alternatives for future living patterns that each man can freely choose for himself.

Men's Liberation

Chapter 1 ❊ INTELLECT
The Blind Man's Bluff

*To notice is to select, to regard some bits of perception,
or some features of the world, as more noteworthy, more
significant, than others. To these we attend, and the rest
we ignore—for which reason conscious attention is at
the same time ignore-ance (i.e., ignorance) despite the fact
that it gives us a vividly clear picture of whatever we
choose to notice.*

—ALAN WATTS[1]

Alfred, Lord Tennyson, gave poetic expression to the fact
that men have long enjoyed a reputation for rationality,
whereas women have not, and that women are thought
to be emotional and intuitive, whereas men are not. "Man
with the head," he wrote, "and woman with the heart."
Not surprisingly, therefore, most men point to their heads
when asked to locate themselves imaginatively, and most
women point to their chests.[2]

Few members of either sex, however, care to think of
themselves as lacking the best qualities ascribed to the
other. No matter how rational he may be, a man likes to
think he also has a heart, and a woman is insulted if told
she cannot reason. And yet society conspires to create
individuals who do, in fact, fit Tennyson's malconforma-
tions. Members of each sex who regard themselves as
mentally complete may remain unaware of powerful cultural influences that shape consciousness so that deep divisions between the sexes and their perceptions do indeed
exist.

One of the purposes of this book is to examine the
disadvantages of sexual segregation. I use the term "segre-

17

gation" in quite a different manner than it is used to describe racial divisions. Men and women, after all, do drink from the same water fountains, live in the same neighborhoods, and sleep in the same beds. But forms of segregation, subtly enforced and difficult to perceive, proceed beneath the surface of male-female relationships. In spite of their proximity, men and women begin and end their lives excluding each other from some of their most fundamental activities and suffering fears and varieties of loneliness that both sexes take for granted.

Superficial differences between the sexes are emphasized too much in discussions of men and their roles. People seem content to chat about fashions and occupations. Should men wear dresses? Should they change diapers? Such queries strike a false note and rise from cramped views of the topic. To treat social roles as matters of mere manners, dress, and opinion is to be preoccupied with trivialities and to lose sight of the underlying sources of these roles. The sources are more difficult to see because they lie curled at the foot of unquestioned assumptions about our civilization. We assume, for example, that if men *are* rational, rationality is a good thing. Many women are skilled at it. Far Eastern cultures, we think, are adopting its ways. But is rationality as practiced in our society a good thing? Is a reputation for possessing it something that men or women or Easterners ought to desire? Is it of such great *value* that it deserves the mind's fullest devotion?

Because it involves using the intellect, rationality draws certain mysterious veils over itself, so that those intimidated by the intellect shrink from questioning rationality's value. To most people its value seems beyond question, because the intellect claims credit for the development of so many marvels. It is the pride of Western nations. Our academics point to the Greeks and most particularly to Aristotle and his disciples as founding fathers of mind-use.

This usage is said to have led to scientific clarity and to those systematic foundations on which our culture stands. Who then would be so arrogant as to question the value of rational thinking?

The products of rational thought are outpourings that are easily seen: technology, mathematical structuring, astronomical perceptions. But the outpourings of "the heart," that inscrutable region classified as woman's own, are hardly as ostentatious. One cannot point to a building or some other structure and say with the same materialistic assurance that it is a product of intuitive sensibilities. If intuition figures in the construction of a building, it is generally a first "flash," an inspiration that must give way to scientific structuring. Action based on the heart is seemingly modest. Its effects are not usually visible. Its province, as a rule, is human relations, and these are enhanced or mended without fanfare and by methods that bypass questions, diagrams, and explanations. There is no question that in our culture the ability to express feelings is not thought nearly as important as the ability to reason logically.

Masculine roles and praise for rational use of the intellect are based on values that are at the bottom of our culture's ways of perceiving. When these roles are cumbersome, it is difficult for men to discern that they are so because rigid thought patterns cast shadows across their minds. The "adjusted" male does not appreciate his predicament. It is so ingrained in the way he uses his everyday mind that he takes it for granted. The tensions that account for the fact that men comprise by far the greater number of successful suicides are simply seen as life's tough facts, which men in particular must be tough enough to "handle" or must succumb to in the process. Loss or defeat are equated with abject failure, a condition that robs a man of status in his own eyes. At the time of the great 1929 crash many Wall Street tycoons jumped from skyscrapers, equating their loss of status with utter subjugation.

From the standpoint of an objective outsider a suicide committed because of some monetary overthrow has its origin in the dead man's erroneous presumptions about his daily requirements. Such presumptions are difficult to change because they are derived from customary ways of thinking about thinking. Few men go so far as to question thought methods themselves. They inherit those bestowed upon them by their environment. To use the mind to turn inward on itself is a task for "professionals." "Sounds like a job for a shrink," said a clergyman to me when I suggested that he assist his congregation in this kind of inner exploration. As is true of most men, he was all too ready to classify what he must or must not do on the basis of prescribed functions alone: a sign of poverty of imagination.

Questioning the supremacy of the intellect is not to disparage it altogether. It has its rightful uses, and these are many. If, however, we are to strike down antiquated roles and barriers to improved human alliances, one of our first steps must be to make intellect stand trial under its own auspices. When this happens, it will be taken down a peg and will release us from considering its methods as the only ones that are truly vital to our perceptions. This holds true not only for men but also for women.

Only recently have large numbers of women attended institutions of higher learning. Woman's capability en masse to "think like a man" (which is to say to order thoughts according to the traditions of Western rationalism) is a new development. Since females once occupied lower educational rungs, it did not occur to men to desire for themselves mental characteristics associated with beings who had second-rate credentials.

Woman protested the status quo after she got what education provided: tools for presenting her case logically so that she could communicate revulsion at her own repression, a revulsion that many women have long *felt*.[3] The liberation of man, which will include new modes of mental awareness once thought "womanly," could occur only after woman had first learned to utilize an ability reputed to belong only to males. This ability, although quite necessary, now needs curbing, since it is dangerous to rely upon the intellect alone. If the curtailment of a rational modus operandi leaves men with a feeling of deficiency, they, as men and ostensibly as the admirers of women, can discover and adopt new qualities in the so-called feminine psyche. The outcome, not surprisingly, may be a mind with wider capabilities and deeper dimensions.

The mind is the measure of the man. Whether or not this axiom is true, it was taught me at my mother's knee, and hence it seems to me a commendable starting place for an examination of men.

How is the mind measured? The conscious. The un-conscious. Emotion. Intellect. Intuition. Memory. Sensory perception. Where to begin? With a diagram of the brain? Will it help if we know precisely where mental occurences occur? Or is it enough to know that they do occur? And even if we admit the existence of the mental divisions just mentioned, can we be sure that they really exist?

An approach to regions so intangible as those of the mind through physiological mapping seems the long way. Each of us knows by direct experience that major mental characteristics exist, and it is a distraction, at best, to try to diagram them.

Nor am I anxious to engage in argument about various mental faculties and subdivisions. If Bertrand Russell wished to downgrade intuitional perception in favor of what he was pleased to call rational perception, based primarily on logic and the intellect, I am too fond of that now-departed philosopher to stick pins in his cadaver.

Russell is this century's supreme wielder of a faith in rationality that enabled him to jump over most of the idiocies of the age. Nevertheless, aspects of that same faith are choking present-day intellectuals who have not yet attained Russell's stature. It is here, into the classrooms of the adamant academics, the teachers of men and women who wear "faith in reason" buttons pinned to their brains' lapels, that I carry my own notions. They may end by regarding me as not only weak and fuzzy but also at a considerable distance from those rocks to which they have tethered their perspectives. They may, in fact, fear that I am floating. I would accept such an observation as a compliment.

The discomfort these teachers experience at my presence in their classrooms is occasioned by my criticism of their unimaginative praise for rationality and by the fact that I suggest that here, under the banner of Western civilization, rationality has given birth to monsters and has gotten all out of hand. The people singing its praises may believe they are rescuing poor victims of retarded religious notions and providing them with a firm substitute; but they fail to see, as most proponents of new faiths do, that the scepter each of them carries is weighty in its own way and makes of itself a new kind of burden.

We are experiencing today the crumbling of religious systems. This fact has had enormous effects on our approach to life-consciousness. Intellectuals have been doing some extraordinary scrambling. Bertrand Russell's essay *A Free Man's Worship* offers a stark rationalist image with which to identify: that of humankind on a raft, sailing nowhere in particular, surrounded by giant waves threatening to capsize the raft at any moment. If we are no longer facing dangers known to our forebears in jungles and on prairies and if we are no longer pressed by the need to be physically tough, we are now being offered a new kind of toughness, a mental toughness, by those who believe that we may grow weak without our religious crutches. Adrift in a "hostile" universe without God or Santa, humankind is told that it can still wax strong, that its intellect is powerful, and that if necessary, it must shake its clenched fist in defiance at Nature, a capricious old mother who cares nothing for human designs. Omnipotent matter rolls on its relentless course, Russell tells us, and if we are shielded, at least for the present, his perspective pulls the rug from under projections of future safety and gives us, in our plush offices and suburban homes, an abstract reason to feel heroic, to experience bravado, and to be above all things realistic.

Realism, which is usually interpreted as a kind of tough cynicism or pessimism, is seen as the antithesis of the naïve faith of our grandparents. Realism tells us not only that religious hopes were hollow but also that our socially induced confidence in progress promised by Western civilization's continuous upswing is a matter for serious doubt. Now we acknowledge that from miraculous pinnacles men may flip backward to barbarism or even to extinction.

Hence the academic community calls on us to bite our lips. We must not cry. From stern rationalists come demands for the suppression of emotion, which may cloud the entrance of the new god: reason. We men try to get with it by stifling our feelings, explaining to ourselves that they are unreliable as guides. Our forefathers based too much faith on intuitive insights, and just look at the absurd beliefs they thought were facts! Wasn't it reason that smashed their delusions? Then, our academic shamans say, it must be reason alone that will light our way to safety. Thus we see that the destruction of faith has given birth to a new credulity in intellectuality-rationalism. And rationalism, we know, claims a foremost seat in the pantheon of the masculinist temple.

We have no right to feel smug because we are abandoning certain superstitions. The transition between a superstitious past and a present that is installing more superstitions may go on indefinitely. It is likely that the rationalism surrounding technological marvels and credited with unlocking the powers of the atom will continue to claim—in the guise of scientific thought—more than its share of converts. The problem, however, is that an emphasis on only one function of the mind, the intellect, creates imbalances.

Elevating the intellect above other mental faculties creates baseless pride. A man, armed with his "logic," proceeds to act on his environment, acting "reasonably" without regard for feelings while scoffing at quiet consultations of the intuition, condemning both intuition and feeling as sentimental drivel associated with deranged mystics and women. It seldom occurs to him that he may actually be flipped into a corner far from the center of what is really going on. Watch him as he fingers his "facts" with the glee that a child fingers marbles; watch him shoot down every impulse or perspective that fails to fit into his "logical" hypothesis. If we ask such a man to regard the constructs of his intellect as a singular aspect of reality and to admit the intellect as a tool rather than as the sole arbiter of truth, it is tantamount to requesting that he give up his whole mind altogether. The reason for this is that he has confused, as have so many "intellectuals," his rational processes with the sum total of his mind. The intellect is seen as the mind itself. There is thought to be a need to cleanse it of unrelated phenomena that might sway it from its logical course. Emotions, feelings, and intuitions must go. Thus men have long held "womanly" thinking in contempt, regarding it as of a lower order, lacking clarity and precision. Women in turn have maintained a wise skepticism about the clarity of "manly" thought. Jungian analyst Florida Scott-Maxwell said: "Thought sometimes has the inevitable fault of ignoring feeling, and when this happens, feeling says truly that thought is incomplete and almost unreal."[4]

And yet there have always been men of genius whose minds reflected perceptual abilities associated with women. Plato wrote enthusiastically of such mentalities, and Samuel Taylor Coleridge insisted that "every truly great mind has been androgynous," possessing the strengths associated with both sexes.

Mind characteristics that have thus far been divided between genders by social conditioning now await their diffusion between both sexes. Those who resist intersexual integration of mental tendencies say that they are rooted in nature's constitution by biological fiat. They warn us that tampering thus with sexual divisions invites disaster. They miss seeing that interpretations of the mind based on biology are simplistic and that the mind's capabilities can hardly be halved between the sexes with such assurance. That they should assume themselves capable of seeing exactly what nature has intended and how its social arrangements among men and women must be protected from artificial interference is amusing. They forget that it would take revelatory powers from on high to tell each person that he or she must do precisely what nature intended. Technology itself would wither if we always pursued such reasoning to its conclusion. We would walk instead of using artificial conveyances and would sit on the ground instead of on rugs and chairs. The Roman Catholic Church has been a leader as nature's interpreter, and who will deny that its views on sexual matters are open to serious doubt?

The belief that men are the inheritors of one set of tendencies and women of another has led to a deplorable kind of separatism. Its effect has been to limit the percep-

tions of both sexes, making men narrow in their judgments
and women ineffectual. Luckily, like racial segregation,
divisions between the sexes are coming to an end. Explor-
ing the nature of limitations in consciousness may help
us see how they have damaged man's relations with himself, with other men, with his environment, and with
women.

That the mind is open to expansive new vistas should
hardly surprise us, since only an infinitesimal portion of
the human brain is used as a person grows. During the
past few centuries humanity has become more conscious
of its outer environment, witnessing discoveries of galaxies
and far-flung solar systems. The exploration of our inner
spheres has proceeded sluggishly. Is it more difficult to
turn the focus of the perceiving instrument (the mind)
upon itself than to turn it toward the stars? Just as old-
fashioned constructs of the universe which were once
commonplace needed to be abandoned, so now do outdated concepts of the mind. There are many that are keeping men in special bondage. A certain kind of rational
thinking does this.

The end product of rationality and logic is a prize that
every man would believe is his: objectivity. Much of
Western philosophy has been a history of man's attempts
to claim this prize while at the same time disparaging its
opposite, subjectivity. The "objective" man sees existence,
he thinks, as it really is. Devotees of subjective philosophies
admit that what they see is not necessarily factual but
may be mere reflections of personal feeling and perspective. The difference between the two is the difference
between men who are often willing to admit that they are
certain and those who are often willing to admit that they
are not.

The notion that men are rational has proved true most
clearly in their relations with inanimate objects. In the

putting together of materials, tools, diagrams, calculations, and other structures, men have excelled through logic. In the animate kingdom, however, rationality as practiced has not yet proved itself of value to truly equitable arrangements. Ecological and political problems bear frightening witness to this fact.

"Possibly the greatest of all the insidious frauds of civilization," wrote Joe Adamson in his celebration of the lives of the Marx brothers, "is this idea that the mind is a logical organ. In any tight situation, logic can be counted on to be consulted last."[5]

Men are deluded into thinking themselves rational under the most extraordinarily contradictory situations. The existence of wars and the behavior of whole populations as they are waged amply mock rationalistic pretensions. A survey of the political rhetoric of our leaders during the recent ten-year war in Southeast Asia is instructive. No little energy was expended in "proving" the necessity of killing hundreds of thousands of fellow mortals. Today virtually no one can say with reasonable certainty what that sorry conflict was about, and yet civilized statesmen who reveled in their rationality called university students traitors for daring to question their motives.

Following are a few characteristics usually found in those men who evince misplaced pride in the strength of their intellectual-rational formulizations:

• *A tendency to confuse thoughts produced by the intellect with realities, something that they are not.* Eastern philosophers have said that "the Mind is the great slayer of the Real."[6] This is to say that the intellect, assuming itself to be all-comprehending, misses what might be called wider realities. The Eastern solution to this problem lies in a practice that many Westerners are adopting today: meditation. One purpose of meditation is to still the thought-producing instrument—to quiet the rush of mere speculations that stream from our intellect, often producing acute anxieties, and to realize that thoughts are only speculations.

• *An over-reliance on words or symbols as vehicles of communication.* What physics has taught twentieth-century men about their inability to grasp what Omar Khayyám called this "scheme of things entire"—that is, to have a clear picture of the material world—was seen intuitively by the Chinese sage Lao-tzu six hundred years before the birth of Christ. "Existence," said Lao-tzu, "is beyond the power of words to define. Terms may be used, but none of them absolute."

A man who relies too heavily on words is apt to be aware of only the most superficial qualities of the phenomena he observes. Take the word "dog." To some men, particularly those who have had direct and extended experiences with dogs, the word bristles with meanings. To a man who has never had such experiences, "dog" evokes little in the way of associations. And yet for the latter man, words and reality may be so inextricably bound that in some strange way they are almost equivalent. He assumes that when he hears the word "dog," he knows what the word communicates, having seen a photograph of the animal or having come in contact with it on occasion in the homes of friends. Dogs, on the other hand, are often credited with a kind of dog intuition when it comes to spotting those who lack feelings for them as sensate, animate beings.

Over-reliance on words is part of an unconscious trick played by the intellect, and it leads to abstractions. It is primarily responsible for the inability of so many men to come to grips with the realities of suffering in the world. Thus although a "rational" man might feel somewhat distraught at the news that a local school bus has crashed, killing twenty-odd youngsters from his neighborhood, the deaths of two thousand napalmed Indochinese children do not move him. Why? Because he has accepted what he believes are the "realities" of mathematical divisions of distance, discarding John Donne's dictum that "every man's death diminishes" us and that the "bell tolls for thee." The reason for this may be that he has permitted symbols (in this case numbers) to convey to him the intensity level of his own feelings. If a map says "far away," even though such a designation is meaningless in today's rapid-transit world, he will not bother himself about occurrences in that "zone." Even more likely, however, is the possibility that the word "children," particularly if he has never been close to children, will leave him lacking in empathy for the disaster either on the home front or in distant lands. Those killed will simply be "children."

This lack of empathy, rising from the translation of experience into symbols (into inanimate, meaningless terminology), lies near the very base of the complaint that men lack feeling. That American men deal well with inanimate objects as opposed to living creatures is due in large part to the reliance placed by our culture on words as things in themselves. If men are to regain their natural sympathies, symbol worship must go.

• *Ignoring occurrences that do not seem to fit into systematized thinking.* A man who relies too heavily on formulations is apt to be hypnotized by the elaborate brilliance of a thought structure itself.

Men who follow causes, whether religious or political, that are bolstered by ornate intellectual frameworks are affected by this quirk. Such men are easily regimented, and once they have seen "reason" for a course of action, are likely to act not on their own impulses but on a course that stems from that "reason."

High regard for systemization causes many men to bypass feelings and to express themselves only along particular lines, those that indicate their acceptance of certain well-established principles as governing their behavior. When questions about male behavior patterns arise, it is wise to keep this fact in mind.

Cerebral mutations of this sort are partly responsible for the longtime preoccupation of men with status within their systems. Systemization requires classification, and the first response of such a mind is to classify others according to how they stand in relation to its own constructs. Not only may those others (if they do not fit into prescribed patterns) appear useless to him, but also more often he believes that they pose threats to his carefully structured system, and so he regards them as dangerous.

Systemization is an almost natural product of rationality as practiced in our society. It fails to see that existence cannot be systematized any more than it can be pictured or described. To meet experience with coordinated interpretations, to shake hands with a stranger while classifying him, is to rob not only the stranger of a chance to be seen and appreciated but also to rob oneself of the chance to truly see and appreciate.

Rationalistic classification is a protracted means of getting to know people and obstructs direct contact between them. It requires lengthy questioning about position and background. It is an "intellectual" way of getting to know a person through a bit-by-bit piecing together of his caste.

• *The neglect of the senses as instruments of perception.* Ludwig Wittgenstein, a military hero who was also a philosopher, tried to convince us that we can never really know something we cannot describe. Other philosophers have insisted that we will not even see an object unless we have first named it.

In response I say that it is quite impossible for me

to describe the faces of those I love. Try as I might, no words could encompass the range of my feelings as I look at them. Certainly there are odors, colors in nature, forms and contours, that we encounter regularly and know immediately but for which we have no descriptive words or phrases.

Wittgenstein's hypothesis would deny the reality of experience not based on verbal processes. Acted upon, it leads to a drawback in Western culture: the inability on the part of many men to respond to what they see with any degree of fervor unless it can first be labeled. Hence such a man wanders through an art gallery deprived of his senses and noticing not the artists' dynamic visions but their names and the prices asked for their paintings. His experience of nature would be equally impoverished. Looking at unnamed existences in the forest, he would bypass them as unworthy of attention. His imagination would not reach out to encompass shapes for which he had no name. In his relationships with people, he would be stripped of a wider awareness because he refused to open the searchlight of his curiosity to possibilities his vocabulary had not yet encompassed.

This tendency has extraordinarily negative consequences for the average male's psychic responses. These negative consequences affect his sexuality itself. Classification is one of the prime instruments men use to maintain control. In another chapter I will examine the effect of this penchant upon sex.

• *An overemphasis on rationality which restricts other sensitivities.* Rationality can delude a man into thinking he knows precisely what is going on and how it can be controlled by the application of specific formulas.

While this approach may work in certain limited environments, it makes for disaster in human relations. Insistence on control meets head-on with multifaceted levels of experience and knowledge. The resulting spectacle finds men applying narrow plans devised by the intellect to situations requiring wider sensitivities.

Economist Kenneth E. Boulding accuses the men in his field of having become so preoccupied with their numerical models that they have severed all ties with the decisive factor: human conduct. Their abstractions, which fail to take this factor into account, have left them twiddling with high-sounding theories and a false sense of security. Boulding doubts that under such circumstances today's economists can truly predict a downturn in time to stop even a major depression.

• *An intellectual approach that often mistakes a culture's most bizarre rationalizations for truth.* "Men in general seem to employ their reason to justify prejudices which they have imbibed, they cannot trace how, rather than root them out." This observation was made in 1792 by Mary Wollstonecraft. To show that it is accurate we have only to consider the more recent histories of the psychological "sciences." Both psychologists and psychiatrists have long supported the status quo. Sigmund Freud himself was a product of Victorian times, and the prejudices of his era are imbedded in his work. It is no small matter to complain that psychology and psychiatry have worked to adjust men and women to the societies in which they live rather than to question the sanity of the mores prevalent in those societies, neglecting Friedrich Nietzsche's observation: "Insanity in individuals is something rare, but in groups, parties, nations, and epochs, it is the rule."

• *Rationalistic tendencies, including classification and systemization, that prevent even utilitarian perceptions.* Aristotle's lifelong occupation involved naming and classifying whatever he observed in his environment; those who have followed him in this pursuit have usually restricted themselves without knowing it.

To classify a bottle, for example, as a receptacle into which one pours liquids may result in failure to use the bottle for other purposes. And yet children who have not yet fallen into the trap of classifying things only by their function might be likely to use a bottle for secret rites. It could serve as a musical instrument, perhaps, or as a prism. It could be spoken into or, like a seashell, listened to. Classification that is removed from direct experience can serve as a blinder. The classifier may find himself facing in only one direction.

• *Reliance on rational debate as a means of settling matters.* An old saw reminds us that a man who has no retort and has been silenced by a given argument is of the same opinion still, yet too often we have heard "intellectuals" express their pride at having silenced an opponent. "When I raised that particular point," they say, grinning almost perversely, "he had no response."

Eastern philosophers remind us, however, that winning is at best quite temporary and is certainly no basis for conceit. Nor does the winner carry with him the whole truth and nothing but. Those who win debates, taking the outcome as proof of their positions, suffer self-deception fluttering on the edge of vanity. At best a debate may produce clarification, but the spectacle of adults measuring truth by a stopwatch is ludicrous in more ways than one. This application of the intellect encourages a demanding mentality with very little respect for the unique parts played in life's dramas by the man who does not seem as smart.

Observers of Far Eastern custom tell us that it is not merely ceremony that makes judo experts bow low before one another prior to a match. In each altercation there must be a loser, and his status—unlike that of the loser in masculinist Westernized terms—is on a par with that of the winner. The man who wins knows that the fact that he has won is dependent on its opposite: the fact that someone else has lost. His victory, therefore, is not an independent achievement.

• *Systemization that imposes on human behavior plans that often do not fit.* Occurrences don't always happen in accordance with plans conceived earlier. The person who is wedded to specific plans might be called a 1-2-3 thinker. He hopes that the plans he intends to impose on his experience-to-be will coincide with what actually occurs. Often, however, experience comes about in sequences that do not match his planning. Instead, things may happen in a 3-2-1 order. The careful planner, unable to flow effortlessly with the actual experience, feels frustration but usually does not know why.

• *An overbearing intellectual consciousness that prevents men from letting go and forgetting themselves.* Skills are best performed when a man can turn off his thoughts and forget himself as the performer. Self-consciousness brings about a stiffness (as in dancing). What is this talk, after all, about letting go of the ego, assuring us that our sense of ourselves as being separate from our environment is an illusion? Freed from this illusion, it is said, we will act with great ease. At the bottom this view sees a human nature that is intrinsically good. It also trusts environment. It has been suggested that Jesus may have indicated something like this when he said, "Those who try to save their souls shall lose them," meaning, perhaps, that good works and beliefs which arise from the core of a man's being are unconsciously performed.

Chapter 2 ❄ FEELING
"I Feel, Therefore I Am!"

But men so often do not know what they feel, are afraid to face their feeling, and when a woman dares not be true to what she feels, thinking that for safety's sake she must mirror the man's feeling, then feeling as true assessment is unowned and absent. The resulting confusion is constant enough to make both men and women despair; for if we do not feel what happens to us, we have not lived our own experience. We have not been ourselves.

— FLORIDA SCOTT-MAXWELL[1]

This is a discussion about a great loss that many men are now experiencing. Tendencies lauded as "intellectual" have created noxious blocks in male approaches to living. The illusion of objectivity, with its insistence on calm appraisals and unruffled balance, prevents many men from daring to admit that they have been deeply affected. They believe that if they do, it will reflect badly on their ability to look cool and unbiased, qualities they think are needed in difficult circumstances. That a man feels he must be stone-faced not only creates a phony view of what he truly thinks but also works to subvert the whole basis of integrity itself. Exhibiting an invulnerable exterior, therefore, is a bow before rampant hypocrisy and also has dangerous implications for human relations on a world scale.

If hiding feelings affects those who are denied access to those feelings, such behavior affects the hider himself even more perversely. Not showing one's feelings often results in not being able to feel.

A psychologist once told me that in his practice he had

noticed that many men seemed to lack feelings altogether. On one occasion, he said, he asked a patient how he felt about certain aspects of his wife's infidelities.

"How does it make you feel?" he asked the man.

There was no response. A bland silence prevailed.

"How does it make you feel?" repeated the psychologist.

Still there was no response until the man dazedly admitted that he did not feel much of anything at all.

In today's confusing, rapidly changing cosmos, not being able to feel may very well serve as a protective device. There is evidence that men are suppressing their feelings to shield themselves from the multiplication of adjustments they must make. Ingrid Bengis, in her ruthlessly honest essay on man-hating, complains that it is precisely in this unwillingness to show feelings that men fail. "They would rather lie, would rather do anything, than admit to what they genuinely feel," she laments.[2]

Lurking beneath the problems men have with their feelings is a relentless antagonism that our culture has shown toward feelings in general. Feelings and their free expression have been disparaged because they contain truly revolutionary seeds. They jump over "civilized" structures. They are reactions to direct experiences minus intellectualized interpretations of those experiences. A man who openly expresses his true feelings often runs counter to accepted mores. If he is fond of a neighbor's wife, for example, and hugs her in public, he brings wrath upon himself. A person who expresses feelings too openly is usually judged as unstable or unreasonable.

Society's antagonism toward feelings is supported by rationales that hope to frighten us. "If people acted on their feelings," say antagonists, "then it's likely that they'd kill us without recourse to reason if they felt like it!" At first this argument seems plausible. But then it occurs to us that with all of humankind's emphasis on reason, human beings are still killing each other with astonishing regularity. Turning the argument around, we get: "If we rely on reason alone, then people may consider killing proper if they persuade themselves that they are rational."

Our astonishment at those rare misfits who kill for "kicks" indicates we are surprised at murder that seems "without reason." The greater number of killings, mass or mini, are usually backed by what the killers call good reasons.

If men were more insistent upon the nurturing of feeling, as opposed to exclusive fixation on intellect alone, it would seem that sensitivity to pain and suffering might have a better chance for development. Feeling is closely associated with intuition and empathy. If feelings were cultivated and men were permitted to respond directly and openly to experience instead of suppressing their responses, it would seem that better mental health would be likely to follow. There might, in fact, be some reduction in the number of males who are admitted to mental institutions. As it now stands, they far outnumber women. Men have emotions, after all, for a reason. To suppress emotion is to prevent it from fulfilling the functions it was meant to serve.

The deprivations men suffer because of their paralyzing inability to express what they feel distort and maim their personal relationships. Some may reject this fact as mere theorizing, but many more will realize that their own personal relationships are shallow and curt. The sense of frustration which hangs over their lives seems to have no explanation. C. Wright Mills suggested that "men in masses are gripped by personal troubles, but they are not aware of their true meaning and source." In every intimate relationship with parents, mates, and children the absence of feeling has a negative result.

Men who grow old maintaining "stiff upper lips," for

example, are frequently unable to communicate with others as well as do older women. Because such men do not express feelings, they do not elicit comparable sympathetic responses from others; an elderly man is seldom an object of neighborly concern to the same degree as is an elderly woman. Although the man may be equally infirm and in need of companionship, the fact that he is a man is often seen as reason enough to let him struggle on his own, wallowing, however helplessly, in his "independence." Suicide rates for the old are shockingly higher among men than among women. Reputable U.S. studies state that for every older woman who self-destructs, there are seven older men who do the same.

Suicide rates bring us to another facet of the feeling problem. The ability to express feelings makes one better able to adjust to life's hardships and shocks. If a person can "let it out," not only is his or her capacity for absorbing repeated shocks enhanced, but also his or her grasp on reality is keener. A man who restrains his feelings risks harboring unbalanced perspectives. It is likely that he will lack empathy for the suffering of his fellows, and his sense of humor and his ability to laugh can be stultified as well.

Two professors of sociology, Drs. Jack O. Balswick and Charles W. Peck, called attention to the American male's plight by pointing out that our culture glorifies his "inexpressiveness." They concluded that this is a "tragedy of American society." By using the term "inexpressive," Balswick and Peck allowed room for two different types of men: those who do have feelings and do not express them and those who do not have feelings and hence cannot express them or at best can only simulate them. The second type pretends to feelings primarily in those situations wherein he hopes to gain something. When his gain has taken place, he reverts to his nonfeeling self. The fictional hero associated with this type of behavior is

James Bond. As for the man who has feelings but cannot show them, screen star John Wayne serves as his archetype.[3]

High U.S. divorce rates give startling testimony to the fact that there are sources for marital strife that may be as yet unexamined. The sorry state of organized marriage is evidence of how the male's inability to express feelings has often prevented him from enjoying the satisfactions of companionship.

Feelings represent perhaps the most direct connection a man can have with himself. Without them a powerful bulwark of individualism is missing. If a man is not moved by feelings or is not in touch with his own, he is far less likely to break out of constricting frameworks. The impetus to do so is lacking.

In the early days of women's liberation (the second wave, 1970) a feminist group known as the San Francisco Redstockings saw fit to break away from the Left and from socialist doctrines, censuring the treatment of women under socialist regimes as well as under capitalist ones. They issued a statement showing they were searching for new ways of creating nonauthoritarian methods. They entitled their statement, "Our Politics Begin with Our Feelings." "Our first task," they wrote, "is to develop our capacity to be aware of our feelings and to pinpoint the events or actions to which they are valid responses."[4]

Men may find difficulty in becoming aware of their feelings, remaining somewhat isolated from them as perceptive instruments as long as they take pride in a socially programmed outgoingness, an active stance that gives them very little time to absorb, to take in, to be passive in relation to the environment. Such passivity requires that they learn to be touched rather than to touch, to be felt rather than to feel, to listen rather than to be heard—in short, to cooperate in making associations fun and adventurous for everybody. Only with such passivity can a man absorb his surroundings and see them with a degree of balance. If a man fears being passive, he will not absorb and hence will lack a fuller capacity for feeling. To have feeling one must absorb passively.

Feelings provide a mighty impetus to autonomous action. When we are spurred by them, life assumes new meanings, all of which are lacking if we interpret it only in intellectualized terms. The mechanistic view of life, encouraged by overreliance on the "scientific method," is spiritless. A man who has seen his environment exclusively through a mechanistic prism and who suddenly becomes aware of his feelings beholds his surroundings in startling ways: not as a series of objects and items but as marvelous and mysterious particulars, each, no matter how inanimate, with its own soul. Without feelings, a man can never experience the awe that is the key with which existence opens.

Chapter 3 ❄ INTUITION
A New Flash
on What's Happening

*Can your learned head take leaven
From the wisdom of your heart?*

—LAO-TZU

Once men are in touch with their feelings, they share with women access to a mind phenomenon known as intuition. This is not to say that men too do not experience intuitive flashes but simply that such flashes are harder to evoke in a consciousness that is closed to feeling. Men, in fact, have their own word for intuition. It is hardly as colorful and is therefore somewhat expressive of the poverty of the present-day male's intuitive capabilities. Men call intuitive flashes hunches.

That intuition has traditionally been known as a woman's province is shown by the phrase "a woman's intuition." Men's capacity to be intuitive, however, is demonstrated not only by great works of art but also by the most profound scientific observations. Albert Einstein wrote that his initial comprehension of the theory of relativity was a kinesthetic image: a certain sensation received through his body. Harvard physicist Gerald Holton tells us that it may very well have been Einstein's disinclination or incapacity to speak until the age of three that led him to mature with an extraordinary cognitive faculty that bypassed spoken categorizations and concepts. Thus Einstein broke beyond demarcations of space and time. He found it difficult to express what he felt and for a long time remained in a quandary about what to do, but as long as he could feel the image he perceived, he continued to search for a way to deliver it.

While it may seem inappropriate to some by reason of the charlatanry surrounding it and of the scientific opposition and ridicule which have attached to it, extrasensory perception is a field in which intuitive flashes predominate. That the study of ESP is still in its formative stages and that the ridicule heaped on it has come mostly from rationalistic thinkers should give us pause. It is quite probable that the scientific studies conducted at Duke University may end by telling us more about the capabilities of the mind than we once anticipated. Famed ESP expert George Kreskin speaks of visual perceptions that come to him impulsively and spontaneously. "The minute I start reasoning," he says, "I'm dead."

Intuition occurs when we perceive things directly. We do not simply believe something to be so, we know it. We perceive not the outward configuration but the inner dimension. Intuition may happen as a quick flash, or it may stay as an all-embracing vision we cannot shake off. Andrew Weil gives men a hint as to how to develop intuition when he says, "It develops spontaneously as we unlearn habitual ways of using the mind."[1]

Perhaps, as Weil says, there is no intellectual explanation for intuition, and the intellect may very well remain unable to grasp its reality. Nevertheless it helps if we seek to comprehend it at least to some degree. By doing so, we may be able to foster it among youngsters, something that Weil complains has not been done.

Dr. Helene Deutsch describes intuition by saying, "In each intuitive experience the other person's mental state is emotionally and unconsciously 'reexperienced,' that is, felt as one's own." In order to be able to intuit, says Dr. Deutsch, one must have "love for a spiritual affinity" with the person who is comprehended. The degree to which this affinity exists, she says, will depend on the richness of the intuitive person's own emotionality. Intuition is, therefore, the ability to understand one's own feelings and psychological associations and "by analogy, those of others."[2]

Many of the most profound seers in the world have given praise to the intuitive faculty. Until the advent in the West of thinkers like D. T. Suzuki, Christmas Humphreys, Thomas Merton, Henri Bergson, and Alan Watts, this faculty has been prominent only in the writings of a few great mystics like Meister Eckhart. These thinkers have charted their conviction that every man has within him a power to grasp the essential nature of things without depending on the circumlocutions of the intellect. Knowledge, they have told us, can be direct and immediate.

During the Middle Ages the intuitive faculty was a source of concern to the church fathers. It is said that this faculty in women led in many cases to their executions as witches. More recently philosophers like Bergson have made church authorities less jittery about it.

Mystics, ignoring verbalization and the printed word, turned rapturously inward rather than toward the church. Even the Scriptures were treated by these mystics as unnecessary to their vision. More than once they were branded heretics. In Islamic countries, where reliance on the Koran is deemed essential, mystic schools like the Sufis arose, promoting "God intoxicated" visions that came not from the holy verses of Muhammad's book but from "the heart."

The sages of India, having given birth to both Hinduism and Buddhism, have long understood and spoken about the "inner eye" or, as the Tibetans call it, the third eye. Buddhist scriptures like the Lankavatara Sutra describe the dawn of intuition in terms strikingly similar to those we have just considered in Dr. Deutsch's dissection of intuition itself: "While intuition does not give information that can be analyzed and discriminated," says the Sutra, "it gives that which is far superior, self-realization through identification."[3]

The examination of faculties like the intellect in these Far Eastern scriptures bears marks of mind-awareness that are startling for their psychological insight. In recent years Western psychoanalysts have turned to them for new knowledge. Noting the limitations of the intellect, the Lankavatara Sutra continues: "If things are to be realized in their true nature, the processes of mentation, which are based on particularized ideas, discrimination and judgements, must be transcended by an appeal to some higher faculty of cognition."[4]

Buddhist scholar Christmas Humphreys writes:

> It is one thing to realize, as stated by Porphyry, that "of that nature which is beyond intellect many things are asserted according to intellection, but it is contemplated by a cessation of intellectual energy better than with it"; it is quite another to accommodate one's mind to a state in which the god of reason is triumphantly dethroned. Here is a world as puzzling to the student as the change within him may be to his friends. Logic and reason are the architects which build the hovels or palaces of intellectual thought; the intuition rises above the world of forms . . . and the builders of forms are accordingly left behind. Good sense is no longer the sole criterion of a proposition's truth or falsity, for the higher mind may see that what is nonsense to the thought-bound scholar is in fact magnificently true.[5]

Chapter 4 ✳ MIND
Toward an Androgynous State

Once it is possible to say it is as important to take women's gifts and make them available to both men and women, in transmittable form, as it was to take men's gifts and make the civilization built upon them available to both men and women, we shall have enriched our society.

— Dr. Margaret Mead[1]

Janet Chusmir has written about a decision she made with her husband after they had been married only a few months. By using her intuitive faculty she left "the builders of forms" behind and rejected her husband's carefully structured solution. He had attacked their problem with a legal pad, drawing a line down the center of the sheet. At the top of the page he wrote, "Yes," on one side of the line, and on the other side he wrote, "No." Together the two of them began to list the pros and cons of the decision they were about to make. After adding them up, the yeses had it, and Ms. Chusmir's husband decided to proceed. She begged him not to, and he was quizzical. "Look at all the logical reasons we should," he insisted. But his wife told him of the "gut feeling" she had which told her they shouldn't.

Her decision, she writes, was made in the pre–women's liberation days. She didn't feel that it was "inadequate, female, or illogical" but only that she had "that awful gut feeling that was signalling" her to say no. Her husband conceded to her wishes. As it turned out, the intuitive decision was correct. Ms. Chusmir says that her husband never again pulled out a legal pad to assist them with decision-making. During the last twenty-five years of their marriage they have always sat informally, she says, and aired their views—touching on pros and cons and arriving at decisions that both can live with. Through the years, she recalls, she has often thought about her husband's legal pad and her own emotional, illogical approach. She indicates that she would not be altogether comfortable today with the same approach she took twenty-five years ago but writes: "Now I'd keep both sides of the line in mind."[2]

What Janet Chusmir's experience tells us is that her husband decided to respect her intuitive reactions. Thereafter he abandoned his strictly structured approach, sensing, perhaps, its inadequacy. Ms. Chusmir, on the other hand, learned the value of listing pros and cons, and together they arrived at a synthesis: thought and feeling, or logic and intuition.

The anti-intuitional joke about the woman who sat alone on an all-male jury and listened to her colleagues debate the evidence illustrates the dilemma of intuition. "Oh, why can't you silly men forget about the evidence," she said, "and think for yourselves?" While her proposition seems a bit absurd under the circumstances, her point deserves consideration. The evidence, by itself, is often not enough. Those who cling to evidence alone may miss certain purely human factors, those that other senses may give more readily; evidence alone may prove insufficient and highly limited. In real-life situations we often do not have time to accumulate piles of evidence, and it is then that a well-developed intuitive sense demonstrates its usefulness.

If we are to develop androgynous mind states wherein intellect and intuition are synthesized, it is wise to remember that although more women are adopting logical analysis as an addition to their talents, few men are developing intuitional capabilities. Intuition requires a certain degree of mental passivity, an openness to circumstances, without an imposing of one's own prejudgments and classifications. It requires that the mind be tranquil, like a pond, perhaps, in which experience can be reflected. If the mind is too active and its speculations disturb its repose, a person will find it more difficult to receive intuitional flashes.

Men whose training has given them an abhorrence of passivity in any form and who link an active mind with what they believe are masculine traits are not likely to sustain durable intuitive insights. Building outer structures around his encounters with premises, terms, data, inferences, analysis, and logic, a man may fail to fly straight to the heart of a matter because he busies himself so with pointed distinctions. Chopping his experience into categories in order to break it down for "proper" study, he misses the instantaneous flow toward what has been variously labeled clairvoyance, perceptivity, and premonition.

Passivity of the mind is associated with the female not because of biological necessity but because women have not always received the kind of training that leads them to value logic. Germaine Greer admits that "women often refuse to argue logically."[3] That men do resort to logical disputations shows they have been so dazzled by the discovery of such techniques that, as with most good things, they have overused them. As humankind hurls toward the year 2000, it will quickly discover that survival depends on the circulation of alternative ways of knowing and that such ways will place high value on the ability of the mind to assume a passive stance. Rationalistic knowledge, which is certainly effective in technical realms, will continue to wield strong influences; but a great deal of analytical processing, an area that was formerly a mind province, will be taken over by machines. Technology will leave people free of what we have called their 1-2-3 concerns, opening the prospects of mind-use to creative levels where intuition will be a highly valued aptitude.

Marshall McLuhan predicts the withering away of the printed page as well as what has come to be known as linear thought. The entrance of such technological phenomena as television presents people with new ways of knowing: ways that no longer insist, as academics and scientific thinkers have, on formal processes involving data, experiments, and hypotheses leading to conclusions. Now, instead, both men and women receive information that no longer requires of them the kind of logical comprehension needed to sustain understanding of a newspaper or a book. Now they imbibe—passively—unorganized raw data. This undifferentiated mass of perceptions, most of which go directly to the senses, is a wholly new way of learning.

What happens to a generation reared on television? Greer believes that we have taken steps toward the reintegration, among men as well as women, of thought and feeling, or of what might be called the scientific and the intuitive processes. She bases this belief on the activism of young people who are responding in almost immediate ways to what they see as political skulduggery. If Greer is right, the world can be said to be taking care of itself in its own mysterious ways. At the time she made this observation, however, youngsters of the TV generation were more active in their opposition to political tyrants than they seem to be now. While the Vietnamese war aroused their ire, the Watergate scandals found them concerned and aware but silent by comparison.

If we are to integrate thought and feeling on a wider scale, we must depend on more than television for assistance. Our educational institutions are still promoting strictly rationalistic modes of thought, with little or no emphasis on a student's intuitive development. The male's pride in his rationalistic skills is still a mighty force in the mental life of the nation. Overseas the withering of religious superstitions promises new life to the use of intellect in imitation of the United States, where foreign professors in their studies acquired methods they praise as gospel. Although television promises to be of great assistance in dispensing information in nonverbal ways that will no doubt have some effect on the disruption of argumentative learning, educators are still caught in the webs of such modes and are inculcating them with considerable passion.

It is clear that educators today are confused about their methods and the state of their profession. The careful organizing that once provided teachers and professors with rationalistic sanctuaries is under unprecedented attack. Once educators were able to lean on accepted educational customs and fashions, presenting their theories in highly systematic (if not esoteric) form; today their students are demanding direct access to experience minus those embellishments provided by polemics. This may be due partly to television, although Aldous Huxley and Timothy Leary might say that the application and investigation of their ideas have had no little effect on the new generation. Drugs such as marijuana, mescaline, and LSD-25 have had enormous consequences for traditional ways of perceiving. Great numbers of students and others, having on occasion used these drugs, have been turned on and tuned in to their senses in novel ways. Thus there has been a growing impatience with the 1-2-3 mentalities of structured expositors.

Some college women, it is true, are making exhaustive attempts to absorb traditionally masculine cognitive procedures. Such efforts are perfectly respectable unless these women root out their own mental strengths only to replace them with nonintuitive methods. This, unfortunately, is what happens to all too many under the influence of certain academics. These women accept intellectualisms as the best way to truth. This has happened to a few women's liberationists who think they have been left behind by missing the "higher education" generally reserved for males. In their attempts to be recognized as equals, these women adopt the styles of the dominant group, failing to be skeptical about the adequacy of such styles. Thus blockages that must be removed if men are to free themselves from dangers, tedium, and anxieties are insidiously shifting into the minds of certain women as well.

Luckily, though, most women remain unaffected. It is conceivable that women, because of intuitive faculties, are better prepared to influence their surroundings and accommodate themselves to this changing world than men. Where a wide perception requires both thought and feeling, the ability of women to make such a mental marriage work can lead them to make important adjustments. Such accommodations are already taking place, and it is clear that men are having greater difficulties adjusting to change. One is tempted to ask why men—on the whole—die so much earlier than women. Is it possible that the pressures of society and the inflexible nature of so many "masculine" minds contribute to their early demise? Men who have not learned to "bend like the willow," a feat more easily accomplished by their female counterparts, are more than likely to snap and break when forceful social winds begin to blow.

In any case, given the changing nature of learning processes, it is obvious that men must widen the scope of their faculties and begin to cultivate qualities that have been traditionally seen as peculiar to the female. To resist such a widening can only result in worse hardships than those men now suffer. Already in almost every facet of their lives frustration, concealment, insecurity, and an overwhelming burden of competitive struggling have made men increasingly uncomfortable in their roles. The nature of the new male's struggle involves unlearning as much as it involves learning. It means acquiring a true respect for women, based not on protective predilections but on imitative ones. For if a man truly admires women, he must not admire them because they seem weak and helpless. Instead it must be because certain of their abilities or qualities complement or are equal to his own or because he can learn from such women and thus add to himself. To speak of admiring women, other than physically, under any other pretext is absurd.

Yet most men refuse to imitate women for a singularly frightful reason, indicating a total lack of genuine admiration: They believe that to imitate them is to become like them, which is ostensibly thought to be the most grievous mistake a man can make. "Imitation is the most sincere form of flattery," says an old adage, and yet men who congratulate themselves on an ability to dish out less sincere forms of flattery have been unwilling to take this decisive step consciously.

Why? Because imitation is pursued on superficial levels: cultural mannerisms and the like. Clothing, posturing, and other activities draw attention away from the mind. Thoughts of imitation are squelched because men fly from socially shaped notions of femininity. In times past these notions were expressed outwardly when women feigned helplessness, dependence, flaccidity, empty-headedness, and the like. It appeared that fainting was inherently feminine instead of a contrived art used for survival. The physical affectations accentuating such traits bolstered men in need of a domineering and authoritative self-image. When these affectations are mimicked by men, they draw disapproving words like "effete" and "effeminate." That men have not wanted to imitate these mannerisms and have assumed they were outer manifestations of innate mind-states is not surprising. Conversely, the thoughtful, independent woman would not want to mimic physical mannerisms attached to male norms. She would reject them as pompous, stiff, and callous, although as we have already said, some women have adopted stiff masculinist thinking patterns and abandoned their own.

Women who affect "manly" mannerisms as well do not arouse the savage condemnation reserved for female impersonators, however. After all, it seems obvious why male patterns are more acceptable: They are traits that "get one ahead" in the world. The male impersonator is "smart" for utilizing them. The female impersonator, though, arouses masculinist fears about so-called feminine sides of the human (male) psyche and is thought to have abandoned the advantages of being a male. From the standpoint of the average male this kind of behavior is insanity in a most unsettling package. Perhaps this is why man-hater Valerie Solanas wrote: "The farthest out male is the drag queen."[4]

The inability of most males to bring about "feminine" changes needed for psychological health and for survival is rooted in faulty associations. The average male connects tenderness, receptivity, and intuition with old-fashioned stereotypes of feminine behavior. Fleeing from stereotypes emphasizing insipid, prissy fragility, he ends by cutting himself off from the great mental strengths traditionally associated with women. What he does not realize is that these stereotypes are not components of justly admired "feminine" psychology and that what he admires in women (aside from their proportions) can be his. Both of these realizations are destined to come, however. The swooning "lady" of the nineteenth century is giving way to the independent, equalized woman of the twenty-first century. As the new woman arrives, the old associations between admired values and feigned weaknesses will disappear. Men will feel free to incorporate in themselves what they will begin to perceive as qualities needed to complete mind-wholeness.

This process would be speeded if educators and the media could clarify the inadvertent misperceptions that have too long prevented men from renovating their consciousness. In the first place the need to learn "the profound lesson of reception"[5] is plain. That is, men must incorporate in themselves the enormous strength inherent in the ability to accept and contain experience as well as to give and eject it. The male's abhorrence of passivity has led him to reject passivity in almost every form, and this leads to a state in which the mind is using only half its wits. Certainly it is clear that a mind that is perpetually aggressive, involved in activity, motion, execution, and diligence, is one-sided. It lacks essential depths: the abilities to accept and to absorb.

An active mind that never knows the quietude of passivity approaches the world from a singular angle. It conceives only itself as provider, never allowing ingestive repose for discernment. In relationships where one partner is continually active and the other is always passive, the passive partner sees the stress and strain of activity. Because so few men are willing to adopt the passive role—even for a moment—they remain unaware of the passive person's sights and thus lack the ability to see themselves or their activity with any appreciable degree of what they ardently desire: objectivity.

The passive person who never knows what it means to give, to act decisively, to utilize skills, and to strive energetically is also half-witted. To the extent that women have been conditioned to such exclusive passivity, they have been maimed. The same must be said about men who are conditioned to exclusive activity. There must be a merging of these methods of mind-conduct so that both sexes can achieve perceptive growth. Rigid roles remain because of rigid values, and these distort our ways of perceiving.

Passivity is thought to be the exclusive province of women. Even though its manifestations have been accorded veneration, still they have been rejected for men. To be gentle, tender, compliant, soft-spoken, sensitive, artistic, loving, and cooperative has been to possess the most treasured traits of the human race. Women have been elevated to pedestals for supposedly embodying these traits. And there on their pedestals they have been kept, along with qualities men have not thought "manly" enough for themselves. Soft men have elicited hostility. Why? Because such qualities seem to subvert traditional masculinist values. In certain quarters of Europe to say that a man is "artistic," without specifying which art and with a slight hesitancy, is to accuse him of homosexual inclinations. So pervasive is the connection between creativity and notions of femininity that some think artistic endeavor has a straight connection with gayness. It is true that there have been many homosexually inclined geniuses, but this view, if it is categorical, is extravagant.

These varied disarrangements between the sexes and the disavowal of the qualities each mistakenly believes to be the sole possession of the other cause a suffocation of potential. American males have been conditioned to use the mind in certain limited ways. They have been frightened by cultural artifice into rejecting capabilities that would make them in every sense more fully human. Many such men are loose on the international scene (which is at best a sequence of fragile diplomatic truces) with only half their wits intact.

Chapter 5 ❋ ROLES
Our Turn to Curtsy and Their Turn to Bow

Society sets up its rules for what constitutes masculinity and femininity, but masculinity and femininity are after all just words, whereas human beings are not. Too, human beings have an enormous range of possibilities in terms of traits and in the ability to play roles of all kinds. These possibilities are severely foreshortened by the process of sex differentiation too rigidly applied and by masculinity and femininity too narrowly defined.

—Myron Brenton[1]

If the mind repels its own dissection, it should easily comprehend how difficult it is to locate what is so casually called identity. And yet each person hopes to hold on to his own identity, making sure that none of it, whatever it is, is lost. Identity implies certain unique or individualistic characteristics each person feels are his own.

Robert G. Ingersoll claimed that individuality was nonexistent if a person accepted an opinion or a mode of behavior without question. Inherited thoughts, he said, having merely become a part of a person's mental baggage, are hardly what the mind wins for its own. Those who only follow, copying rituals shown them by others, have given up their individuality, he asserted. "Nearly all people stand in great horror of annihilation," he wrote, "and yet to give up your individuality is to annihilate yourself."[2]

If nearly all people do stand in great horror of annihilation, perhaps one of the ritualistic mimicries they most fear losing is their sex role. Sex roles are central in the average male's self-concept. Because roles are taught (at very early ages) and are not innate, men take pride in mastering them even if they make themselves tough and unpleasantly stone-faced in the process.

Those who have failed to fit into prescribed molds generally try to hide the fact. Instead of pride, they experience a shameful anguish, which their liberation—when it comes—will teach them is unnecessary. If it is true, as many researchers are beginning to tell us, that sex roles are not absolute allotments doled out by nature, then we are left with the thought that like our religious attitudes, sex roles are cultural products.

The implications of this realization are just beginning to dawn on the Western world. Tomorrow men will look back on the 1970s and remark on the constrictions affecting their sex. In future decades today's male role will be remembered as a straitjacket.

Late nineteenth-century and early twentieth-century freethinkers questioned the validity of religious claims to sole possession of the "way" and the "truth." Among the most effective means they employed was making clear to "cultured" folk that the religion of their region was only one of many in a constellation of religious perspectives. Early defenses of antiquated religious positions were made by theologians who wrote books slandering the founders of other religions, "proving" by comparison that their own religions were "best" and that acceptance of any other was a sure road to hell.

Today's sexual freethinkers and iconoclasts are met with a phenomenon not unlike that which took place in the religious field. With well-established sex roles under fire, defenders of the status quo have come forth to do battle, warning us, in ways that evoke the theologians, that a change in our sex roles will lead to racial suicide. This, in fact, is the theme of a recent tome, *Sexual Suicide*, by

George Gilder.[3] Where once religious apologists blamed nonbelievers for world ills brought about by unbelief, so Gilder informs us that the unhappiness and confusion now attending personal relationships are the results of mass deviations from the straight and narrow.

George Gilder has done nothing more than express the uneasiness of today's male at assaults on once-accepted sex roles. Whenever human beings find that the ground is shifting under what they once thought were secure bastions, they balk. As a rule it is the older generation that balks, looking with dismay at changes taking place which they cannot comprehend. Women too are affected. Journalists like Harriet Van Horne and Midge Decter vent their uneasiness about women's liberation in books and articles, providing an interesting dialogue between the generations. They are joined, occasionally, by inheritors of the Ernest Hemingway mystique, males like Mickey Spillane and Norman Mailer, who hope to prove that writing is indeed a masculine occupation and that they are men in the old-fashioned sense of the word.

And yet as with religion, which often seems such an innate part of one's being, sex roles are many and varied. Dr. Margaret Mead has told us: "Many, if not all, of the personality traits which we have called masculine or feminine are as lightly linked to sex as are the clothing, the manners, and the form of head-dress that a society at a given period assigns to either sex."[4]

There are more than a few cultures wherein behavior according to gender is markedly different from that in the United States. Gender roles are extremely flexible, and drives that many people have been taught are instinctual do not actually exist in people of other cultures. It seems that this very flexibility has been necessary since earliest times for men and women to be able to divide tasks among themselves according to circumstance.

Adaptability would seem to point, in fact, to the likelihood that no single pattern of sex-role behavior is innate. This has important ramifications for men, since the difficulties faced by so many could be much relieved if certain behavioral demands were seen for the cultural artifices they truly are. The man who suffers because he believes that he must adhere to the patterns subscribed to by his neighbors would experience relief if he saw that his role was open to serious question and that he was free, if he wished, to abandon it altogether in favor of one more suited to his individual nature.

If men and women are going to coexist with some admirable degree of proximity while absorbing the best qualities from one another, new realizations about roles are indispensable. Being born into a culture was once sufficient for role implementation and fixation. Until recently men did not question the traits expected by their culture. It was a settled matter, and a man might go from cradle to grave secure in his behavioral mold. That this is no longer the case is beyond dispute. The world surrounding today's male is changing with a most unsettling rapidity. His long-established roles, if he clings to them too tenaciously, threaten to make him at best ponderous and an absurd burlesque, at worst a menace.

Roles, if they are not innate, have their origin in our environment. Industrialization, urbanization, mobility, and changes in the requirements of the economic system all create new conditions under which old roles no longer fit present needs. Retrogressive theorists who demand a return to traditional male-female formats offer no adequate explanation of how this can be done, given the major changes to which American society has become subject. What these theorists do not seem willing to acknowledge is the very real possibility that role adaptability exists to meet the exigencies of an era. What is more, roles *are* changing, and today's young male is moving in directions that were heralded under the banner of unisexualism a few years ago. That this is not only a local phenomenon is clear. P. J. O'Rourke, who was one of the eighty-seven newsmen accompanying Richard Nixon to Peking, wrote:

> Unisex is the very first thing that hits you in China. Not that ersatz continental garçonette haircut business or high heels for men, but real unisex. The clothing that they wear—it's not masculine or feminine, nor is it as dumpy and sexless as it looks in those *Daily News* centerfolds, it's just the same for everyone, UNISEX! And the effect of those millions and millions dressed alike without regard for age or station is more spectacular than any Ken Russell costumed outrage.[5]

The millions to whom O'Rourke refers are, of course, a quarter of the world's population. To say that all these males and females dress alike is to indicate to those who are somewhat globally minded precisely what is going on next door. Admittedly, clothes do not, as they say, make (or for that matter, unmake) the man. There can be no doubt, though, that they do go a long way toward erasing what George Gilder and his ilk must think are essentials in the male-female continuum, making it much easier for the propagandists of sexual equality to slip in an acceptable word or two.

U.S. psychologists like Dr. Fred Brown, of New York's Mt. Sinai Hospital, are sounding the arrival of unisexualism in America. This is hardly any surprise, given the fact that the late sixties saw America's young men sporting shoulder-length hair and America's young women donning blue jeans and work shirts. The psychologists finally administered the famed Rorschach inkblot test to determine the degree to which this unisexualism has gone.

In the past, approximately 51 percent of both sexes saw male figures or symbols in an ink spot used as a test of sexual identity. A man who saw female figures was adjudged feminine, and a woman who saw female figures was adjudged masculine. Today only 16 percent of both sexes tested see the inkblot as male. Fifty-one percent see it as a female figure.

I prefer firsthand observations to tests, however. Visits to colleges throughout the United States have convinced me that males in these domains, at least, are decidedly more gentle in outward manner than their counterparts ten years ago. There is no reason to call them feminine or to call the decisive women I have observed masculine. Instead, both sexes are simply beginning to adopt characteristics once thought to belong to one sex or the other. Today we realize that these traits are interchangeable and that they belong not in one camp but in both.

Television commercials show role changes in progress. A recent one for Emeraude, a perfume by Coty, shows an attractive male and female commenting on what their sex roles used to be and what they are now becoming. The male says: "Being more of a man used to mean having sixteen-inch biceps or driving faster than anybody else. Today it means being strong enough to be gentle." The woman says: "Being more of a woman used to mean acting hard to get. Today it means not acting at all."

Female and male impersonators play a role that is necessary today: emphasizing culturally manufactured differences between the sexes. They exaggerate in posture, clothing, speech, and movement the most stereotyped "female" and "male" behavior, mimicking stances and conduct that are culturally induced. The value of male or female impersonation, therefore, lies in the ability of the performer to mirror, however exaggeratedly, the cultural affectations unconsciously adopted by the general public. That these peculiarities have little to do with biological ordinances is something impersonators amply demonstrate.

Unisex fashions enjoy a certain popularity in the United States; in other nations, like China, they are the rule. Impersonators and transvestites resist this trend, since their stock in trade is a magnification of sex differences. Similarity in clothing styles robs the impersonator of "his" or "her" distinctiveness: It allows men the same degree of color, flamboyance, and variety that was once the sacred province of women; it gives to women the right to comfort and simplicity once thought "manly." It makes the practice of impersonation a nostalgia trip in which stars of the last few decades are imitated in preference to those of the present. Bette Midler, a seventies phenomenon whose repertoire reaches back through the 1940s, has been accused of being a female who imitates female impersonators. "They say I'm a drag queen from Chicago," she says with a laugh, adding in a serious tone: "I am *not* from Chicago."

That great confusion still exists about roles and sex identity is clear. Organizations like the International Institute of Sexidentity have arrived on the scene. Headed by an attorney, Cathy Douglas, wife of Supreme Court Justice William O. Douglas, the institute seeks, with the aid of research grants, the truth and consequences of the sexual roles that are generally played. Ms. Douglas sees her research program as "an ultimate quest to find out who we really are and to determine which behavior patterns are dictated by our culture and which are determined by the real nature of men and women." She believes that if the real nature of men and women can be located, "laws can be adjusted to meet those needs so that we will have a more orderly and productive society."

Commenting on male roles, Ms. Douglas said: "I think women have a much easier time changing their role patterns than men do. That's because men traditionally have only one role, that of provider. For example, in childhood, there's never a time when boys can act feminine or be the counterpart of the tomboy role for girls."

Cathy Douglas has set for herself an ambitious project. On the surface it would seem that she intends to draw inferences about the "real" nature of men and women from biology. I trust that her reliance on biology will not sink in the muck that has swallowed snipers on both sides of persistent role debates. On one side are those who claim that "natural" behavior (by which they usually mean conventional behavior) stems from biological necessity. On the other side are those who use anthropological finds to show how roles vary and how the sexes in different societies have flouted the inferences drawn by biological instinctivists.

Biological arguments against sexual equality and role variation are unimaginative. They assume that human beings are not capable of transcending their bodies in ways commensurate with changing circumstances. This means that the mind, even when being assaulted by utterly new circumstances, must remain faithful to a traditional pattern of behavior and that it is therefore the prisoner of biological necessity. This concept of mind hardly leaves room for creativity or, conceivably, for survival.

Perhaps any pronouncement with so grand a scope as that which Ms. Douglas envisions will realize its own limitations. Thinkers have been trying to locate the essential natures of the male and the female since earliest times. The task has evolved through theology, philosophy, and psychoanalysis. All three of these disciplines have failed to produce theories of lasting repute, although each has left contributions both negative and positive.

Organized religion provided some of the earliest role definitions. In the Christian system St. Paul gave men the reins of power and warned women not to talk in the church, a command that more than a few have ignored, including such go-getters as Mary Baker Eddy and Aimee Semple McPherson. Most of our current sex-role practices stem from the Judeo-Christian tradition, and most look to the obviously unbalanced neuroticisms of St. Paul for their source. The Genesis story of the Creation and the commandment on adultery retained woman as property along with servants and mules. She was, after all, a sort of afterthought, a reshapement of Adam's rib. The Judaic tradition has always shown the most concern for males, segregating the sexes at worship through the centuries so that women were able to look out of shuttered chambers while their husbands, sons, brothers, and nephews took care of supplications to the Divinity.

Philosophy struck some of the first sustained blows at sex roles in the Western world. As the doctrine of natural rights evolved toward the end of the eighteenth century, the idea of sexual equality took hold. John Stuart Mill developed the concept and emphasized the need for legal and political equality between the sexes. Even so, there were other philosophers like Nietzsche who warned against the acceptance of any view that did not take into account "the abysmal antagonism" between men and women and "the necessity of an eternally hostile tension." Philosophy's bachelor misogynist, Arthur Schopenhauer, insisted that women had only one role: that of propagators of the species. He is echoed by moderns like Gilder, who claims that "the woman in the home performs the most important work of civilized society." As corollary to this, of course, the role of the male for both of these traditionalists is clearly that of provider.

Psychoanalysis has elicited more abuse from sex-role

skeptics than any other discipline. Perhaps this is because the psychological professions have wrenched control of public confidence from priests and theologians and are maintaining conventional codes in the guise of "science." Armed with this knowledge, Gloria Steinem said: "Sending a woman to a Freudian analyst is like sending a Jew to a Nazi." Freud himself, poor fellow, was the victim of prudish mores that abounded in his day. To implement the social codes that he mistook for the real world, he invented ingenious phrases like "penis envy" to describe the condition of those women who refused the dubious satisfactions of their role assignments. Speaking thusly as the Father of Psychoanalysis, Freud revealed not only the high value he placed on the male organ but also the fact that he assumed that value to be universally shared. In short, he lived before the advent of transsexual operations.

Debates about roles and role-playing have their cutesy side, and the flak raised between traditionalists and iconoclasts that fills the airwaves and books can certainly be amusing. There is another side, however, one that is hardly seen and yet is tragic and depressing. It is not seen because it has not yet been articulated, and those who suffer under the burdens of sex roles do so in confusion and silence. Fearing ridicule and in fact often sustaining it or worse, these victims are more numerous than we ever admit. They are not misfits but everyday citizens who lead "lives of quiet desperation," aware that they are not being themselves, adopting phraseology and speech foreign to their natures, standing up for ideas they detest but which seem to assure protection of their best interests, and going to social events with sweat on their brows. These are the young men who are taught to "make it" in the rough-and-tumble world of hard knocks. Shaven, clean-cut, and orthodox in behavior to a fault, they fill government and industry posts en masse, taking their places in the pecking order without so much as an audible whimper. The frustrations they feel are worsened because they do not believe they have any other choices. A few become violent. Dr. Janet McCardel, a prison administrator, says: "People are driven to a point of violence by lives made gray and drab from lack of options. If you don't have choices in your life, if you don't acknowledge or have never been taught that there are all sorts of opportunities open to you, then you hold on irrationally to one position."[6]

A primary step forward in the liberation of men, therefore, is the opening of role options. Strict classification and systemization have limited imaginative perceptions about role possibilities. Men have not only been classified, but their roles, borrowed from the economic and environmental situations of the past, have also been narrowly functional. The whole of society conspires to force such roles upon them, starting in the very earliest years.

A total role reversal won't help ease the disquiet felt by many young men today. It is not that they want to stay home and clean house or to be womanly but that their families and neighbors expect them to follow a certain course to "fulfill their responsibilities as a man." These responsibilities are too narrowly defined, and the interpretation of such words as "independent," "self-regulating," and the like does not allow for deviations from a norm that makes these words little more than suspenders for the Calvinist work ethic.

Chapter 6 ❄ INSTINCTS
Will Men Always Be the Same?

The lower an animal is on the scale of evolution, the more complex are its inherited instinctual patterns and the less modifiable they are by environmental conditions. As one moves up the evolutionary scale, however, one finds that inherited instinctual patterns become less complex but more subject to modification by learning. This development reaches its apogee in human beings, who are born, not with complex instinctual adaptive patterns, but with relatively unfocused basic biological drives. The direction these drives take in human beings and the objects to which they become attached are subject to enormous modifications by learning. It is precisely this fact that gives human beings their remarkable adaptability.
—DR. JUDD MARMOR[1]

Rapidly changing circumstances have made obsolete many motivations a man admires today but which were better suited to a former age. Sitting at his desk, pencil in hand, he feels the "call of the wild" and resents the white collar that rubs his neck raw and the tie he dons each morning without knowing why. Accepting his role as provider, he pushes himself to limits in dreary bureaucratic rounds, doing jobs he knows could very well be handled by machines with as much efficiency if not more. Much of the rage he feels at the misuses of his life may fly out at unfortunate times (men still commit far more crimes of violence than women); the real source of his dissatisfaction is in the structured system of values he accepts as his own.

Today's male has been trained in subtle ways by both

parents and peers to revel in merits that may very well have aided the pioneers but have little relevance to his office routine. Many young men are resisting this kind of socializing. For those who are not resisting, though, business affairs smack of implanted desires (created by values) to get back to the jungle, where survival of the fittest is thought to be the law. This value also runs deeply in the core of the company he works for, covering its nature under innocuous-looking memos that are often, nevertheless, knives and arrows that maim and wound competitors. That companies and corporations should have so often become the wolves in sheep's clothing which they are is no surprise. They are run by men with jungle values who have clawed their way to the top.

Some jobs, of course, still give men a chance to delight more directly in the old masculine virtues. Those who fill them have become male symbols in our culture: longshoremen, truck drivers, marines, and football players. Brawn. The use of the body's strengths. Traveling the open road. Brawling. Pushing. Punching toward victory. These capabilities, even though they no longer relate to the jobs most men fill, are still admired, whereas the gentle influences of Jesus are considered too impractical.

It would be a comfort to believe that these images of brawn are nothing more than the last vestiges of a disappearing psychology. Certainly it is time for millions of men in the office brigades to latch on to more realistic role models, or even better—*to become themselves!* But thus far it is clear that the old idols have simply been reincarnated in gray flannel suits. Old wine is being poured into new bottles. Men who do not show outward signs of brawn find other ways to express such inclinations. Often they strive to be "classy," hoping to one-up the he-man's show. Money becomes a substitute for muscles. Today's office he-man wants to strut his stuff on weekends (at least), so he must suffer carrying his ever-heavier pencil, and when his superiors walk by, he pretends he wields it as regularly as an ax.

If man, once the proud hunter, has been reduced to a furtive pushing of pencils, can he help but feel mocked? Certainly the images his culture presents to him of his manly ancestors have robbed him of the glamour he feels —by reason of Hollywood—is his male birthright.

He reads pseudoscientific jargon about his "innate" aggressiveness, brutality, and his killing "instincts." These writings confirm him in his old-fashioned value set as he strides manfully across the office floor and pours himself a drink at the water cooler. The pseudoscientific jargon hits its mark. Why? Certain books achieve popular status not because they are constructive but because they evoke a chill. It would seem that men are too often willing to believe the worst about themselves. To be created in God's image is, as a rule, too highfalutin a self-reflection. The result is that a new kind of book has swept the publishing market, one that provides savage images of man, couched in semiscientific chatter, and that tells him —poor confession-prone serf that he is—what his guilty conscience has been taught to believe: He is a brute!

The sales of such books are no more startling, really, than are the sales of the violence tabloids whose headlines say: "Grandfather roasts boy in backyard barbecue and serves to neighbors." Although such lines are pure myth, there are more than a few who will stop to read—and quite possibly believe.

The difference between the violence tabloids and these "scientific" tomes is that the tomes—which are the intellectual's equivalent of *Gruesome Horrors Comics*—are making sweeping pronouncements about human nature. Their effects are felt on higher rungs of the social scale, and their reverberations, far from being elevating, keep men in a pessimistic state about their futures. If these books succeed in proving to a man that his nature is essentially brutish (something that the church doctrine of original sin has helped to do with incredible efficiency), he is not likely to consider milder manners as the best policy. His dissatisfaction with the technological creation of a clerical-world-turning-leisurely will continue to make his life hellish as long as he feels that his "natural right" to be a brute is somehow thwarted. His values, which these tomes encourage, must be changed so that they accord with changed conditions in the world. Then he will be happier.

The "scientific" books to which I refer are those by such men as Desmond Morris (*The Naked Ape*),[2] Konrad Lorenz (*On Aggression*),[3] and Robert Ardrey (*The Territorial Imperative*).[4] Their conclusions have been received against a background of preparation by such speculators as Freud, whose ability to weave webs of bizarre enchantment ranks him as Scheherazade's rival. The prominence of Freud in American academic circles is shown by the fact that his name appears in the index of virtually every nonfiction book published between 1940 and 1960. In Europe he has been merely regarded as the Austrian guru that he was. In other words, he was the founder of a school, and like many others of his kind, he gathered a following. The esoteric nature of his subject plummeted him into the spotlight at a time when various new sciences examining man were emerging from pretechnological times. Other gurus whose speculations could have received equal treatment from the media came into prominence at the same time, except that their prominence never equaled Freud's, since he was the *first* of such gurus. A naïveté that needs pruning in the American vantage point is that the *first* anything is necessarily the best or the most profound. Hence our society's eagerness to accept this Austrian guru's message reached an unfortunate and even an absurd pitch. If Freud's view of man's nature was too pointedly gloomy, it was no matter. The shamans and witch doctors of our day—psychiatrists— seized the opportunity to promote the Freud mystique in order to add to their own stature. There were many only too eager to believe when he gave the kind of dejecting news about man that follows: "The element of truth behind all this, which people are so ready to disavow, is that men are not gentle creatures who want to be loved, and who at the most can defend themselves if they are attacked; they are, on the contrary, creatures among whose instinctual endowments is to be reckoned a powerful share of aggressiveness."[5]

What man, after reading these words and accepting them as gospel, could fail to utter a growl or two to measure up to his "innate" aggressive nature? Having been taught by clergymen, Freud, Morris, Lorenz, and other bogeymen-in-repute that they have an "essential nature," a terribly dark and mysterious side that is nasty and will always seek to express itself, millions of U.S. citizens growl even when it isn't necessary. They are trying to show that they know who they are. The truth is, however, that more than a few are suffering what Erik Erikson called "an identity crisis," and far from perceiving precisely who they are, are grasping along with everybody else for clues about it.

The "aggressive violence" theories have special appeal to many because they offer complacency. They can be accepted because they give little hope for the future in these days of nuclear peril. A man need not bother himself about upgrading his scene. Reform? Revolution? Why bother? It seems easier to continue to express at least a few of these less admirable habit patterns until we are eventually eliminated by hydrogen warfare. In the meantime such thinking leads to fascism because there is no room for doubt that others need to be controlled. To unshackle the masses, says such a philosophy, is to invite them to kill you.

So we are left in this last quarter of the twentieth century to cope with some difficult transitions. Man the hunter and the protector of his tribe has become man the pencil-pusher who has been fooled by gurus mouthing high-sounding intellectual gibberish into thinking that his ancestors were rough and tough and that he has inherited from them especially ferocious tendencies. It remains for the proponents of liberation to explain that behavior, contrary to Freud, need not seek its roots in the past. What we think our parents once did is not a sound or sufficient basis for our own behavior. It would help if we ceased this incessant preoccupation with origins and looked instead at our present circumstances. As Charlton Heston said in *Planet of the Apes*, "We are here and it is *now*." Any sound action must stem from present conditions and not from bogus ideas about the instinctual patterns lodged in the rather gruff images we carry with us about primitive man.

If, however, man is now supposed to be aggressive and domineering, he must also be disappointed in himself. One does not have to be a sociologist to realize that the corporate state that America has become leaves great numbers of its employees with feelings of coglike futility. To change the social order seems too gargantuan a task if not an impossible one. And yet almost every level from business through government is hopelessly out of touch with the daily needs of its citizens. Powerful technologies, instead of releasing man to pursue his fonder dreams, have created Kafkaesque mazes from which exit seems hopeless. Man glorifies speed because it is considered daring and therefore "masculine." The image of Alice in Wonderland running in place but falling behind is a poignant one, for it describes the condition that even the most advanced technologies have been allowed to foster because of the values at their base.

The automobile provides a startling example of Alice-in-Wonderland speeds. The average American ("the horse-less cowboy") spends fifteen hundred hours annually driving some seven thousand—odd miles and earning the capital needed to keep his vehicle in tow, shelter it, park it, and pay highway taxes. For each hour of his life invested, he covers only five miles in his car. In nations where highways are few, citizens cover such distances on foot. The difference between Americans and these "backward" nonindustrialized folk is that Americans spend 25 percent of their time each day concerned with getting to and fro, and the walking citizens of other lands spend only 5 percent.

Although the American male may not consciously realize such facts, he does sense that his society is making him impotent in more ways than one. Though he spends long, boring hours in the office, hoping to enjoy the fruits of his labors, he finds himself enmeshed in rounds that rob his life of luster. If he growls, flexes his muscles, speeds, or struts across the floor, it may be that he is trying to recapture his own sense of command over his life.

There can be no doubt that he is protecting himself too. His clinging to belligerent postures is his outward way of showing that he shields himself from the very cruelties he sanctions in his culture. These cruelties are not of a physical nature. They are assaults on his personality which he allows to be administered by respected institutions. They begin when he is quite young. Patricia Sexton tells us in *The Feminized Male* that boys are bored with what she labels feminized educational procedures. She says that this accounts for their restlessness, rebelliousness, and the tendency of many to drop out in disgust.[6] By using the "feminized" label she equates feminization with a willingness to be regimented academically.

On the contrary, education is too "masculinized" and lacks the feelings, emotions, and sensitivities that should give it meaning and excitement for boys, who are led to believe they have a greater stake in education than do girls. Women have not been pressured to succeed and thus do not feel the competitive strain of schooling as much, nor do they take it as seriously.

Rebellion in school, particularly elementary school, is simply a boy's natural reaction to regularly suffered psychic attacks. Rationalistic myopia is unleashed on him in full measure. He is thrown into competitive postures with the taking of his first tests and examinations, told he cannot be trusted when he is handed his first hall pass to go to the rest room, and experiences his first cold, cataloged responses to his young personality in the form of grades from A to F. "F," of course, stands for "failure," a word that in our success-oriented society is a terrible blow to the self-image. Since women have tended to think of their images as shadowed by those of the men in their lives, intellectual failure has not had the same personal meaning for them. In the past it was conceded that a woman could fail only if she picked a "loser" for a husband. His success, in other words, was hers as well, even though she may not have been involved in it in any crucial way. In any case, the male is told over and over that he will "never get anyplace at all" without that sheepskin and that now good grades count with companies too!

It is of interest that Walt Whitman congratulated Horace Traubel for his "failure" to attend institutions of higher learning and told him how much better off he was because he had not been regimented by them.[7] Whitman scoffed at tests and examinations and in *Leaves of Grass*

counseled: "Mind not the cry of the teacher." Educator
Max Rafferty, who writes an educational column syndicated in more than one hundred newspapers, lectured to
university audiences, saying that public education in
America has for several decades stressed conformity and
adaption to group standards as the goal of learning. He
described student grievances that led to campus riots as
caused by "creeping facelessness" and a "loss of identity."[8]
If such riots were responses to identity problems, which
may be at least partly true, it is not difficult to conceive
how men would hold to brutish mannerisms to indicate
that on the physical level, if nowhere else, they are
self-protecting. Professor John C. Raines, of Temple University, observes that America's middle classes are "up
against the wall" and "going nowhere."[9] If this is so and
men are indeed cornered like caged animals, it is no
wonder that they punch at the air and give evidences of
their readiness to strike.

Theorists who blame aggressive stances on "innate"
tendencies may very well be misreading defensive postures
adopted by men which are not unlike those we see in
otherwise gentle animal species. That these postures exist
even when there are no outward signs of violence or threat
does not mean that they are instinctual inclinations seeking
a needed outlet. Instead, as we have seen, man is subjected to subconscious sieges from subtle if not invisible
social influences, and like every animal, he waxes fierce
because something (in his case values) has made him
fearful.

Since the American male still views himself largely in
one-dimensional terms—as provider—he sees the increasing complexity and competition in the social life around
him as a threat. He might not be able to put it into these
words, but there is no doubt that he is forced to compete,
not in a robust and vital way but in frenzied rounds of

intense one-upmanship. America, with its unholy emphasis on consumerism, has no sooner provided him with a salary advance than he finds himself thrown once again into a meaningless race, his advance eaten up quickly by consumer items he deems necessities. In recent years the cost of living has reached unprecedented heights, and there are more than a few indications that natural resources that citizens have long believed are theirs by right are disappearing. Books that tell how to leave a so-called civilized life and return once again to more primitive formats are popping up on the market. Increases in crime and reports of mass murders convince many men that a somewhat savage demeanor is their best protection.

What occurs under these circumstances is a spiraling of uptightness in which competitive drives meet ominously with the search for security. Arching over the depressiveness of this structure is the merciless, runaway nature of the state machine itself, impelled by economic "logic" that speaks in the relentless, mercenary tones of big business.

In past centuries serfs tilled the lands for their overlords, hardly aware of the deprivations they suffered and unwilling to seize and share land among themselves. Today, dominated by the naïve masculinist myths that bigness is better and that fastness is finer, as well as rationalistic distortions that extoll organization and efficiency, men toil, pencils in hand, in a society where most are puppets of their companies. Technology threatens to eliminate their jobs. They feel little sense of accomplishment as they look at mere stacks of paper on their desks. Overshadowing everyone is a feeling of helplessness which comes with the contemplation of nuclear extinction.

If men are expressing themselves in tones that seem more appropriate to the Stone Age, it is little wonder. We must not assume, though, that Stone Age men were necessarily brutal, for that would be bad scholarship. Anthropological studies of primitive societies still extant prove that there are many men living in almost direct contact with nature who are indeed gentle and whose manner and posture—even to modern strangers with utterly alien ways—is warm and hospitable. Far from being threatened by the unknown, they are merely curious, not fearing, as perhaps they should, the destruction of their placid ways of life.

Myron Brenton suggests that men are experiencing difficulty reconciling the sedentary, inactive aspects of modern life with the primitive contact their forebears experienced as fighters, hunters, and workers at tasks requiring strength. Although this is no doubt true, it would be a mistake to assume that functional roles assumed by men of the past are in any way beckoning to men of the present by reason of race memory calling for reful-fillment. Today's men, after all, have *not* experienced what their forebears experienced, except, perhaps, vicariously through Hollywood's lens. If men spend their weekends in the woods hunting and fishing, this is no evidence that they are responding to the natural call of their species. If they jump into sports cars, racing for the horizon at lawless speeds, nothing except a kind of romantic credulity need convince us that they are being manly in any primal sense. The thrills derived from high speeds are no respecter of gender, nor is antipathy to them. The adoption by men of avant-garde sports is likely to be a method of making it seem that they fit their roles in society by engaging in animated pastimes thought to be suitable accompaniments to those roles. Usually in such cases there is very little real commitment to the peculiar new sport. It makes, hopefully, for a strikingly different image, something racy that the young business tycoon can use effectively as a ploy for esteem. His feelings for this sport are not a consuming passion but rather a segment of his divided life that is kept well in its place. It may provide him with some esoteric gab when the question of sports arises.

Any office worker might well wish for bodily activities to keep him from losing his physique, and the desire to fuse with nature is well-nigh universal among members of both sexes. There can be little doubt that many men do utilize hunting, diving, and other sports to demonstrate their masculinity, capitalizing on popular myths that still connect such recreation with primal potencies. Their demonstrations are likely to convince not only others but also themselves of their robust natures, and the invigoration they experience on contact with nature is often misread as a reveling in their "natural masculinity."

Hunting itself is often used to demonstrate that man is the only species that kills for sport (i.e., for fun). This argument is simplistic. A man who hunts may pretend that it's all fun, but he is proving himself as well. He believes that he is practicing ancient masculine virtues.

In some societies where hunting is no longer a necessity, tribesmen still spend their time rather futilely doing what their forefathers did. It could not be said of them, certainly, that they are *all* inclined to continue hunting because of some primitive instinct that reasserts itself. Nor, in fact, would these tribesmen be regarded by unbiased outsiders as adding to their masculinity thereby. What has happened is really rather simple. They have not yet found something else with which to occupy themselves. Like southern Democrats whose forebears have voted only one ticket since the Civil War, these tribesmen continue to hunt. One hesitates to suggest that far from being masculine, they might more easily be thought of as atrophied.

In fairness we must admit that the phenomenon of

hunting has causes besides these few motivations we have discussed. A testing of skills, perhaps, or a true search for a weekend's meal may be some other reasons. American sportsmen are also looking for the spaces they do not find in their offices. It could be, though, that the cloistered frustrations of the man who works may be only a temporary condition. He is destined, no doubt, to experience abuse and dissatisfaction through a period that may well last beyond the sights of the present generation. But pencil-pushing itself may be slated for an overhaul. Technology could easily create a society in which the confining offices would no longer be built as basic units of the economy. Robert Theobald's projection of a workless America,[10] although by no means an overnight possibility, provides us with a vision in which human energy is replaced by mechanical energy (automation) and human thought is superseded by computer thought (cybernetics). Accordingly, the need for human labor will decline. What stands between us and the realization of this vision is the emphasis our society puts on increasing production rather than on the distribution of wealth and abundance promised by technological advances. If only the national government concerned itself more with the welfare of its people than with the prosperity of its production processes, this could mean an end to unfulfilling labor. Basic goods might be distributed without the demand that citizens work to pay for them. In other words, it is quite possible that pencil-pushing may be only an aberrant stage between the Industrial Revolution and the technological era, an era that, if it ever fully arrives, will advise its children to play.

Chapter 7 ✷ PLAYFULNESS
Recovering the Missing Ingredient

*From all the widened horizons of our greater world a
thousand voices call us to come near, to understand, and
to enjoy, but our ears are not trained to hear them. The
leisure is ours but not the skill to use it. So leisure becomes
a void, and from the ensuing restlessness men take refuge
in delusive excitations or fictitious visions, returning to
their own earth no more.*

—ROBERT M. MACIVER[1]

Whether society is at the threshold, must wait, or has
already entered the Age of Leisure is beside the point if
we acknowledge that men are ill-starred in leisure roles.
Even now, when men enjoy more leisure time, few as yet
have learned to use or appreciate "spare time" when they
are away from the daily routines provided by their jobs.

It is estimated that four-fifths of the average American's
leisure time is spent either watching television or listening
to the radio.[2] These estimates, gathered for use on the
stock market, say that of the 113 waking hours per week,
38 hours are spent working and 25 hours commuting,
dressing, and eating. This means that 50 hours are left
each week for leisure.

If society is on the brink of the kind of leisure boom
wherein either technological advances or unemployment
will provide men with short work weeks or even unin-
terrupted free time, how will such time be used? Isn't it
true that leisure will be difficult to adjust to because there
are values rampantly on the loose which weigh heavily
against its enjoyment?

Few precepts are so firmly woven into the fabric of

79

American society as is the work ethic. This ethic permeated the nation as the Industrial Revolution got under way, teaching every citizen that no man of worth or integrity should be without a job. According to Robert Theobald, it was necessary to inject this belief if the Industrial Revolution was to succeed because people in the early nineteenth century had a tendency to quit working as soon as they had accumulated enough to satisfy their basic needs. Maxims such as "The devil finds work for idle hands" were introduced onto the scene, and even today the unemployed man—even if his unemployment is no fault of his own—often feels a kind of shame.

But the work ethic is facing its decline and fall. As Sydney J. Harris writes: "The young breed of workers will not eagerly trade more time for more money. . . . The revolt of the young is not so much against capitalism as against mechanization; not so much economic as esthetic; not so much in terms of the class warfare Marx predicted as class restructuring in favor of more time, more leisure, more personal pursuits."[3] Nevertheless, a great deal of the shame of being unemployed is everywhere apparent. This shame is compounded by other factors that make enjoyed leisure a stranger in America. Part of the problem lies in the mentality that follows suggestions of advertisers and big business about what to do during off hours. The average man is bombarded by recommendations on how to structure his leisure time. He is told that certain activities will provide him with that elusive "fun" he has been hoping for and that he must simply follow the crowds to places where "fun" is to be had. Usually, although he may not realize it, the man who follows such suggestions finds that instead of relaxing, he is caught up in a complex of activities within an established system requiring concentration and effort—either he must drive for some distance, staying carefully in line with others who are headed in the same direction, or he must stand in lines with people who are hoping to have the same "fun." The fun, as a result, is diminished.

The greatest barrier to man's psychic adjustment to leisure lies in our culture's rationally structured attitudes toward play. Since so many people are ill at ease with unstructured time, they fill it with other structures, unable to accommodate themselves to the kind of flow and spontaneity necessary to true playing.

Small children at play seldom submit themselves to the elaborate prearrangements that spoil adult recreation. Methods of inductive reasoning have not yet warped their approach to their games, and consequently they are able to pretend without self-consciousness, to speak without worrying about proportion, and to forget themselves in the midst of frolic. What separates their amusements from most adult play is precisely this absence of consciousness of themselves as enthusiasts. When self-consciousness intrudes, trying to bring *order* and trying to impose that order on sequences of events, spontaneity evaporates. To bring rationalistic order into the arena of play is to rob festivities of the core of their jollity. We laugh when something unexpected, unplanned, touches our funny bones, and we enjoy ourselves most when we cease analyzing and forget for a few moments as we enjoy. We are not conscious of enjoyment as something we must measure and calculate.

Gunther S. Stent, a professor of molecular biology at the University of California and author of *The Coming of the Golden Age: A View of the End of Progress,* took special notice of the "hippie" phenomenon of the late sixties. He was persuaded that the appearance of this group signaled a new development on the evolutionary scale, a "human psyche which is perfectly adapted" to repose and creative idleness.[4]

The growing popularity of marijuana is directly related to the relief experienced by men and women in our culture who relax under its influence in ways they find difficult otherwise. Marijuana has been of particular assistance to men in this regard because men more than women have been socialized to believe that any display of silliness on their part is taboo. Women, on the other hand, are allowed to be giddy and to giggle uninhibitedly without losing, in a chauvinist's eyes, the natural grace that is theirs. The desire to alter consciousness with such drugs as marijuana originates with a man's need to be released from these cultural tensions, and after a joint or two, he lolls indolently:

> All these people are making their mark in
>   the world,
> While I, pig-headed, awkward,
> Different from the rest,
> Am only a glorious infant still nursing at
>   the breast.[5]

His conversation, no longer dominated by a need to appear logical and orderly, surprises him with the turn it takes toward the ridiculous, a turn that often delights him. At other times he appears to himself to be more direct and more pointedly in touch with his surroundings. What is most wonderful of all is liberation from the social requirement that he protect his dignity by appearing—as a man— to be in control of his thoughts and his bodily movements at all times. The fact that he can allow his mind to wander uninhibitedly, without forcing it to stay on one course, and that he can permit his body to be loose instead of concerning himself with its manly carriage is a deliverance from learned inflexibility. It is this emancipation that invests marijuana with what seems to be its messianic significance. Under its influence many men have learned for the first time what it means to "let go" of themselves, to giggle, and most particularly to play.

It is a sad commentary on American society, however, that men should feel the need to resort to cannabis to reclaim their right to loaf and enjoy frivolous moments. It portends of danger as well, for surely a society of men who find it difficult to relax except under the influence of drugs is ill-equipped to handle its affairs with objectivity and balance. Therefore even if an Age of Leisure is not just around the corner, it would help significantly if we relieved men of the conventions that make playfulness awkward and difficult. If leisure is closer to actualization than we think, the knowledge of how to utilize it becomes more urgent than ever. In fact, teaching men how to relax could conceivably be the most important educational task of the century. Certainly, if society is to overcome the effects of the shame it feels at being idle in a conventional sense, more than a few decades of reindoctrination will be required. The reindoctrination would not involve a new set of cultural rules but a throwing off of those already accumulated. Education for leisure would be, in fact, a kind of unlearning, so that minds, instead of walking club-footed as they do with a sense of regulation, restraint, modification, and direction, would find the ability to flow unchecked and to abandon what we called 1-2-3 reasoning in Chapter 1.

Such "letting go" implies, certainly, that a man who is no longer concerned about structuring is just as likely as anyone to behave well. There are some 1-2-3 thinkers who believe that it is necessary to wait until a man is better educated, socialized, or in fact, *tamed* before certain restraints are eliminated. These people opt for strict formalities and are comforted by the barriers provided them by custom. They do not trust their fellows' spontaneously expressed impulses. Sex and violence are linked in their minds to such a degree that they cannot conceive of affection in public, for example, without carefully translated rules that everyone follows. Each occasion for affection is seen as an opportunity for assault. If rules were lifted, they fear, there would be only barbarism. The fruit of all this is their belief that *control* is a necessity. Bodies must be controlled so that they do not bump into each other; minds must be subject to channeling devices called etiquette.

Each recreational experience is hedged in by proprieties, so that when these people gather, a great deal of time is spent determining mutual sympathies and similarities. This is done primarily by keeping close to hypocritical customs and by concealing impulses that are often affectionate if not sexual. The sympathies and similarities mutually sought are those of restraint and prohibition rather than of abandon. They are those that assure the timid that others are "safe." They protect alarmists from direct expression of their feelings by insisting upon behavior that denies the importance of the very feelings they do have. What is not granted is that they might find true similarities if they spilled their pleasurable fantasies. If those impulses were indeed related to pleasure and not to control, restraint, and power, they would be found to be quite harmless. Difficulties begin only when power-playing and domination are introduced. When this happens, genuine playfulness comes to a halt. Coercion intrudes, and people behave so as to protect rather than extend themselves. A turning away from direct confrontation takes place, and genuine communication fails.

No amount of waiting until people are better socialized is going to unlock the bind that domination-trips place on our relationships. It is in accepted social customs themselves that domination through control is indulged and allowed to spill over into lives that might otherwise be spontaneous and joyful. The person who is convinced of the necessity for restraints would have us believe that steps must be taken before any proscriptions can be lifted. The effect of this view, however, is to leave men wallowing in the grind while the "elite" think of some way to release them with no damage done. The constrictions themselves, though, are shaping mentalities routinely accustomed to power manipulation. It may seem that certain controls prevent damage, but they are in fact causing it. At present the damage takes the form of the intermittent assaults we count as crime statistics. As the incidence of crime climbs higher, we wonder why, failing perhaps to realize that unnecessary constraints and controls are helping to manufacture crime. Having rubbed out possibilities for playfulness, play fails to satisfy. All work and no play make Jack not only dull but dangerous as well.

Playfulness must—by definition—cut through social convention to find its life. Demarcation lines determining *how far it may go* keep it from blooming. Play within limits and without trust is soon felt to be the dreary routine of daily bantering that it is, and it ceases to be play. Today's attempts at playfulness are stymied by a trustless pall of regulations. A spritely and imaginative bounce to life is effectively squelched. Since men feel but do not understand their unhappiness, they continue to try to have fun in a dreary round of attempts that are always thwarted unless they break customs and taboos. When men have "played" in a controlled environment, they feel restive but cannot explain why. Play, which should be a form of release to them, becomes one more of many inhibiting factors kneading them into sorrowful forms.

To play is to learn to trust that the environment will not wound or maim and to relax long enough so that one's own vulnerability can be enjoyed. Children on sleds provide an illustration: They race quickly down a slope toward a destination that is not wholly settled. In the process they may be flung from their sleds, but they trust the snow to cushion them sufficiently. When they topple, they frequently get up laughing. The fact that they are in an awkward position is, they realize, part of the fun! Their self-images are not threatened by the experience because it is taken for granted that everyone will spill at one time or another.

As long as men methodize their leisure, regulating, coordinating, and collating their animation, it will lack zest. This is not to insist on an end to every kind of control or the destruction of every type of systemization. These, certainly, have their place not only in the sphere of playfulness but also in more serious activities. But what is meant is this: Control must be devalued as a prime element in activity. It has been granted too prominent a place, been thought too necessary and useful. Like rationality, it has extreme drawbacks that prevent both mind and body from expressing those instinctive, unforced pleasures that rise to the fore when we act in accordance with what Eastern philosophers call our original natures.

Before men can learn to renounce control—particularly in personal relationships—they must learn to trust themselves in unstructured social settings. The man who trusts his own uninhibited self to act well will not only be more expressive, and hence a source of delight to others, but will also learn to trust others too, which increases everybody's chances for tomfoolery, joviality, and carefree sport. Leisure challenges men to unlearn control so that they may play, and when this unlearning takes place, it pervades life in its more critical facets as well. Even politics might benefit.

Politicians who have a sense of humor have long been advised to make witticisms only on occasion. A Presidential candidate who has an outrageous sense of humor is not considered likely to win. The case of Adlai Stevenson (who joked his way through two Presidential campaigns and lost both) is an example. Some critics felt that he did not take matters with a sufficient show of solemnity and that this worried the voters. If his losses were indeed due partly to this factor, then they demonstrated a deficiency not on his part but on the part of the voters. They indicated, in fact, that voters may have been uncomfortable with a man who could turn to a serious matter and draw an un-expected laugh. That he could do this was seen as indica-tive not of quick wits and a sense of proportion and balance but of the fact that he was not *serious* enough. On the other hand, foreign politicians are praised by Amer-icans for their playful humor, and in the case of adversaries it has made them seem less fearsome—sane, perhaps. When Nikita Khrushchev toured the United States at the invita-tion of President Dwight D. Eisenhower, he bit into his first hot dog. "Hmmmm," he said. "The Soviet Union may lead the world in rocket-making, but the United States leads the world in sausage-making." Somehow when we laughed, we trusted that this man would not rush to put his finger on the nuclear trigger. Over a decade later it was he, rather than our own President, who drew back from the nuclear brink of the Cuban crisis. Personally, I prefer a man who can laugh heartily and who is playful more than I do one who calculates.

The person who trusts himself can trust others because his understanding of self opens him to understanding those around him. When he sees clearly in such a fashion, he does not fear. His empathies are strong. He understands what others need and what they feel. Since he knows him-self well, he is not made inferior in his own eyes when he flounders or stumbles. He can laugh at himself comfortably. If others laugh too, he knows that it is because they are laughing with him and not necessarily at him. And if they do laugh at him, it is because, he knows, they need to feel more competent than they do. Therefore no anger wells up within him.

Such understanding paves the way for playfulness without strict control and for a flight from structured behavior on many levels. Certainly the man who spends long days in an office where order, discipline, and precision are the emblems of production needs to know how to throw off these components when they are not urgent. If he carries them over into his everyday life, subjecting his wife, children, friends, and neighbors to controlled congeniality, his life will sink into an abyss of gloom.

Later on I will examine how control and domination limit men in other areas of their lives, particularly in the sexual sphere. There they will be seen to be particularly debilitating forces.

Reichian therapists believe that there is a stream of sexual energy through the body and that because America has been keyed to the denial or repression of pleasure, infants cultivate shields to keep the flow of this energy from expanding. If this is not done, according to work-ethic moralists, our attention will be diverted from important tasks involving our jobs, food-gathering, and shelter. In the meantime, however, love and play are blocked and paralyzed. Our abilities to express our feelings, to relax, and to go on sprees, larks, and romps, are crippled. Wilhelm Reich believed that such crippling manifests itself in our bodies, extending its stiffness even into our musculature. One might add, "into our environment," as well. Reich recommended breathing techniques to release resultant tensions in the individual and accounted a full orgasm as a sign of good health.

As long as men shy from spontaneity on account of sexual repressions and fears, assuming that social chaos and rape are consequences of instinctive behavior, they will be unable to enjoy leisure. Only when the fear of contact between people is eliminated will the trust that fosters impromptu activity grow. Men will no longer feel the need to keep up their guard, and human conduct will flower with less paranoia and less premeditation in wholly natural ways. New horizons of giddiness and joy will thereupon be discovered.

Chapter 8 ❊ COMPETITION
Winning Isn't Everything

*There was another side to the American character—
the harsh side of self-interest, competitiveness, suspicion
of others. Each individual would go it alone, refusing
to trust his neighbors, seeing another man's advantage as
his loss, seeing the world as a rat race with no rewards
to losers. Underlying this attitude was the assumption that
"human nature" is fundamentally bad, and that a struggle
against his fellow men is man's natural condition.*

—CHARLES A. REICH[1]

As if it were not bad enough that competition exists in
the rough and tumble of business and barter, it has been
introduced into our moments of playfulness as well. Sometimes characterized as the go-getter spirit, competition is
a value so deeply embedded in the American male's
psyche that removing it seems an impossible task. Women
have allowed themselves to accept this value too, although
more covertly. It is among men, however, that competition
occasions loud boasts.

Perhaps total removal would be an irrational course, for
there may be isolated instances in which competition promotes public or personal good, although I can't think of
any. What is most needed, however, is the destruction of
competition as a *primary* value.

Ashley Montagu challenges the commonly held belief
that commerce through competition is the "lifeblood of a
nation" by suggesting that "such greatness as America has
achieved it has achieved *not* through competition but in
spite of competition." He insists that "social welfare

through cooperation" rather than competition leads to progress and national survival.[2]

My own objections to competition are not quite so far-ranging, although it seems clear that in most instances of social interaction, cooperation is certainly superior to competition. The time has come to knock it off its pedestal and warn about the dangers that surround it and that have made of the male psyche an unbalanced and often deranged mechanism. Competition stems partly from the intellectual tendency to make comparisons—a tendency that is overused in assessing others. It leads to comparing the self with others instead of allowing it to appreciate its own uniqueness, irrespective of what others do.

A strange juggling of ethical perspectives takes place under the influence of a competitive standard. When a man competes, it seems *winning* becomes his primary objective; other concerns grow dim. As he struts toward pinnacles of success, too often he forgets the whole spectrum of rectitude and integrity which should, hopefully, line his avenue to the top.

This happens because competition as a value is taught as a good in itself. Those who approach it with unlimited praise, inculcating it in little boys and girls and preaching it to young people on the brink of their careers, fail to see that competing has an amoral coloration and that without this recognition it will be pursued with no thought of the harm it does as long as men think it an ultimate value in its own right.

"Competition is . . . the motivating feature of our system," wrote former Texas Governor and Secretary of the Treasury John B. Connally.[3] His enthusiasm for the competitive ideal was shared by Richard M. Nixon, who claimed himself heartened by the "reaffirmation of our competitive spirit." Nixon linked work and competition with achievement and self-reliance: "America's competitive spirit, the work ethic of this people, is alive and well. . . . The dignity of work, the value of achievement, the morality of self-reliance, none of these is going out of style."[4]

Only the philosophically inclined might have explained to the then-President that the presentation of his ideals followed wholly arbitrary sequences. Competition cannot be said to have any specific connection with the dignity of work or with achievement and self-reliance. Israelis on a kibbutz are not competing, yet their work has dignity and their sense of achievement and self-reliance is intact. The fact that Nixon lumped these ideals together was indicative of his own approach to work and morality and bespoke of the spirit of capitalistic enterprise. To invoke "the morality of self-reliance" as a supportive concept is simply to scramble high-sounding phrases for heightened effects.

The competitive ideal as it is now practiced is out of hand and promises to be among the nation's more resistant menaces. If it continues under its present guises, the ruination of the nation is inevitable and will proceed along with a growing neuroticism of its people and the threat of world destruction.

And yet competition is enshrined as a foremost value in the sanctuary of masculine virtues. Among young boys each "win" over others is rewarded with gifts and praise. American children are ready at a frighteningly early age to see life as a race—a race requiring constant vigilance and great energy lest some other runner should win. The leisure time of the young is distinguished by the great number of competitive games to which they are introduced.

Even before he enters elementary school, a male is encouraged to win over others. Once in school, he is told to get good grades. Success counts. He is frightened by constant talk of falling behind and is advised to keep his nose to the grindstone in the compulsive race to the top. In school, it seems, high marks count more with parents than does the nature of the perceptions absorbed. The development of intellectual curiosity or the love of knowledge is seen as secondary to the all-important task of keeping up with the Joneses' children. It matters not if Johnny has learned to enjoy reading and can compose well-written essays. If his grades fall below Billy's, who lives across the street, he is in disgrace.

The competitive ideal strikes at the root of his education, making him a product of instruction rather than a learner in his own right. Along with other children he is forced into a tight social mold and told to keep abreast of his companions. If he fails to march in unison, it is not taken into account that, as Henry Thoreau suggested, he may be hearing a different drummer. In the competitive race there must always be high degrees of uniformity. If there were not, there could be no way of measuring who is ahead and who behind. The nature of our current educational process is exacting, with little or no room for individual variations. Education is dispensed as a series of compartmentalized apportionments, each structured to insure that Johnny, no matter how different his approach to the world may be from Billy's, is following the very same orders that earned Billy his high grades. Competition is less concerned with the innate abilities of an individual than with how those abilities stack up against the abilities of others in a given line of endeavor, a line that a particular society insists is important. For this reason it is anti-individualistic, and for the purpose of winning it would wipe out or ignore all unique characteristics that do not seem relevant to the contest at hand.

The intensity of competitive arrangements in American society is responsible for a great deal of the pressure felt by the average male. Being successful by conventional

standards takes precedence over other values. Although
there are many who do not see their predicaments in this
light, competitive values override concern with happiness.
It matters little if, in the race, a man is huffing and puffing
or if he is overwrought and uncomfortable. The important
thing is that he hastens and that he advances under any
and all conditions to the forefront. Other values can be
trodden under foot along the way. It is triumph that
matters.

In the business world this is translated into obtaining
contracts for one's firm and doing so before such contracts
are awarded to another bidder. Or it may mean making a
sale before another salesman from the same or a different
firm can do so. To accomplish such goals almost any means
are used, some that endanger the very foundations of our
society and others that are more innocuous. What is obvious, however, in many bids for contracts and in attempts
at sales is a depressing amount of bribery, political maneuvering, and downright dishonesty.

Like other concerns that society promotes as male
"musts," competition has been glorified to such an extent
that recourse to it is totally out of proportion. Instead of
being the healthy spur to activity that our national myths
imply that it is, it has become a grim struggle to stay on
top, regardless of the course taken.

In the business world we have been led to believe it
is the competitive spirit that lies at the core of our
"healthy" economy. What has happened, in fact, is decep-
tive. There has been competition, yes, but not of a nature
that opens a wide range of economic possibilities to small
businessmen. The ideal of competition has become a mask
hiding power struggles between monopolistic firms that
lay claim to "fair competitive procedures" but are actually
using colossal sums of capital to eliminate smaller rivals.
The "morality" of the competitive spirit—*all's fair in busi-*

ness and war—has led these large firms to use any and all means to maintain monopolistic holds, slugging it out with each other while giving outward appearances of competing fairly on an open market. The real morality that guides them in their reach for profits and that stands blithely behind competitive jargon is *winning is all that counts.*

Estes Kefauver described the competitive mask behind which monopolies hide in his posthumously published book, *In a Few Hands: Monopoly Power in America.*[5] Until his death in 1963 Senator Kefauver conducted extensive examinations into fundamental changes that had taken place in the American economy because of industrial concentration. The political pressures brought against him for his role in such an inquiry were immense. They did not stop him from saying: "In our society the practices of monopoly are often secreted behind a front of 'competition.'" Kefauver knew that "competitive facades" had been erected by a multitude of businesses, and he singled out the automobile and oil industries as examples. Describing the retail outlets for gasoline which are located next to each other along highways, he said that "the appearance is one of intense competition" between the stations. None of the stations, however, will dare to shake the sensitive price structures in gasoline sales, he said. The type of competition that takes place he called "non-price forms of competition." This is the form that competition takes when price rivalries are eliminated. Sailing comfortably under the banner of competitive activity, this kind of competition "builds unnecessary costs into the fabrication of the product, representing sheer economic waste for the general public." Instead of making real improvements on products sold and holding out the possibility of lower prices, these business competitors actually construct their goods so that they do not last, attaching to them ornate and pretentious gimmicks but concerning themselves little with the true usefulness of their items. Prices climb, and in this phony competitive spiral both the public and the economy lose. Giving all of the outward signs of competition which the American public has been conditioned to accept as practical if not just, the spiral continues to eat away at the quality of life in every sector.

Kefauver cited the history of the Ford Motor Company to demonstrate how competing automobile manufacturers finally usurped Ford's leadership in the field and produced inferior products in the process. Ford remained the leading auto manufacturer until 1930. Between 1909 and 1923 the company adjusted its prices dramatically to fit fluctuations in the economy. Although it was not stylish, Ford built a product that was nevertheless made to endure and give good service and which enjoyed a reputation for reliability. Often Henry Ford announced drastic cuts in the prices of his product. In 1909 the Ford touring car sold for $950. In 1912 Ford reduced its cost to $600. In 1916 it sold for only $360. World War I sent prices up again, but afterward Ford prices dropped from $600 to $440 for touring cars and from $975 to $795 for sedans.

His competitors were furious. They insisted that sales would not be stimulated by price reductions. By 1930 Ford's supremacy in the field was challenged by General Motors, which had been bolstered by substantial investments from the Du Pont Company, helping it to assert its dominance in the auto industry. From that time forward, styling, speed, gadgets, and the like took precedence over durability and reliability. Prices climbed with each new "improvement," never to be reduced again. Even today, when cars could easily be constructed to get more mileage and when safety features might be easily introduced, a car's stylishness has remained a prime selling point; its lifetime, which is usually embarrassingly short, counts for little.

What this demonstrates is that the competitive motive has been ill-used by the automobile industry (an industry, incidentally, that accounts for eleven of the nation's twenty-two largest manufacturers) and that integrity has not mattered nearly so much as fast turnovers in sales. It also shows that success, the consummation of effective competition, is a motivating feature in buying. This is to say that the public has been hoodwinked by the "successful" look. If style and newness count, it is because they show. In their ostentatious way they seem to say, "Look at how well I have competed!" The automobile industry pays some four billion dollars annually in its quest for better styling. This amount, of course, is ultimately paid by car buyers.

Why are there not more automobiles on the road which are old, odd, but trustworthy? Why are our natural resources such as steel and oil being used to construct and fuel the perpetual output of ever-new styles that lack the integrity of inner substance? Is it possible that on the business level competition justifies such idiocies? Is it also possible that on the personal level, the success motive—the quest for a flashy exterior—has irrationally overcome the citizen's basic needs?

A reassessment of competitiveness is a prerequisite not only in the sphere of personal relations but also in relation to the nation's lifeblood as well. Too much fraud and deception passes easily by invoking the sacred mention of competition. Thoughtless emphasis on competition destroys meaningful relationships between consumers and producers, and it also often curbs productivity itself. The employer as well as the employee loses.

Men who are taught to be competitive are often thrown into working situations where competition creates desperate strains rather than facilitating progress. Problems of morale, harmony, and norms which are hardly worrisome when men are working alone intrude on projects and lead to pugnacity. Many firms simply assume that competitive behavior is a good thing, little realizing what dilemmas are created in their midst and how production is often slowed thereby.

Morton Deutsch conducted experimental studies of the effects of cooperation and competition upon group processes by contrasting cooperative with competitive groups. Since little research has been conducted in this area and since Deutsch's experiments were the first of their kind (1949), his findings are worth reporting. He discovered that cooperative groups coordinated their efforts to greater degrees, were much friendlier with each other, and had more productivity per unit time than competitive groups.[6] Further studies conducted in 1954, 1961, and 1964 obtained similar results. Martin M. Grossack reported that "cooperative Ss [subjects] showed significantly more cohesive behavior,"[7] and Leo K. Hammond and Morton Goldman found that "non-competition is more favorable for the group process than either group or individual competition."[8] Some researchers state that "cooperative conditions are likely to result in a greater division of labor and hence more effective performance."[9] Thus, it seems, in work groups where cooperation predominates over competition, production is increased and group harmony is facilitated. Such research unsettles the commonly held assumption that competition is at the heart of all business success. Such a perspective may have encouraged enterprising young men in earlier times, but as a national spirit, contrary to Presidential pronouncements, there are signs that it is definitely going out of style.

Unchecked competition has created a situation in which the American dream is in danger of extinction. That dream rejects arbitrary power, and yet men retain a bigger-is-better philosophy that admits unlimited competition. What threatens the dream is the accumulation of boundless and thoughtless power that resides only in those who have the money to effect the most successful competition.

On the personal level studies have been conducted to show how the competitive spirit is producing a culture in which youngsters are "systematically irrational." Linden L. Nelson and Spencer Kagan discovered that ten-year-olds in Los Angeles failed time after time in attempts to get rewards for which they were striving.[10] The reason? They competed in games that required cooperation. What was worse, these children expended a great deal of energy, even giving up their own rewards, in order to deprive their competitors of prizes. This type of irrational behavior, it was found, increased with age. In short, the drive to compete, even among adults, crushed rational self-interest and struck petulantly at others.

Nelson and Kagan's studies demonstrated that the competitive spirit is not a global phenomenon. Mexican children from rural areas cooperated in their tests and won prizes that escaped their American rivals. Nor did the Mexican children become embroiled in conflicts to get the rewards or try to prevent the Americans from taking them. "They avoided competition," wrote the researchers, "even when it was not to their benefit to do so."

Nelson and Kagan accounted for differences between Mexicans and Americans by suggesting that Mexican parents rewarded their children whether they succeeded or failed, whereas American parents gave rewards only for success. The Mexicans believed that what they get is not related to what they do; the Americans learned that their receipts are totally related to what they do. The Mexican children submitted to their rivals in hopes that someone could win. The American children gloated: "Ha, ha, now you won't get a toy!" They persisted in competition in situations in which it was detrimental to them. Nelson and Kagan said that the American approach "tends to create a lack of sensitivity," which means, of course, an absence of empathy for others.

This finding is hardly surprising when we take into account that competition tends to consume all values that get in its way. Since it is woven into the fabric of our value system and emphasized at every level of endeavor, men are blind to its destructive effects, and the "means justifies the end" as long as the end is success.

Unfortunately, much of what goes by the name of sport and play has been co-opted by competitive values. Worse, many sports have been organized in structured ways so that even when men are purportedly relaxed, they are calculating and measuring, assuring themselves that they are following carefully fashioned rules. In the life of every male youngster there comes a time when noncompetitive games like leapfrog cease and when competitive games like baseball begin. Why do youths begin to play these constructed games? Who encourages them to do so? Is it possible that competitive sports are only one more way of assuring that men must follow strict guidelines? Such "games" teach that it is important to win, that it is shameful to be last, and that those whose dexterities in this area make them last are hardly worthy of esteem.

Competitive games are also a way in which men have ritualized their relationships with one another, making sure that time spent in each other's company is organized time. If there is anything that a competitive sport does, as a rule, it is to crush opportunities for anything more than very occasional spontaneity. A man may jump into the air and catch a fly, for example, and the spontaneity of his jump may be hailed as such. During most of the game, though, he stands waiting for that moment— waiting and watching as his companions in "sport" wander about the field in accordance with the rules. When the opportunity for spontaneous behavior presents itself, it is of such short duration that it can hardly be said to encourage the development of either spontaneity or playfulness. Instead there are the same elements of grim determination to win that propel men in their professional lives. Thomas Boslooper and Marcia Hayes write:

> Pro sport and, all too often, amateur sport are no longer play but work, not relaxing but anxiety ridden, not a test of prowess but a proof of maleness and an often corrupt contest for personal wealth, not an outlet for but a contributing cause of aggression —in short, the mirror image of male activities in politics, in industry, and on the battlefield.[11]

Competitive games teach men to "follow the game plan" that is devised ahead of time. If the 1-2-3 thinking involved does not work because conditions are 3-2-1, it is little matter to the player as long as the coach's instructions have been followed. Only if he departs from those instructions has he reason to feel guilty. Thus Little League players are tomorrow's big-league goose-steppers, hoping for a win and following a coach's directions. The entire circumstance turns a man away from self-regulation and puts his body at the service of the team, in the rough and tumble of authoritarian, if not totalitarian, training.

Competitive playfulness robs men of the time they might spend enjoying aimless pleasures, putting them once again into the position of being not only rule-bound, but time- and statistic-bound as well. Most competitive games, certainly the more popular ones, are divided into segments by well-defined time limits. As has been stressed before, genuine playfulness cannot develop under structures. Play is more extemporaneous than structure allows for. Most of a baseball player's time spent waiting for others to act out their parts in the game's structure is passed with startling resignation.

In the last decade there have been a number of books published which reflect growing cynicism about the nation's athletic endeavors. Disgruntled baseball players, unhappy football players, and others have been exposing the grim nature of the games with which they have been involved. The "important" thing—winning—has all but drowned out other values supposedly taught by sports. The cold commercialism, players' unions, doped contestants, and political maneuvering on the playing fields have all but robbed professional sports of joie de vivre except among the most naïvely devoted fans. Russell Baker, humorist and columnist for *The New York Times,* complains that television sports are getting out of hand. He says that there is a new "world championship" every week, and once a month a new "game of the century" is milked beyond its worth by publicity.

Even the Olympics, long thought to be free of such juggling, have been shown to be cesspools of Machiavellianism. Mark Spitz contributed an introduction to Sherman Chavoor and Bill Davidson's book *The 50-Meter Jungle: How Olympic Gold Medal Swimmers Are Made.*[12] Chavoor was twice coach of the women's Olympic swimming team for the United States and is credited by Mark Spitz as being the man who truly helped him to get his seven gold medals. Here is what a publicity release for the book says:

> The phony amateurism of the Olympic committee, the pain of the endurance training, the bitter rivalry among parents, the exclusionary practices of the WASP-dominated country clubs (Spitz was a Jew, and it is said to be no accident that there are no

Blacks competing for swimming medals), the destructive squabbles of the NCAA and the AAU—
these are some aspects of the "50-Meter Jungle" exposed. [In addition there is also] the hypocrisy of a
sport in which a little money on the side is okay,
but too much is sure grounds for disqualification.
There are harsh words for parents who push their
kids too hard and for those who interfere unnecessarily. Chavoor says swimming is so cut-throat that
a child of eight has to learn to defend himself against
a psych-out from a competitor's parent.

The Lombardian ethic, based on coach Vince Lombardi's famous remark that "winning isn't everything, it's
the only thing," has become the ethic of other athletic
giants. This ethic filters down into the public school
system. That no one there questions it is mute testimony
to the value concerns of many educators. Lombardi himself
often "inspired" his players by telling them that winning
was a demonstration of manhood, and one of his best-
known players, Willie David, emerged from a Green Bay
Super Bowl victory saying, "We went out and won the
game and preserved our manhood."

Certainly there is no doubt that sports in America
are undergoing the same kinds of critical evaluation that
have been the lot of other institutional endeavors. Some
football players have admitted to leaving the game in
spite of their love for it because they have found their
opponents treated not as challengers but as enemies. They
have lamented how they found themselves "out there" to
"destroy" those opponents; to do so they have been told
it is necessary to despise and hate them.[13] When players
are taught to hate each other in order to win a game, a
process of estrangement takes place between teams and
in the psyches of the players themselves.

Some players have turned to organized religion as their way of asserting that "winning isn't everything." Ray Tesner, a football star and Orange Bowl contestant from Penn State, said that he found that following Jesus "is not a sissy's way out but that it takes a real man to trust God." Consequently, he plays not to win but for God. He is echoed by others like Penn State's offensive right tackle, Charlie Getty, who says, "I no longer play for the coaches, my parents, the fans, or even myself.... I play to bring praise to the living God because without him I am nothing." One wonders what the living God must think when he sees young men, their bodies protected by leather padding, savagely banging into one another on the "playing" field. There is something "heavy" about religious motivations finding their way into one's games. It might be argued that games can hardly produce much in the way of leisurely relaxation if they must always be invested with such cosmic significance.

Some competitive athletes loved by fans for their "manliness" have admitted to hating their roles. Mando Ramos, the champion boxer, said: "I should have been an actor. ... Everybody thought I was a fearless fighter. I wasn't. On the way to fights I would wish that my opponent was sick so I wouldn't have to fight. Yet everybody thought I was brave and cocky. It was all a sham. I didn't even want to be a fighter." If Ramos or any other fighter were to link his profession with religion, the thought of the Deity clucking approval as two contestants beat each other into insensibility would make for amusing theology.

Jack Scott, director of the Institute for the Study of Sport and Society, proposes what he calls a "radical ethic" in sports, which would ask that competitors not seek excellence at the expense of others. The radical sports ethic, he says, attempts to build an approach to sports which avoids the abuses and excesses of the Lombardian ethic on the one hand and the "dilettantism" of the counterculture antagonists, those who suggest abolishing even scoring while enjoying sports for sports' sake, on the other. Neither of these opposing approaches, says Scott, is sufficient.

What makes sense as innovation is the development of new games and their popularization in public educational programs. Precisely what they might be is not the question here, but rather how to create them is of concern. Perhaps backgammon might provide a model. The world's champion backgammon player, Tim Holland, praises the game by saying that it combines aspects of every popular game known:

> It blends the pure luck of craps and roulette, a lot of tactical skill, and a large element of personal judgment. . . . You can cooperate . . . with an almost unlimited number. . . . Then, it's so clean and candid: Cheating is just about impossible; no one is hiding any cards; there's no bluff as in poker. It's also very democratic and good for the ego, because, with occasional luck, beginners can beat the most advanced players. . . . It's the most pacific game I know of; it's totally devoid of any element of human aggression. You're never angry at your opponent, as in rummy, or at your partner, as in bridge. Whatever anger you feel is directed at the dice, at some abstraction of Lady Luck. . . . One of the most important and sensitive aspects of the game is learning to refuse doubles. . . . Most people tend to take doubles too easily. It's like Vietnam—they think that refusing is admitting failure or defeat. That's why backgammon is the greatest possible thing for the American psyche—it forces us to play a game in which you just have to lose very often.[14]

The difference between this kind of game and competitive Super Bowlism is arresting. Doug Swift, a player on the Miami Dolphins, described how it was necessary for him to stay in a motel room for a week before a Super Bowl game. "You need a laugh," he complained, "but the lesson of experienced teams is that emotions must be harnessed and saved for intensity on Sunday." Playfulness indeed. The American sports arena, instead of promoting mass participation, has become a stage for peacocks who strut about, reinforcing antiquated masculinist values, while thousands of screeching passive male spectators look on.

If sensitivity for the needs or feelings of others is lacking, we need no special sight with which to see the effects of an unchecked competitive ethic on international relations. If world peace is to be achieved, the fact that nations are interdependent and should cooperate must be stressed. Although the term "friendly competition" may sound acceptable in the international sphere, it becomes considerably more ominous when financial power is standing behind one friendly competitor. In a world of abundance, cooperation regarding the distribution of goods and natural resources is a must, and competition can only lead to ruin.

The use that has been made of Darwinian theories about the "struggle for survival" in the human province is probably unfortunate. Social Darwinism, emanating from the philosopher Herbert Spencer and from the brood that acclaimed his notions, captured the imaginations of men at a time when laissez-faire capitalism was scrounging around for a philosophical base. Since it seemed that animal species had survived by wiping others out, an attitude began to take root which applied a similar approach in the realm of human relations. Hitler, no doubt, perverted this theory (or perhaps, extended it) to emphasize that his was the "master race," justifying the extermination of "inferiors." Freud, much influenced by social Darwinism, created the fancy that aggression is an instinct, thereby casting a cheerless fog over the future of mankind, particularly with the onset of the nuclear era. The influence of these two giants, far from providing a realistic or scientific view of man, has merely fettered intellectual forces of the twentieth century, leaving them thrashing in a mire of appallingly retrogressive pessimism.

Ashley Montagu admits that competition and aggressiveness can be observed in the behavior of animals and humans but insists that these arise only when circumstances create conditions "largely, if not entirely, of a frustrating nature."[15] He rejects the negative emphasis of social Darwinism by citing such works as *Cooperation Among Animals* and *The Principles of Animal Ecology*, by W. C. Allee, quoting this latter "monumental" work appropriately as follows:

> The probability of survival of individual living things, or of populations, increases with the degree with which they harmoniously adjust themselves to each other and their environment. This principle is basic to the concept of the balance of nature, orders the subject matter of ecology and evolution, underlies organismic and developmental biology, and is the foundation for all sociology.[16]

Montagu, after wide-ranging studies of human behavior in many sectors of the globe, categorically rejects the myths about human beings being innately competitive, and research such as that conducted by Nelson and Kagan with Mexican children would seem to bear him out. Among these children competitive drives were lacking *because they had not been taught.*

In any case, the liberation of men demands a restoration of balance in such fields as have been ravaged by the competitive ideal. Until this balance is found, men, and particularly American men, will suffer individually and collectively. It is high time that parents and educators gave more careful consideration to the matter before sending men into the world, impelled haplessly toward nothing more than competition and winning.

Chapter 9 ✳ VIOLENCE
A Dead-End Ploy

Because war is as ancient as man, unthinking people suppose it to be a necessary evil; but cannibalism, the burning of virgins as sacrifices, and similar barbarities are as ancient as man, yet social evolution has relegated them to the primitive past and we do not think it extraordinary.

—SYDNEY J. HARRIS[1]

Encouraging competition is a way of encouraging contention and rivalry. It is a path, conceivably, to violence. As a feature of urbanized America, violence has become so routine that we feel able to say, as Tolstoy did, "One speaks and writes nowadays about executions, hangings, murders, and bombs as one formerly spoke of the weather."

The American male has been nursed by a violence-prone ethic. Why this has been so requires complex inquiries, but that it *is* so is obvious when we consider crime statistics or remember the bandying about of such slogans as "The army will make a man out of you."

What is meant by this, perhaps, is not that killing itself or the infliction of injury on others is a prerequisite of manhood, although there are more than a few who may understand the slogan in this way. More likely, however, the slogan means to say that the army will bring social contacts of a wider nature, with the challenge that opens a young man to maturity. It will offer travel and a sense of orderliness; rowdy youths will be tamed and made accountable to others. In short, it will provide men with what many feel is necessary regimentation. The fact that all of this is done within the confines of a group that is organized for killing is hardly taken into account.

And yet violence is taken for granted, particularly since the advent of television, which has brought the haggard faces of homeless civilians and the screams of napalmed youngsters into American living rooms, year in and year out. If the American public spends 80 percent of its leisure time preoccupied with TV and radio, there can be no doubt but that the horror of rising crime statistics invades psyches on daily news programs or on the variety of fictional crime programs. Instead of disassociating human nature from violence, many have come to believe that far from being a socially induced reaction, violence is simply innate behavior.

Once again we are face to face with a morbid image of our species, one that popularizers of "innate aggression" theories would encourage. Like proud fathers who teach their sons to box and wrestle, jabbing at opponents when they seem to leave themselves "wide open," the popularizers aim to instill a belief that we are all endowed with aggressive tendencies and that it is "perfectly natural" for us to kill and, in fact, to enjoy killing.

Robert Ardrey, playwright turned ethologist, is among those theorizers whose work has been taken as proof that men revel in bloodletting. Ardrey himself revels in saying so. Failing, I hope, to see that he provides, in a sense, justification for murder on scales both large and small, he hastens to tell us what passed through the minds of men who lived 500,000 years ago.[2] "Those men who had an efficient capacity for violence," he recalls, "who enjoyed violence, were the men who survived." Such bursts of assurance about what *enjoyments* transpired a half million twelvemonths past are mystifying at best. Perhaps it is Ardrey's same self-assurance that leads him to describe it as "perfectly natural" for a modern man to hit his wife over the head and kill her, adding with aplomb: "We had the same instincts in the old days." While Ardrey may have been around in the "old days," I was not, and so I don't feel competent as a commentator on values in those times. I do wish that Ardrey, in making such statements, would be a bit more explicit, however. There have always been communities where murder is practically unknown. My own grandfather came from one: Stornaway, on the Isle of Lewis, in the North Sea off the coast of Scotland. There, for example, not one murder occurred in two hundred years. When it did finally (recently), it was not the work of an islander but of an outsider. Perhaps Ardrey would account for this two-hundred-year lull in "the natural order of things" by calling it a wave of repression.

It is not my province to debate Ardrey's theories, however. As a former Hollywood script writer, he possesses a sense of drama and highlighting which have simply led him to draw colossal conclusions from small particulars. When members of the species Homo sapiens try to account for their own often baffling images in order to discover what sort of motivations are at the core of human behavior, they turn to different divining rods. Some choose local religions, others prefer astrology, and in recent times there has been a tendency to examine and gloat over what other animals do. Ardrey has become something of a well-known fortune teller, using animals for his cards. Whatever they do is a *must* for us! The trouble with this kind of spirit-rapping is that it always encourages people to look elsewhere rather than at themselves for whatever will be their fortune.

There are more than a few experts bemoaning Ardrey's conclusions. I wish them well while suggesting that healthier individuals and societies are living rebuttals to Ardrey's focus on perversity. Violence and aggression are certainly used as often meaningless means, but among animals they are likely to arise for the most part only in situations in which vital interests are threatened. Aggressive behavior has a defensive function. An animal responds to menacing onslaughts by either fleeing or attacking. More often animals flee except when they have no chance to do so. This would seem to be the more clever route to survival, since there is no telling what ugly deformities most animals would sustain if they fought at every turn of the path. In his recent book *The Anatomy of Human Destructiveness*, Dr. Erich Fromm asks a logical question based on the fact that most animals do flee: "Why, then, do instinctivists talk exclusively about the intensity of the innate impulses of aggression, rather than speak with the same emphasis about *the innate impulse for flight?*"[3] Many men may find it possible to push Fromm's inquiry a step further by recalling their military training, a process meant to eliminate what the high command could consider mild manners.

A form of brainwashing, it has aimed at instilling in men attitudes toward killing which are new and different from those they seem to have had before entering the military. Young men charge across practice fields, screaming, "Kill, kill, kill," and the requirement that they take orders is meant to assure that they will do just that when they are on the battlefield—no questions asked. One wonders whether much nationalistic indoctrination from public school through "basic training" is meant to suppress what Fromm calls man's "flight instinct." At the same time, if it is indeed so difficult to suppress this instinct (and judging by the intensity of masculine taboos and constrictions, this would seem to be the case), perhaps this indoctrination is itself responsible for much of the violence that proceeds unchecked in our society.

What is necessary in war is to destroy a soldier's *empathy* for those he fights against. This fact may account somewhat for the reluctance of our public institutions to encourage the development of feelings or emotional responses in men. Those selfsame feelings might lead to empathy and might prevent him, it is feared, from killing. Eastern philosophies teach man's kinship not only with other men but also with the lower animals. The Jain sect in India encourages the wearing of cloth masks so that its members won't destroy insects by accidentally inhaling them. Both Buddhism and Hinduism teach that all existence is an extension of the self. Fromm believes that men can be persuaded to kill each other when they have been taught to regard their opponents as something less than human—as alien beings. Thus, he says, Anglos called Germans Huns and Krauts in World Wars I and II, and the North Vietnamese became Gooks in the Southeast Asian war. When men do perceive the humanity of their opponents, however, killing becomes difficult and repugnant.

Taking these reflections into consideration, it is a chief task of our generation to examine the canons we promote in the name of defense. American concepts of defensive needs are hopelessly old-fashioned and are geared not to self-preservation but rather to ultimate destruction. If violence is an aberrant response to social strangulation, discomfort, and frustration and is fostered among men by the demotion of concerns traditionally considered "womanly," such as tenderness, there remains in any justification for its use only one still reputable premise. This is that violence must sometimes be used either for defense or to change intolerable conditions.

This premise accounts for a great deal of strutting, chest-puffing, and muscle display. Those who engage in such brandishings are dating themselves. American technology, in the form of nearly 100,000,000 guns, many of them handguns, has made muscles obsolete. It is impossible to estimate how many brutes and studs have been eliminated on urban streets by tiny bullets. If the federal government took away its citizens' constitutional right to bear arms, it is hard to say how long it might be before muscles came back into fashion. One could hope that a more peaceful society, sustained by finer values, would make them obsolete forever, except, perhaps, as emblems of good health.

Defense, if our species is to survive, must assume a wider meaning that men have not yet accorded to it. But Americans, thus far, seem little concerned with knowing truly how to defend themselves. The nearly sixty thousand persons killed in automobiles annually and the four million who are injured each year in these conveyances (the "horseless cowboys'" horses) make it clear that the public has not yet gotten around to demanding protection through the construction of safer vehicles and the engineering of superior runways for them. A great outcry over American lives lost in Vietnam finally brought protection to the unfortunates being killed in that conflict. In the ten years that the fighting was perpetrated, as many Americans were lost as are lost in only one year of auto fatalities. In the same decade ten times as many died on highways in our own "safe" nation, and yet very few balk. It is considered newsworthy when Ralph Nader refuses to ride in automobiles that do not provide safety belts. Why? Because knowing how to defend oneself, it seems, means being free of silly conventional attitudes about masculine or warlike posture and learning to perceive how defense must take on new meanings and adopt new procedures.

Much of what goes by the name of defense is productive of little more than acute paranoia. The person who would defend himself has become so conscious of his defensive posture that it brings upon him, like self-fulfilling prophecies, those misfortunes he is ready to expect. In the heat of expectation, as he looks about anxiously for an attacker, he often finds that those deranged misfits who believe that masculinity requires *attack* catch his eye at the very minute he spots them. His aggressive carriage— oh, so defensive—is an open invitation for compulsive assailants to prove their skills.

If defense is always conceived of as a state of readiness to do battle, then it may very well lead to the destruction of the person or nation so conceiving it. "Living by the sword" means not only striking others with it but also swinging it around and continually suggesting that its use is possible.

If men are going to construct meaningful defenses, these must include gentleness, sharing, generosity, and a host of other peaceful characteristics. They must be both active, like generosity, and passive, like the willingness to share. Our ideas of defense are primitive because they are based on tribal fortifications. We have carried the idiocies of the duel into the international arena. A public insult finds us ready to demand restitution of our honor. In a nuclear age, however, being trigger-happy can mean universal death. The more ominous our supply of weaponry, the more likely it seems to others that we may be tempted to fight. If defense is our true motivation, we must give every sign that we are peaceful, restraining implanted aggressive impulses in any sphere where we have sublimated them, especially in our economic dealings.

It can be argued that there is a viable stance that might be called intelligent nonaggressiveness. Such an approach would stipulate that a superior defense could succeed without vehemence, managing to ward off aggression without a struggle. Although this stance seems idealistic to some, it has extremely practical foundations and relies on degrees of passivity which may overcome in the long run.

Lao-tzu, perhaps one of the world's most outspoken opponents of violence as method, gave maxim after maxim to
illustrate this method. Water, he said, is considered weak,
but when it invades traditional citadels of strength, "nothing surpasses it, nothing equals it." What is implied in
this concept is that whatever seems hard and tough or
whatever shows a tendency to undue resistance is subject
to weakening and decay. It is a law of nature. The American adage "The bigger they are, the harder they fall"
might also read, "The harder they are, the more easily
they fall."

While gentleness, frugality, and humility may sound
like strange defenses to some, Lao-tzu suggested that gentle people do not live in fear of retaliation. Frugal people,
he said, can afford to be generous, and those who are
humble find that no one challenges their leadership. What
is offered here is the other side of the aggressive stance,
a glimpse into the great strengths that are inherent in
passivity. The reverse sides of gentleness, frugality, and
humility are rudeness, extravagance, and pride. These
qualities lead to devastation.

New weapons exist for the waging of peace. Sharing is
one of the greatest of such weapons. Reciprocity, or the
demand that we always receive a return equal to the
thing we have given, is not necessary under the banner
of sharing. Reciprocity has Calvinist overtones, and to conceive of the damage it often does one need only conjure
up the image of a small boy who, lacking generous impulses, scraps with and scolds playmates because they
have not given him what he seems constantly concerned
about: an exact return.

Those who have accumulated great wealth must eventually share it or face the destruction of their fortresses
and the increasing clamor of ruffians. Marie Antoinette's
reputed comment about the ravaging poor, "Let them eat

cake," has been translated into modern idioms and is repeated time and again by successful and wealthy members of society. The hope they retain of escaping from the ramifications of economic imbalances and social unrest is fading, however. The well-to-do no longer feel safe from marauding cutthroats. Sooner, hopefully, than later the rich will see that sharing means surviving. This principle applies on both the local and the international scenes.

It is significant that the idea of a guaranteed annual income for every citizen was voiced openly by Senator George McGovern in his Presidential campaign and that it was greeted as "radical." McGovern's proposal was in fact not so different from the suggestions of President Nixon, who promised much the same thing but couched it in better-camouflaged terminology. Both political parties see that technological advances will deprive citizens of jobs and that a guaranteed annual income is the least a society of "great abundance" can do for those in its domains, particularly as joblessness climbs.

More research into death-dealing diseases would be an excellent form of defense and a weapon, if we shared our knowledge, for peace. It is certain that many citizens will lose loved ones this year to cancer, heart disease, and other dreaded ailments.

Another weapon with which to wage peace is communication. Television is now the most potent of such weapons in humankind's arsenal. If powerful networks were dedicated to promoting world harmony, giving men everywhere a much-needed sense of neighborliness and neighborhood, whole populations might share appreciation of each other's unique perspectives. This could be done without stepping on ideological feet. The eighty to ninety billion dollars spent each year on bigger and better bombs might be spent in part, at least, establishing close ties between nations through a vast web of international communication. Perhaps the concept of an international auxiliary language is too abstract for most admirals and generals, but if they began to allot at least part of their budgets to such research and to international cooperation toward such ends, mankind might at last find that real and quite practical steps had been taken toward the establishment of peace. Defense would bristle with new implications.

The nuclear age has brought about a situation in which superpowers know that "winning" is no longer possible. As it stands, if either "wins," both lose. This means that victory as a goal is no longer feasible. No political ambition could possibly be important enough to warrant the use of old-fashioned weaponry like hydrogen bombs and multiple warheads. In fact, even conventional warfare has proved itself incapable of achieving victory in localized conflicts. The Vietnamese experience demonstrated this fact. For ten years the most powerful nation on earth rained bombs and imported well-equipped soldiers into a tiny Asian country. At last it was forced to withdraw, after threatening to "bomb them back into the Stone Age," without reaching its goals.

Hannah Arendt, whose book *On Violence* is a valuable political examination of this subject, tells us how so-called rationality among "scientifically minded brain trusters in the councils of government" plays a frightening role in the making of hypotheses that include violence as a solution for national problems. She writes:

> They reckon with the consequences of certain hypothetically assumed constellations without, however, being able to test their hypothesis against actual occurrences. The logical flaw in these hypothetical constructions of future events is always the same: what first appears as a hypothesis—with or without

its implied alternatives, according to the level of sophistication—turns immediately, usually after a few paragraphs, into a "fact" which then gives birth to a whole string of similar non-facts, with the result that the purely speculative character of the whole enterprise is forgotten.[4]

Arendt examines the flaws in theories that propose violence for various purposes. There are instances, probably, when it seems to be the only recourse, but these are *apolitical* and rise spontaneously from on-the-spot conditions. Planned violence, utilized to highlight long-term political goals, nearly always fails, according to her analysis. Even if it is used, as some revolutionaries propose, for short-term goals and for demonstrations, the danger exists that "the means overwhelm the end." If the goals are not reached quickly, there will be not only failure but also an implantation of violence as method into the particular civilization. Arendt tells us: "The practice of violence, like all action, changes the world, but the most probable change is to a more violent world."[5]

If change and reform are what are sought, the successes of the world's foremost nonviolent strategists provide us with examples of political and social revolution. Mahatma Ghandi in India and Martin Luther King in the United States both achieved a radical alteration of the systems in which they lived among the oppressed millions they represented. A lesser known but effective nonviolent movement was that conceived by Kwame Nkrumah, who achieved political independence for the Gold Coast (now Ghana). Nkrumah thought of his nonviolent resistance movement as "positive action." He used nonviolent weapons, including noncooperation, strikes, boycotts, and propaganda through the media, to gain the ends he and his followers sought.

The significance of these facts for men who have been indoctrinated with a readiness to fight either for self-preservation or for dignity is that alternatives—often more sensible—exist. The flexing of muscles and a naïve faith in physical power inculcated in childhood may seem harmless enough on the surface, but if such responses become widely accepted, as they have been in the United States, their effect will be felt in the councils of government. When "threats" emerge from any quarter, collective fists will rise to smash them with brute force as long as voters believe that "getting tough" is the best policy. As a solution to problems posed by threats, violence is short-sighted. It prevents people from putting healing salve on exposed irritations and from eliminating peacefully the causes of a threat. It keeps them from expanding in their understanding of themselves in given situations. "To understand all is to forgive all," says an old French proverb. A violent solution is the end of even the initiative to understand. Finally, one wonders precisely what was meant when Jesus, often described as the Prince of Peace, said, "The meek shall inherit the earth." It may be that his comment contains more truth than poetry.

Chapter 10 ❋ WORK
The Making of Dull Boys

In so-called developed countries like those of Western Europe, the United States, the Soviet Union, and Japan, growth is going to cease. They are going to find themselves in a permanent state of siege in which the material conditions of life will be at least as austere as they were temporarily during the two world wars.
—ARNOLD TOYNBEE ON HIS EIGHTY-FIFTH BIRTHDAY

A great deal of violence is done to men without their being aware of it. The obligations they feel in connection with working, for example, often cause psychic damage. This is because men are assigned only one role: provider. Those who do not fancy a designation signifying they are beasts of burden are invited to follow this discussion of the contretemps that providers suffer as they are fed into industrial machinery.

Dr. Joan Gomez says, "Some 200,000 American men between the ages of 15 and 55 will die this year [1974] as opposed to 121,000 women." Dr. Gomez believes that the most likely candidate for early death has drive and energy:

> He married early, works hard and takes on responsibilities. He is restless and active and his mood swings from anxiety to boredom, but he cannot spare time for exercise or relaxation. His only recreation is eating and drinking. He drives fast. He has business lunches.

Scanning the obituary page of the daily newspaper gives

121

a vivid sense of how many years *young* many men are when they die. What can be done to discourage this spiral in which so many are caught?

First, men must see that the priorities for which they have chosen to labor are frustrating their real needs. These priorities, many of which have nothing to do with basic needs, are supported by vague concepts like "security." They help to create the provider syndrome, the formula for which is this: Job = money = possessions = security.

It would not be fair to blame only capitalist barons for this syndrome; they are caught in questionable quests as often as anyone. They are simply at the wheels, although they have no real idea of where they are driving everybody. Almost everyone, both entrepreneur and employee, is struggling so that he may possess and be secure, often with little or no thought given to a different emphasis on requirements and necessities. Men suffer discontent without knowing why, or if they feel truly successful, they may wonder why their sons refuse to follow in their footsteps, rejecting life-styles to which they have accustomed themselves for so long.

Could it be that young people are seeking a new sense of adventure in their lives? They see that even the executives of major corporations are taught to be mild, conventional, well-behaved specimens who, no matter what the provocation, will remain seated. If inspired creativity, excitement, and pride are the workingman's hopes, it is clear to American youths that these incentives are rapidly disappearing.

The daily life of the corporation employee seems bland and boring. The rugged individualism projected in capitalist lore is lost as he sits in lushly carpeted offices where the faint clacking of typewriters can barely be heard above Muzak. When corporation men meet one another in elevators or in the cafeteria, conversations are pathetically devoid of anything resembling passion for mutually shared activities. In some cases not even *effort* is any longer required of men, and workdays consist of long coffee breaks, longer lunch periods, and afternoons spent waiting for 5 P.M. The joy of production, of watching the growth of one's own creative projects, is impeded because employees deal with products having nothing to do with their own interests, products they rarely even see. Karl Marx suggested that men at work experience themselves as strangers, but he was mistaken when he said that only at home, during leisure hours, are men truly themselves. There too, unprepared to deal with domestic life, they are disinterested and bored.

If the economy survives as we presently know it, changes in men's values might be slow to appear. If, however, it is now in flux on a grand scale, as I believe it to be, searching reconsiderations about priorities are long past due.

Men might find release from many stresses if only the corporate state were better harnessed to public interests. If more public parks and beaches graced Floridian or Hawaiian coastlines instead of today's massive oceanfront condominiums, for example, men of the future might find those quiet places they are clearly going to need.

Monied interests (which now means big business) have never been terribly concerned with public welfare, however. Production, efficiency, organization, and profits are what they like. As long as profits pour into corporate coffers, long-range goals involving the common good get little thought.

Business tycoons, it is true, have allowed reforms, but more often they have fought them. As far back as the nineteenth century prominent businessmen opposed legislation in the public interest at every turn of the road. They have opposed unemployment compensation, Medicare, the Antitrust Act, an end to pollution of the environment, ecological reforms, building codes, mine safety, zoning laws, load limits on trucks, and even the dating of milk cartons in grocery stores. Still, American men have been reluctant to criticize an economic system that has provided such abundance and have plodded to work each morning, believing that it will continue to so provide. Until recently, that is.

A Louis Harris survey made public by a Senate subcommittee found that public confidence in big business declined dramatically during a five-year span. At the beginning of that span 59 percent of the public spoke well of the business community, but in September, 1973, the Harris poll found that enthusiasts for the major American companies had dwindled to only 29 percent of the population. Among younger people the figures indicated an even greater distrust.

Fred J. Cook's *The Warfare State*, written in the early sixties, was a first of its kind. This book detailed the intimate love affairs that go on between industrial tycoons and Pentagon generals. Eisenhower's last statement as President warned against the acquisition of unwarranted power by what he called "the military-industrial complex." The military peacetime budget climbed from seventy-nine billion dollars in 1974 to almost eighty-five billion in 1975. As early as 1961 certain senators like Henry "Scoop" Jackson encouraged bigger and better military budgets. The simple fact that Jackson came from the state of Washington, where Boeing Aircraft, the state's largest employer, was in need of military contracts, was too good to let pass unnoticed. There was no doubt about it: What some critics said about our economy needing war to perpetuate itself seemed too close to the mark, although the reasons were perhaps not the ones they gave. There are obviously grave inequities in business ethics as practiced, and they are eating away at the foundation of everyone's securities. By the end of 1973, however, the "system" was already tottering visibly. Nixon's 1974 State of the Union message, which glossed over growing hardships faced by Americans, was not well received. A Herblock cartoon at the time showed an American man eating a few beans for supper and saying to his wife, "Our dollars are buying more, the country is in great shape, he's innocent [the President], and this is a lovely steak dinner."

In discussions of business motivations many people were expressing insecurities about the economy. Present in those conversations were persistent doubts about the morality, virtue, and integrity of the corporate state. Those who chose to defend it did so not on ethical grounds but on the basis of its practical successes. Only there was a kink in this approach too. The successes had come to a halt, temporarily at least, and while the President was promising that there would be no recession, things looked bleak indeed. While only a few years before it had seemed appropriate to point to spectacular material progress under capitalism and to laud the miracles of mass production, by this time few were willing to say that capitalism would once again be its old sweet self.

No one, in fact, gave any ethical credit to raw capitalism at all. Rather they spoke in Ayn Rand's tones of the selfishness of human nature, which will not strive to accomplish without materialistic incentives. Only personal profit, they insisted, can provide such an incentive. This view of human nature fails to inspire; it is a mythic view that is tough- and hard-sounding and seems, therefore, "realistic."

Many of the evils passing under the banner of the corporate state might as well be invisible, so accustomed to most of them have we become. Yet this system has been hailed as a necessary accompaniment to our freedom. This is nonsense. The freedoms we laud in America are not the products of corporate ingenuity but rather of the Bill of Rights and the Constitutional guarantees that have kept our society open to critical evaluations and the possibility of change. Major companies, on the other hand, have been shown to be meddling in the affairs of foreign governments, attempting to sway their elections, and concerned primarily with their own survival and expansion.

Political analysts have long believed that despite their deficiencies and cruelties, immense concentrations of corporate power would continue to maintain their hold as long as they satisfied material wants. They have told us that Establishment businessmen will make a few reforms at a rate that meets the demands of the average citizen. As long as this is done, they have contended, there will be no clamor for sweeping economic change. Perhaps they have underestimated the common man.

Until the onset of the famed energy crisis, which gave the American people a closeup of the Great Profit Motive walking hand in hand with Negligence, the political analysts' contentions may have seemed sound. Suddenly, however, the land of plenty was struck by shortages in everything from wheat, plastic, and paper to the very lifeblood of the entire industrial economy: oil. Although solar energy could have been harnessed years before and although the heat of the sun might have provided free energy to warm living rooms, run elevators, and propel other machines, no one had been willing to research and implement the use of such energy. Why? In part because the profit motive was missing, and also because oilmen set up effective blocks to solar energy development. Sunshine, so readily available, so unlimited, does not require mining, and so no one can get too rich accepting its bounty. In other words, major corporations in collusion with an influenced political machine preferred to drain the very bowels of the earth, to allow poor citizens to freeze in their living rooms, and to wax indifferent as profits for scarce goods piled high.

Suddenly an aroused citizenry shouted, "Why didn't someone tell us this was going to happen? Why didn't someone keep an inventory?"

Senator "Scoop" Jackson, blaming the Administration in power, said, "What is apparently lacking is the will to impose some order and common sense on an economy that is approaching chaos." In an honest moment Jackson might have admitted that no single Administration could be held accountable. Both political parties have waltzed with a fossilized economy for years, measuring success in circulating dollars, the *symbols* of wealth, rather than keeping track of real wealth in the form of food, natural resources, and shelters and offering more than urban jitters, inflated rents and mortgages, and a growing sense of insufficiency.

Oil and gas shortages, electrical blackouts and brownouts, and other strains on a burdened populace have upset family balances, sometimes even causing death for the overtaxed. A couple in their nineties, Catherine and Frank Baker, were found dead in their two-story home in Schenectady, New York, after the local utility company shut off their heating power. A spokesman for the Mohawk Power Corporation defended the move by saying, "We try to use personal discretion in these cases. Obviously we are more reluctant to turn off power in the winter than we are in the summer." The Bakers' heat was shut off because of unpaid utility bills. Another company representative said, "We're running a business," but the chairman of the Schenectady County Human Rights Commission announced that he was "disgusted and heartsick." He added: "I am sure this tragedy will not be the last occurring to older folk." In fact, rising food prices found some oldsters eating canned dog food. The government rushed gallantly to their aid by instituting nutritious daily meals for the elderly poor, but food prices for everyone else climbed, as did the cost of gas and oil.

Supreme Court Justice William O. Douglas blamed collusion between big business and the government for shortages. Such crises, he said, are caused by powerful corporate lobbies, and the nation's tax system is "designed to protect those out to destroy our natural resources."

In the 1972 elections major corporations gave money both legally and illegally to campaigns waged by political incumbents. This shattered illusions about the existence of a two-party system for federal elections.

The New York Times expressed the insecurities voiced by citizens in an editorial titled "American Perspective": "The United States is a nation adrift. From almost any vantage point, thoughtful citizens have difficulty gaining a steady perspective on the country's problems and prospects."

The editorial bemoaned two years of "roaring boom and rising inflation," noting that the American economy has begun to drift downward at "an increasingly rapid rate." Unemployment figures have been taking alarming jumps, and most economists agree, says the editorial, that "joblessness will continue to climb sharply."[1]

In the face of such apprehensions men can no longer harbor illusions about the work world. It is not dependable. A retired labor leader put it to me this way:

A young man prepares himself for a career through long, hard years of schooling. He is told that he needs such preparation so that he will be able to step into a top position in the company. But when he gets into the company, he often finds that the qualifications he has aren't as important as he'd been told they were and that promotion depends on many factors besides ability and knowledge. While he spends years waiting for promotions, he finds that his paycheck is buying less and less, and he begins to say to himself, "This isn't living."

Highly successful men, those who have had a chance to be creative and independent while taking risks and making decisions, see things differently. Money, because they often have more than enough for their own needs, is seldom a problem for such men. The challenges provided by their work are what keeps them loyal to a corporate structure, even though it may be riding roughshod over the necks of employees on lower rungs, polluting the environment, or currying political favors to extend its boundaries. When challenges to the system are proffered, these men defend it by saying that there is opportunity for those with initiative and ability. They often forget that the achievement of a success comparable to their own can only be the good fortune of a few. Most corporate structures stand on a hierarchical base, a pecking order, with an elite directing vast numbers who toil with little satisfaction below. Some successful men, however, opt for satisfactions of a different sort and have dropped out of the system to recapture a more vibrant sense of living.

Men who are not in top management positions seldom feel an invigorating pride in routine corporate jobs. Not only must they face daily routines that are neither challenging, engrossing, nor productive of results they can actually see, but also their leisure time fails to satisfy them. Dissatisfaction is growing because these workers can now see how dog-eat-dog values have ravaged the continent, drained resources, and spawned materialistic armies of consumer robots doing the bidding of corporate superiors.

Such men recall little of their early idealism as they search in mirrors for their souls. Although their eyes once shone brightly, the brightness began to disappear after they entered the rat race and became twentieth-century serfs.

Workers striving to "get ahead" follow rules laid down by their companies, but they are becoming increasingly aware of what they miss when they structure life around clerical drudgery. The two-week vacation with a promise of a month's vacation after ten years' service is not enough. Children may share family outings on weekends or be squeezed between morning golf and afternoon shopping, but the relationships between working fathers and mothers and their offspring often wither.

While dissatisfactions continue to build, advertising and other forms of social pressure bear down on the worker, convincing him he needs commodities his neighbor has already purchased. Thus the economy, instead of being geared to public welfare, has become a boiling pot of impractical articles, and men judge each other's successes by the number of possessions they have amassed: automobiles, clothing, and bigger and better TVs.

It is quite possible that for many men the amassing of possessions becomes their way of identifying themselves. Certain items not only demonstrate identity to others, they hope, but also become reflections or perhaps extensions of themselves: "I am a man who owns two autos." "I am a man who affords a house in Scarsdale." "I am a man who has provided his son with an education and a sports car." Liberace has quipped, "The difference between the men and the boys is the price of their toys."

A society encouraging this kind of thinking fails to emphasize riches of a more personal sort. When a man's ownership of particulars long taken for granted comes to a halt as the economy suffers reverses, those who identify themselves through positions and possessions face especially difficult times. They will feel impoverished and lost, no longer using either jobs or toys as guideposts on the path to self-definition.

Some Jewish survivors of Nazi concentration camps have detailed their discoveries of themselves after being stripped of all possessions. One writer, who had his doctoral thesis taken away, the gold removed from his teeth, and his clothing stolen, spoke of how he had found himself in a primary sense as never before. His possessions gone, he was forced to meditate on what he did have. What he discovered were the values that stood at his core: those facets of character giving him dignity as a human being.

Scotland's muse, Robert Burns, pointed, as have sages in all centuries, to holdings more important than material goods—those that make a man of worth not only to others but to himself as well:

> What though on hamely fare we dine
> Wear hodd'in grey and a'that
> Gie fools their silks and knaves their wine
> A man's a man for a'that.
> For a'that and a'that
> Their tinsel show and a'that
> The honest man though air sae poor
> Is king of men for a'that.

What this means for today's beleaguered male is that he may feel greater exhilarations if he does not become "demented with the mania of owning things." Nor need he feel, given the fact of technological change and even the possibility of economic collapse, that he must remain tied to conventional jobs that are draining him but giving little in return. Men have been all too ready to identify themselves *as men* through the work they do, the possessions they own, and the successes they have achieved through competition. This has put undue stress on vast numbers who feel that failure in the work world stains their masculine identity. Young men are told they must have leadership ability, power, control, competitive spunk —qualities and values for which most present-day jobs simply have no room, or if they do, they create the very problems of which we complain.

For those who choose to remain in the system, a redefinition of masculinity is necessary and is, in fact, already occurring. Redefining, which is also the task of this book, allows men to treat themselves more kindly instead of measuring themselves against the harsh standards of the past.

Surely in a world of such bewildering complexity and change, no man can hold himself responsible if he is unemployed. Surely he learns not to define himself only through his work. As technology puts more and more men out of their jobs or as economic earthquakes rumble on every side, such self-recrimination can lead only to psychological hysteria on a mass scale, as it does now among the poor. Ghetto dwellers, in a rage because they think they have failed, find belligerent outlets for those pent-up aggressions they have been taught are their natural heritage. In every land we hear the clamor of the nearly one-third of the earth's population presently living in dire poverty. Manouchehr Ganji, an Iranian scholar, presented a report to the United Nations' Commission on Human Rights which says that a billion men, women, and children survive on incomes "estimated in United States purchasing power at 30 cents a day."[2]

One of the first things men can do to avoid being caught too painfully in the grind of social breakdowns is to inquire into what social changes are transpiring as the disjunction of the entire system proceeds. They can make themselves fully cognizant of the fact that enormous upheavals are taking place, that the established order is crumbling, and that new social constructs are rising in our midst. Certain philosophers have told us that no truly profound philosophy can be built except on the firm foundation of "unyielding despair." This is a bit extreme, perhaps, but there is some truth for our age in the idea. Translated in a different way, one might say, as the Buddha did, that each man must build his life on an awareness that nothing lasts and that everything is subject to change. There is no reason to despair, however, or to insist that things are hopeless. Quite the contrary. Once men have tasted what has been called the wisdom of insecurity, the dance they do to life will be imbued with greater passions, freedoms, elasticities, and spontaneities that find them taking risks leading to autonomy.

Judith M. Bardwick, in her study *Men and Work,* said that the most outstanding characteristic of highly successful men was that they were not only risk-takers but also risk-creators. This means that such men seemed willing to throw security and all the safety and comfort it implies into the air, gambling on the possibility that they and the world they have juggled will land upright. These men created risks and kept their lives in flux, never sedentary, never secure. No matter how safe they felt in a given spot, no matter how convenient or calm were their surroundings, they were usually willing to throw themselves headlong into new areas. Their success, according to Bardwick's study, has seldom been guaranteed. They have been confident nevertheless, not because of money hoarded or because of possessions but because they felt within themselves those qualities needed to build meaningful relationships in any sphere.

Granted that millions of American men can hardly be expected to abandon "safe" ships overnight. Many will cling to small life preservers, hoping that the ship's captain will do something clever, that rescue boats will appear miraculously out of nowhere, or that the ship itself will stay afloat and save them the trouble of swimming.

Except for the most imaginative, a high standard of living is too great a price to pay in exchange for exhilaration experienced in the whirl of metamorphosis and uncertainty. Many men, though, are now considering a jump into the sea. They are, after all, strong enough to swim. They are asking themselves exactly what values they hold when they refer to a "high standard of living." Perhaps the concept is leaving its materialistic implications behind and taking on spiritual ones. Perhaps the repetition of seditious Christian maxims are finally having their cumulative effect: "It is easier for a camel to go through the eye of a needle than for a rich man to enter the kingdom of God."

There is no doubt that financial security is at best shaky in these times. No insurance can guarantee the survival of our currency as we know it. We have watched with mild surprise as the foundations of one institution after another have fallen before rushing change. Somehow it seldom occurs to us that those same winds might blow through the United States Treasury Building, leaving in their wake comtemporary equivalents of Confederate cash.

A quest for security, no matter of what kind, is actually a search for the unattainable. An ultimate security cannot be guaranteed. It exists only when there is no change, no hint of alteration, diversification, or transformation. When a man is utterly secure, he is untouched. There is no room for meaningful choice, for animated movements, or for those extremes that give men reason for courage, ingenuity, or appreciation. The secure man need not risk. He does not have to devise new routes for himself. If security is his goal and he has reached it, he no longer realizes the worth of experience outside of his framework. To empathize with adventuresome souls he might have to leave his lair.

Even if the economic structure of society were not

endangered, insightful men would still hope for better values than those that consumer capitalists have wished on them. Even if the ship were not sinking, they might still persuade themselves that their little life preservers—the jobs they cling to and by which they define themselves—are really the poorer half of a bargain whose better side would be to welcome the hazards of authentic living.

The man who finds self-worth and identity solely through his work is in a precarious position during fluctuations of the economy. Just how precarious it could be may be judged when we consider that a quarter of a century from now there will be twice as many human beings as there are at present. Automation by that time will have been developed on new levels, and armies of the jobless will abound. The amount of college training a man has may scarcely matter. If there is not rapid change in our role expectations, calamities will follow.

With the unemployed feeling worthless because they have been taught a worn-out ethic, we may expect reflections of their feeling in behavior. The jobless poor now feel worthless and strike irrationally at their surroundings. Deprived of the esteem society gives to those who have had success as breadwinners, jobless men lose their self-esteem, the base of their respect for others. The nonachiever doubts himself and shares with those like him an envy and antipathy for those who are successful. The Calvinist work ethic may very well be manufacturing criminals.

What remains to be said about work in these pages will be directed, nevertheless, to those who *are* employed. Men who work are subject to different kinds of pressure, and these can often cause great psychic damage because the average man is not aware of them. The man who has no job may be able to pinpoint his dejection, but when a man feels anxiety and frustration while on the job, he wonders why. His condition worsens if he accepts bread-winning as his most important function. There is little doubt then that he feels guilty about his dissatisfaction, considering that he, at least, is working while many march in the ranks of the unemployed. Seeing himself mainly as provider—a one-dimensional self-appraisal—he gets little joy from his other roles: those of husband, father, or community guru. Looking for his satisfactions in narrow spheres, he, the provider, becomes an alienated worker.

A man's alienation from his work has many sources in masculinist tradition. Playing the role of provider is only one such source, but others are equally important. A look at long-accepted beliefs about what it means to be masculine will explain not only a man's alienation from work but also his estrangement from other facets of his life.

There are outmoded values that operate throughout the American male's work world and that call for skeptical scrutiny. As we examine these values, we shall notice how they affect the very core of a male's ability to perceive as well as the kind of business world he moves in.

Chapter 11 ❊ DOMINANCE
An Impediment to Awareness

There is no evidence for unalterable drives for ownership or dominance or to kill.

—Drs. John Lewis and Bernard Towers[1]

Men claim praise from one another for being dominant. As with competition, the means to this end are given little consideration. The praise is accorded to dominance *for its own sake.* Men are taught from birth that they must be on top. The man who is on top is considered "manly" because he controls. Ideally, he has complete control. Whether such "mastery" is the result of promotion (as when men climb hierarchical structures) or refers to governing behavior in the home (even intimate behavior), the attempt to dominate for its own sake is made unashamedly.

Since most men have little chance to dominate in their offices, this acquired urge finds its outlet mostly in the home. If a man is not Master of All on the job, he can at least lay claim to such a title under his own roof. Social custom supports him.

Dominance for its own sake, elevated to a primary appetite, leads to anxiety, destruction, and the crushing of spontaneity. What is seldom realized is that the dominant man is more than half blind. His concern for his position turns off his awareness of small detail and can lead easily to his demotion.

It is questionable whether domination can ever be truly successful. Each creature has its own intrinsic nature, and that nature is wont to fulfill itself in its own way. Although an attempt to dominate it may change it outwardly or reroute its behavior temporarily, whatever is immanent in its nature will try to reassert itself. Enforced taboos, for example, do not wholly succeed in dominating human sexual conduct.

Dominance seems visible in day-to-day life, but it can only uplift and enhance experience if tempered by other traits. The trait with which dominance is best superseded is cooperation.

To illustrate how dominance creates imbalances because of the value ascribed to it, it is only necessary to consider its opposite: yielding. A similar overattachment to passivity and yielding would warp civilization. This is not to say, of course, that yielding is unnecessary. As it now stands, men have given it too little consideration. To create needed balances in American culture, yielding as a source of strength needs exploration. It may be that a much greater emphasis on yielding will result in more cooperation between men. To see that this is done is a social task of the age. In the meantime the will to dominate begs examination.

Domination can never be total, is always temporary, and is based on an illusion of power. The illusion may very well be nearly real, as the power assumed may be very strong indeed, but it is not complete. Since existence is in flux, power cannot retain its hold. Most instances of domination by individuals or by groups is accomplished by trickery. Those dominated, accepting their domination as inevitable, believe that rulers, priests, or councils have a monopoly on power. They think there is no way they can possibly circumvent that power. A dominating man like Hitler may convince them in his more megalomanic moments that he is all-powerful, but any objective observer will tell him he rules by the aid of social superstitions and myths and that his climb to the top has been largely a fortuitous sequence of events. If he credits himself wholly for his seeming control, his egocentric perspective will only hasten his fall.

Priests dominate by appealing to mythical powers. The powers lie only in the minds of those dominated. A powerful ruler lays claim to being "top dog," but his dominance is mostly a matter of appearance or, perhaps, of definition. Ruling cliques can be rendered impotent before an idea. Aleksandr Solzhenitsyn, who defied the Soviet state and was exiled therefrom, could easily have been thrown into jail, for example, or tortured and executed. He was, after all, only a writer challenging the dogmatic hierarchy of an extremely powerful nation, a single human being disputing authorities who could dominate him outwardly with ease. No matter how complete might seem their ascendancy, however, Solzhenitsyn's pen would prove mightier. Though those in power might very well have imprisoned him, their control could only extend to his body. His thoughts could not be dominated, and these circulated worldwide. As Ingersoll put it:

> Surely it is a joy to know that all the cruel ingenuity of bigotry can devise no prison, no dungeon, no cell, in which for one instant to confine a thought; that ideas cannot be dislocated by racks, nor crushed in iron boots, nor burned with fire. Surely it is sublime to think that the brain is a castle, and that within its curious bastions and winding halls the soul, in spite of all worlds and all beings, is the supreme sovereign of itself.[2]

There is a nagging observation that must haunt every man who seeks domination for its own sake. Lao-tzu made it long ago:

> Those who would take over the earth
> And shape it to their will
> Never, I notice, succeed.

Those who pride themselves on being dominant risk the dissolution of their hopes because they concentrate too pointedly on the position they have achieved. They see themselves as unique and separate from others and from their environment. Doing so, they miss nuances, events, and actualities passing on every side. The energy consumed by pride that requires retaining a dominant position makes them blind to the reality of life as it proceeds. While they sit on top, unable to see in every direction simultaneously, incidents occur that eventually undermine them. If it is not a personal failure they experience, it is one in which what they stand for is eventually dispersed. As I write, I cannot help but think of Mao Tse-tung, who is near death and who will leave his image linked to his administration, hoping that it will be strong enough to hold compactly. A verse by Omar Khayyám comes to mind, in which the Persian muse tells what became of the court of a famous Iranian king:

> They say the lion and the lizard keep
> The courts where Jamshid gloried and drank deep.

The man who hopes to completely dominate or control is whistling in the dark in this age of such bewildering variety and change. This is so not only in the social realm; it applies to man's relations with nature as well. The illusion, encouraged by Western philosophies, that man is *apart* from nature or *above* nature and that it is his destiny to control and dominate nature may lead to cataclysms every bit as damaging as could flirting with nuclear domination in the social sphere.

Nature has its intrinsic character, and attempts to change or reroute it rather than cooperate with it may often, in the long run, create more serious difficulties than those that domination proposes to solve. The Western concept of "dominant" man at the apex of creation, deciding by fiat what he will do to "conquer" nature, sets him aside as unique and separate. This view of himself as detached or above things blinds him to the reality that he is part of nature and that he must cooperate with his environment.

Control in the scientific sphere is often plodding, mechanical, and rigidly categorized by rational calculations. Scientists are finding that nature is not obeying or altogether following precise and uniform patterns and that those we do observe are our own descriptions of nature rather than its determining motivations.

In earlier times the scientific world view saw nature as a kind of machine. Initially the machine was said to have been created by divine law. Later this hypothesis began to change as it became apparent that the "machine" was running by itself. Finally came the realization that nature, no matter how exact our picture appears, is changing as we watch it, interacting with us, and demanding that we meet it anew at every turn of the road.

The methods of science have been primarily concerned with classification until relatively recently. With the onset of technological expertise, however, control and domination became a seeming possibility; the fragmented, sectionalized approach science had accustomed itself to using became a hindrance in applying such control. What "controllers" began to see was that nature is interrelated, that it cannot be chopped up piecemeal and dealt with one section at a time. All the drawbacks of old rationalistic methodology come into play in dealing with nature when the intellect conceives man as distinct from nature, missing reality as ensemble. Overreliance on terms leads to abstractions, and those controlling and dominating nature become hypnotized by their word structures. Existence cannot be systematized in this way, and yet many scientists still arrogantly assume they can do so.

Interference in one sphere produces unexpected and injurious effects in others. It is only necessary to read Rachel Carson's *The Silent Spring* to see what "scientific control" has wrought in nature.[3] The use of insecticides, she says, threatens man's very existence. Nature has its own ways of checking and balancing. If man needs speedier methods, perhaps he might cooperate with natural processes by introducing more insect-devouring species to certain areas. Or perhaps crops that need protection could be surrounded by vegetation preferred by crop-eating insects so that the primary crops would be left untouched. Such methods might have more beneficial results in the long run than do insolent attempts at elimination by force.

Analytic, intellectualized approaches to nature are producing what Alan Watts called "an ever-growing accumulation of extremely complicated information, so vast and so complex as to be unwieldy for many practical purposes, especially when quick decisions are needed."[4]

What is lacking is the intuitive perception that sees man as part of the whole, as united with existence rather than separate from it. Henri Bergson said that intuition can never be as precise as intellect (the analytical approach) nor can it act as a substitute for it. "But what it lacks in precision," he wrote, "it makes up in immediacy. It comes into play whenever our vital interest is at stake. It pierces the darkness of night in which our intellect leaves us."

Scientific disciplines are highly specialized. When scientists in one field decide upon a course of control which deals with natural phenomena that crisscross many disciplines, they find themselves at a standstill, hardly knowing how to approach questions requiring mastery of more than one field. Watts suggested that technological progress is beginning to have the opposite of its intended effect. Experts know only what lies in their specialized areas, although they are consulted when problems arise. "Mastery of a single department of knowledge," said Watts, "is often as frustrating as a closetful of left shoes."[5]

While pride in his "ability" to dominate produces bitter fruit in man's environment, the effects it has on him as an individual are just as sour. Having achieved the "upper hand," he revels in his position, and his satisfactions become dependent on the rating he gets from others.

The problem behind this approach is easily exposed: The man at a high level, contrasting himself with those "below," fails to appreciate that his relations with others for his own good are just as interdependent as are his relations with nature. Achieving a high rating and enjoying it for its own sake, he becomes fearful of its loss. Thus protecting his rating becomes his most compelling task, and if he finds that he is losing it, he believes that this is the worst of calamities. With retention of dominance for its own sake as his chief end, he is stricken not only with anxiety but also with the fact that he will do almost anything to retain his rank even if it means interfering with the common good. If others have more to offer than he and the results will be beneficial but will detract from what he once did, he prefers to ignore or crush their offerings. In this way dominance for its own sake can become a highly conservative force, hiding contributions from others.

A man who takes pride in being dominant makes himself vulnerable in many ways. Without knowing it, he loses self-awareness, appreciation of others, and the abilities to act uninhibitedly, to play, to enjoy, to feel secure, to love, and to be free and socially adept.

The dominating man must wonder if those he dominates are actually showing their true feelings to him and relating to him honestly. If he is too sure of his right to be dominant (most men do not even question it), he may bypass their feelings and step on their sensitivities without consulting or giving them due consideration.

He may be foolishly inclined to accept only the word of peers instead of consulting, on occasion, those he considers his cortege. One of the worst blind spots he has shows when he assumes that certain people are his inferiors. A dominating employer, for example, may rush through his plant to see if it is truly on fire, as reported. He bypasses employees on lower rungs, assuming they know nothing, while he searches for managers or foremen.

Dominant men, fearing loss of position, may deal about important matters only with those who seem unlikely to topple them. Often they miss insights that could be gained from men of ability. If they are unduly attached to their positions, they derive pleasure only (or primarily) from facets of life that enhance their status without being aware that this is what they are doing. Often they miss whatever does not contribute in this way, as does any obsessionist.

The dominant man is sometimes surprised when he hears that others have high aspirations. When he receives preferential treatment because of his station, he doesn't hesitate to accept it, even at the cost of trampling on those he considers less worthy. He feels free, in fact, to inconvenience others so long as he may impose on them his idea of what their activities should be.

Finally, the dominating man runs a most dangerous risk both to himself and to others: losing the ability to distinguish between spontaneity and impulsiveness. This happens when he is convinced that what he does is best, since he is on top.

The theme of dominance will be touched upon in other sections of this book. Before leaving it as a topic, however, it may be wise to consult those who use dominance and submission as highlighted patterns for their relationships: the sadomasochists.

Sadomasochism is a growing phenomenon in the United States for reasons we will soon probe. Here it is enough to say that overt S&M couples frankly admit that their sexual patterns are games. The dominant figure, although appearing to impose his or her will on a submissive partner, is in fact a phony. It is his or her partner, in the final analysis, who determines to what degree domination will take place. In such relationships, therefore, it is the submissive partner who is actually in control. If he or she walks away, the game is over. Thus even those who base their love lives on power plays refuse to allow power a full reign in their affairs when the chips are down. This would indicate, it seems, a basic distrust for those whose will to dominate is strong.

Chapter 12 ❊ POLITICS
The White House Staff as Football Team

We are all in it together. This is a war. We take a few shots and it will be all over. Don't worry. I wouldn't want to be on the other side right now. Would you?

—President Richard M. Nixon, speaking to his aides on September 15, 1972, as recorded in the Presidential (Watergate) Transcripts

If men are innately aggressive or (as some religionists would have it) depraved by reason of Adam's sin, democracy is in serious trouble. Those who believe that men are ferocious beasts must cringe, in fact, at the thought that these same beasts have access to voting machines where they can express their ferocities.

The unique faith vouchsafed in democracy's vision, however, is that it trusts men to behave benignly as long as there is a free exchange of information among people, an optimistic view. It sees them as fair and peaceful, likely to choose the best for themselves en masse as long as they have access to information about what is really going on. The optimism, however, is only justified if viewpoints can be freely stated and circulated and if elected representatives carry out the people's will. If citizens do not know what is really going on and opposing views are never heard, a society can be expected to march all too confidently in one constricted direction. Otherwise, according to democratic belief, as long as the teeming multitudes remain suitably informed, it may be said of them that "they go toward something great, toward the best."[1]

U.S. politics has been the province of men, and that it should be permeated by old masculinist values is understandable. To the extent that these values are prime movers of the political processes, crushing everything that blocks their way, political machinery is a scourge rather than a help. The competitive politician who is prepared to take any steps necessary to win may care not at all for the means he uses. A new task awaits political scientists, and that is the discovery of ways in which politicians can be divested of opportunities for exercising masculinist values, as they do. Parliamentary procedure and the compromises practiced in a republican form of government are major concessions of masculinist values, but the accumulation of a politician's power, based on assistance from those who already wield power (like corporate barons), evokes masculinism and brings about competition fought with the iron fists of financial power.

To the extent that the citizens of a democratic society are imbued with masculinist values themselves, they will be reflected in the political structure. A politician wielding power in competitive, domineering, and violent ways is only acting by principles his community takes for granted, unless, of course, he resorts to violence in secret. The thirty-seventh President did this when he lied to the American people about the bombing of Cambodia, carrying on a secret war there.

The hard, inflexible "logic" characteristic of politicians who flee "permissiveness" because they cannot trust their fellows to spontaneous action and must see to it that they are structurally regimented and securely under control is everywhere apparent. It is expressed in the United States primarily by the politicos of the Right, although in Communist nations masculinist characteristics are just as obvious. Those few U.S. revolutionaries (leftists and rightists) who resort to violence are placing their faith in masculinist method; eventually, if they continue political assassinations, hijackings, and kidnappings, they can expect to meet their opponents' artillery, which will possibly be considerably more destructive.

The democratic Left in the United States has been traditionally antimasculinist, however. Long before the time when Harry S. Truman fired Douglas MacArthur, there were distinct cleavages between those who favored aggressive military ventures and those who did not. After World War II, for example, the United States, having had exclusive possession of the atomic bomb, might have waged "preventive war." There were those who favored such a policy. Instead the nation under Truman made a decision that has been called historically unprecedented and began to share its wealth with other countries, purportedly to keep them independent. During the Korean War General Douglas MacArthur, hero of the Far Right, was relieved of his position because he did not see eye to eye with his Commander-in-Chief about the prospect of bombing Red China. Truman did not want Korea to become the starting place of another world war and wished to contain the conflict if possible. He felt that it was enough to demonstrate to the Communists that the United States would not tolerate aggression. He entertained, in fact, a nonmasculinist definition of victory: It consisted of keeping all fighting to a minimum and refusing to be provoked into a general conflagration.

Truman, interestingly enough, recalled later that he never liked fighting. He said of his boyhood that he was not popular among some of the neighborhood boys. "The popular boys were the ones who were good at games and had big, tight fists," he told Merle Miller. "I was never like that. Without my glasses I was blind as a bat, and to tell the truth, I was kind of a sissy. If there was any danger of getting into a fight, I always ran. I guess that's why I'm here today."[2]

MacArthur presented the masculinist case by saying, "There is no substitute for victory," by which he meant military victory. It was a deceptively simple slogan.

The arrival of Senator Joseph McCarthy on the national scene complicated issues by bringing demands for "firmness" coupled with the fear of "pinko queers" in politics. McCarthy insisted that the threats facing Americans existed not only abroad but also at home, and he leveled a charge at his opponents which associated them with an "effeminate" attribute feared by many men: *softness*. The phrase "soft on Communism" became a rallying cry for political hopefuls. The right-wingers, because they pursued masculinist values and were eager to march against enemies both hypothetical and illusory, did not stop to think that their hero, MacArthur, had been canned because he had repeatedly called for an extension of the Korean War through the use of nuclear weapons on the Chinese mainland in direct defiance not only of his superiors but also of the nonmilitary authority on which the United States Constitution rests. It took considerable courage for Truman to fire the general, given his popularity as a World War II hero.

As MacArthur "faded away," Joseph McCarthy became even more shrill. He inherited MacArthur's followers and linked nonmasculinist images of political opponents with Communists, calling them queer and charging that the State Department was overrun by homosexuals. The purges he led of such institutions have recurred for years. For a time McCarthy successfully repressed dissent and made his brand of thinking the sole standard of loyalty to the nation. He watched with grim satisfaction as the constitutional foundations of the United States trembled at his touch.

Into the hubbub surrounding McCarthy and his followers came a right-wing Congressman from California who won his seat partly by charging that his opponent was "soft" and who won his reputation by prosecuting a man suspected of Communist ties. His name was Richard Milhous Nixon. A spiritual son of McCarthy, Nixon was later destined to take perhaps the most colossal masculinist strut across the American political stage ever, outdoing even President Theodore Roosevelt. Years before, "Teddy" had out-Hemingwayed Hemingway, carrying his "big stick" belligerently as a substitute for God only knows what. Critics have said of him: "He worshipped the strenuous life, was a lover of nature, an imperialist. His foreign policy was a kind of preview of fascism."[3] Roosevelt's letters are full of evidence of how virile he considered himself, poking fun (years before Nixon and Spiro Agnew did) at "effete society" in England and on the East Coast.

About Franklin Delano Roosevelt there are differing opinions. His son, James Roosevelt, said of his father that "he was not the sort of man who ever cried under any circumstances. I don't think there is a man or woman alive who ever saw him cry." There are others, Roosevelt appointee Supreme Court Justice William O. Douglas among them, who credited F.D.R. with the ability to show his feelings, even the ability to cry, in fact.

Eisenhower, a military man, was not, strangely enough, a strict masculinist. Having served his country as a five-star general, Eisenhower knew about Pentagon mentalities, and the military bigwigs found it difficult to pull the wool over his eyes on questions of "preparedness," strategy, and budget. Even so, Eisenhower accepted the military strategy known as massive retaliation, which is to say that the United States would reply to any violation of non-Communist soil with a nuclear attack. His Secretary of State created "brinkmanship" as a way of dealing with suspected foes. Its method was to flex nuclear muscle and stare at the foes nose to nose even to the very brink of war. This posture was thought by "rational" men to be the most effective deterrent to any conflagration, but congressional liberals saw it as dangerous and silly. John F. Kennedy saw the strategy as one that had reduced the United States to the alternatives of "inglorious retreat or unlimited retaliation."

Nevertheless, it was Eisenhower's warnings about the "grave implications" of growing unchecked military power that called attention to how big business had been in collusion with the spenders in the Pentagon and to the way that the quest for "bigger and better" bombs and missiles could go on indefinitely, with corporations raking in the profits:

> The conjunction of an immense military establishment and a large arms industry is new in the American experience. The total influence—economic, political, and even spiritual—is felt in every city, every State House, every office of the Federal government.... We must not fail to comprehend its grave implications. Our toil, resources, and livelihood are all involved; so is the very structure of our society.... We must never let the weight of this combination endanger our liberties or our democratic processes.... In the councils of government we must guard against the acquisition of unwarranted influence, whether sought or unsought, by the military-industrial complex. The potential for the disastrous rise of misplaced power exists and will persist.[4]

What this means, in effect, is that huge private corporations, propelled by profit motives and competitive drives, can only survive if there is a need for their products and that this need can only be assumed if the nation has more than a little tension in its trigger finger.

John F. Kennedy took Eisenhower's warning to heart and refused to allow his generals to challenge him publicly, as had happened to both Truman and Eisenhower. When Kennedy fired General Edwin Walker for making extremist statements, only the Far Right hurled charges of "muzzling the military" at him. Kennedy's aides claimed that his Bay of Pigs fiasco was an inheritance from the previous Administration's military advisers and that Kennedy learned, as a result, not to depend on those advisers thereafter. Lyndon B. Johnson, on the other hand, listened carefully to his military advisers and as a result found himself enmeshed in a conflict he hardly comprehended and which brought about his eventual decision not to run for reelection.

Richard M. Nixon, when he took the reigns of power, was delighted that at last his dream of being President (top commander) had come true. He was known to be a friend to the Pentagon, and few expected that he would deny his generals the pleasure of bombing the Vietnamese mercilessly. Although public pressures demanded a cessation of American involvement in Vietnam, Nixon utilized every opportunity to drop as many bombs as he could. He succeeded in using more explosives in Southeast Asia than were dropped by this nation during World Wars I and II. The futility of this policy was apparent.

"We will not be humiliated," declared Nixon in his speech to the nation after the invasion of Cambodia. "It is not our power but our will and character that is being tested," he claimed. One of his most revealing arguments against immediate withdrawal from Vietnam (a policy recommended by his critics) was to insist that such a withdrawal would be tantamount to the country's acceptance of "the first defeat in its proud 190-year history."

I. F. Stone characterized Nixon as "a fighter," albeit a

"dirty, lousy, stinking" one. Other columnists, even those who had rooted for him, have been given to character analyses of Nixon which, in the light of the theses of this book, are telling. James J. Kilpatrick, in his column "The Conservative View," called Nixon a creature of "established order" who "goes through channels" to get things done, rather than doing them himself. "He is a private person," wrote Kilpatrick, "reserved, restrained, tightly controlled." Even so, Kilpatrick believed that these qualities, which "in their place" and to a "reasonable degree" might be called *great* in other Presidents, were in Nixon faults. He carried them to extremes, unable to "let go," as had Presidents before him. Instead of picking up the phone and demanding immediate information about Watergate, for example, Nixon is said to have let matters slide by going through established channels and asking his aides to investigate. "The President," said Nixon, referring to himself in the third person to excuse himself for overlooking the Watergate charges, "doesn't pick up the phone and call the Attorney General everytime something comes up on a matter. He depends on his counsel or whoever he's given the job to." Kilpatrick suggested that Truman or Johnson would have jumped to the telephone themselves to find out what was going on if such wayward revelations were disclosed about their subordinates.

If Nixon was unable to show his feelings, however, he was not ashamed of the fact. He preferred the cool, masculinist exterior to any show of feeling. In the midst of his Watergate troubles, Nixon compared himself to Abraham Lincoln at a Lincoln's Birthday address at the Lincoln Memorial. "But perhaps more than anything else," he said of the Civil War President, "people admire the strength, the poise under pressure. Lincoln was perhaps the most heavily criticized President in history, but he had that great strength of character never to display [his feelings] no matter how harsh and unfair the criticism might be. This particular fact is an inspiration for us today."[5]

Comedian David Frye, a Nixon impersonator, characterized his model by saying, "Nixon is as neurotic a President as we can imagine." A.F.L.–C.I.O President George Meany accused Nixon of "dangerous emotional instability," and even Nixon's own choice for Attorney General, William Saxbe, wondered aloud during the bombing of Hanoi (while peace negotiations were taking place) whether or not the President had "taken leave of his senses."

Nixon added fuel to the fire about such speculations when he announced at a press conference that he had "what it takes" and boasted that "the tougher it gets, the cooler I get." At a later date he told an audience, "We always become stronger when the going gets tough. We didn't cross the mountains and prairies because we were made of sugar candy."[6]

Years before, Nixon himself admitted in an article he had written for the *Saturday Review* that his own colleagues and friends in "the business and professional world" often said, "Anyone who becomes a Communist must have been queer and unstable to begin with," thus showing that even near the beginning of his career the man had surrounded himself with peers who saw deviation from certain norms as evidence of unmanliness or homosexuality. Perhaps, in fact, many of his reactions since have been efforts to keep himself from deserving any labels indicating that he is less than "manly."

Dr. Eli S. Chesen in his book *President Nixon's Psychiatric Profile* says that Nixon has shown a regular pattern or tendency to "over-control," trying to stay on top of everything so as not to be left without a feeling that he is dominant. Dr. Chesen suggests that the Plumbers' incident, in which Nixon aides were indicted for breaking into a psychiatrist's office, was "an inevitable extension of Nixon's psychological need to have total control over himself and his environment."[7]

Richard Nixon's lifelong concern with strength, winning, competition, and domination has been reflected in his choices for government leaders and for his own aides and friends. His Vice-Presidential choice, Gerald Ford, a former college football star devoted to football metaphors, is an example. Ford showed an inordinate amount of support for the embattled Nixon, and continued this support right up to the final days of Nixon's Administration, long after it had become obvious that impeachment or resignation was inevitable. Criticized for doing so, he explained he had no fear of dissenting from the President's position on any issue but that once a decision had been reached, he felt bound to support it. "I learned long ago," he said, "that after a play has been called, you don't go out and tackle your quarterback."

Senator Harrison Williams called Ford's bluff by indicating that he distrusted the application of football analogies to governmental processes. He asked Ford what he would do if his quarterback (an obvious reference to Nixon) got turned around and "started running with the ball to the wrong goal line." "Would you tackle him?" queried Williams.

"That's the exception more than the rule," Ford insisted.

"These are exceptional times," Williams instructed him.[8]

On another occasion Ford used similar metaphors to describe the condition of the nation: "I only wish that I could take the entire United States into the locker room at halftime," he told assembled guests at a Chicago dinner. "It would be an opportunity to say that we have lost yards against the line drives of inflation and the end runs of energy shortages." Describing his countrymen in competitive masculinist terms, he announced: "We have a winner. Americans are winners."[9]

Vice-President Agnew had also utilized football analogies to make his points. In his first long TV interview, with David Frost, he explained that it is the right of citizens to elect their "team," but that while the team is playing, citizens may not get down on the playing field and tell the team what to do. If they wish to change things, said Agnew, they may elect a new team four years later. When he resigned from office after pleading nolo contendere to criminal charges, it came as a disappointment to many; in his early days in office he had called for a return to old values, by which he meant an end to "permissiveness." He believed in putting children "in line" so that they would follow prescribed parental rulings. He did not allow his own daughter to wear an armband protesting the Vietnamese war. And finally, it was Agnew, we must recall, who characterized antiwar Senator Charles Goodell as "the Christine Jorgensen of politics" and referred to his own opponents as "effete."

Nixon's choice for White House Chief of Staff was a military man, General Alexander M. Haig, Jr. Haig has said that "politics and soldiering are very close" and that "it's only a soldier who can respect and admire a politician. Both are fields where a man lays everything on the line to win or lose. . . . When they don't win, the results are fatal."

Haig had worked closely with General Douglas MacArthur in Japan and has spoken of him with great admiration: "He was one of the dying breed of American bureaucrats." Haig too has been a hard-liner, as was MacArthur. In April, 1969, when North Korean planes shot down a U.S. reconnaissance (spy) plane, Haig recommended that U.S. planes bomb North Korea in retaliation so that in Haig's own words, "the Indochina war could be a whole new ball game."

The question of nuclear bombing power has come forth time and again in discussions about a President's mental balance. Haig, relaying a Nixon order to Deputy Attorney General William Ruckelshaus, was abashed when Ruckelshaus refused to comply. "Your Commander-in-Chief has given you an order!" said Haig, demonstrating that those within the military hierarchy are not likely to say no if a President gives orders to fire nuclear missiles. George E. Reedy, once President Johnson's press secretary and author of *The Twilight of the Presidency*, says that he doubts if a President's inner circle would do anything to stay his hand were he to irrationally declare the necessity for nuclear war. "To them, everything he does is rational," says Reedy. "He is the center of their universe." Reedy's book argues that the President, as the nation's leader, "sets the standards of rational conduct. If he reached into a bowl of spinach with his hands, the people around him would make excuses for him."[10]

It was apparent in various public announcements on Watergate that the men surrounding Nixon were anxious to follow "team rules." Nixon himself often visited or called members of various football teams, suggesting to them how they might fare best on the playing field. It should have been no surprise, therefore, to hear the scheduling director for the Committee for the Reelection of the President (CREEP), Herbert L. Porter, pleading guilty to lying to the F.B.I. and telling the Senate Watergate Committee that he had kept quiet for fear he would be accused of "not being a team player."[11] James W. McCord's testimony before the Senate Watergate Committee produced a similar revelation. McCord recalled how John Caulfield, a Treasury Department official, had tried to persuade him to remain silent about the Watergate incident, to plead guilty, and to await executive clemency. McCord said that Caulfield told him: "Everybody else is on track but you. You are not following the game plan. You seem to be pursuing your own course of action. Do not talk if called before the grand jury. Keep silent and do the same if called before a congressional committee. . . . You are fouling up the game plan." It was McCord's letter to Judge John J. Sirica, of course, that loosed the Watergate flood on the President and his team.

The significance (local and global) of masculinist politicking should be clear. If we elect politicians who adhere to such values, there is every chance that they may plunge humankind over the brink of war in the name of "honor" and with a refusal to consider nonmasculinist solutions. "The focus of the problem does not lie in the atom," said Henry L. Stimson. "It resides in the hearts of men." By "hearts" I presume Stimson meant men's values.

At present China and the United States seem to be trying to refine the language in which they discuss the still unresolved question of Taiwan. If they are not able to reconcile their opposing positions, it may be possible, at least, for them to keep those differences from getting in the way of other matters. China's invitation to the U.S. President to visit Peking illustrates how nations may arrange to circumvent mutual obstacles, avoid belligerence and aggression, and find cooperative ground. John F. Kennedy, defining defense in nonmasculinist terms, addressed the Soviet Union with these words: "I would say to the leaders of the Soviet Union, and to their people, that if either of our countries is to be fully secure, we need a much better weapon than the H-bomb, a weapon better than ballistic missiles or nuclear submarines, and that better weapon is peaceful cooperation."

And yet General Thomas D. White, former Chief of Staff of the U.S. Air Force, was content to say (during

Kennedy's term in office) that "prudence requires us to carry as big a stick as the bully carries and a bigger one if possible. Our scientists," he said, gloating, "tell us we can build a fifty-megaton or a one-hundred-megaton bomb quite easily. If this is so, we should consider building them for psychological reasons if no other. But other reasons suggest themselves. ... We have now dropped behind in one aspect: the big bomb department. We should lose no time in catching up."[12]

The United States, according to internationally recognized authority on military science Martin Caidin, has poured its resources into hundreds of "billions of dollars worth of huge rockets, submarines, supersonic bombers, and many other delivery systems, all to perform but one basic act over and over—the delivery of nuclear hell to 'the enemy.' " Caidin asks, "If we really believe that activating these systems must destroy civilization, then why do we continue their production? Why do we spend more billions to improve the weapons and the delivery systems?"[13]

Anyone who has read Martin Caidin's descriptions of a nuclear doomsday should be sufficiently frightened to take particular concern with the values politicians express. At the time of this writing the most recent worldwide alert of U.S. troops (to be ready for global war) took place under Nixon in October, 1973. National leaders who cling to old-fashioned ideas about what it means to be a man never want to lose face and might choose the option of plunging the planet over the brink.

Nikita Khrushchev's behavior during the Cuban missile crisis of 1962 was extraordinary under such circumstances and illustrates that sanity in such matters may sometimes prevail. Bertrand Russell, who acted as intermediary between the United States and the Soviet Union during that tense period, acclaimed Khrushchev as a great statesman for refusing to be bothered by the consideration that he might lose face. Those who claim that Khrushchev was trying to install missiles in Cuba, only ninety miles from U.S. shores, forget that U.S. missiles were, prior to that time, aimed at the Soviet Union from Turkish bases situated equally close to Soviet borders.

The introduction of women into politics is not sufficient as an antidote to masculinism in politics. The dangers will persist if women step into roles vacated by men without instituting revolutionary changes. It may be, however, that fewer women would assert themselves by resorting to war. Too few women have held high government posts. In the last twenty years only one woman has been a member of a President's cabinet, and no woman has ever been allowed policy-making status on the White House staff. Marc F. Fasteau's study of the Pentagon Papers says that none of the U.S. officials whose names appear in the six-hundred-page summary of those papers is a woman.[14] The war was conducted by men.

Token women in government service will not do the trick. When certain women find themselves heads of governments, they are not likely to welcome other women into the system, and they may manipulate men into keeping them out. They enjoy their unique status and the praise it brings them, and they are likely to identify with male political colleagues rather than with women who have not yet "made it" into the system. Golda Meir, former premier of Israel, is a case in point. She told *Ms.* magazine that women's liberationists were "crazy."

Both token women and masculinist men accept the rank and structure of governmental hierarchy without question. Various kinds of protocol, seniority systems, and opportunities for misplaced power persist. Martha Mitchell, telling about her life in Washington, called attention to what she believed was responsible for her discomfort in that city:

> Probably the main reason for my unpeaceful co-existence with the nation's capital was that it operates on a set of rules of etiquette that goes by the name of "protocol," whereas I was brought up on a completely different set of principles known as good manners.
>
> Protocol, for example, dictates that a guest's position at the dinner table is determined by his or her rank. The higher the rank, the closer the guest is to the head of the table (or, by tradition, nearer the salt). Your hosts couldn't care less if this arrangement put you next to your worst enemy.[15]

This kind of grading is an attempted justification of the whole status-oriented sickness at the heart of U.S. values. It is profoundly antidemocratic and flies in the face of the equalitarian standards by which the country pretends to abide. Robert Burns would have laughed scornfully:

> The rank is but the guinea's stamp
> The man's a gowd for a'that.

What is most unsettling about this kind of ranking is that the U.S. government is setting the tone for behavior throughout the rest of the nation.

Communist governments too suffer from what some analysts have called political arteriosclerosis, which keeps younger aspirants to political office from taking their rightful place in decision-making processes. At present North Vietnam is ruled by a Politburo whose members' average

age is sixty-four. The Soviet Union's Politburo members also have an average age of sixty-four. The top men in China are even older. A "young" Communist leader is Fidel Castro, forty-eight, and even his reign has been exceedingly long for one man. The chiefs of the "Young" Communist Leagues are often middle-aged. Yevgeni Tyazhelnikov, of the Soviet Union's Komsomols, is now forty-six, and China once boasted a Young Communist chief who was in his sixties.

Reliance on so-called rational proceduralism and an unfortunate inability to show feelings hinder meaningful relationships between diplomats and between their states. Whenever men are stiff and formal with one another, they find it difficult to express their feelings openly, and this leads to distrust. The fact that many diplomats converse through interpreters proves words nearly useless as conveyors of meaning. Receptive capacities might show more readily and lead to trustful relations if men relied more on nonverbal methods for communication, methods that allowed them to express feeling.

Theodore Roszak, in his brilliant essay "The Hard and the Soft," shows how language covers the brutal values that lie underneath the fancy pronouncements of nuclear strategists and diplomats. "In recent years," he writes, "the language of violence may have shifted toward semi-mathematical jargon, but the tough-guy posturings of our nuclear strategists are an obvious extension of the same tradition."[16] He shows how language covers reality by neatly coining words such as "megadeath," which somehow fail to convey the ultimate horror of nuclear battle. Such jargon may claim rational origins, but Roszak suggests that the trend toward such phraseology may end in "wargasm," the insecure male's final solution:

Our international political leadership may talk high

politics and heady ideology. But its space rocket and ballistic missile rivalry is all too clearly a worldwide contest of insecure penises out to prove their size and potency. It is the sort of pathetic competition "real men" often come down to at the end of a long, boozy night out.[17]

It is beyond the scope of this book to delineate precise steps for the reformation of political machinery. Only hints and suggestions can be made. These, as is clear, lie in the values men now cherish and those that must replace them. Working in a kind of evolutionary way, new values will bring major changes to political structuring. Charles A. Reich says in *The Greening of America* that there is a revolution coming. "It will not be like the revolutions of the past," he writes. "It will originate with the individual and with culture, and it will change the political structure only as its final act."[18] The question, as Justice William O. Douglas puts it, is "Can we develop a new consciousness that places the individual and humanistic values above the machine?" By "machine" I presume Justice Douglas means not only technology but also the whole structure of governmental processes, which takes its cues from masculinist values.

Reich's vision of revolution sees a general decline in the quality of citizens' daily lives as the revolutionary motive and foretells the system's self-destruction as a consequence. Certainly there will be a falling apart of various facilities once taken for granted, and much of politics in the near future will revolve around immediate concerns: organizing locally to circumvent and reform political behavior that no longer benefits humankind in this period of unprecedented transformation.

Chapter 13 ❄ SIZE AND STATUS
The Bigger-Than-Thou Penis Syndrome

Congressman Joel Wachs has incurred the moral wrath of his colleagues in his first month in office at Los Angeles City Council. The young tax lawyer circulated a petition to raise revenues by taxing men's cocks on the basis of size —ranging from a nuisance tax to a luxury tax. The reactions of the other councilmen quickly called the joke "despicable" and "inappropriate." Wachs, undaunted under fire in a recent council session, grinned boyishly and exclaimed, "This is fun!"

—Screw[1]

Men have accepted certain kinds of hierarchies, which fit collectively into the Bigger-Than-Thou Penis Syndrome. These hierarchies are concerned with size and position, and they are closely related to all of the games of one-upmanship, status, dominance, and control so prevalent in our society. Their effect on everyday life is staggering.

Prior to the technological revolution, when physical strength bore some relation to fighting capacity, size may have mattered, although the axiom about being big and falling hard was invented partly to discount a man's size in battle. As technology removes man from the battlefields and places him behind buttons, the entire size question ought to be irrelevant, except in barroom brawls. The man who brags about the size of his penis should by now have received notice that generally speaking, its size is irrelevant. Masters and Johnson's experiments with clitorally induced orgasms show that depth of penetration matters little in comparison with the stimulation of a woman's clitoris.

164

That physical size should be discounted on both the battlefield and in bed almost simultaneously is a coincidence of timing. It almost seems that destiny intends male attitudes, shaped in the long-ago, to undergo fundamental revolutions in this era. Concern with size has plagued men for centuries and threatens to undermine good judgment in present-day circumstances. Many employers admit to prejudging prospective employees if they are not "tall enough." "I'm afraid to hire little men," said one, "because I'm afraid they'll try to act too big for their britches." This commonly held attitude stems from the efforts of some smaller men to play tough in lieu of their inability to stand tall. Social emphasis on size works in their disfavor. The connections I am making between size-concern, status, and the elongated penis are theoretical, naturally, but preoccupation with size does derive from the male's hope to play dominant and to do so successfully.

Penis size is one of the more sensitive sides of this preoccupation. Artist Betty Dodson notes that laws prohibiting the display of the erect penis were obviously written by men. "But to protect *whom* from exactly *what?*" she asks.

If men are truly committed to the idea that "bigger means better," then it seems likely that they may actually be protecting not women but themselves by prohibiting photos of erections. There is, as any sexologist knows, an inordinate amount of concern among men about genital size. In the pages of almost every sex tabloid there is usually more than one display ad featuring quack "remedies" to lengthen the penis, with some promising to add as many as three inches. In *Screw* these ads are carried in almost every issue. Skin bookstores, usually found in urban red-light districts, feature display cases with various ointments to "make it grow." These ointments actually sell for five and ten dollars a tube, indicating how some men will try almost anything if it offers a chance of increasing genital size.

There are many reasons why men believe in the importance of size. It is a taught prejudice and derives some of its importance from competition. It may start early in life, when youngsters compare and play "I'll show you mine if you'll show me yours." Hearing the "bigger is better" philosophy expressed by fathers who buy bigger cars and mothers who encourage bigger muscles, young boys, by the time they have reached puberty, are exceedingly size-conscious. Subtle influences add to that consciousness. Movie screens, billboards, and statues show famous public figures as larger than life.

Professor Seymour Fisher's studies suggest that bigness is definitely seen as evidence of masculinity. Larger parts of the body are even regarded as "masculine," whereas smaller parts are not. Fisher found that certain personality quirks are related to size. The man who feels the need to exaggerate his height is also more anxious to show that he is a "go-getter, a dominant and achieving person." Among Fisher's most interesting finds was that the man who places emphasis on size is usually convinced that men are superior to women, and that concern with demonstrating that he is bigger derives in part from "a desire to prove to himself that he is psychologically bigger than other people."[2]

A great deal of blatant suffering is caused by sizism. If it is wrong to judge people on the basis of race, sex, or age, it is equally wrong to discriminate on the basis of size. Sizism is so pervasive that multitudes make negative evaluations of themselves and of others on its account.

"Bigger is better" is responsible not only for the worries of American men about penis size but for fixations on large breasts too. It has been suggested that women, feeling inferior because they are usually smaller, use their breasts as a way of saying, "I am big too." In a number of cultures breast size is not emphasized, nor are preoccupations with breast shapes. Dimensions determined by brassieres are unheard of. There are primitive cultures, in fact, where a woman's breasts are not even thought to be objects of sexual interest.

Anthropologists describe the peaceful psychological transitions of children in cultures where there is no undue anxiety about bodily sizes. This occurs, it seems, in societies where nudity is common. If we applied the implications of these anthropological findings to American life-styles, it might be found that more nudity in our culture could erase the qualms experienced by our children.

Freud thought that young boys undergo a great shock when they discover that their fathers have larger genitals. Understanding this fact, he wrote, is a key to comprehending personalities. He went so far as to say that feelings of inferiority are introduced by a young boy's glimpse of a naked father. What Freud failed to emphasize was a proper remedy for such traumas. If a child were able to watch steady transformations (as he does in nude cultures) of children becoming youths, youths becoming adults, he would have a better sense of the meaninglessness of size, seeing so many of its human variations and realizing how regularly hidden parts of the body will grow.

Cultural emphasis on size has led not only to a great deal of unnecessary worry and anguish but to certain kinds of hypocrisy as well. The man who arranges to appear larger than he is, whether with the aid of platform shoes, padded shoulders, or a top hat, is engaged in fooling others. To the perceptive observer, these items are as obvious as a cheap toupee. What is distressing about the attempt to create a bigger image is that the hypocrisy of appearance is accepted in other areas of life as well.

The man who strives for status is also seeking ways of standing tall and appearing to be larger than he is. The climb to the top is often climaxed by looking down on those over whose backs one has scrambled, but the sensation experienced is not often one that brings conviction that the position is truly deserved. That status can fail to bring meaningful rewards is no surprise. Its symbols, coveted by men who relish appearances, are hollow. A private office. A nameplate on the door. A title. Although these unconvincing badges tell of a man's rise to a certain corporate stature, they reflect but little of his actual self, since, unfortunately, he has often spent a lifetime circumventing his real feelings in order to fit in with corporate demands.

This may account, in part, for what Charles Drekmeier believes is the most unnerving form of discontent. It appears, he says, not among those whose status is considered low but where it is high. "Discontent," he writes, "appears to be greatest among those who have attained positions of status possessing at least a limited authority."[3]

Drekmeier's observations do not apply to all those who have attained high positions. Certainly there are many who have had a chance within corporate structures to show their abilities and have demonstrated those abilities freely. The stuffy surroundings in which they have worked have not choked them as they might have others, since these men have been so involved in their work that they scarcely notice even spatial limitations.

Status is not often a motivating factor among successful men, however. Judith Bardwick says that the highly successful men in her studies were often quite unaware of status as a goal and that these men felt, for the most part, that their station in life did not come from charting beforehand a series of objectives which they sought and accomplished. They saw their successes as results of their own efforts and abilities, without regard for position, income, or status. "It all just comes," was typical of the responses they gave in answer to questions about such matters.

The man who arranges to appear successful and does so in order to climb the social ladder both at his job and in his neighborhood concerns himself with show. Clothes, particularly those that register expensive tastes, are helpful in this regard. Businesses may deny it, but every man who holds a job involving any amount of public contact knows that his appearance counts almost as much as his performance. He is his firm's *image,* and the message from high in the pecking order is clear: The man who appears to have stepped out of *Gentlemen's Quarterly* gets a better corporate position than does one who attaches little significance to clothing.

Tax laws prove that image and appearance are more important to men than is commonly admitted. Even men high on the corporate scale may deduct the difference between a Dodge and a Mercedes Benz if such symbols are thought necessary to maintain the image of a successful businessman. A salary paid to a chauffeur from eight to five o'clock is deductible as a business expense. What would a client think of a man who had to drive his own automobile? One wonders why the Internal Revenue Service allows such a businessman to charge off the bill for a new yacht and its crew simply because he invites potential customers to go for a cruise.

Lionel Tiger looks, as does his mentor, Robert Ardrey, for justification of status play among men by referring to behavior among the lower animals. In his study on male bonding, *Men in Groups,* Tiger performs a feat even more staggering than psychoanalysis. Instead of merely reverting to childhood for explanations of male behavior, he jumps species barriers and tells about status among Japanese monkeys. The male offspring of high-status females, surprisingly, "identify" with high-status males.[4] How nice. Monkeys, it seems, are fully behind various tycoons and capitalists, exonerating elitists as nature's own.

The structural hierarchies that promote status are hardly

visible to a nation accustomed by rationalistic overemphasis to classification, systemization, and the like. If it is accepted that our perceptions should always be stately, orderly, and identifiable, there is nothing to stop us from accepting similar alignments in business arrangements.

The "bigger than thou" consciousness that keeps status and position in the forefront of the American way gets impetus from a desire for the approval of others. The best way of getting this approval, under present conditions, is by presenting a favorably distorted appearance, one that gives others the idea that a man's size, both financially and psychologically, is bigger and thus better than it is.

The belief that status and success are available to all Americans is widespread, and yet most are dissatisfied and literally hate to get up in the morning because their jobs bore them so. One of the most pointed reasons so many men are unhappy with their work is that it seldom provides them with the means of experiencing and taking pleasure in their own capacities.[5] Too many pursue recognition, success, or money, all of which are petty alternatives to self-discovery and acceptance. And those who pursue status and success die young.

In 1974 Dr. Robert J. Samp conducted a study of more than 1,700 people over the age of eighty, including 129 who were one hundred years old or older. "We didn't find any intense, driving, highly competitive business executive types in the whole bunch," he reported, noting that today's "uptight" world is a major factor in killing men before their time. Dr. Samp suggests that the key to living a longer, healthier, and happier life lies in identifying the primary stress factor in a person's life and changing it. In most cases, such stress factors are related to employment status.[6]

The rush for status is reflected not only in gaudy trimmings and in the consumer goods that lie so lavishly on store counters. Jobs themselves are rated in such a way as to bring, depending upon what they are, a higher or lower rank to those who fill them. Some men fear to take certain jobs because they do not seem "masculine" enough. This kind of concern is full of dangers for the whole nation. It ignores the perspective that says there is no occupation at which a young man may not become a hero and strikes at the very basis of the belief that work has its own inherent dignity. Class concerns add to a male's burdens. A father who is an accountant makes it clear to his son that he does not want him to accept a position that fails to reflect his own class status. The son, on the other hand, may derive a great deal of pleasure from picking grapes or pruning trees. Instead he is guided into an office, where he dons a starched shirt and occupies himself with activities that are not amenable to his nature.

In an economy where a man is judged on hierarchical scales, only a few positions offer the kind of repute sought by status-seekers. The man who appraises himself and others by their functions is afflicted with a sore superficiality. Since most jobs are neither glamorous nor expressive of power, he fails to accord those who hold them the same honor he gives men who enjoy positions of renown. An expert bricklayer, a master barber, or a good cook are not allowed the same degree of respect accorded to a commonplace lawyer or a mediocre doctor. Capability counts for little. It is position that is important. Whenever men tend to self-estimates based on position, most are sustaining poor assessments of themselves because of misplaced values. These values, unfortunately, are the rule rather than the exception in U.S. society.

In certain Asian societies in which regard for position is carried to ridiculous extremes, social hypocrisies combine to highlight these extremes. An Iranian high-school teacher in the United States told how he returned to Tehran for a visit and was introduced as a professor from an "esteemed university" in the West.

"No, I am a high-school teacher," he remonstrated.

"High school?"

"Yes, secondary school."

"Surely you are being too modest," said his hosts, laughing. They continued to introduce him as a professor.

Men who lack self-approval can seek approval from others. In some cases outside approval helps a man, but not if it rests on false footings (i.e., appearances). In a healthy society men gain fundamental perspectives on themselves by making themselves vulnerable to the responses of associates and friends. If they covet status symbols, using them to disguise themselves—if they attempt to convince others they're bigger than they are, elevated on shoes of position and possession—they fail to get from others what they need most: meaningful reflections of themselves. Without realistic feedback, they have few ways of knowing themselves. Without the openness and honesty of valid relationships, there is no one present to give a man confidence in his real merits or an awareness of his faults. Quests for status stand in the way of genuine self-appreciation because self-knowledge comes about only when a man thinks he is appraised for his real qualities. He cannot be seen, however, if he is camouflaged by symbols and is appreciated instead for what he *seems* to be. Size, rank, respectability, and other forms of stratification make him blind to himself and distrustful of others. Certainly he cannot trust the members of a society who are so committed to accepting and reflecting mere appearances. He needs to know that others see him as the person he is, and yet he masquerades. He knows they see only a caricature.

Naturally, the status-seeker hopes the acknowledgments he gets will help him think better of himself, but this is unlikely as long as he is aware that he is decorating himself to cut a figure that really isn't his own. As long as he solicits approval by surrounding himself with externals, he isn't likely to achieve self-confidence. Therefore even the man who achieves status remains disappointed and is plagued by feelings of inadequacy. Since men in our culture are given to proving themselves as *providers* and since work itself is a prime means for self-validation, it is tragic that it has been poisoned for so many by misdirected points of view.

The tragedy is compounded when we are fooled by the myth that men are truly free to choose their line of work in a democracy and to change their positions with ease if one line of work fails to bring its own rewards. Theoretically this is so, but in practice, men shrink from self-expression, following status-conscious guidelines created by those around them. Competition in America is fierce, and a move from one position to another cannot be made without great trepidation. Often, even though a man wishes to make a move, he fears that to do so would be a "step down," meaning a reduction in salary. His values might change so that material goods became less important to him and love, companionship, and freedom assumed greater consequence in his life. His family, however, accustomed to the trappings of status, would balk if he were suddenly to suggest that they seek happiness and fulfillment in these nonmaterial experiences. He himself might find it difficult to conceive of how he could "do without." He may know that he is suffocating and that the socially acceptable goals he accepts as his own prevent him from realizing what he really wants to be: a loving friend to his mate and children, a relaxed and humorous personality, and a man whose values strike higher than the plasticity around him.

Bigger is not better, of course, and the emphasis on status, with its accompanying demoralization, must give way to new values. A thoughtful man will reject its price as too high to pay and will seek instead joy on his job, the kind of joy that once produced what is seldom seen today: pride in workmanship.

Chapter 14 ✻ WOMEN

Those Who Know How to Open Doors by Themselves

New relations of flesh and sentiment of which we have no conception will arise between the sexes; already indeed there have appeared between men and women friendships, rivalries, complicities, comradeships—chaste or sensual—which past centuries could not have conceived.

—SIMONE DE BEAUVOIR[1]

For many men relationships with the opposite sex are becoming increasingly difficult. Values associated with masculinity have disrupted personal ties.

Traditional ways of relating, based on old masculinist custom, are already obsolete. Clinging to them provides a kind of security for men who feel safe following well-established guidelines, but to people aware of the nuances of the new age, these men reveal their insecurities without realizing it. Men who are aware of the need for changes are bringing the attention of their brethren to drawbacks caused by old values and are helping to release them from discomforts experienced in the presence of today's changing women. While such discomforts are privately acknowledged, men have been taught to deny their existence publicly. Men are supposed to be *sure* of themselves in relation to women.

In a later section of this book women who are not active and self-confident will be discussed. The varied ways in which old-fashioned manipulative "ladies" have contributed to unhealthy male-female relationships need underscoring. At present, however, it may be wise to consider difficulties

t that genuine courtesy is not one-sided. Th
vays rushes ahead to open doors lacks a sens
be his: that he is being cared for too! A doo
not heavy, and it might be wise to sugges
r gets to it first should open it for the othe
courtesy becomes a meaningful exchange
m the realm of mere ceremony, because it

Katz, director of research for human develop
ducational policy at the State University o
ays that since 1969 he and his colleagues hav
lic surveys of male-female relations on cam
data," he writes, "show that great change
king place in the last decade."
believes that the "double standard" in sex
most recent surveys indicate that nearly a
nts feel that it is as right for a young woma
al intercourse prior to marriage as it is for
What startled the good doctor most, perhap
ling that women who are sexually active i
a greater frequency of sexual experiences "an
r degrees of emotional and sexual satisfactio
responding group of men."3
rcent of the college women in Dr. Katz
ated that they wished to have a career. "I
s, "having a career is *more* important to mo
having children [italics mine]." Although D
ally sure whether the evidence he has gathere
ast few years is indicative of major change
e, he is willing to admit that "for this colleg
personal and professional equality between th
ached a point unimaginable in their parent

study conducted at Stanford University
lass of 1974) found similar changes takin

men face with nonmanipulative women who consider themselves equals. To do this it is necessary to postulate an
ideal woman, as seen through the eyes of the young, the
well-informed, and those who are weaving new values
into the fabric of their lives.

The ideal woman postulated here is a person who is
self-regulating and self-sustaining. If she is not the equal
of a given man in every respect, she may have dexterities
in some areas which make her superior, and he, naturally,
may also be capable in ways that she is not:

> By my side or back of me Eve following,
> Or in front, and I following her just the same.[2]

For purposes of discussion it must be assumed that she
is self-confident for sound reasons and not because of some
psychological imbalance. I say this because I have noted
in my conversations with men about self-confident women
that they often believe such women are emphasizing confidence to make up for lack in some other segment of their
lives. That males who emphasize their self-confidence may
also be doing the same does not seem to occur to these
men. What is even more amazing is that men fail to see
that it is proper for women to feel confident. Nor does it
seem to occur to them that women—having been socialized
for millennia into submissiveness—are, if they are emphasizing self-confidence, bucking the traditions of centuries and
that their first steps may be somewhat awkward.

The point is this, however: Many more women than ever
before are beginning to buck traditions openly. If they
are not yet ready to change, perhaps they are reading in
women's magazines about the disadvantages and handicaps
they suffer. Their periodicals and publications are suggesting to them that they make new demands—not upon men
but upon themselves—and that they seek the satisfactions

of self-reliance which were denied them under the old systems that taught subservience in marriage as their proper goal.

The question facing today's male, and it is a difficult one indeed, is: How can I build relationships with such self-reliant women? Accustomed to a woman who leans on him for support, advice, finances, and protection, a man faces reversals in his relationships with women which, although they may not be total, are at least far-ranging and unsettling. Men have forgotten that women can take their places beside them as equals. Certainly the pioneer women who crossed the plains in the last century did so. They stood next to their mates with rifles, defending themselves and their families from hostile marauders. They worked hard on the wagon trains and on building their cabins and communities. They were strong, competent women, and their male mates accepted their strengths as necessary to the implementation of those hopes and dreams that went into the construction of this nation.

Once settled, however, American men proceeded to enforce antiquated patriarchal values, combining them with praise for the then-prevalent Victorian conduct that glorified women who were fainting, fawning, helpless "ladies." Now, not quite a century later, as women break Victorian shackles, men are in a quandary about how to behave in their presence. Why? Because masculinist values conflict with what women today are asking for: cooperation. Since today's male does not read women's magazines and hears only bits and pieces of argument, pro and con, about "liberation," he finds it difficult to digest the new viewpoints and reacts with doubt, dread, ridicule, antagonism, or paternalism. Usually when a man thinks of women, he has certain women in mind, or he sees them as he has been *taught* to believe they *must* be. For the most part women have remained a mysterious breed to men. They

seldom consider that virtually
reproductive organs) between
created by long conditioning,
contrasts in external appearan
to the other. Thus men are ri
fronted by beings who no lon
passive, dependent, and weak.
that they themselves are the
and that positive traits like ac
are what they have to offer w
rather helplessly themselves i
tiveness. What, after all, is th
use are we, think men, to bein
we would offer them?

What becomes of chivalry
the point or at least uncalled
women with chivalrous activi
clumsy and wonders whether
victim of exaggerated poses.
situations where there seem
taught mannerisms and rout
bundle of bizarre affectatio
chivalry now makes him feel
women behind him to exit fr
that he has a habit that is har
secure in his chivalry, he is

Offering a woman a seat o
table to light her cigarette, o
seat quickly to open her
manners that are either fad
doubt about it," says Elizabe
Post Institute, Inc. "Manners
ners are being written abou
elegantly as they were fifty

What is seldom acknowle

the plain
man who
that sho
after all,
that who
In this
removed
reciproca

Dr. Jos
ment and
New York
made per
puses. "O
have been

Dr. Ka
gone. His
college st
to have se
young ma
was his fi
college ha
report high
than the c

Eighty
studies ind
fact," he sa
women tha
Katz is not
during the
in our cult
generation,
sexes has r
generation."

A simila
California (

place. Dr. Warren Miller, director of the Laboratory of Behavior and Population at Stanford's medical center, discovered that the school's coeds were more sexually experienced than their male counterparts.[4]

One wonders how uncomfortable many men will become as the equalization of the sexes proceeds from the stand-point of women. The male's culturally induced tendency to direct and protect the women in his sphere may, of necessity, give way before the new woman's discovery that she can take care of herself. As more women make this kind of discovery, where will it leave the man who is accustomed to directing and protecting as his particular offering to a relationship? What, in fact, is he going to do if he begins running into women of the kind described by Whitman in *Leaves of Grass*?

> They are not one jot less than I am,
> They are tanned in the face by shining suns and
>   blowing winds,
> Their flesh has the old divine suppleness and
>   strength,
> They know how to swim, row, ride, wrestle, shoot,
>   run, strike, retreat, advance, resist, defend
>   themselves,
> They are ultimate in their own right—they are
>   calm, clear, well-possessed of themselves.[5]

There is little doubt that many men would feel uncom-fortable with such equals, although others might welcome the company of women with whom they could play un-inhibitedly and with whom they could share a fuller number of their best-loved pastimes and satisfactions.

Today's youths are giving signs that they may be capable of accepting reversed dating roles and that some young men do not shrink from what their elders called aggressive women. Men who are incapable of accepting invitations from women may ask themselves why. A kind of sexual puritanism is at the core of male objections to this kind of role reversal. Reared in a society that has taught him that sexuality is base—although he often seeks its pleasures for himself when he asks for a date—a man who objects to being asked out by a woman is apt to think that she has "designs" on him or that she may be seeking satisfactions for herself similar to those he seeks for himself. Since he has not accepted sexuality for the healthy expression that it can be, he finds it hard to admire such a woman. By asking him out, she seems to him to be saying in effect that she is moved by the same motives that he is, motives that he feels guilty about and therefore cannot countenance in a love object. Like John Wayne, who admits, "I have never thought of equality when I thought of women. I have always put them on a pedestal," he is suffering from pedestalitis. In the United States the woman who indicates too openly that she may actually enjoy sexual intercourse is in direct conflict with the Virgin Mary. It does not usually occur to such a man that a date need not have sexual implications. Most men feel uncomfortable as sex objects.

Most men are not at all comfortable with the thought of being physically admired. Old-fashioned roles insist that it is the man who does the admiring—ogling—and the woman who accepts his compliments. Whatever compliments a man receives are usually for attributes other than his physical beauty. His status symbols may be acceptable substitutes, or better yet, his character is something a woman may admire after she has known him for a while. The woman who admires men bodily, however, is asking, in many locales, to be considered "a pig."

Another reason a man may find role reversals difficult to countenance is that he suffers from the rationalistic limitation we called 1-2-3 thinking. If a woman were to actively pursue him, he would be face to face with a 3-2-1 situation.

The man who values domination and control is frightened by an active, self-confident woman. He is accustomed to "making his moves" at the time that suits him best. In a reversed situation he fears he is at the mercy of another's whims, something that seems to take control out of his own hands so he cannot schedule his own fun. Ideally, however, whatever "fun" there is to be had would be unscheduled and would result not from careful rational planning (the right time and the right place) but as a spontaneous outgrowth of mutual communication. If he were to realize this fact, he might not feel so "put on the spot" to perform sexually should he not want to. This last worry is probably all too widespread among those who object to self-reliant women. It is part of the masculinist mystique that men are ready, willing, and able to "go" at all hours with almost any woman. This is a myth, of course, and is cause for more unhappiness and concern among men than is generally admitted.

Some men seek relationships with women who are willing to hide the fact that they are active and self-confident. A bright and attractive young woman from a suburb of New York City told me how she was forced to hide her intellect when she moved to another part of the country, a sparsely populated area. Her new boyfriend was not threatened by her when they were alone, she explained, but he did not want her to express her intellectual capabilities too openly among his friends. She sat quietly when she was in the company of those friends.

Why are so many men comfortable with women who are seemingly not as intelligent as they? Or to put the question another way: Why are so many men uncomfortable with women who give evidences of being their equals? Why did

Marilyn Monroe, who usually played a dumb blond, become America's number-one sex symbol? Because of maculinist values.

Rationality is purported to be the province of men. If a woman is capable of rational discourse on a high level, she is believed to be exhibiting masculine characteristics. In a society where homophobia is rampant, this is anathema. A man must feel utterly positive that he is in the company of a 100 percent woman, and in our cultural milieu such a creature is deemed incapable of intricate reasoning. What he fails to realize is that rationality is only one kind of mind dexterity and is not necessarily evidence of the highest mental development.

I have known women to pretend to stupidity on first meeting a man, asking about his occupation, for example:

"What do you do?"

"I'm a philosophy professor."

"What's philosophy?"

I have watched men take a woman's ignorance for granted and painstakingly explain themselves, unaware that the woman is simply having fun at their chauvinistic expense.

Competition is also thought to be the province of men. A woman who appears as equal, who asks men for dates, makes her own choices, and directs her destiny, is removing herself from the competitive market. Where once a man could compete with other men for her attention, she has, by assuming equality, changed the entire competitive game. This demotes her as a status object. If she cannot be won in a race with others, what good is she for status display?

The fact that he cannot exercise dominance aggravates the old-fashioned male most. During courtship, at least, he is accustomed to taking each and every situation into control. It is by seeming to show that he is in command that he hopes to attract her, and by guiding her gently but surely so that she does his bidding that he woos her. Finally, in the sexual sphere, he is "on top," which may account for the prevalence of the "missionary position" in U.S. society.

When a woman will not play passive, he is mystified. If she does not give him reason to feel that he is in control, he feels rejected. If he guides her but she fails to follow, he is lost.

Public displays of extreme masculinist dominance can be seen among motorcycle gangs. The flamboyant "studs" who clog sidewalks on New York's Lower East Side clutch their ragged little girl friends by the back of the neck, pushing them along or yanking them backward as though they had no minds of their own about walking to and fro. The girls, yielding willingly and submitting themselves in an almost grotesque fashion, are unabashed. They are "property" and may be passed between their masters on agreement between the males; or if a struggle erupts, the winner takes his pick.

Among less ostentatious masculinists I have seen how the need to feel dominant has prevented contacts with the opposite sex. A young man sitting on the beach may watch a woman for hours, fearful of speaking to her. Imagining that she is somehow pointedly different from himself, he can hardly think of what to say. Since he is expected to be in control, he thinks that the burden of the conversation rests with him rather than being the mutual matter it is. Counseling such a young man one day, I said: "Just go over and say, 'Hi. May I sit down?'" No line or witticism is nearly as welcome among women as is unstructured, reciprocal gab. The male who believes that his conversation must be carefully mapped, full of interesting tidbits, masterful, forceful, alluring, and knowledgeable, all at the same time, labors under a heavy strain when he simply wants to say hello and get to know a woman. His structured approach, which tells him there must be a series of carefully planned steps in which he leads a woman without seeming to overdo himself, is more often than not a pathetic comment on human relations.

The fact that so many men do see women as essentially different from themselves instead of as beings with thoughts, perceptions, hopes, and desires not unlike their own destroys *empathy*. What can one talk about with them? What in the world might be likely to interest them? How will they feel if one slips and fails to be Mr. Strong at a moment during the conversation? What many men discover in the women who do draw close to them is that they can be talked with and that the communication gap is not as wide as it seems with other women. This fact alone is capable of making them devoted husbands. Many other men never discover this fact, however, and continue to talk with men, leaving women in a corner with "the girls" to talk "girl talk."

When conversation with women is difficult, it is not because of innate (gender) incompatibilities but because women have been socialized as creatures who take little or no interest in those "affairs of the world" that engage men. On the other hand, since women have been trained to look to men for guidance, men are often reluctant to accept women's viewpoints as of much value. When a woman is as knowledgeable about certain subjects as is the man she converses with, he may find her exciting as a conversationalist but worrisome as a prospective paramour. "She's so quick intellectually," said a man to me about a woman he had conversed with, "that I could never make a move toward her without her being aware of exactly what is going on." Men who think in this way believe that they lead women into bed without those women having the slightest idea of what is transpiring. Just as the motorcyclists lead their girl friends by the back of the neck, which seems to be a presumption that the women are not capable of going places on their own, many men who put women in a different class from themselves (pedestalitis) find it hard to believe that a woman may enjoy sexual relations as much as or more than they do. Dr. Katz's finding that women who are sexually active enjoy their relations more than do men and engage in intercourse more frequently gives men pause for thought.

More than likely the inability of men to countenance relations with self-confident women (that is, relations that extend from shoptalk through bedroom banter) stems from the fact that the sexual revolution is only imperfectly advanced. It has been less than a decade since sex as pleasure became an acceptable topic in media, and it is only little more than two decades since Alfred Kinsey investigated sex behavior and reported his findings to a disbelieving nation. Kinsey and his associates made it clear that there were actually several codes of sex mores in society. Different religious castes, social classes, and nationalities, as well as varying value systems, have made discussions of sexual behavior, already hampered by Victorian ethics, even more difficult. The sexual ignorance rampant in society has meant that men are ignorant of women, of their likes and dislikes, and of their emotional makeup.

Lisa Jacobs, writing about Will Harvey's book *How to Find and Fascinate a Mistress (and Survive in Spite of It All)* says of Mr. Harvey what might be said of the American male generally: "His ideas about sex and women are avant-garde, for the 50's. But times have changed. Women, for Mr. Harvey's approval, must still be thoroughly complacent and idolatory. With the first signs of independence he runs like hell. . . . Her life must revolve around his."[6]

Why does a woman's independence frighten a man? First, because the male's ability to be sexually aroused—

his so-called voracious sexual appetite—is something of a myth. It is subject to conditions and feelings more than he is willing to admit. He fears that if he is not in control of a sexual situation, calling positions in as carefree a manner as he calls all the shots until he and his intended climb into bed, he will not be able to perform. Every man knows he cannot command himself to get an erection. If he does, he fails. Therefore he fears that an equalized woman is likely to be demanding and that if she is able to call even a few of the shots, she may call for his erection at a time when he cannot will it into existence. Since it is believed—wrongly—that men are "always ready," he is panicked by the possibility that he will seem less than manly, not only in her eyes but also in his own. Men fear women who show capabilities similar to their own, therefore, because they fear exposure as being "less" than men.

Intellectual capability is particularly frightening because a man has been conditioned to believe that rationality is the supreme dexterity. If a woman can wield her intellect quickly and sharply (more so than he), he feels less than whole in her presence. This works in reverse for women, naturally. Some women may secretly sense that Reason is not King and may quietly balk at a man's confident use of logic to win an argument. Since these women have not consciously arrived at a point where criticism of reason-as-method is possible, though, they may still feel less than whole in a man's presence and will keep their doubts to themselves. Since rationality is not the supreme dexterity but simply one way of using the mind and since it is a hindrance, in fact, if relied upon too heavily, men can be liberated from their fears of "smart" women by grasping this simple fact.

Old-fashioned guides to "catching a man" written in the forties, fifties, and early sixties stressed the importance of letting a man think himself smarter than a woman who is doing the "catching." The secret, according to these guides, is to allow the male to think that *he* is doing the pursuing and that the decisions are all finally his. It is important, say these guides, to make the male secure by making him seem more intelligent.

What has occurred in the United States is this: Occasions for male aggression have been minimized, but the male's belief that he must be aggressive still reigns. The mythical cave man who drags "his woman" to his lair by the hair is not being mannerly by today's standards, and so today's male looks to other methods to express his acquired aggression. The modern method is more refined, he thinks, but just as potent. It is the method of intellectual one-upmanship. By mistaking the intellect for a more powerful force than it is, he seeks to "drag" a woman away through its persuasion. If she can use her own intellect and allows him to know it, he feels that the "dragging" can only be made more difficult if not impossible.

As the liberation of women proceeds and an increasing number of women refuse to hide their capabilities in order to protect men from such anxieties, it is necessary for men to see that intellectualism does not provide the omnipotence that was once thought possible. This may be a difficult lesson to learn, but it could provide one new base for male-female relationships in which intellectual chatter proceeds unchecked without one partner or the other withdrawing with feelings of inferiority. When it is appreciated that "winning" intellectually is not the point of conversation and that intellectual views are only partial, a person with few rationalistic dexterities need not feel uncomfortable.

When this happens, relationships open up on new levels in which physical relations are possible but not necessarily obligatory. As it now stands, women are seldom men's buddies, although there must certainly be many more men and women who could enjoy one another's company without believing that it means they must copulate or marry. If such relationships did take place on a wider scale, many happier unions or, perhaps, marriages might result. A man who is able to relate to a woman on all fronts, not needing to dominate nor fearing her intellect, finds himself in touch with a situation in which dependency has less of a chance to work its concomitant resentments. A man can love a woman who owes him nothing much more easily through the passing years than he can care for one who depends on him for bread, butter, and her knowledge of the world. Similarly, a woman who cohabits with a man because she wants to and not because her bed and board are contingent on his pleasure is in a much better position to love spontaneously and meaningfully. Her attention is therefore truly flattering. If she must pretend and depend, an inner resentment builds of which neither she nor her mate may be aware.

How can a man continue to care for a dependent without feeling some measure of contempt? Is love aligned with admiration? If so, can a man continue to admire an anthropoid whose capabilities are seemingly inferior to his own? Can he continue to assume that she is inferior and maintain respect? In some ways, perhaps, he thinks he can.

He may "respect" her for her "virginal" mind, which gives the appearance of rejecting physical pleasures he himself craves. He may "respect" her because she bends to his wishes so well, submitting herself without complaint. This latter kind of "respect" is rampant in the United States. It is associated with the guilt felt by many husbands who have treated their wives with too great a will to dominate. They reason that their wives possess a kind of "womanly" strength which allows them to accept domineering blows like a punching bag. In many cases these blows, mostly psychological, may be manifestations of contempt.

The husbands who provide them condemn themselves for their own insensitivity. Submissive women may take advantage of the resultant guilt and manipulate their husbands accordingly. Finally and somewhat paradoxically, a man may "respect" a woman because she is "weak." Later he finds that she is exceedingly capable in times of stress, something he did not realize about her at first, since she kept the fact hidden from him. When hard times erupt and she acts coolly and with precision, he is astounded. Ashley Montagu reports that an important study made during World War II found that in heavily bombed areas in England, "almost 70% more men broke down and became psychiatric casualties than women!"[7]

These kinds of "respect," based on puritanical assumptions of chaste thoughts, guilt, and misperceptions, are unhealthy. Although they may provide a working basis for a long-term relationship, they give a man little in the way of genuine knowledge and appreciation of a woman *as she really is.*

What men may genuinely respect in some women is their ability to bypass intellectual formulations and grasp essentials intuitively. This ability, men may or may not realize, can be responsible for women's skill in coping during difficult predicaments. The fear that men have of a woman's intellectual skill is an unnecessary fear, since the intellect seldom provides half the insight given by intuition. A woman who shows intellectual strengths may not see a man nearly as clearly as a woman with intuitive ones. Thus the insecurities experienced by men in the presence of intellectual women have been unnecessary and have protected them not at all from feminine scrutiny. Without their realizing it, men have often been seen quite accurately by women they have assumed are not bright.

Relationships based on mutual knowledge and genuine respect (which comes when partners enjoy each other's abilities and accomplishments) can lead to the unification of platonic, romantic, and enduring love. In any relationship that has been blessed by shared appreciations and joint perceptions, rigid classifications of these three types of affection become meaningless. Since such a relationship is founded on a rock, so to speak, the fluctuations of romantic notion and physical desire may enter without consuming it or becoming its raison d'être. As it now stands, too many men and women believe that when sexual desire is not present in a relationship, it is dead. This is a woefully unimaginative viewpoint that sees relationships in hollow, one-dimensional terms.

Men need not insist on one set of values for platonic relationships with women and on another set for relationships that are romantic in nature. And yet many behave in just this schizophrenic manner. Ingrid Bengis writes of how she was accepted as "not quite a girl" on male baseball teams. Men, she said, enjoyed many of the same delights she did, and yet when she attempted to share pursuits with male friends, they put demands on her because she was a girl which they would not have put on themselves. She was required to hit a home run on every occasion or to face expulsion from the team. "It was impossible to be real with them," she complained of the men.[8]

Platonic relationships with women are so rare, in fact, that they became news at the University of Michigan when students chose roommates by lot in a two-week experiment testing the feasibility of coed roommating. The publicity that was generated amused campus old-timers, and one remarked, "Cohabitation has been going on on college campuses for years. It's rather paradoxical that when we do it on a nonsexual and platonic basis, it becomes a news issue."

Until men and women can think together, play together, as well as make love with one another, whole and robust relationships between them will be laborious if not impossible accomplishments. To play means to cooperate rather than to assume that one must lead while another either follows or simply watches. As long as competition reigns, however, there will be a combativeness present in relationships, a fear of losing, and a stress on winning. Since most men can't comfortably accept what they think would be failure should they lose to a woman, neither can they relate to such a woman except on a superficial basis.

A dominant figure in any relationship is an obstacle to personal freedom. When one partner imposes his or her particular design on life, individuality is crushed. The joy experienced when a lover feels appreciated for him or her *self* evaporates. Any arrangement in which a partner's "trip" is paramount and in which he or she becomes a director welcomes the end of spontaneity and the growth of prearranged style. One lover accepts, and the other administers. Sooner or later this arrangement is certain to exact its toll. If men wander from their spouses, perhaps it is partly because they wonder if these women have minds of their own. Perhaps men secretly wish for partners who will bear more of an equal share of life's burdens. If women wander from their husbands, perhaps it is because they grow tired of pretending to follow directions and want to seek for themselves a partner who will appreciate them for their own personal qualities, aside from those connected with their roles.

Finally, it remains to be said that men often find it difficult simply to make *friends* with women partly because sexual relations with a greater variety of women after the onset of a certain age is denied men in a society that does not practice sexual freedom. They may be likely, therefore, to overcompensate for this denial by too readily regarding women as potential bedmates.

The fact that women have often presented themselves

as inferiors has also led to disregard of them as friends. And might it not be possible that the poor estate of friendship among men themselves, in which same-sex touching is strictly forbidden, has made the extension of the concept of friendship to women difficult or, perhaps, hardly worthy of consideration?

Chapter 15 ❊ SEXUALITY
Releasing a Revolutionary Force

Sex is fun and subject to the morality of fun.
      —DRS. WILLIAM SIMON AND JOHN GAGNON[1]

If men flee from active, self-confident women, their flight is propelled mostly by sexual fears. The fears are evoked by the specter of competition with women, for it seems that most men are unsure of their sexuality, particularly if it is matched against what they believe are inexhaustible mines of feminine desire.

How could this be otherwise as long as men's self-images are so vulnerable? Snakes and snails, of which little boys are reputedly made, are hardly inspiring phallic symbols. Even in other cultures sexual insecurity is often a problem. Margaret Mead reports: "In marital quarrels among the Iatmul, the men complain bitterly because their wives demand too much of their copulatory powers."[2] Dr. Mead believes that "if a culture is patterned so that men are required to make love to a particular woman at a particular time and place, then rebellion may set in."[3]

This may be particularly true of U.S. culture not only because of its strict adherence to schedules but also because sexuality is no longer justified by an Old Testament morality that insists it be enjoyed only for procreation. Birth-control devices have given sexuality a new mantle: pleasure. To enjoy pleasure with another person is to introduce the necessity for cooperative and communicative play. If a hallmark of sexuality is playfulness, men, who have difficulty utilizing leisure because of their inability to be playful, are at a distinct disadvantage. Intellectualized approaches to living have accustomed men to structured behavior. Sexual contact within structured frameworks can proceed only if a woman cooperates within a set structure. If she begins to manufacture her own kinds of playfulness, however, and these do not fit a male's expectations, he becomes uncomfortable.

He finds it difficult to imagine how it is possible for him to retain his own concept of manliness when face to face with a woman whose appetite for pleasure is voracious. Previously it was he who decided how lengthy a given sexual encounter would be, but with a woman who seeks pleasure for herself, he can no longer quit when he wants. His excitement must continue unabated, he believes, as long as hers does, and if it does not, he feels robbed of manliness at its core: the "staying power" of his penis.

People who have observed the behavior of men in group sexual encounters (such as writers for *Screw*) have reported that it is the women in such encounters who take the active role. The men often lie back in a state of semi-disablement, worrying about their inabilities to perform and concerned with their status as compared to that of other men who show, on occasion, that they are able to perform. For the most part, however, women run to and fro from one man to another, trying to keep each in a state of excitation. Sex as play-pleasure has provoked a plethora of personal fears.

If the number of men faced with such fears is growing, as reports on the incidence of impotence would seem to indicate, the solution rests in rescuing men from those values that make cooperative sexual play (as opposed to domination and submission) difficult. The new sexuality, which is to say *post-contraceptive sexuality*, helps those who seek its pleasures to relinquish old values and to discover the new ones it upholds as the price of enjoyment.

There has been little mutual pleasure and virtually no ecstasy in lovemaking through the centuries except between those couples who have been sexually playful, but through these same centuries, during which sexual repressions have reigned, hedonistic procrastinators have been rare. Generally men have simply satisfied an urge to orgasm without concern for their partners' pleasure, and sexual intercourse has not been characterized by prolonged, leisurely feasts of mutual enjoyment.

To be free of anxieties with active, self-pleasing women men must first free themselves from the intellectual constructs that inhibit their ability to play, and they must relinquish dominance (and its accompaniment, violence) as well as competition (which introduces measurements that do not belong in the sexual realm). Otherwise all sexual experience will be tinged with structuring, which provides little in the way of mutual satisfaction unless both partners are particularly enthralled by a given structure. Even so, however, repetition of a particular structure soon exhausts its mystery, and boredom sets in. Domination in sex as practiced traditionally insures that a woman follows a man's structure. If she does not and introduces playful innovations of her own, he has one of two choices: to abandon his structure and attempt to cooperate with her playfully or to pick up his marbles and go home because the game is not being played according to his constructs.

The difference between old-fashioned female behavior, which involved submission to phallic probings, and the type of sexual enthusiasm celebrated by Germaine Greer, who suggests embracing and stimulating a man instead of merely *taking* him,[4] is a significant one. In the psyche of the traditional male it seems like the difference between copulating with a lamb and a tiger. That he maintains such frightening visions of sex with straightforward women, finding it difficult to play with them, is because his vision comes from his own interpretations of their attitudes. Using the traditional values he associates with active sexual behavior, he discovers that he would not want done unto him what he does unto others. In short, he mistakes enthusiastic playfulness or activity for aggression, and the aggression he envisions is fraught with the negative complications of masculinist values.

It may be that some women, striving to put old roles behind them, do make the mistake of adopting masculinist values, and instead of embracing and stimulating men gently, they do so with determination and pressure. Since what they do is the product of ideology rather than of feeling, the intensity these women exhibit is not sensual but strained. Such women do teach a man what the impedimenta of male attention, selfishly structured, can be like, however.

Germaine Greer cautions women (as men should also be cautioned) against adoption of what she calls "the performance ethic," in which rationalistic shortsightedness places emphasis on the genitals in lieu of a sexuality that is fused throughout the whole person, finding sensual release on a wider scale.[5] This "ethic" bypasses or avoids any touching to which it has given no specifically sexual connotations. That men and women allow this to happen is due to approaches that strip them of a wider awareness because they refuse to be open to possibilities not specifically defined. Instead they focus on their genitals, the area that they think about specifically when they engage in sexual relations, and the result is narrowly functional behavior and a horror of what they imagine to be perversions.

Since birth control has removed sexuality from procreative concerns, today's male in heat begins to see himself not as a potential father but as a pleasure provider, an almost machinelike phallus that must be capable of perpetual motion and always has staying power. The fact that men enter into physical relations within strict definitions of their roles is again as unfortunate as are fixed roles in any human encounter. Sexuality is not suited to structuring of any kind and soon becomes little more than a kind of programmed masturbation if its fulfillment is always preplanned. Thus men must be freed from 1-2-3 thinking about what they are supposed to be able to do when they relate to women sexually. The idea that sex must always be a lengthy pleasure bout is just as restrictive in its way as the idea that it is for procreation only. Although prolonged sex can take place if it is playful, playfulness is not subject to time regulations and is quelled if presented with a schedule.

Psychologist Dr. Paul Cameron reports that males spend a great deal of time thinking about sex. In a survey of four thousand people he found that males between the ages of twelve and seventeen think about sex once every two minutes. This rate continues into young adulthood and drops to once every five minutes in middle age (forty to fifty-five) and finally tails off to once every ten minutes after sixty-five. Females give thought to sex every two and a half minutes as teenagers, once every three minutes in young adulthood, once every ten minutes in middle age, and once every twenty minutes after sixty-five.[6]

Precisely what is meant by "thinking about sex" in Dr. Cameron's studies is not altogether clear, since ways of thinking are so varied. The lesser incidence shown by women could very well be reflective of social conditioning rather than biological fiat. What is amazing about figures for either sex, however, is that sexuality exists *in thought* so much more than it does in actuality. This means that ways in which men have been taught to use their minds also become ways in which they think about sex. Rationalistic enthusiasms that are supposed to be the province of males in particular enter into these thoughts and give male fantasies highly structured casts.

Women, whose training is less rationalistic and who are allowed to revel at least to some degree in *feeling*, are less affected. The fact that they have been placed by society in the position of receiver has made it almost unnecessary for them to think about precisely what they will do, and instead they accept what is being done. Now, of course, this is changing. As it does, women must be warned about the pitfalls of preprogramming themselves along masculinist lines so that spontaneous enthusiasm and activity on their part is not transformed into a sexuality marked by structured aggression. In other words, women must not relinquish the ability to play as they learn at the same time to become erotically active.

At Wright State University in Dayton, Ohio, an avantgarde class called Problems in Human Sexuality attracted some forty students, most of them married women. Homework included skin flicks, erotic books, and trips to gay bars for chats with homosexuals. The absence of men in the class puzzled journalists and others who were watching its progress with interest. Assistant sociology professor Ellen Murray explained male absence this way, however: "Most males are pigheaded," she said, "and think they know all there is to know about sex."[7]

Dr. J. Dudley Chapman, speaking to the American College of Osteopathic Obstetricians and Gynecologists, echoed Murray's belief that sexual ignorance abounds. In spite of the sexual revolution, he says, sexually related hang-ups of shame and fear have not disappeared, and new ones have developed. "Our desire to please and to be pleased in return," said Dr. Chapman, "forms one new hang-up, and if we all fail in this there is shame, lack of self-esteem, and depression."[8]

The success ethic operates among couples in the sexual realm as rampantly as it does in other spheres of their lives. Difficulties multiply when men try to achieve success as it has been defined for them by outspoken sexual "liberationists." Many sex manuals have taught them to believe that their sexual performances can be faultless if only they will follow the rules and directions specified in those manuals. Once again, the belief that rules (structured observances) can help create better human relationships intrudes mercilessly on those relationships. A rule points to fixed behavior patterns (roles); human relationships and feelings are larger and wider than formulas and regulations for improving their expression. The great trouble with rule-making in the sexual sphere is that a rule is apt to be used at a moment when it is not particularly needed. This accounts for the forced nonplayful quality of sex about which so many women complain.

If men are "pigheaded," as Murray believes, it is partly because if they admitted to sexual ignorance, it would suggest "some kind of demented incompetence," according to Dr. Chapman. No man wants to seem either demented or incompetent, and so instead of learning more, men stay shy of classes that might teach them more. At the same time they feel intimidated by locker-room boasting in a society that is just beginning to be able to speak about sex without snickering.

It is a fallacy, certainly, that men are knowing about sex. This is not to say that women are as knowledgeable or more so, but men pretend to know because such knowledge is part of the facade required by masculinist values. Cool action, based on careful experimentation and objectivity, is the image that these values demand. To be "in control" one must "know," and hence a know-it-all pose is used as a means of convincing others that one is masterfully erotic. Technique is often mistaken for knowledge.

As we have said, however, eroticism is not subject to any technique unless, of course, it is a highly specific type and focuses on mere physical release. The problem, however, is that mere physical release is often not release enough. Satisfaction through orgasm is not sufficient. If the whole person is not involved, the release experienced can be only partial. It is possible to be a master of technique and yet to emerge from the sex act more tense than before. Why? Because there has ensued such punctilious and exacting concentration on technique that no other components of the mind and body are given leeway to relax. What is built when men pretend to knowledge, and most particularly when they master technique instead of widening their abilities to feel, is a wall of ignorance around sex which maintains the status quo of sexual ignorance and creates the anxieties so prevalent today.

Masculinist values provide many of the aggressive, success-oriented, sex-conqueror fantasies that fill thousands of so-called erotic books crowding today's market. One prize fantasy object, valued by men for centuries, is the virgin. Just how extreme the demand for fulfillment of the virgin-deflowerment fantasy can become is illustrated by the recent case of an Italian groom, Salvatore Nappo, who said that he discovered his wife of four days was not a virgin. "She did not have the courage to tell me," said Nappo to the press. So armed with a small hand weapon, he took his wife for a drive in the country, shot her in the neck and throat, and left her in a ditch forty-six miles from town.

Why is virginity important to so many men? First because it assures them that their virgin partner is ignorant of sexual matters herself and is therefore not likely to make comparisons with their prowess. A virgin is believed easier to lead and to dominate. A man can guide her according to his own compulsions, and there is no way she can judge his performance. Virginity is also important because it assures a man that he is *the winner* in one more childishly competitive game. If a woman is not a virgin, this robs a man of the most cherished bonus of the competitive drive: the status that comes from being first on the block.

The values impinging upon sex today are obvious in the language used to describe it. "Screwing," for example, is a word that does not accurately describe what takes place between a man and a woman. The word implies that someone, presumably a woman, is being restrained or pinned, either above or below, and hence the word is tinged with a degree of hostility. Germaine Greer complains that all of the names used to describe the penis are *tool* names and that words describing the sex act, except for the word "ball," are all poking words.[9] My objection to this sad fact, and I presume Greer's as well, is that a poking word does not sufficiently account for participation on the part of a woman and hence sounds anticooperative. Secondly, it focuses total attention (once again) on the poking instrument, which places undue emphasis on genital sex without suggesting the suffusion of sensual feeling through the whole body and personality. In the long run this approach produces the boredom and sexual antipathy for each other which many couples develop. It ignores the fact that sexual contact of an extremely intense nature can take place not only when two people are fully clothed but also when they are not even touching except, perhaps, with their eyes.

The ways in which men talk about sex also belies their claims to knowledge of the subject. Dr. David R. Mace has noted in conversations with thousands of husbands covering a forty-year span that men almost always discuss sex "impersonally and indirectly, in stories and jokes." Seldom, he says, do they descend to the personal level, describing their own experiences, bewilderments, and frustrations. Dr. Mace, a marriage counselor, says that the first thing he notices about men, in contrast to women, is that they are *self-conscious* when they discuss sex.

Ann Welbourne, founder of Community Sex Information in New York City, said that her organization, after handling over fifteen thousand telephone questions about sex, had determined that eight out of ten callers were men. Most of these men, she says, were in their early twenties, and most were single. She believes that the questions that more than any others perplexed these men involved the *mechanics* of sex. Women, it seems, asked medical questions about birth control and abortion.

At first, says Welbourne, her own attitudes toward callers and their questions included "smug, know-it-all" feelings. As the calls increased, however, her attitudes quickly changed through shock to "empathy toward people who were profoundly misinformed and disturbed." Calls poured in, asking if anal sex or oral sex were normal activities. After listening to so many problems, she was deeply moved. "I cannot possibly convey in words the profound sorrow," she said. "I was nearly moved to tears." The calls succeeded in making her "acutely aware once again of the universality of sexual repression and its dehumanizing consequences."

Before proceeding in this discussion of sex, it will help if I clarify my own attitudes about the so-called sexual perversions. I heartily reject the Babbittry exhibited by Dr. Alexander Lowen, who views all types of "deviant" behavior as emotional illness. He insists that "healthy" people have no desire to engage in "such practices" as homosexuality, group sex, fetishism, or pornography.[10] As critic Michael Perkins put it, "Evidently the neurotic and abused body Lowen is attempting to save in his book *The Betrayal of the Body* is not to enjoy its freedom once it is out of its straitjacket."[11]

Against Lowen's sexual provincialism I would introduce Dr. Eustace Chesser's position:

> Perversion and deviation are terms that express individual moral judgments. They do not belong to any scientific language. In order to study the problems that arise from sex objectively we need an entirely new way of classifying behavior. The dividing line should be between what people do with mutual consent, and what people do against another's will. In other words between social and antisocial acts.[12]

Such antisocial acts would include indecent assault, rape, offenses against children, and so on.

It is important that the reader understands what Chesser is saying because if men are to lose their self-conscious, mechanical perspectives on sex, they cannot afford to worry themselves about crossing old-fashioned sex barriers erected by definition-makers. Lowen's position would require that a man stop in the midst of mutually shared sensual pleasures and determine whether or not they fit a prescription. If men are to relax sexually and learn to play, this kind of burden must be put behind them.

Sexuality, after all, is one of the most profound and satisfying means by which men can transcend the pain, monotony, and limitations of their daily lives. If it is true, as Aldous Huxley said, that the urge to transcend "if only for a few moments, is and always has been one of the principal appetites of the soul," then sex as a way to such transcendence is unsurpassed as a nontechnical avenue (i.e., one that needs no drugs or other aids to produce its ecstasy). What is more, sex is also a means for integrating ecstasy and affection with experience, thus removing the alienation, boredom, and poverty of feeling which afflict humankind as it plods along in the midst of seeming limitations. As man learns to use technology to increase abundance and provide leisure, he will turn to sex to transcend himself even more than he does at present.

If both leisure and contraceptive devices are creating a new perspective on sex, so too is women's liberation. Until recently many women seemed content to forgo sexual pleasures, making themselves mere receptacles for men "to get off on." Now that women are asking for pleasure too, however—and according to the college studies we have mentioned, succeeding *more* than are men—new predicaments arise for men, who are as yet unchanged to any appreciable degree.

The major predicament as viewed by marriage counselors, psychiatrists, and other social observers has been a startling increase in impotence. Dr. George L. Ginsberg, in concert with two other psychiatrists, presented a report to the *Archives of General Psychiatry*, stating that more cases of impotence have appeared than ever before. "Until now," said Dr. Ginsberg, impotence "has been very unusual to see in younger people." The three doctors said that the cause was the "liberation" of women and their subsequent sexual demands. In the past, they implied, a woman was expected to be passive and less threatening to the male. Anxiety about whether women can be satisfied is now on the increase, they said.[13]

Active women and contraceptives are making it uncomfortably clear to men that they must maintain sexual intercourse over longer and longer periods of time to avoid reputations as "wham, bam, thank you, ma'am" types. The women with whom they copulate are looking for prolongation of the sex act, and the quick release equated with premature ejaculation is not appreciated. Such a release does not, after all, give women the time they need to achieve satisfaction. Thus the self-confident woman who asks for sexual pleasure on an equal basis frightens any man who has not yet acquainted himself with procrastination as the soul of sensuality.

If men are to avoid or to overcome impotence, they will need cooperation from women in the sense that women must understand how demands for sexual performance can destroy sexual desires. Male passions can vanish as quickly as can female passions. Sexual feelings are aroused as a kind of spontaneous play. They do not come forth on cue but because of a constellation of factors, the least of which is self-conscious determination. Dr. Daniel Goldstine observes: "One, if not the major, cause of the new impotence is performance pressure." Men who complain of impotence have signaled the "do-it-now" stresses on lovemaking as a foremost factor in their anxieties.

The authors of *Human Sexual Inadequacy*, William H. Masters and Virginia E. Johnson, report that their clinic enjoys a 78 percent cure rate in its treatment of men suffering from impotence. Sex-therapy clinics have sprung up in major cities, basing their programs on Masters and Johnson's methodology, and are assisting the distraught males who flock to them with this problem.

To assist in the elimination of impotence women are advised not to treat men as sex objects. By this is meant, of course, that sex per se must not be seen as a woman's only concern when she slips into bed with a man. If it is, the pressure on him to perform will be more acute. Sex is an aspect or an extension of communication rather than an entity by itself. If it is treated like an entity, it will often resemble a conversation that begins in the middle without any beginning.

Women whose bedmates find themselves unable to perform must acknowledge that they are disappointed but in a sympathetic, supportive manner. To berate a man for his inabilities only makes matters worse. A man suffering impotence must be told that his partner understands his

disappointment, does not condemn him for not perform-
ing, and only wants to make him feel appreciated if he
is insecure.

It helps to examine the environment in which sexual
relations take place. Ideally, the environment should
change from time to time and should be comfortable and
clean. If children can wander through the bedroom at will
or if there is too much pressure not to make noise on the
account of other people in the vicinity, occasions for impotence may be multiplied. Other causes of impotence may
range from worries—whether sexually or otherwise motivated—to too great an anticipation after a lengthy separa-
tion. If a woman insists on sex too regularly, she introduces
unnatural time-consciousness. Timing must be abandoned
to give way to a cooperative spontaneity.

As with most male problems, impotence has its roots
in the values associated with masculine tradition. Perhaps
hyperintellectuality is among the most damaging encum-
brances of all. This is so because thinking is responsible for
the vicious circle that produces the fears creating impotence. If a man experiences a single failure in the midst
of sexual intercourse, he may allow his intellect to enlarge
his failure out of proportion to its importance. Although
it might have remained incidental, his thinking apparatus
produces abstractions that pour into his consciousness with
crippling rapidity. Unable to still his mind by stopping
thought production as do the Eastern meditators, he
watches helplessly as his mind weaves a single incident
into a blanket of anxieties, none of which have any solid
basis in what actually happened at the time of his first
failure. When he approaches his partner on the next occasion, his fears have become so enormous and his anticipation so acute through thinking that he fails again. A
vicious circle ensues, and in its dizzying spiral he wonders
if escape is at all possible. His problem is indeed one of

the most heartbreaking imaginable, and more than a few men have ended their lives in the grip of fears that have overcome them.

If a man has been taught to neglect feeling, the problem is intensified. If he categorizes sex, as do many intellect-conscious men, as a function of the genitals, he is in even greater trouble. If he is programmed to achieve, as is today's working man, and believes that every second counts, he has divided his sexual life into technological time categories and is in a rush to consummate his affection. This prevents him from relaxing *in the present* and puts him in a debilitating state of anticipation.

Since competitive drives prescribe comparisons, men are unduly concerned with maintaining high sexual performance standards. To enter the arena of play armed with standards, however, is to eliminate the possibility of spontaneous movement. When this kind of self-consciousness abounds, a man is forever checking himself against his experience to see if he has met self-set standards. This prevents the uninhibited flow of bodily motion which stands at the center of physical play. Only when a man forgets set standards, letting them drop, will the level of his sexual performance rise.

The psychology of play demands an end to arrangement and speculation about what might be, what was, and what is. It asks for the realization that *we are here and it is now.* Instead of thinking about doing—pondering, deliberating, considering, and brooding—a man must simply do. This means that he must abandon what Ann Welbourne referred to as the mechanics of sex. To do so gives his behavior a direct quality. When he spends time thinking about the mechanics of sexual action rather than just acting, his experience is diminished, and he performs less adequately.

To be absorbed in the present it is necessary for a man

to be able to feel. Feeling—the enjoyment of touch—can hypnotize a person so that he or she forgets time altogether. With men, however, feeling is only partially developed. Perhaps this is true of everyone, but it is particularly true of men. I make this statement confidently because passivity and receptivity (the ability to absorb) are at the bottom of feeling. If a man flies from passivity and receptivity, as most American men do, then he cuts off major avenues to feeling. Passivity and receptivity are needed if we are to fully sense things. Without them, our senses can be only partial.

If a man is to forget himself and cease worrying in the midst of sexual intercourse, a taste for prolonged sensual self-enjoyment must take the place of the stern commitment to satisfy an active woman which he has so seriously made. This cannot happen until a man ceases to see himself only as the active one or the one who acts upon another (the vulgar phrase is "gets to do it *to* her") and becomes instead both active and passive, *cooperating with* rather than *doing to* and passively enjoying the sensations that come to him.

If any man is not sufficiently passive, he will never be acted upon in any significant way. Therefore he will lose out on a great measure of experience both for himself and for his lover, who in turn might enjoy the pleasure of being active. If a man uses his sexual energy only actively, he will never experience the heights of feeling that require passivity for the fullest exhilaration.

If rigid thinking patterns cause a man to believe that there are only a certain number of ways in which the sexual act can take place, he will be overconcerned with *what* is taking place rather than how it feels. The hippie slogan "If it feels good, do it!" is a novel suggestion for these overconcerned men. Ignoring such advice, men allow neither themselves nor their partners sufficient room for self-expression, and playfulness is cut out at its core.

Until Masters and Johnson exposed the myth of vaginal orgasms, it was assumed that the coital position was the most satisfactory means of achieving mutual pleasure. The noncoital orgasm, brought about by direct clitoral stimulation, was generally frowned upon, and men and women were both brainwashed about its undesirability. If they removed themselves from the "missionary position," it was feared that they would end by assuming all sorts of positions bordering on perversion. Since it is now clear, however, that women reach orgasm clitorally and that nonpenetrative stimulation by the male assists in bringing the female to satisfactory sexual climaxes, new possibilities for playfulness have been introduced.

Sexual technique becomes secondary in a playful state. The word "technique" itself is counterplayful. It is *attitude* that is of primary importance, because attitude alone invests sex with the characteristics it needs to be most gratifying; cooperation, spontaneity, feeling, trust, and openness create the best conditions under which meaningful sex thrives.

If negative values such as dominance and competition prevail, specific aims and particular goals will fetter the mind. In physical relations dominance is expressed by restraint and easily evolves into violence. That there is a considerable degree of violence in sexual language is clear. Men "take" or "make" women, for example, and when they do so, it is a "conquest." Women "submit" or "surrender." They are "violated" and allow themselves to be "possessed."

Kate Millett devotes considerable space in *Sexual Politics* to an analysis of Norman Mailer's obsession with violence, quoting from *The Naked and the Dead* to show that Mailer thought of violence in connection with sex:

> All the deep dark urges of man, the sacrifices on the
> hilltop, the churning lusts of night and sleep, weren't

all of them contained in the shattering, screaming burst of a shell ... the phallus shell that rides through a shining vagina of steel ... the curve of sexual excitement and discharge, which is after all the physical core of life.[14]

Mailer's closest rival for the Bull of Literature title was Ernest Hemingway, who praised "manly" violence on too many occasions. Alan Sillitoe writes: "An intellectual obsession with violence is a sign of fear. A physical obsession with it is a sign of sexual impotence." I am forced to remember that Hemingway took his own life and that *Screw* once titled a Hemingway book review, "The Impotence of Being Ernest." Mailer, in turn, once stabbed his wife and has been engaged in more than one public brawl. Why?

Furthermore, why is sadomasochism growing so rapidly in the United States? It has always existed, of course, but there are definite signs that it is on the rise. Its connection with the dominance value and with a resultant impotence is clear. Sadomasochistic devotees say that S&M is a "further step" waiting for those who have tired of conventional sex and are looking for new expressions. In short, they view their practices as the end product of a wide and growing sexual awareness. When a man has found other sexual acts "boring" because he has "done everything" and becomes impotent, he refers to himself as jaded. Jadedness, though, is merely a glamorous term used as an excuse for enfeeblement, since it casts no aspersions on one's sexual stance. Jadedness and impotence both arise from a rigidly structured approach to sexual relations, however, in which each sexual movement is experienced intellectually and seen as a distinct deed.

Such mental posturing bypasses tenderness and concerns itself primarily with physical positioning and a hyperconsciousness of each movement as it takes place. The sexual experience is chopped into categories: kisses, caresses, cunnilingus, fellatio, coitus, and other predilections. It is not seen as a passing sequence of spontaneous, playful flux. Because society is rife with demands for sexual competence, men worry about maintaining high sexual performance standards and become nervous about whether they are touching properly, whether they are "good," and the like. Part of the difficulty stems too from puritanical training that came early in life, woven from the thread of a sexually retarded society. People who consciously label each sexual movement they make do so because the movements, spotlighted by society's puritanical emphasis on them, seem unprecedented and unique each time they occur. Instead of accepting the movements as a matter of course, an intellectual awareness returns to these people in the midst of sexual passion. Therefore they are self-conscious, and an erection is hard to come by.

Only when the mind does not concentrate so precisely on what is taking place does the body attune itself to a natural rhythm and pulsate uninhibitedly and unselfconsciously.

Sadomasochism is structure-oriented and concerns itself with power and control. Its practitioners seem preoccupied by bondage, and sadomasochistic ritual is accompanied by handcuffs, ropes, and chains. Long-term S&M relationships cannot survive without distinct allocations of observance and function.

What this means is that the undue emphasis intellectualized approaches have placed on positioning and performance has made some men into sadomasochists. Being unable to perform, they create strict games (sadomasochism) in which instead of pleasure, dominance and submission become paramount. This is done only when it becomes apparent to them that pleasure, because of their rigidly structured psyches, is not within their reach (i.e., they think they have become jaded). Hyper-self-consciousness has created impotence, and since they cannot rid themselves of this consciousness in the midst of sexual passion, achieving the spontaneity that is necessary to play, they embrace the structures of dominance and submission instead. Role-playing in S&M circles is rampant. Motorcycle gangs adopt S&M poses because they have not learned to play. Perhaps even war is ultimately an S&M game.

If a man relinquishes dominance, he can learn to revel in the passive state of being, learning what Whitman called "the profound lesson of reception." Such a man would allow openings in himself for vital, active ingress—and would welcome the ministrations of an active woman. "The man who cannot cope with a female on top of him is a male chauvinist," says Germaine Greer, who suggests to women that they throw their legs over their lovers to detect, if they can, sexual imperialism. "The man who is frightened by his woman's erect body over him," she writes, "is full of castration fears which will poison all his relationships and ruin all his orgasms."[15]

If men are to understand the new feminine sensibilities and relate to active women, then they must learn to understand, appreciate, and draw on those qualities in themselves traditionally associated with femininity: receptivity and passivity. Society has told men to repress these capabilities, and so men must learn to ignore society's admonitions.

Simone de Beauvoir says that "through her erotic experience woman feels and often detests the domination of the male." If this is so, it is time to ease her situation. The new sexuality may be more akin to a dance. When the partners hold each other too closely, clutching, dominating, and trying to step, they are clumsy. Their dance lacks sensual pulsations, and the partners appear to be uncomfortable with each other. When, however, the dance is not forced and the partners each give themselves to the musical beat without being conscious of every movement, they seem to take on an aura of rhythm and sensuality.

I would say, in fact, that under such conditions (and this is a major thesis of this book) the new sexuality becomes a great revolutionary force. Learning to *play* in concert with others is at the root of the new sexuality, and since play cannot be structured, it is antiauthoritarian. Sexuality today, if it is to be fully enjoyed, is the one drive that demands recognition of its values: cooperation, spontaneity, passivity (openness), sharing, sensitivity, trust, and freedom. If prolonged pleasures are to be drawn from sexuality, these values must, of necessity, accompany the lover who seeks them.

Chapter 16 ✳ LADIES
A Few Words
about Manipulators

*In the not so distant future women who continue to play
the game with each other and with men in order to
vicariously advance their own status will elicit amusement
and pity more often than respect. As the falseness of the
old roles becomes more and more apparent, women who
continue to hide behind them will seem superfluous,
out of place—like costumed Halloween tricksters ringing
a doorbell at high noon in midsummer.*
—THOMAS BOSLOOPER AND MARCIA HAYES[1]

There are always "liberators" who like to call names, to
feel put upon, and no doubt it helps make liberation more
dramatic if they feel they are rescuing one sex or the other
from the clutches of living monsters. Among extremists
the "names" have escalated from "sexist" to "oppressor" to
"enemy." If there were no devil, these people might invent
one in order to enjoy self-congratulation for doing battle
courageously.

What prompts some liberationists to define other people
with such gusto as oppressors? Perhaps occasional definitions help to promote a viewpoint, but it can be argued
that there are oppressors among both genders and that it
will do no good to say that either gender, per se, is oppressive. Defining others as one's enemy has one unintended
effect: It gives the so-called enemy a proud badge to wear.
Witness how many men own up to the charge that they
are male chauvinists.

It has taken Esther Vilar, a female misogynist, to reverse the arguments of those women's liberationists who

call men oppressors. Vilar says that it is women who are oppressive and men who have been enslaved by them. Her book *The Manipulated Man* contends that men are rather dense in some significant ways, and she condemns women for enslaving them.

What Vilar has managed in her book is an elevation of certain mental dexterities she regards as superior. I would like to think that she has done this (as Ashley Montagu did in *The Natural Superiority of Women*) with tongue in cheek, but I am afraid she cannot be allowed such an escape hatch. In her book she emphasizes and reemphasizes with italics that women are *stupid.* She writes: "Women just sit back getting lazier, dumber, and more demanding—and, at the same time, richer."[2] Just how dumb can women be if they are richer? And if women are dumb and yet manipulate men, which sex is dumber: the women or the men?

Before an entire gender is saddled with a reputation for stupidity, the standards being used to define this stupidity should be determined. When this is done, both stupidity and superiority will be seen against a value background that is purely subjective. Calling names and characterizing all members of one gender or another with such positive vengeance is hardly conducive to intersex harmony.

I am not convinced that when human beings enslave each other in various ways, it is a deliberate and conscious act. Social motivations push both sexes toward a destiny that is often far below the heights they might attain if each were more prone to skepticism about socially acceptable behavior. Since most people are not very skeptical, though, they accept what seems to be going on around them, and generally it is left to a few to explain to them what they are actually doing in the hope that changes will ensue. In the long run, however, defining another group as the oppressors will only stiffen the resistance of its members to legitimate changes.

The charge that women oppress men is no more important, therefore, than is the charge that men oppress women. Calling names may help generate indignance and give focus to grievances so that some image against which to vent frustrations and anger is available, but it is not going to ease the situation, particularly when easement depends on reconciliation of the sexes instead of estrangement.

It is social pressure, after all, that affects men and women so profoundly as to make them robotlike in its grasp. If anyone doubts this fact, they need only refer to the histories of organized religions to see how hundreds of millions embrace their precepts without seriously questioning them. If men oppress, it is not because they are inherently domineering, and it would be a mistake to assume that if women manipulate, it is because they have evil motives.

There are many women who manipulate with the very kindest motives, believing that what they are doing is good not only for themselves but also for the men they love. The point is not their intentions, however, but rather the kind of relationship which ensues when a woman is fully aware of her manipulative capabilities.

The relationship must be one, of necessity, in which the excitement of genuine reciprocity is dulled. To those men and women who refuse to complain about a situation that they can recognize (in some degree at least) but have no will to change, it can only be said that they are doomed to suffer the increase of boredom. This may be particularly true from the woman's standpoint, and although she may seem content on the outside, her pleasant demeanor is only a pose that hides an often-condescending attitude toward a mate she no longer finds exciting. This is not to say that she does not continue to love him but rather that her love is more akin to a mother's love, one that is functional and protective rather than flourishing anew, challenged by the vision of a male who has not settled into a routine that she can all too easily pinpoint and use to her own purposes, if she chooses to do so. The kind of boredom that sets in under such circumstances is behind more than a few divorces, because once the boredom becomes conscious, it finds expression in irritation, exasperation, and provocation. Sexual intercourse under such circumstances is not any longer a new or imaginative surprise but a habit whose characteristics are all too well known.

Certainly the misplaced confidence men put in logic and other intellectual processes has made it easier to manipulate them. The person who is wedded to systematic procedures, believing that they are bound somehow to reality, is easily duped. He has applied certain fixed patterns to his life. The woman who is likely to manipulate him understands that real life is not fixed but spontaneous and unpredictable. Once she has determined the patterns that motivate him, she is then free to use this knowledge to her advantage.

In any case, it should be clear that when women as oppressors are considered in these pages, women as a class and even individual women are not being blamed. It must be understood that their tendency to oppress is socially induced and that they are in the grip of cultural deceptions which mold and warp their behavior. It is these deceptions that should arouse legitimate ire. As Clarence Darrow said, "I hate the sin but not the sinner."

Hopefully, women's liberationists who complain of male dominance might adopt a similar approach. If they did, they would far better understand male behavior patterns, and the legitimate angers that ignite them would be unlikely to erupt in personal attacks on oppressive men.

It is flattering to one with masculinist values (particularly a believer in dominance) to think of himself as a dominator. It is not flattering to a woman's image, however, if her role as manipulator is exposed. This is precisely what Vilar attempts to do by casting scorching searchlights on ways in which many women have manipulated men for their own purposes while men have retained the most unrealistic images of women imaginable. If only Vilar did not seem so motivated by a hatred for women and better realized that oppression works both ways. Her book does alert men to manipulative behavior made possible by dominance and submission, and it could have been, if only it were a more compassionate work, liberating for men. In her hatred for manipulative women she has done them a service, freeing them by uncovering their attitudes and asking that they seek that independence that will help bring about men's independence as well. If men and women are to continue intimate associations, a man must choose associations with women who are independent and free also. It is foolish to believe that decent relationships can be built on dependency. Dependency creates resentment for both partners in a relationship. Who can continually accept without feeling indebted, and who can only give without feeling that he or she is owed?

In what ways are some men oppressed and manipulated by some women? They are often difficult to detect for the simple reason that the props and artifacts of manipulation are subtly woven into American culture and are accepted as part of the natural scheme of things. The props include the whole artillery of the feminine mystique —those items that assist women in making themselves seem more helpless than they are. And it must not be forgotten that there are a growing number of manipulative women who are both "helpless" and "equal" at the same time, a tactic that confuses unliberated men, who have been taught to be protective and who still respond to such

women in old-fashioned ways. Most of the following discussion will concentrate on traditional manipulative techniques, but a mention of ways in which manipulators are
using women's liberation to their advantage is apt.

Since men are accustomed to what they somewhat
laughingly refer to as feminine behavior, they often over-
look the ways in which that behavior is used deliberately
to motivate them. To catalog those ways is too great a
task, although a few general observations can be made.
Most of what will be said here applies to married women
who are not employed outside the home. In no way do I
mean to imply that "career" women do not often face
sacrifice and conflict, being wedged between domineering
employers and family "duties" thoughtlessly dumped on
them by dominant chauvinist husbands.

Examples are set for men and training given them in
proper male-female deportment by parents—including
mothers (a fact that feminists who angrily denounce men
as their oppressors should remember). If men are conditioned to believe that women are helpless, it may be because many mothers believe in using a man's romantic
interests to inspire him to financial achievement. Since this
method is the accepted one, love is used to trap a man in
the service of the corporation for more years than he
might otherwise be likely to stay. Mother assumes that
this is the kind of "security" he needs, and since his work
is a mysterious realm to her anyway, she can think of it
only as good (or at least proper), especially since it requires
of him that he be disciplined. In his father a young man
is subjected to the force of example, which is perhaps the
most potent teacher of all.

Society and self-interest often conspire to teach women
that it is the province of men to support, defend, and
work and that it is their province to "inspire" them to such
activity. The "inspiration" tendered is perhaps the reason

that most manipulative women use to justify their behavior. In many cases it works effectively as a goad to making a higher salary, since men hope that through working hard and "getting ahead" they will show their love and shower life's good things (most of which are now plastic) on their beloveds. The dependence of women is heartily welcomed, since it is just one more way in which men can flex their muscles and prove themselves "worthy." In the throes of early love and affection it seems no task at all to take on heavy-duty employment. When a man returns home in the evening, he looks to his new bride to provide him with the small comforts that make his day complete. As time passes, he earns the money for various items that will make his loved one's lot a bit easier: precooked foods, washers, dryers, dishwashing machines, and other technological assists. These do ease her day, and she is left with leisure, which she accounts for with little innovations: frills, flowers, and clothes for herself.[3] Men are taught what is meant by "gracious living" because it is an aspect of life that they generally leave to a woman's taste and take on a woman's word.

In the meantime, however, much of what was formerly called house*work* and which once did indeed call for hard work on the part of the housewife has become simple and swift. Even cooking is no longer the household chore that it once was, since women now seem to prefer synthetic instant meals, already packaged and seasoned, to those home-cooked dinners of the past. If anyone doubts this, a trip to the local supermarket will serve as confirmation.

That women are not helpless is often difficult to explain to a man. Woman's helplessness has become a part of her image which is aesthetically pleasing to many men for some odd reason. To insure that it is effective as a means of manipulating him to do her bidding, makeup and other artifacts conspire to make a woman appear babyish, since babies are thought to be the most helpless creatures of all. Many men even call their mates baby, which adds to the whole illusion. High heels, which must certainly be the most uncomfortable footwear imaginable, have given women a kind of unwieldy appearance, making them seem vulnerable to a fall. Many men still believe that women, when they cry, are experiencing a profound unhappiness. Since they themselves have been taught not to cry, it does not occur to them that crying on the part of a woman is not indicative of as much pain as it would seem to be. Some women can cry at will and do so. Men assume that when it happens, something deeply, terribly upsetting has occurred, since they are judging outward appearances by their own standards. Women do not have to explain themselves, and so it may be that they cry only to effect some minor change in their man's planning. More than once I have heard men say, "I can stand almost anything except hearing a woman cry. That really gets to me." The manipulative woman knows such things and uses them accordingly.

Scarlett O'Hara in Margaret Mitchell's *Gone with the Wind* was a woman who manipulated easily and well. This was obvious in her relationship with Rhett Butler, who finally walked out on her at the end of the book. The feminine wiles she adopted were mere put-ons, difficult for men to see, since dominating men seldom have an adequate sense of themselves and are encouraged by any sign that they take for weakness, thus making their "conquest" easier after a suitable amount of titillation and teasing (called flirting) has taken place.

Manipulation can take place only within a dominant-submissive framework. Slaves were often manipulators of their masters. They allowed their masters to believe that they were always subservient, and in doing so, often arranged matters so their masters believed themselves to be making the decisions, whereas many of them were made by the slaves.

If a manipulative woman wants a fur coat, for example, but does not want to appear to be making the decision that it should be bought, she may say to her husband, "I don't believe we should spend the money necessary to buy that coat." A domineering man who nevertheless loves his wife will say to himself, "What right has she to make decisions about how my money will be spent?" Because he wants her to be happy, he will reply, "Of course we'll spend the money," which is what his wife hoped to hear in the first place.

In order to make a man believe that he is making decisions when in fact he is not, a manipulative woman may ask his permission to do any number of things which are not really important to her. This provides her with the opportunity to play helpless and needy, which will be to her great advantage when there is something she really wants.

If there were a greater degree of sexual freedom in society of the kind that has developed among many of the young, men might look for different values in the women whose companionship they seek. If the precious halo surrounding women because of their purity and virginity were shattered, as the young are shattering it, there would be less unrealistic thinking about women. As it now stands, women are lifted onto their pedestals in great part because the Madonna image—the Virgin—is so strong in our culture. Sexual abstinence is somehow connected with purity and goodness under this system, and hence we get the kind of assessment made by husbands that borders on lunacy in its belief that because their wives abstain from sex with others, this makes them candidates for medals. All too many men have romanticized women to their own detriment and to the detriment of their relationships. When they think of these women in such idealized terms, they spout words such as "angel" and "princess," characterizing them as "too good for me" or "too good for the world." With the additional weight of the "baby" images of helplessness and the need to be taken care of, men carry around with them an often heavy responsibility: to protect and make life easy for their defenseless little "chicks." And yet Esther Vilar tells us that "when women are among themselves, discussing the desirable qualities of a specific man, they will never declare that they want someone to look up to, someone who will protect them. Such twaddle would be greeted with the laughter it deserves."[4]

The movement for women's liberation has given some women a double-edged sword to use in their manipulative arsenal. A woman who gives the impression that she is "liberated" may do so by adopting masculinist values: competition, dominance, and other instigators of one-upmanship. She openly vies for control, challenging a male to win and flaunting her ability to equal him in earning capacity. The male, since he still accepts old values, is faced with a whirlwind of confusing images. Although he may wish to admit her equality and her right to "personhood," he has also been taught to respond in protective and defensive ways "for her benefit." The manipulative woman knows this and takes full advantage of the knowledge in her relationship with him. She can strut and demand, or she can purr and coo. When she purrs and coos, he feels comfortable. In many instances purring and cooing has taken the place of sex as a reward when a male has been "good" to his mate. His conditioning makes him appreciative of this bizarre behavior, since he is merely hoping for a response to the offerings that males traditionally make, and he equates her tendencies to dominance with the movement for women's liberation. It is little wonder that many men are opposed to that movement, since so many unliberated women make use of it in such negative ways.

Again, if sexual freedom were widespread, sexual favors or their withholding would not threaten a man so. That tens of millions of men are threatened in this way is obvious in that each sexual contact, except among the young, is difficult to come by, even with minimally desirable partners. Few men are attracted to garish prostitutes or female bar flies, and until quite recently very few women have been openly, joyously, and actively sexual; those who have been have unfortunately been held in little regard by the men who have enjoyed them.

Laws that prohibit extramarital behavior are useless because no relationship can be held together by laws.

> Were you looking to be held together by lawyers?
> or by an agreement on paper?[5]

Such laws should be removed from the ledgers. Extramarital sex is consensual behavior between or among adults, and it injures no one except a jealous or possessive person. This is not to encourage fornication among those who are not so inclined, but it should most certainly be removed as a condition that invalidates marriage or any healthy relationship. A marriage needs only one partner to decide it is invalid, and then any available law can be used to force its dissolution.

It is certainly true that men wrote such odd laws. They may have justified doing so by saying they were protecting women or in their more honest moments by saying they were insuring emotional and financial investments. By making extramarital sex a cause for divorce, they merely followed antiquated religious rules. These rules placed women in a kind of obligatory spot, sitting under the apple tree with one man at a time: the man who has married and paid for her. They put men themselves in the position of being manipulated for whatever sex is doled out to them. They have prevented married men from expressing their feelings to others—and have prevented married women from doing the same. This setup has created either-or marriages, which are the very worst kind of marriages to have because few relationships are either-or, even though people treat them that way. A marriage should not base itself primarily on sexual fidelity and only incidentally on other qualities of character. In fact, I wonder if men, by providing women with support and demanding sexual fidelity as the return on their investments, have not made love and a more profound fidelity a bit weaker, a bit less full of the camaraderie that comes from being with a woman who has obviously chosen freely to be a very close friend and companion.

What is even more important is this: A woman is not being protected if she is encouraged to be weak and helpless. Her vulnerability, which the present system encourages, is nothing more than a man's way of making himself indispensable *with money*, which is only one more way of assuring him that he can win her on a basis other than that which requires his own merits. If a man accepts this kind of arrangement for the reasons given (and a great many do), he has done nothing more than reveal that he does not believe he himself is sufficient as bait for a woman's long-term interest. In other words, he is simply expressing the insecurity he feels as a man, as a person, and as a sex and/or love object.

As long as the demand for sexual fidelity allows no other expressions for either men or women (outside of their marriages) and is regarded as the hallmark rather than simply one possible outcome of a good relationship, both men and women will be enslaved because they are not allowed to find other people through whom to experience positive feedback and to gain a greater sense of themselves. The present arrangement makes one single woman a man's only way of assessing himself. To give such a position to any person is to see one's reflection through too narrow a focus and to place too large a stick in that person's hands. We love our parents too, in many cases, and yet we would not want to deliver our entire sense of ourselves into their hands. Since most men are on shaky ground about their masculinity, they are in an inferior position with regard to women if it is stacked against feminine staying power. When men are free to express themselves on a wider scale, their feelings of sexual inadequacy will not be used as a club to keep them in line. They will no longer crawl on their knees to a single individual for the kind of self-validation they need to feel whole.

The best way to insure that manipulation has little or no chance to corrode a relationship is by encouraging women to be strong and independent, giving them the same kind of sexual freedom which men would like for themselves:

> Stranger, if you passing meet me and desire to
>   speak to me, why should you not speak to me?
> And why should I not speak to you?[6]

If a relationship between two people is really on firm ground and is based on genuine conviviality, trust, and mutual admiration, it will not ask partners to make demands on each other concerning where they go, whom they see, and what they are doing.

If sex is no longer to be used as a bludgeon, it will be because men and women are free enough to draw close to each other for ennobling reasons that step beyond its perimeters and are not calculating their own worth by the manner in which other people freely express themselves. To judge a relationship's value by the degree of sexual fidelity it inspires is to miss its most essential ingredients. If a man encourages his mate to be free and promotes her chances to be self-supporting and self-reliant, he is assuring himself that she remains near him because he is truly appreciated. A loving person helps to promote his mate's independence as a matter of course.

It is a great compliment to women that they have formed women's liberation groups. If many women are manipulators, at least some have seen through the social structuring that promotes this kind of behavior and have rejected it. They are striving to make women independent so that manipulation of men will no longer be either necessary or possible. Women who oppose moves to equalize their own status are suspect as manipulators, especially if they are vehement in their opposition.

Men's liberationists should not allow themselves to feel spite or antagonism for individual women, but rather they must become aware of the manipulative techniques used by some women, examine their own vulnerability to them, and kindly reject the techniques whenever possible. This does not mean that they must reject the women who utilize them but simply that these women must be put on notice that manipulative behavior is passé. A genuinely loving and thoughtful man will feel only pity for a woman who is manipulative, and he will realize that the male's tendencies to dominance have made it necessary for her to use such techniques. On each occasion that brings him an awareness of manipulation, he will not strike bitterly in retaliation but will help the woman overcome her tendencies if both can agree that these tendencies stand in the way of a meaningful relationship.

Men have refused to believe that manipulation by some

women really goes on. Why? Because men have preferred to think that they themselves are dominant, that they are actually guiding and directing. Dominance as a value has impeded their awareness. To accept that one may be manipulated is to concede the fact that one is not in control, which is impossible for anyone who clings to masculinist values.

Chapter 17 ✳ COUPLING
The Decline of
Organized Marriage

KUWAIT—(AP)—*Fist fights broke out in Kuwait's parliament during a debate on polygamy. Many of the 50 legislators took part in a 10-minute brawl, trading punches and lashing out with ekals, the black camelhair ropes that hold the traditional Arab male headdress in place. Fighting was touched off when a delegate insisted that Kuwaiti men were entitled to four wives in accordance with Islamic law. He represented the rightists in the parliament.*
— ASSOCIATED PRESS DISPATCH[1]

I would like to see more varieties of life-style. We don't need the idea of monogamous marriage for life— till death do us part. Death used to part us much sooner than it does now.
— DR. JOHN MONEY, PROFESSOR OF MEDICAL
PSYCHOLOGY AND ASSOCIATE PROFESSOR OF
PEDIATRICS, JOHNS HOPKINS UNIVERSITY[2]

In 1963, when discussions of far-out sexual arrangements were hardly as commonplace in the media as they are today, I discovered an article about incest in *The National Insider,* one of those numerous tabloids dealing with scandals and erotic oddities.

The National Insider was characterized in those days by a touch of grace which other scandal rags lacked: It carried genuine articles of social interest, often written by people who were personally involved. The article in question was by the mother of a large group of brothers and sisters who was arguing passionately and earnestly for the practice in which her whole family was engaged: affectionate relationships that stepped over sex taboos and often culminated in sexual expression. There is no proof, she insisted, that incest produces malformed babies. (And no less an informer than Ann Landers has said: "It is impossible to predict how gene patterns will develop. Some incestuous relationships have produced healthy and brilliant children, others have produced children who were defective both physically and mentally."[3]) Therefore, concluded this fiery writer in *The National Insider,* incestuous behavior opened prospective parents to the same risks that everybody takes. What impressed me most about her arguments, however, were the pleas she made for authentic, loving relationships within the family structure which did not require, as in most families, refusing those natural expressions of feelings. If her children had loving thoughts, she said, they were encouraged to share them in physical expressions with other members of the family:

> What is less or more than a touch?[4]

Furthermore, if there were men or women outside of the family structure who were cared for by this woman's children, they too were invited into the bosom of the family on what were exceedingly literal terms:

> If your lover, husband, wife, is welcome by day or
>   night, I must be personally as welcome. . . .
> I am a free companion, I bivouac by invading
>   watchfires,
> I turn the bridegroom out of bed and stay with the
>   bride myself.

I tighten her all night to my thighs and lips.[5]

The result of this experiment, she said, had been gratifying. Her children had grown up without feelings of shame about touching and enjoying themselves and others, and the family structure (expanded beyond the limits of the nuclear family) was a happy one. Strangely, I felt that the article was a true-life account, and even if it were not, I decided that it contained some exceedingly compelling criticisms of family structures today.

More recently one hundred members of an avant-garde Unitarian church formed nine separate extended families. The "family" members were not sexually involved with each other, as far as I know. Sexual alienation was not the problem they were trying to overcome. Instead they aimed at reducing the loneliness members felt either in their biological nuclear family units or apart from them. In any case, the concept of an extended family was one ingenious way of circumventing biological fiats. It is not necessary that a family consist of blood relatives, these people seemed to be saying.

The local newspaper carried color photographs of these extended families and quoted their joyous comments. One of the family facilitators appointed by the church said: "You share a lot with your extended family that you don't with your own families." More significantly, another commented: "I've gotten some of the security that I had from a large family as I was growing up. It's an interaction with people [who are] not interested in status or economic roles. I've found a sense of community and neighborliness that I thought no longer existed."

Pessimism about the community and the neighborliness surrounding family life is widespread today. The isolation felt by millions who are members of nuclear family units is intensified by television programs promoting idealistic characterizations of the family. These characterizations add to the consternation and confusion, and men, particularly, wonder what is going wrong in their own spheres. Why isn't marriage and family life the happy, carefree, warm, and loving experience seen on TV? If our parents were capable of maintaining the family unit with some degree of dignity, why can't we? The suburban wife-swapper's guilt at being unable to maintain his ties according to the old-fashioned mold is considerable. Why is it that the Louds became *An American Family* on the first real-life portrayal of a family filmed and shown on educational TV? Bill and Pat Loud who actually decided *on television* to get divorced after two decades of marriage!

Many suggestions have been offered as to why the nuclear family structure is crumbling. Some of these suggestions are wide-ranging and profound, others are close range. Close-range reasons given include the belief that kitchens are too small, a suggestion offered by educator Ethel Kahn, of Rutgers University. Kahn believes that post-1940s housing created the efficiency kitchen, destroying the communication enjoyed among family members for almost two generations. The living room, which became a place set apart for entertaining (the status room), was not considered suitable for family gatherings, and interaction was therefore discouraged. Kahn's suggestions are valid. Certainly it is true that the arrangement of furniture and room structures can alienate people who live side by side if an inviting atmosphere for conversation and closeness is not created.

There are more consequential reasons, however, why the nuclear family is facing unprecedented breakdowns, reasons that point to the economic and social structuring of the Western world. Significantly, it is just now becoming necessary to criticize the nuclear family structure itself and to point out that like other institutions that are changing, it too must suffer its metamorphosis as various other types of family structures did in centuries past. If church members are experiencing doubt and voters are seeing through the once-impregnable citadels of political machinery, if old-fashioned moral codes have vanished in the twinkling of a condom and more and more men and women are in divorce courts, is there any reason why the nuclear family should not be subjected to criticism and doubt?

It is the basic unit of society, so we are told. To attack the family unit is to shake the foundation on which society stands. And yet can anyone truthfully say the society standing today is so satisfying and so productive of human happiness that it could not use a bit of shaking? The nuclear family is a fixed structure. It is an arrangement that seems natural because it has existed for so long. As is true of any structured arrangement, though, it faces extreme problems if the structure is not fluid enough to flow with changes in life's varied patterns. Marriage vows create just such rigid structures.

Someone may say that no relationship is possible without structure, but the reverse seems to be true. Relationships that depend on structure for their sense of meaning have enthroned *expectation* and *demand* in place of relationship. A genuine relationship requires one person's constant rediscovery of another, since others are no more static than is life itself. To expect anything of anyone (a promise to think and behave in a certain manner over an extended period, for example) is to deprive that person of the right to express any changes in perspective which either threaten or fail to coincide with the promise.

Marriage vows are promises. In an age in which changes

in perspective are easy to effect because the media bring us knowledge of the great variety of possibilities open to us as individuals, no one can be sure that another man or woman is going to want to maintain the same outlook or basic life-style for the rest of his or her life. What is more important is that love, if it is to have depth, must include knowledge of another so that one may meet that other's needs. A marriage vow militates against genuine knowledge, however, because it requires of men and women that they maintain a front of conformity to that vow. If a partner expresses thoughts that conflict with it or behaves in a way that violates it even temporarily, the still-conforming partner becomes angry and resentful and more than likely will admit that he or she does not know why the wandering partner behaves in such a way. This is tantamount to saying that there has been a rupture in communication between the two. As soon as the contract's provisions have been broken, the conforming partner is face to face with a mate who is altogether mysterious because of not having followed the plan prescribed by the vow. The conforming partner, in other words, is surprised because his wandering mate is an unknown. This should be no surprise, though.

Because vows give men and women the right to expect certain kinds of thoughts and behavior from each other, they create a situation in which couples *think* they know each other as long as the rules are being observed. Following the rules, they are attached to external measuring points, and their relationship is judged by each on its conformity to an outside scale. This prevents them from being in touch with each other internally, however, because instead of seeing and accepting each other as they really are, they are concerned with seeing each other only in relation to the rules.

In the nuclear family the same solemnity that encircles

marital vows insists that members of the family unit *do not doubt* the unit itself and that if they think they might be better off unrelated to one another, they must keep these thoughts private. The nuclear family is perhaps the one institution in our society about which doubt and skepticism have seldom been expressed. While other social institutions are bearing the full brunt of a tendency to unbelief, few are willing to turn their critical faculties against the family. What was once assumed about religion —that it is necessary to the well-being of the nation whether it is true or not (even Voltaire said that if there were no God, we should have to invent one)—is now assumed about the family unit: the so-called basic unit of society which is also the last citadel to admit that it is falling before the probing incredulity of a changing civilization.

If family members are unwilling to doubt the unit to which they belong, neither is it possible for them to know one another with the kind of direct knowledge that might come from seeing each other outside of the "sacred" bonds of the family circle. The son or daughter who feels compelled to "honor" both father and mother whether they deserve it or not, who thinks that it is only right and proper, in fact, that they should be *loved* even if they are not lovable people, is in a dilemma under such circumstances. The possibility that mothers and fathers can be truly known under present conditions is diminished because hardly the same objectivity that applies in relations with others can be applied if all doubt is squelched. Thus the nuclear family works *against* rather than *for* interpersonal recognition as long as it requires its members to accept its sanctity without question.

Is it possible that men's liberation, which is freeing men from structures and values of the past, will wreak havoc in society if it criticizes the anatomy of the nuclear family?

Not at all. It has set itself the task of creating new kinds of possibilities for relationships between men, women, and children: relationships based on adherence to new values which do not demand a blind belief in the hallowedness of groupings that if viewed by any outsider would be regarded as unfulfilling, abortive attempts to regulate persons who are often strangers to each other but who feel bound to keep this fact to themselves.

Neither men's nor women's liberation is causing or promoting the breakdown of the family structure. Instead, these movements are ways of seeking alternatives to the cruelties inflicted on men and women by the already rampant decay of that structure. Before either movement began, the nuclear family was already crumbling, and its beams and pillars were crushing and trapping human beings as they fell. Liberationists have simply wandered among the ruins, lifting the ancient, decaying "supports" so that those pinned painfully beneath them can once again get up and walk confidently.

"The state of marriage is a calamity," say William J. Lederer and Don D. Jackson in their book *The Mirages of Marriage*.[6] Vance Packard in *The Sexual Wilderness* tells us that "a marriage made in the United States in the late 1960's has about a 50-50 chance of remaining even nominally intact." The high divorce rates do not account for less visible forms of marital breakdowns. Sociologist Harold T. Christensen believes that the number of divorces are equaled by separations and desertions. When it is considered that 25 percent of the American population is Roman Catholic and that Catholic teaching forbids divorce, the situation looks even more ominous. *The New York Times* reported that "the clerk of Los Angeles County caused an uproar recently by disclosing that for every five marriage licenses issued he had recorded four divorces or annulments."[7] Statistics show that the divorce rate climbed to an all-time high in 1946, when many marriages dissolved after World War II. Now, however, the record for 1946 has been broken, although the marriage rates have remained approximately the same. According to government figures, seventy-four thousand more divorces were granted in 1973 than in 1972, passing the all-time 1946 high mark.

Thus it is clear that antimarital and antifamilial propaganda (which has been rare anyway) has had nothing to do with the breakdown of the traditional structures. In fact, little attention has been given to these structures which has not been maudlin, supportive, conformist jargon, written by men and women who promote conventionality with soppy sentimentalism. One woman reporter, writing for a major daily news service, quotes a number of sociologists who cling to the belief that traditional marriages are here to stay. Describing the nuptials of Lynn and Al, who were blessed with a chocolate wedding cake decorated with fresh flowers, this reporter allows her readers to think that unconventional speculations about marriage are mere rumblings—a patronizing view. Using Lynn and Al as her prototypes for the future, she says that they will probably end up by rearing a family not unlike the ones in which they grew up. The academic "authorities" she quotes speak of how young people strike out against authority but end up embracing structures similar to the old-fashioned ones.

What is significant about Lynn and Al, however, is that they lived together in college for two years before they decided on marriage. This step is certainly a revolutionary one and little more than a decade ago would have been cause for parental consternation. Although the news-service reporter may not have realized it, it is a step recommended by less conventional sociologists who are making suggestions for orderly steps in the breakdown of monogamous structuring. Rustum and Della Roy, writing affirmatively in answer to the question, Is monogamy outdated?, say of premarital sex (which is being slipped somewhat covertly into the behavior patterns of Americans under the label of engagement) that whereas it need not become the universal norm, "Pluralism of marital patterns should start here."[8] The Roys watch with interest as they see what they believe are modifications of traditional monogamous patterns taking place.

Such modifications frighten the timid, who would prefer to cling to the comforting notion—as the news-service reporter does—that tradition itself is stabilizing. The Roys, speaking of such timidity, say that those who refuse to consider profound changes in marital structuring may do so "because of personal involvement—either their marriage is so successful that they think the claims of disease [marital breakdown] exaggerated, or theirs is so shaky that all advice is a threat."[9]

To think that acceptance of new patterns is characteristic only of the young and the rebellious is to be blind to what older citizens are saying. No less an authority than Max Lerner sympathetically reviewed Nigel Nicolson's *Portrait of a Marriage*, in which young Nicolson describes the marriage of his parents as triumphant. Both husband and wife had extramarital affairs, even homosexual ones, and yet had two sons, a number of close friends, and a well-ordered castle and garden which they tended together. Lerner speaks of their "comradeship" and says that "in some ways it was a marriage of true minds, and they did not admit into it the impediments that would have destroyed it." He continues, "We have learned that marriage can have a variety of sexual and affectional bases, with shared ties that give both people the continuities all of us need." Such commentaries on married life from scholars like Lerner, who are on the aging side of the generation gap, reveal how far-reaching are the changes in attitude.

No humane thinker would insist, as society presently

does, that monogamy is the only virtuous, fulfilling, and loving expression of a relationship. To those who would maximize the possibilities for affectionate and sexual relationships among all segments of the population, monogamy must seem a primary obstacle, since it demands an exclusivity that shuts out all those who do not fit within its narrow construct. This is of particular significance to all single men and women, who are forced into second-class citizenship until they marry. The married male enjoys certain legal and social benefits, but to attain them he must, under the present system, promise to forgo deep relationships with all other members of the opposite sex, a hideous price. If he ignores this stipulation, he is subject to social humiliation and may find himself paying handsomely for his transgression unless he happens to be one of those many thousands who desert their wives to avoid alimony regulations. Because of employment, desertion is out of the question in many cases, however, and men find themselves bound by rules that prohibit the expression of otherwise natural affection, an affection that would be winked at if the man were not legally encumbered.

The denial of admittance to single people at domestic social gatherings occurs because a single man is thought to be "on the prowl," as is a single woman, and hence is a threat to marrieds who wish to retain their exclusive holds on their mates. Few think to question this kind of discrimination. If they did, perhaps it would cease, as it would be obvious that society as it is now constituted provides literally thousands of opportunities for men to meet women (and vice-versa) in nonsocial (business) situations. This was not always the case but has become so as the nation's working force has accepted more and more members of both sexes; perhaps it may be seen as part of the reason why monogamous family units are dying like flies.

"Monogamy decrees that the price of admission into the complex network of supportive relationships of society is a wedding band," write the Roys.[10] That literally millions live outside the bonds of matrimony is often not considered by those who have entered into this self-congratulatory state. A great percentage of those millions will never marry or remarry and hence are denied socially acceptable affectionate relationships *as well as social ones* for the rest of their lives. Since platonic relationships are almost unknown or are at least open to critical and gossipy evaluations and skepticism, this means that all significant heterosexual friendships have almost no chance to grow. Thus current monogamous ideals impede and prohibit the maximization of affectionate and sexual relationships in society, leaving those who do not adapt themselves to external standards emotionally and sexually shipwrecked. The widowed, the divorced, and those who have thought it essential to remain single are all subjected to isolation in various ways unless, of course, they consent to conform (if they can) to the nuclear family pattern.

Hitler knew, as have other authoritarian rulers, that the family unit is an extension of the government. He, the führer, was the father of his nation, and individual fathers (linked through employment to the state) became his emissaries to whole families. Before him, the kaiser too was the supreme father in the fatherland. Wilhelm Reich clarified this fact in *The Mass Psychology of Fascism:* "The authoritarian state has a representative in every family, the father; in this way he becomes the state's most valuable tool."[11] It is no surprise, therefore, to hear the Nixons and Agnews of this country railing against "permissiveness" in the treatment of children. Children, they are saying, must not be allowed to grow on their own account but must be subject to those rules and regulations which enjoy the state's sanction.

All of the demands made on men and women to achieve socially acceptable nuclear family units are utterly absurd. This is so because whenever a man submits himself to a relationship in which he is told what he may or may not do, where he may or may not go, whom he may or may not know, what he may or may not say (both to his spouse and to others), how he may or may not feel, what he may or may not touch, and how he may or may not think, *he is a prisoner*, plain and simple, who has been regulated in all of the most significant areas of his experience. He is a slave who is not trusted by society to demonstrate his feelings wisely. The great guilts that have been unnecessarily associated with sex have made him think that in this area of his life he is particularly unsuited to self-government, and he reckons that the depravity associated with Adam's apple episode has turned him into a "luster"; he becomes a sniveling self-deprecator who finds it hard to enjoy the deliciousness of his sexuality.

Attempts to achieve the kind of relationship society demands of men and women have been equally absurd. Lifelong love is required of men and women, and yet most men still find women fill their need for full-blown companionship only very inadequately. They find that discussing matters with them which bear some semblance of mutual interest nigh impossible, since their prime areas of concern are so different. Not even a couple's children offer the kind of mutual tie they need, since most fathers are not prepared for fatherhood—do not conceive of it as a life concern and therefore too often become bored with the state, leaving children to the woman and allowing themselves the pose, in the United States at least, of assenting bystander.

The father who attempts to draw close to his offspring late in life is a familiar wanderer in the land of Babbitt. Trying to patch up relationships he forgot about soon after subsiding from his initial high at hearing himself called Dada, he stumbles toward the young adults he sired, heavy with the realization that he has been absent from them much of their lives. He has not been playful enough to enjoy either his wife or his children. Work has made him a dull boy. He denies himself, because of the masculinist identity he clings to, the ability to absorb them, to feel them, and to love them as themselves. He sees them as role-players instead of as real human beings, and he knows them as rule-followers (unless he is in touch with them regularly and intimately). Since he is embarrassed by intimacy (he cannot even kiss his own son), he is seldom well-equipped for it.

More will be said about children in the next chapter. However, since it is their welfare that lawmakers pretend to be concerned with once it has been determined that most women can take care of themselves (and, as divorce and employment statistics indicate, don't really need the institution of marriage to do it), child welfare is an issue. In 1925 Judge Ben B. Lindsey and Wainwright Evans wrote in their bold and forthright book *The Revolt of Modern Youth:* " 'Preposterous!' say some. 'Why, what would become of the children of these unmarried unions? It would rob children of all protection.' "

The judge, writing from long and compassionate experience on his bench, laughed at this viewpoint, calling it

a distinctly humorous argument, that, from a society that puts the brand of illegitimacy and disgrace on those children.

The obvious retort is, What becomes of the children of conventional and legal marriages? Who looks after *them?* What guarantee have *they* of "protection"? In a recent survey of one American city it was found that 32 percent of the children in a certain school, all of them "legitimate," had no father at home. I am running up against this situation all the time. The assumption that our present form of legal marriage automatically "protects" the future of children would be funny if it were not tragic. . . . Marriage, as at present ordered, does not guarantee to any child the benefit of its parents.[12]

What is being said is this: If men are going to liberate themselves (which is their first responsibility) or assist women in their liberation (there is nothing wrong with assisting as long as it is cooperative and not presumptive), they must begin by refusing to enter into relationships wherein they support those women. In this way they will be assisting women in the most complimentary way: by helping them to help themselves. They will also be complimenting themselves by gaining the knowledge that it is their companionship women seek and not their wallet. At the same time they will remove from themselves heavy "responsibilities" (that term given to financial burdens by insipid system supporters). This is not to say that no thought must be given to the plight of those who have already accepted such "responsibilities," but how many men who are supporting a woman and therefore allowing that woman to become even less self-sufficient have asked themselves how long that woman would stay if she had to be self-supporting?

To circumvent the suffering caused by today's monogamous nuclear family units, men may wish to consider communal relationships among other options. These have an historical precedent, luckily, in some early Christian communities and among the American Indians, the original (extended family) inhabitants of this nation. Present restrictions accompanying marriage and family living will continue to stifle contact, pleasure, relationship, and affection between increasing numbers of distraught citizens, and a brave few must show others that there are viable alternatives.

If a man is disillusioned by monogamous nuclear family patterns (what Nena and George O'Neill call closed marriages) and opts for alternatives, he will fail in those alternatives as long as he carries masculinist values along. If he goes to a commune, for example, his acquired urges to dominate, control, and compete will work to destroy communal life. Jealousy is regarded as the prime problem in communes, the one on which most of such gatherings flounder. This is not surprising when domination and competition among men are not only not questioned but even practiced and encouraged. When these urges step into the realm of affection, they introduce structure, since to be sure of dominance a man must be aware of exactly what he may expect. These urges also introduce measurement, since to determine that he is ahead of a competitor a man must measure the degree of affection he receives and be sure that no one else is as far ahead as he is. If affection is given to anyone else, it is seen as a dreadful loss to the dominating competitor, who has established a prohibition against outside affection, the most sensitive regulation he prescribes. For the woman to copulate with another man would signify that she has capitulated to a competitor. As long as the prohibitive regulation is not flouted, a man assumes that his relationship is in order. Statistics show that he is wrong to make such an assumption.

It is not surprising that a man clings to rules to help him know his woman companion better. Since he finds it difficult to be truly intimate with her, feeling that he cannot enjoy the fullest kind of communion with her, he puts her on reserve to satisfy only a portion of his compartmentalized desires. For other satisfactions he depends on work, television, sports, and theories. Occasionally he has a night out with the boys, and according to Julius Fast, may spend a great deal of time telling them that his wife doesn't understand him, a line with which all extramarital partners are too familiar. A man can be intimate with a woman only to the degree that he is willing to let her express her real feelings to him, even if these conflict with the program for "relationship conduct" that he hugs like Linus's security blanket. If a man could only break away from his neurotic need to be sure of his future with a woman, he might actually learn to enjoy her company in the present by getting close to the self that she feels she expresses rather than to the self he projects onto her. That he confuses his projection with her reality is too often obvious. This confusion may make for a working relationship as long as she does not somehow violate his projection or as long as she can tolerate being appreciated for her perpetual chastity (the Madonna again) except when she is with him. Since she is often financially dependent on him by the time such dissatisfactions set in, she may, if she grows attached to the phony images of herself he projects, continue to repeat the inanities he reveres to keep the image compact and her money coming in.

Since it is characteristic of dominance to miss the meanings of trifles and to accept servility without recognizing it, he remains satisfied with the arrangement as long as she is careful to be what *she seems to be* to him. What many women are now discovering is the pain they have experienced at having pretended to be what they are not for rewards that no longer seem as important as they once did.

Before the nuclear family came along, a woman had others in her circle besides herself to think about, since members of her family often lived with her or were part of her larger family group. There were fewer opportunities for her to meet others. Today she has only herself and her children to consider. The old family pattern gave many opportunities for emotional support within the home even if it was not forthcoming from a husband. Hence women were more readily domesticated. Today, however, if such emotional support is not forthcoming from a man, there is little to tempt her to remain, since domesticity is sterile in comparison with the shared family (communal) tasks of the last century. Domesticity today is a lonely routine, seldom appreciated by men in any intimate sense but only in an abstract one.

Human beings are complex creatures, and in an era when the media add to their sense of options, no single person can be expected to be all things to another. In family groupings of the past other family members provided people with opportunities to express and enjoy themselves in ways that the stark nuclear family unit does not. Today, within the walls of apartments or houses, there are only two adults, abiding by rules for their sense of mutual knowledge and separated in essential ways from each other because of differing roles, roles that do not provide mutual ground for interests. It is little wonder that the sense of companionship needed to impel relationships over long time spans is not felt. Men and women have allowed themselves to be too different from each other.

The O'Neills write movingly of the restrictions imposed by closed marriages on men and women, showing how couples who are jealous of one another keep sociability from developing even in nonsexual situations.[13] The "closed marriage," they say, creates people who may no longer reach out to others to enhance their understanding, knowledge, and appreciation of their world. The husband-wife team is expected to "turn off the outside world and to turn on only to one another." This kind of marriage deprives its participants, as long as they may not have full freedom to reach out and touch others, of their humanity. The altruistic impulses they may feel are blocked by egocentric demands on the part of a spouse whose insecurity as a companion is so great that no other companions, sexual or nonsexual, are allowed in a mate's spectrum if those companions are of the opposite sex. By refusing others physical contact with his mate, a man demands that the healing powers of touch inherent in another's body be his and his alone. This is a woefully selfish demand, since if love is truly transcendent and is as wonderful as he believes it to be, should not its benefits be available to everyone? Or should not a partner at least have full freedom to decide for himself or herself to whom those benefits should go?

What kind of relationship can be built on a basis of restriction? Only one in which intimacy is so fragile that it cannot suffer the loved one's generous impulses toward others. Any man who flies into a jealous rage is revealing distressing facts about his relationship with a woman: He does not know her, he does not trust her, he lacks rapport, and he believes that sexuality is inherently evil, or he would not object to the affection of one person for another spilling over into the arena of touch. He distinguishes, in other words, between having feelings and expressing them. Finally, he places his whole belief in the validity of a relationship on a basis of sexual fidelity, which says precious little for the remainder of meaning in that relationship.

If premarital sex is destroying the requirement for virginity at the time of marriage, perhaps the destruction of concepts making virtue prerequisite within relationships is also due to take place. If two people cannot be all things to each other, neither can they expect of each other that each forfeit all other loving relationships. Such an expectation, in fact, works against the development of intimacy itself. Jealousy germinates in a culture where "affectionate" relationships take place between people who do not really know each other because they base their mutual evaluations on how well a partner follows the rules instead of becoming intimate. The most "important" rule is "Don't sit under the apple tree with anyone else but me," a rule that reveals the poverty of egocentric love as it is practiced in this country.

As it stands now, couples must go almost everywhere together. A man who marries must abandon all relationships with former friends of the opposite sex. Usually he abandons all friends of the same sex who are not yet married. If he does not, their influence on him will be, it is feared, nefarious. Occasionally "old friends" who are still single may be invited to the house, but it is preferred that they be planning to marry too so that they become part of a couple; in this way couples need relate only to other couples. Thus jealousy and monogamous unions prevent friendship and increase alienation for millions. Even when couples associate with one another, they "keep up appearances" with each other, and there is seldom any real sharing of intimate concerns. What happens in relationships that are limited in this way is clear: The ability of the individuals in any coupling to see themselves with any degree of objectivity is diminished because, as the O'Neills say, their chance for "growth and validation through others" is limited.

Not only is jealousy an indication that one partner does not truly know the other (since he has a pedestalized view of that person), but it also says that he or she is dreadfully afraid of being left on his or her own, of being a separate person who is *free*. Jealousy, in other words, is a response to unwanted freedom, and it has its basis in a culture that rears its children to be dependent instead of self-regulating, autonomous beings.

What the struggle for sexual equality means in the long run, and the reason it frightens so many, is that it strikes at the very roots of the dependency habit, requiring of men and women that they prepare themselves to stand on their own. The orientation of the liberated person is expressed, perhaps, in these words of Buddha:

> It is not what others do or do not do that is my
>   concern.
> It is what I do and what I do not do, *that* is my
>   concern.[14]

The new world vision of man and woman, divested of monogamy, of the nuclear family unit, and as we shall see, of other forms of dependency, is that of free beings, able to go where they will and take care of themselves:

> Each man to himself and each woman to herself,
>   is the word of the past and present, and the
>   true word of immortality.[15]

If monogamy and family units are ignored by the new male, does this mean wife-swapping of the suburban variety or anonymous orgies and unbridled promiscuity? Hardly. There will probably always be relationships that will be blessed by special depths of understanding and appreciation. If dependency and domination were removed so that relationships could not be soured by them, person-to-person communication of an intimate sort would grow. Neither a dependent nor a provider is free to explore the far corners of mind and experience.

Those who believe that taking a stand that removes monogamy's special virtue will lead to the promotion of indiscriminate touching and feeling are only partially correct: in a spiritual sense. Ideally, it would be best if we could relate to everyone, even those who are aesthetically displeasing to us. The laying on of hands and the healing power of touch would assume new meanings in a society that did not denigrate its sexual impulses so. Men and women might help by such touching to inspire those millions who are sexually starved to new heights of self-awareness and appreciation. Nearly everyone needs a boost, and if men and women cling to exclusivity and forsake all others, keeping only unto each other as long as they both shall live, it is certain that the good that might come about if affection were allowed a wider basis to work its magic will never have a chance to grow. This means that every man and every woman must think of themselves not as members of a coupling—Tweedle Dum and Tweedle Dee —but as individuals, each self-contained. "The strongest man upon earth," wrote Henrik Ibsen, "is he who stands most alone."

The difference between having a relationship and being the member of a coupling is enormous. A relationship allows one to be oneself, to go anywhere freely, to see anyone affectionately, and to speak openly and honestly about any matter. Being a member of a coupling, however, is like being the member of a cause-oriented organization. The individual depends for his sense of identity on the *other*, on an external (the coupling, the cause) rather than on himself. He follows rules, as in an organization, in order to belong to the coupling. If his partner breaks those rules, his association with the coupling comes to an end. Coupling, viewed in this way, is destructive of individual strength and initiative, and in its shadow individuality withers. Under such conditions it is the relationship that suffers.

Chapter 18 ❄ FATHERHOOD
From Vicarious Immortality to Voluntary Friendship

I think all parents are potential child abusers. . . . The basic way of raising children is through power and authority. We think it is destructive when so many parents have the idea, "It's my kid. I can do what I want with my kid."

—DR. THOMAS GORDON, FOUNDER OF A PARENT-
TRAINING PROGRAM IN PASADENA, CALIFORNIA

"Masculine culture contains a strong vein of antidomesticity," writes Germaine Greer.[1] In support of her statement I say that it is on this "strong vein" that men must rely if they are to gain their freedom. If women are to be relieved of their state of dependency, there is still one other dependent who must be taken into consideration: the child.

Planned Parenthood, which has offices in every major city, is hardly as effective as it needs to be. In some locales it has been denied its share of United Givers Fund monies, and at best it reaches only a small number of citizens. The power of the Roman Catholic Church, forbidding birth control as it does, has been such that dissemination of birth-control information was hampered in many states until only a few years ago. Birth-control opponents like to say that the U.S. birthrate has declined. This is temporarily true, but it does not mean that there has been a decline in population, nor does it mean that the decline in births will continue. The excess of births over deaths in the United States in 1973 was still enough to add 1,164,000 Americans to the population. During 1974–1975 there will occur a

7 percent increase in the number of women in the prime childbearing ages of between twenty and twenty-nine.

If it were not for religious opposition, birth-control information might be part and parcel of every young woman's education. Birth-control knowledge is a primary necessity for women, since it is in their bodies that new life sprouts. If the sexes are to become autonomous, women must understand that it is they themselves who must decide whether or not they will add to the already overburdened population.

John Stuart Mill's principles, as enunciated in *On Liberty*, give each person autonomy over his or her body, and this means that no man should insist on any woman bearing children. The decision to have a child must be reached by the person most affected: the woman who will be having it. A skilled planned-parenthood program would instill in every woman the consciousness of all those reasons *not* to have children. To have a child in order to trap its father into the married state is *not* a good reason, for example. If the mother hopes to cement her failing relationship with the father, she does *not* have a good reason. An enlightened citizenry could not help but approve of such counseling as a major facet of all educational programs for women, *the controllers of their own bodies*.

Before proceeding to consider an alternative to present-day parent-child abuses, it may be wise to ponder precisely what is taking place. What is the role of today's father, for example, and how well is he fulfilling that role? Who would deny that it is wise to seek ways to improve child-adult relationships?

At present the role of the father is that of *provider*. This role has come to mean "fatherhood" to most men. Beyond it, the parent concept for men is literally devoid of meaning. It is safe to say, therefore, that "father" is a synonym for "financial functionary."

Fathers find it difficult to be friends to their children except on weekends, and the major tasks of child-rearing and child-teaching have been left to the mother. This means that while the United States is considered a patriarchy, it is only ostensibly so; it is, in fact, a matriarchy in which it is the mother (and to some lesser extent the public-school system for the child from ages six through sixteen) who has accepted the parental role in a full sense. The words "parental responsibility," as applied to a father, have become a catch-all phrase that means financier.

Currently, although the father may hope to achieve some kind of vicarious immortality through his children, to implant a significant measure of himself in them, with the concomitant hope that they will bypass him (by rising to higher social strata), he is seldom close enough to them to attempt such instillation. His relationship with his children is obligatory rather than voluntary, and like all obligatory relationships it lacks the rapport and the give and take of a cultivated, easygoing friendship. In many homes the father is used to dominate his children as a last resort when the mother finds it difficult to do so. And yet when he performs this task, it is the performance of a semi-outsider whose arrival usually does not take place until after nightfall. It is the act of a person who has little or no connection with the incident that has provoked what the mother believes is the need for dominance. The father is usually ready to agree with the mother's side of a story, nevertheless, and often will inflict penalties for an incident he knows nothing about from personal experience.

Fatherhood, in short, is virtually meaningless to the American male except as an abstract concept. He has no training for the role of parenthood, as do some young women, and as a result little or no interest in assuming it once it has been thrust upon him. He thinks the care of children is a woman's business, and he accepts his provider role gladly, pleased that he does not have to spend hours with a child, who, he thinks, is somehow "better off with its mother." He has relinquished all but monetary involvement.

Whether men like it or not, they have been willing accomplices in the creation of a society in which women alone have been entrusted with society's major responsibility: the upbringing of children and all of the influences that go with it. If the equality of the sexes is to take on some semblance of meaning, this imbalance must be corrected.

In considering corrective alternatives to this condition, it is imperative that any proposed solution should aim at removing the worst aspects of the nuclear family unit's current failures by making relationships between parents and their children voluntary rather than obligatory. This would open the way to possibilities for real relationships. The words "mother" and "father" must not be overemphasized, as they so often are, so that the reality parental figures project conflicts with an idealized idea of what they should be. Nor should it be necessary, if our society is to rear self-dependent children, for those children to feel that the quality of their own existence is dependent on two rather confused, supportive, dominating adults who, if they do not succeed in their parental roles, are creating an aperture for failure—not only the child's but their own as well.

In a society that cares for its young (in the daytime public-school system) from ages six through sixteen and is presently giving income help to one out of every four of its members (while seriously considering a guaranteed annual income), education of the young might just as easily begin at an earlier age. This step would obliterate matriarchal influences that are now sporadic, unreliable, and confused. As it now stands, the child is subjected to too much domination from and dependency on the mother.

If day-care centers were to begin instruction of the child at six months, for example, the mother would have less of a chance to use the child as her doll or her source of amusement. Even better, opportunities for mothers to create tendencies in children to rely on *them* for the satisfaction of needs rather than on themselves would be diminished. A revised educational system would assure that the mother could not, if she were irritated by a child's feelings, intrude on them simply because they inconvenienced her, and it would allow the child to discover independently what *is* so and what is *not* so.

Such day-care centers would be extraordinarily sensitive to the absolute integrity involved in seeing that the child is not assaulted in the cradle by being taught bogus convictions as gospel and by being fed values that accord with old-fashioned gender divisions. Instead schools would insist that the child be free to make sense of the reality he perceives, thus assuring a truly free being. Such an educational program, not unlike the Montessori method, would show the child self-care instead of allowing for dependency. Learning to depend on parents is the worst aspect of the current familial arrangement. The child then manipulates and the parents dominate, thus forming the basis of the child's authoritarian personality. In his reveries Portnoy asks his mother, "Where did you get the idea that the most wonderful thing I could be in life was obedient? A little gentleman? Of all the aspirations for a creature of lusts and desires!"[2] Portnoy does not analyze the political implications of his mother's intrusions, but if obedience is taught to human beings at a very early age (which is what happens, according to Dr. Stanley Milgram[3]), a nation of goose-steppers has been created at its mothers' knees.

The child is told to accept too many hereditary beliefs as essentials, bequeathments that take a lifetime of reversing in public schools, colleges, and psychiatrists' offices.

Most of these "truths" are taught by parents who think it essential to pass down a certain viewpoint, whatever it may be, to the child they conceive. They are not interested in seeing what kind of child will develop independently (with its own ideas and personality) but what kind of reproduction of themselves they can make, given the right circumstances—which means, in effect, good luck, a rare commodity in this age.

The intrusion of the parent on the child's personality is accepted by society at present. This fact will form the basis for yet another much-needed movement: children's liberation. Sixty thousand cases of child abuse are *reported* annually in the United States. Even if the child is not being physically assaulted, there is too often a tragic kind of intrusion on it. Its parents are not passing along to the child physical affection, spontaneous laughter, self-esteem, playfulness, curiosity, and long periods of companionship as good friends, but are passing along rules, regulations, and an actual *lack* of presence which is all the more poignant because parents are supposed to be present, according to their own value system.

Fortunately, the child is only partially crippled by its parents. It is significant that we measure the interest value of a person by the degree to which he has bypassed the beliefs of his parents, having found new horizons alone. "The essence of being a boring person," writes Dr. David Cooper, "is not to have gone beyond, in imagination at least, the limited horizons of one's family and to repeat or collude with repetitions of this restrictive system outside the family. . . . *In short, to be a boring person is to be a family person, a person who finds the primacy of her or his existence in the mirror reflection rather than in the mirrored.*"[4]

Children, unless they are taken captive by dominator parents so completely that they can never again make up their own minds or think their own thoughts, rebel against parental domination to some degree. It is this that produces the negligible variety of independent thinkers who live on the fringes of society.

Are children innately the helpless, dependent creatures of parental fantasy? Hardly. Even Mary Wollstonecraft, writing in 1792, observed that since the child is not left a moment to its own direction, it is thus rendered dependent. Therefore "dependence is called natural," she concludes, although it need not be. Children at birth can stand upright, swim, and grasp objects without difficulty. Dr. Jaroslav Kovch did experiments in Czechoslovakia with children in special environments, finding that they could climb ladders at eight months. Maria Montessori's educational programs demonstrate that children have amazing capabilities between birth and the age of three, the time she believes is most essential for the child to begin a proper course (schooling) of self-regulation and creative learning. Describing the babies in her care, Montessori said:

> Above all they sought to render themselves independent of adults in all the actions which they could manage on their own, manifesting clearly the desire not to be helped, except in cases of absolute necessity. And they were seen to be tranquil, absorbed, and concentrating on their work, acquiring a surprising calm and serenity.[5]

Can we hope to persuade Western society not to take its matriarchal Madonna image so seriously? This image is worshiped in this country and seems natural, but as we have seen, it is creating dependent children, is thwarting the freedom of parents, and has placed the burden of being "all things" on bewildered mothers, with fathers looking on nearby. Instead of allowing the child to learn

during its most formative years, Western societies allow
the mother to learn instead, although more often she may
simply continue to play the games she learned as a child
with dolls. Did the dolls really teach motherhood? Has it
never surprised us when a young girl, instead of cradling
and rocking her doll, bangs its head against the wall or
tears its stuffing out? The games a little girl plays with
dolls are not all identical, since they depend on her values.
By the time she is old enough to play with dolls, she has
already been indoctrinated, and she plays games in which
dolly must *obey* even her mere whims! At other times she
imparts her "mother's wisdom," which is more often social
notion, to the doll. Since social notion is always fundamentally off key in so many ways and, except for imparting
the tenet "love thy neighbor as thyself," is probably better
left untaught, it would seem wise to keep mother independent of the early learning processes of the child, or she
will saddle it with the inadequacies of her own character.
Kahlil Gibran wrote:

> Your children are not your children.
> They are the sons and daughters of Life's longing
>   for itself. . . .
> You may give them your love but not their thoughts,
>   for they have their own thoughts. . . .
> Their souls dwell in the house of tomorrow which
>   you cannot visit, not even in your dreams.
> You may strive to be like them, but seek not to make
>   them like you.[6]

The romantic notions that surround motherhood are
projected onto animals (even piglets suckling at their
mothers' teats) to make motherhood's training seem the
most natural of facts. There are no animal species, however,
in which the mothers are as solicitous of their young as is

the American mother, that lovely gal pinned down in Philip Wylie's *Generation of Vipers* as Mom.

Since it is the welfare of children with which we are concerned here (and the maladaptations into which they are forced under the present regime), I offer the following alternative as only one possible solution to the plight of children as we have considered it. Some steps must be taken.

Day-care centers might assume the burden of early training. Under a Montessori-like program of instruction children would become independent and capable at a very early age. This type of educational program would promote autonomy, each child eschewing assistance from others. Such a factor would assure a bulwark in our educational system for democratic survival. A Montessori-type system also promotes creative capabilities, spontaneity, and calmness.

Astoundingly, most men are not aware that there is no way in which their paternity can be proved in a court of law. The fact that one is a father can be shown only negatively—that is, by saying who the father isn't. No judge, however, can point and say with assurance: "*You* are the father." Thus except as a voluntary friend, there is no reason for a father to assume financial obligations for children. Neither is there any such reason for mothers to do so. Instead, when the mother decides to have a child for her own *good* reasons (which would be, naturally, to give to *life itself* rather than to *herself* for her own ego-centric needs), the educational system (as it presently does) would provide daily meals and extended housing. Thus it would assure a continuing democracy by giving new little citizens an education in which they would experience the freedom to depend upon themselves. They could, conceivably, form relationships with "parent" figures (not necessarily biological mothers and fathers) and others in which there is no relationship between a dominant person (parent) and a dependent one (child).

There will be those who heartily denounce the alternative I have suggested here. I can only reply that the present system is riddled through with destructive tendencies and is producing a rather frightening social environment. Under the present system, men have abdicated, taking no part in the rearing of children. An imbalance of the sexes is in effect. The liberation of people—men, women, and children—must begin by our giving back to children the autonomy that is rightfully theirs and by helping them to establish a real connection between themselves and their wider environment. Although it may be that children must depend on adults for anatomical survival, this kind of early dependence must be disengaged from the affected and socially manufactured dependencies on adults for extraneous details. Our culture must begin to function *cooperatively* so that adults do not invite a child's submission, his ability to be controlled, and his tendency to manipulate.

Words remain to be said about the plight of the contemporary father who has already saddled himself with the "responsibilities" bemoaned in these pages. It has been noted how few are the joys of fatherhood and how many its responsibilities. As Myron Brenton put it, "His duties have expanded while his rights have diminished."

We must, in this practical world, "concentrate unto them that are nigh" without projecting fathers too rapidly into any vision of the future. The foregoing alternative vision (of the processing of the members of nuclear family units into individuals) is as American as apple pie. It need not be in conflict with what fathers today can do to encourage individuality, autonomy, and a host of creative and able characteristics in their young. If the child has already observed a role structure that has been presented as example, he can still be weaned away from depending on that structure instead of on himself. This is the basic issue of child upbringing.

Those who rear children to depend on structures—familial, ethnic, religious, or political—are plainly asking them to depend on institutions that are presently crumbling before the mighty onrush of a new and different world civilization. It is a civilization that is building its foundations not on the tribal idiocies of certain populations (which is what American sex roles truly are) but on a wider basis that makes the currently surviving patterns for human adaptation too limited for the weight of life's spice, variety. In this new world the young will not be well educated if they are trained to fit into strict patterns of behavior which place them in hierarchical slots. The structures will be undergoing such quick changes that education itself must readapt or perish. Educators are sorely confused about their relationships with the young these days. It figures. They are discovering that youths are impatient with them, and they wonder why, not understanding the impatience with linear presentations of those who perceive in a nonlinear way.

If we insist that our children resemble us, we will be doing them the worst of disservices as they face a world that promises to be totally different from the one we know at present. If it is possible for us to believe in the superacceleration of change, we should know that the young must learn to be independent early and to follow their own best instincts, uncovered by educational programs such as those mentioned.

If we are new fathers, our effort should be to avoid trying to make our children over in our own images, allowing them to develop their own images. Children should not feel as though they "belong" to somebody else, to their parents. Children belong to themselves. It is this need to belong that stands as one of the worst features of family upbringing. Dr. David Cooper suggests that nuclear family structuring is such that mother and father think of the child as "theirs" instead of treating a youngster as an individual who has self-discovered plans and perspectives and who utilizes these with a sense of self-esteem.

It is the sense of existential aloneness that is created by the family in a sense. Because families project feelings of belonging which are only temporary but quite pronounced nevertheless, they open the child (when the family unit dissolves) to the experience of utter aloneness, which he thereupon tries to overcome by creating a unit similar to the one he has recently left behind. Relationships that are formed to protect against existential loneliness suffer a frantic compulsiveness, however, and may be unhealthy. They find their foundations in insecurities rather than in shared interests and outlooks. When a person is trying to blot out this stark vision he has of being alone, his judgment is likely to be impaired, and he chooses a mate to give a temporary sense of relief. Aloneness is not something human beings can afford to fear, though. It is finally the condition of each person. We are each one alone and must care for ourselves. In the future, relationships will be entered into by children who have become adults with a consciousness that aloneness is the natural state that it is. We can be surer that when this happens, there will be relationships of peers rather than of frantic souls trying to protect themselves from the imaginary terrors of solitary communion.

To say that a child is like his or her parent is to insult the individuality of the child. It is to comment on the poor job a parent has done at exposing the child to many influences. Instead the child has been sheltered and is encouraged to mimic the parents. If children refuse to mimic, this is often given as a sign of madness, but it probably speaks more for the common sense of children if they have had strength enough to overcome parental interference with their psyches. Each child has a unique mind, and since events shape each one quite differently, no parent has the right to expect a chip off the old block any more than he or she does when meeting a stranger. The parent expects a stranger to be an individual and will discover that the child, hopefully, is also an individual. If parents do not know this and believe it, they are then capable of mercilessly assaulting their children with their own kind of battering ram.

Parenthood is satisfying when it means *friendship* between the generations. No friendship can long survive if one friend is forever trying to write his or her own personality onto that of the other, scolding the friend into line, showing the friend *how to be.* People (a child, for example) feel appreciated if they are loved for themselves and not because they abdicate their seeming follies and absorb those of their comrades. To appreciate the self is the first step to self-esteem. For the child to try to appreciate the self because he or she has conformed to an image projected by another (parent) is to put the self into conflict, since it can never truly be comfortable as an imitator. The self is shaped in ways that differ from the image (parent) it perceives, and since it cannot perceive entirely, it can only mimic partially. This has been a factor in the preservation of our species.

That a child should be forced into mimicry at all is a sad commentary on parent-child relationships. Under the present system adults command a scene in which their communication with children depends on how well those children mimic and do as they are told. Appeals such as these and domination of the children if they do not conform strangle any truly reciprocal relationship. As soon as models are presented, they cease to be people. (That's you, Dad!) Instead they become ideals who, if children are quick, will be seen as unequal to the task in some way, thus making the travesty of the relationship even clearer to the children, who are expecting everything but who find old Dad falling short.

Myron Brenton wrote with high indignation about the plight of the American father in *The American Male*, a book published in 1966 that was quite avant-garde at the time. One of Brenton's most serious questions is whether traits like sympathy and understanding that we label feminine might not also be thought masculine if Pop were around more. Since the proximities of fathers are reduced to bill-paying or business-managing, the absent father is still with us. What can he do in order to contribute to a better future for all offspring? He can give up his dream of vicarious immortality, the most selfish reason for child-rearing that can enter an egocentric mind. The sickness of this kind of child abuse (particularly the abuse heaped by fathers on their sons) is rape with the big ego. Pedophiles invade children only physically and often with far less trauma to the child than is generally thought, but parents invade their children much more certainly. They rape them not only with mere flesh but with their own whole images, attempting to stuff those images—painfully, if necessary, and certainly *permanently*—into the child's mind. The rape is also rendered more painful by reason of the fact that parents are not close enough to their children to see what they are actually doing to them. They do not see their children *as they are* but as they think they should be.

Brenton touched a nerve when he asked if femininity and masculinity might not have shared traits if Pop were around more. If men were communicating with children and were not remote from a child's scrutiny, each child might understand that masculinity does not mean being big, competitive, and domineering.

Even if Pop were around more, let's concede that children need more than one image to relate to so that they may develop a rich perspective by observing possibilities inherent in many life-styles. It seems easy for the mother-sheltered child to believe that sympathy and understanding do come from the female alone. This means that fathers must actually *get to know* their children as other than reproductions, not flirting with daughter to teach her manipulation nor playing the stalwart goose-stepper with son but being a friend to both, without introducing roles that each must follow. It is these roles that often stand in the way of a value a particular parent may wish to communicate but does not. Compassion, for example, may be entirely extinguished by competition.

It would be advantageous to all children if their fathers had more than a few male friends of differing temperaments and capabilities whom he could parade in and out of the child's purview so that some notion of variety could be brought to the child's image awareness. No child, any more than any other individual, should be forced into relating exclusively to one set of parents. In spite of what the iconoclast Ingersoll said about the words "mother" and "father" being sacred, they are not, nor should they be. Nor should any word cast a sacrosanct pall over the relationship it encompasses. Each relationship must be built differently and cooperatively to achieve its clear meaning and beauty.

Fathers are asking if a child educated to be self-regulating and independent of the Establishment in any final sense might not be ill-suited to survival. The time has arrived when this question must be asked in reverse. Is it not possible that the child reared to depend on the Establishment (including the family unit) is in for a rude awakening, since the Establishment itself is crumbling so and "things ain't what they used to be"? If we could count on institutional stability and social sameness over extended periods of time, worry about the survival of a child who is independent of social mimicries might have a more convincing ring.

The belief in the innate depravity of children also intrudes on this discussion. If children were allowed to be self-regulating rather than being made to tow the line, would they not turn into monsters? William Golding's *Lord of the Flies* holds this macabre message: Children are monsters. When a planeload of children is brought down on an island, its passengers become uncivilized brutes and go to war. I do not accept the message of *Lord of the Flies*, however, because the children it depicted were products of Westernized value systems and were infected before their plane crashed. What would the author of that book say about the gentle people of the South Sea islands? *Lord of the Flies* is better drama than it is science.

The American father is supposed to be many things to his children: a wise counselor, a firm disciplinarian, a good provider, an acceptable male image, a "pal," and a link to the world at large. He is made to feel guilty if he cannot fulfill all of these roles at once. Most of the time he cannot, and so a pall of guilt hangs continually over his head. Not only do so-called authorities make him ashamed because he has only two hands, but members of his family are also likely to criticize him for not being everything he "should" be.

Mothers are therefore handy saddles for all of the *believed* virtues of parenthood. The mother's abilities are seldom questioned. The father, however, must try to strike an imposing stance, one that is a mixture of roles and seems appropriately remote so that he won't be accused by psychiatrists of being a "motherly" father and so he can carry on his charade, hoping it will not be observed and then wishing later it had been (by himself, at least).

The nation's courts give ample proof of the sorry state of fatherhood. They award custody, in most divorce cases, to mothers. Fathers, even though they are financially capable, are discriminated against on the grounds that mothers make better parents. The father's role—that of provider—continues even after divorce, even though the pleasures and intimacies of fatherhood are often denied. Surely if equality of the sexes is to mean anything to contemporaries, this imbalance of justice must be corrected.

The ascendancy of the Madonna in our culture has made the position of the father seem inconsequential. Her glorification has been too much out of proportion to that of the baby god's father, Joseph. For as long as men accept this kind of position, in which they are unattached to their children except financially, will the nation's insipid Dagwood Bumstead attitudes about fatherhood persist. Fathers, as men's liberationists, can work to reverse the conditions under which children are reared, assuring the future that it will be receiving autonomous creatures. They can introduce feeling into relationships with sons and daughters, not fearing to hug and kiss sons of any age and not fearing to empathize with daughters. Fathers may learn to feel as their daughters feel or as nearly thereabout as is possible. As it now stands, a full relationship is impossible between a man and his daughter as long as that man refuses to put himself in the position of his daughter, to seek her states of mind, to see the world from her vantage point without worrying about being thought womanly. He can help his daughter to take care of herself, just as he believes he should help his son to do so. Her tools should not be mother-taught techniques to trap a man. Her tools should be the honesty that radiates from any competent person who is reared to be self-sustaining. The father who cops out on providing this kind of education may give his daughter every dollar he earns, but if "father" is to be another word for "friend," he will have failed by that measure.

For this is what the words "father" and "mother" must

mean to the most sensitive parents: *friend*. The state of friendship supersedes the state of parenthood:

> Yet underneath Socrates clearly see, and
> underneath Christ the divine I see,
> The dear love of man for his comrade, the
> attraction of friend to friend,
> Of the well-married husband and wife, of
> children and parents,
> Of city for city and land for land.[7]

Certainly the indignities suffered in the name of work, the "sacrifices" made to assure children of those "benefits" society offers, and the "examples" set by two harried, hurried adults are not sufficient to give parenthood its fullest meaning. It is the fact of friendship, which betokens communication and hence honesty, that is the jewel parents value. In some cases it sparkles. In many it does not.

If it is too late for a father to reverse the early training that has resulted in his child's dependency, it is not too late to begin giving that child a sense of self-esteem for the areas in which he can claim self-gained awareness. The father who assaults his child with his notions of what constitutes ability will know that he has lessened that child's revelry in his or her own abilities. Because the child has not conformed is no reason to disparage the use of those dexterities he or she does have. As we have seen earlier in this book, men have allowed themselves to think too narrowly about the use of the intellect, for example. It is high on the scale of desirable capabilities, but in truth, dexterity in this area is only one variety of capability. If a child does not exhibit it, it does not mean that the child is not capable in other ways, even though an intellectualized father might think differently. The same would apply to a sports-minded father as well. If a man is a friend to a child, he will only wish to assist the child to become more fully realized as an individual, and this means that he needs sensitivity to a variety of roles a child may choose and enough empathy to encourage that child to pursue his or her own interests.

Johnny wants to be a dancer? The old-fashioned father says, "No." Boys don't dance. There's no big money in it. What would the other guys think? No, he may *not* dance around the living room. He must not be encouraged. He may not take lessons. Why doesn't he want to be a doctor or a lawyer? Why doesn't he choose something that offers a future?

Perhaps part of the sickness of our culture lies in the belief that it is necessary to be only one thing, to be plainly identifiable by occupation, to have a lifelong job, and to train specifically for that job. Expertise limits a child's potential for development. Expert Ph.D.'s have gone hungry at Cape Canaveral because space programs no longer required their expertise. Who in the next few years can say what will happen to jobs once thought stable? The child who has been reared to be independent will take note of social conditions and arrange for his own survival and, hopefully, enjoyment.

George B. Leonard shows in his book *Education and Ecstasy*[8] how current educational methods cannot be depended upon. He says that the ordinary classroom is designed to stop a child's spectacular learning career as speedily and effectively as possible. In his interesting book Leonard takes his readers on visits to schools of the future, showing how an ecstatic love of learning can be humankind's today. He proposes that in the coming age lifelong education will be the main purpose of life and that children will begin to realize the awesome potential of the brain.

At present fathers mouth the slogans of the system, insisting not that education be enjoyed for its own sake but that it be used as a means to an end. As a means only, it is denigrated—since its goal is a job of some sort which matches the father's idea of appropriate achievement rather than the absorption of knowledge for its own sake. Quests for achievement and success, which have nothing to do with the insights gained for other possible uses through education, propel many fathers into the slave-driver role, pushing sons to get good grades (to be measured in competition with other grade-getters). After the grades come the degrees, and then a proper position in a firm that calls for the respect of all who hear its name, primarily because of the financial remuneration it pays. Brenton says that although the remuneration may give a young man a sense of accomplishment (because it pleases his parents), it may also cause him serious difficulties with his identity. The fact that he has "accomplished" eludes him. "He can never really be himself," suggests Brenton, "a person with a core, someone who believes in something." The problem is that he has been highly conditioned to associate success with approval and love.

A final word about fatherhood: To be a father one need not sire a biological offspring. Fatherhood is being a sensitive friend to a child, and by this standard there are too few fathers. Men must be liberated from the idea that their fertility is a measure of manhood. This, on the part of men, is an extremely distorted reason for siring children. It is not only cruel, but it is also the cause of untold numbers of thoughtless births. In some countries a man's prestige is dependent on the number of children he has fathered. Dean Harrison writes that in Latin America the concepts of *machismo* and virility are "inexorably linked."[9]

In any case, liberation must mean that males overcome their hesitancy about birth-control measures for themselves. One doctor, according to Harrison, says of his patients: "It's hard enough to get them in here for a yearly checkup. . . . They say they're too busy."[10] Too busy, that is, to discuss birth-control methods with doctors! Before the mid-1950s not much was known about the male's reproductive system, and women's birth-control pills beat similar pills for men to the market, thus grabbing the first headlines. Dr. Harold Jackson, head of the department of experimental chemotherapy at Christie Hospital in Manchester, England, says, "It is now clearly practicable to exercise chemical control of fertility via the male."[11]

Chapter 19 ❋ FRIENDSHIP
Slaps on the Back
from Strangers

John Anderson, my jo, John,
We clamb the hill thegither;
And mony a cantie day, John,
We've had wi' ane anither:

Now we maun totter down, John,
And hand in hand we'll go,
And sleep thegither at the foot,
John Anderson, my jo.

—ROBERT BURNS

"In the past," said Dr. Margaret Mead, "society was very destructive to any male friendship. It was always expressed by that terrible bang on the back."

Now, luckily, James Taylor is singing "You've Got a Friend," the Staple Singers have given us "Touch a Hand, Make a Friend," and Bette Midler has been admonishing, "Ya gotta have friends!" Midler sang "Friends" at New York's 1973 annual gay liberation meeting at Washington Square Park. Homosexuals, organizing to emphasize that they are also just people, have come out of their closets and dared to hold hands publicly, a step that took great courage and has earned them begrudging respect in many quarters. Such respect is due from people who are not homosexually inclined because many of those who call themselves normal have been too cowardly to come out of their closets and hold each others' hands first—as though there were some shame, some awful sexual thought at the back of a friend's mind, the thought that it might mean he is somewhat . . . that he has *tendencies*. If there is anything men have found difficult to do, unfortunately, it is to admit to themselves that each has within him the capability of responding in various ways at unknown times to either sex. We may suppress the physical feelings we have, since they are so terribly taboo, but Kinsey's statistics show that the majority of men at some time wish for physical fulfillment with another man. This, however, does not mean that such men are exclusive homosexuals. It means simply that the human body and personality and mind are aesthetically attractive on occasion and that neither heterosexuality nor homosexuality are particularly exclusive states of being. Friendship has no particular relationship to homosexuality per se, but the fear of homosexuality—of being thought gay—has prevented passionate friendships between men from taking place in our culture except among people who have chosen to band together in defense of their right to enjoy such friendships. These are people who are thought so very unusual that they are jailed in all but six states if their friendships give evidence of physical expression and who are called by the most unflattering sexual epithets. Margaret Mead has called our attention to peculiar tribes like the Iatmul, who wear little stools attached to their buttocks to protect themselves from anal rape. Their taboos about homosexuality, given Kinsey's figures, seem to approximate our own in some ways. Mead writes:

> In the men's group there is a loud, over-definite masculine behavior, a continuous use of verbs that draw their imagery from phallic attack on men and women alike. But there is also a very strong taboo on any display of passivity, and there is no development of male homosexuality within the society. The slightest show of weakness or of receptivity is regarded as a temptation, and men walk about, often comically

carrying their small wooden stools fixed firmly against their buttocks. A male child from any outside village or tribe becomes a ready victim, and Iatmul workboys are said to become active homosexuals when they meet men from other tribes away at work. But within the group, the system holds, and demonstrates vividly how it is possible to distort the upbringing of every male so that his capacity and temptation to introduce sex into his relationship with other males is very strong and yet kept closely in control.[1]

If homosexually inclined people led the battle to open our way to expressing love to members of our own sex, then heterosexually inclined people must help them finish that battle. Otherwise friendship will never have a chance. The homosexuals in our midst are a burning issue in men's discussions with each other, and the whole question aggravates them emotionally to a greater extent than is ever admitted. In men's consciousness-raising meetings there have been those who, gaining the courage to say, "I am attracted to you, even physically," in honest dialogue with other men, have found themselves sitting utterly alone and the group scattered and gone, literally panicked by the mere mention of such goings-on. Such a spectacle: grown, purportedly heterosexual men, unable to sit in comfort in the same room with someone known to be attracted to his own sex. Needing to flee! Why?

Affection can be distorted only by strict cultural conditioning. When we want to draw close to someone, it is a great inhibitor if we must *fear* touching him, if the physical expression makes us suspect. This is in fact the condition of the American male today, however.

If he were not subject to this kind of fear, if it really didn't matter whether or not he were thought to be homosexually inclined, if the arbitrary and unreasonable labeling and pigeonholing of affection were not subject to cliché descriptions like "heterosexual" and "homosexual" (descriptions that are mere niches, corners, and hardly expressive of character or ability), then the American male might not feel so pressed to continually demonstrate his ascendancy with women and in society. He would also be free to pursue deeper and more meaningful relationships with other American males.

Dr. George Weinberg, noted authority on statistics in psychology, author of *The Action Approach*[2] and other psychological works, was among the first heterosexually inclined psychologists to crusade for the concept of "healthy homosexuality," long before the American Psychiatric Association belatedly changed its collective mind and declassified homosexuality as a mental disorder. He wrote:

> I would never consider a patient healthy unless he had overcome his prejudice against homosexuality. Of course if the person is himself homosexual, the prejudice he holds is barring the way to easy expression of his own desires. But even if he is heterosexual, his repugnance at homosexuality is certain to be harmful to him. In my experience, such a prejudice is more rife among heterosexual men than among heterosexual women.[3]

Homosexuality quite officially stopped being a mental disorder in the United States on Monday morning, April 8, 1974. At that time the American Psychiatric Association tabulated the votes from its membership, and by a vote of 5,854 to 3,810, with 367 members abstaining, it switched in midstream and headed in the opposite direction. The confusion reigning over this issue was severe, and psychiatrists everywhere were debating it hotly. For the first time in the history of the 129-year-old organization its membership forced a vote on an action of the trustees, who had declassified homosexuality five months previously. The prominent antihomosexual crusader Dr. Charles Socarides proceeded to circulate a petition demanding the vote on the trustees' decision. The A.P.A. struck down its anti-homosexual minority, however, and confirmed itself as participant in what the excitable Dr. Socarides called "the medical hoax of the century." This action, he said, contradicted a historical fact "that male and female are programmed to mate with the opposite sex, and this is the story of two and a half billion years of evolution and any society that hopes to survive." His call was drowned out in the din of change. Gay liberation had made its point.

What this means to the man in the street is that he may now contemplate and even practice closer same-sex friendships. Even if they do earn him a denigrating epithet or two in spite of the fact that they have no physical overtones and in spite of the fact that he could never—not even in his wildest dreams—think of himself as distinctly homosexual, he can still rest assured that the epithet does not mean he is mentally unbalanced. It is a small gain, admittedly, but it helps if one knows that passionate feelings for another of the same sex are not subject to morose classifications by medical men. A vote has changed the situation.

This vote is more important to men generally than is usually assumed. In fact it is more important to the average Joe than to the homosexual men it has declassified. There are not as many men who classify themselves as exclusive homosexuals as there are men who would not consider engaging in homosexual behavior—but there is a great deal of homosexual behavior going on among men. In case we have forgotten, Kinsey showed us that the number of men who do engage in such behavior is nearly as great as

the number of men who don't. Even so, the vote is important primarily to men who find the very thought of being
considered homosexually inclined *the worst thing that
could happen*. It is this great number of men who need to
understand that they can be free to touch a friend and
that nobody will think the unthinkable. And even if they
do think it, it won't matter because (1) it isn't true, and he
doesn't care what other people think, or (2) he is enough
of a man (a human being) to feel that affection—no
matter how it is expressed—is highly preferable to its
lack. It needs encouragement, particularly if we are to
keep out of wars. Whitman sang:

> Over the carnage rose prophetic a voice,
> Be not dishearten'd, affection shall solve the
> problems of freedom yet.[4]

What did he really mean? It is certain that he did
not mean genital contact between males would solve
freedom's problems, but *affection*. . . . Something, maybe,
like the *love one another* business that Jesus got into with
his twelve disciples. . . . *Love one another as I have loved
you*—that was it! Why was it acceptable for Jesus to kiss
his friends, and why is such a practice not now acceptable
among men in the United States?

It is far more important that men generally feel free to
be close to one another—emotionally and even physically
—without believing they are mentally disordered than
it is for those fewer numbers of exclusive homosexuals to
enjoy their bodies freely. Although taboos against same-sex
affection prevent a few men from expressing themselves
sexually, their worst feature is that they strain the poten-
tialities and upset the balance of a whole culture by making it difficult for men to draw close. As if it were not bad
enough living in a culture where alienation and isolation

are common! Yet to accept the taboos on deep friendships —between grown men—is to welcome destruction's finishing touch. It is to make a farce of those marvelously human feelings we often experience in our relationships with others but must be careful not to express with a touch. The United States is a nation standing on the brink of paralyzation, so afraid are its denizens of touching one another, of *the laying on of hands!*

Even the term "homosexual" has a more frightening ring to most men than does any other. Perhaps it is rivaled by "atheist." There have more than once been amusing combinations of words strung together in right-wing tabloids: "Communist - homosexual - corruption - perversion." How quaint! "Homosexual" is an electric-shock adjective that inspires such horror among men as to make even a closer examination of relationships with other men difficult to conceive. This is what the "gay" taboo has done to society, with staggeringly destructive effects. It is sad when men ritualize their behavior, finding it difficult to show affection except in circumscribed ways, and must protect themselves against a stupid taboo, one that really isn't worth the hassle, just in case some other man with a locker-room mentality might smirk. Big deal, that locker-room joker. The louder he laughs, the more *he* is suspect. If he *is* suspect, he should not earn respect for being himself, as does the overt gay person, but pity for being such a novice in sexual matters that he can communicate his fright only by pointing at people he hopes are worse off than he is. On top of that, he is a perpetuator of the taboo and a potential gossip.

Fearful that they will be called or thought homosexuals, men have organized their relationships with each other into ruts. Those who see themselves as homosexuals have indeed suffered as a result (and many have adopted masculinist values, as have their heterosexual brethren), but the suffering of the gay community has been only the tip of an iceberg of human suffering. Beneath the surface of relationships between males the homosexual taboo has grown cold and seemingly impregnable, souring and distorting male friendships, making them less expressive, limited, apprehensive, casual, cool, and full of competitive, dominating tendencies. Seldom is one friend enamored of another, appreciating him for the great beauty of his character, his manner, his way with others, his self-esteem, and his compassion. If one is enamored, he must contain his admiration. He must keep it in check. He must stifle his impulses. Above all, he must not touch too affectionately. Rough touching is OK. A slap on the back? Yeah. A poke in the ribs? All right. He must not, however, count friendships as too important, too worthy of emotional investment. He can say to himself: "I won't let myself feel too strongly. I shouldn't express what I feel, or my friend will think I'm corny. If I said I loved him, he'd think *that terrible thing*. I'd better stop these thoughts, or I'll find myself gettin' queer or something."

There has long been a most unfortunate connection in the minds of American men between passivity and homosexuality. Few seem to realize that male homosexuals are just as likely to follow masculinist values taught by society as are heterosexuals. Homosexuality has nothing to do with passivity per se unless a man determines that he will explore physical passivity through homosexual stimuli, something that many homosexually inclined men do not do themselves. Physical passivity, after all, can be explored in many other ways and is only one aspect of passivity itself. We do need passivity, says Dr. George Weinberg. "To condemn passivity," he writes, "is like condemning your eyeballs." We need it, he tells us, to see and to discover. And yet American men en masse reject passivity except for a growing minority in the youth culture.

It remains for thoughtful people of all persuasions to destroy the false fences erected between men by social demands. If this is not done with great rapidity on a wide scale, our natural sympathies for each other, deformed and prohibited by negative conventions, will transform themselves into frustrations that may burst on us in waves of hostile reverberation. Alan Watts has seen the point. He wrote:

> If they . . . young and unrealized homosexuals who affect machismo, ultramasculinity, and who constitute the hard core of our military industrial police mafia combine . . . would go fuck each other (and I use that word in its most positive and appreciative sense) the world would be vastly improved. They make it with women only to brag about it, but are actually far happier in the barracks than in boudoirs. This is, perhaps, the real meaning of "Make Love, Not War." We may be destroying ourselves through the repression of homosexuality.[5]

Watts himself admitted to heterosexual preferences, perhaps hinting that he had experimented homosexually. In his autobiography he suggested that a heaven in which he lies (as the old hymn says) "forever on my Saviour's breast" might be fun for nuns, "but for a man it is the invitation to the boredom of a homosexual paradise." "This is not to say," he assured us, "that I condemn homosexuality, but only that I do not enjoy it."

Masculinist etiquette stifles natural sympathies. Men might reach out to embrace, but the staid voice of what they are pleased to call manners reminds them that occasions for affectionate squeezes should be few and far between. They aren't altogether proper. Shake hands instead. It isn't *proper*, they feel, for men to hug one another, to kiss, to embrace publicly or privately. It isn't *proper* for a son to kiss his father and vice-versa. It isn't *proper* for men to get too close, to be too expressive. Someone, the ever-present and proverbial someone, might think that something is wrong.

Is it possible that American men are starved for affection from each other? I think so. They are, in fact, terribly deprived, and most men are afraid to depart from their rigid, mechanical images. They become petrified and calcified: hard, unbending, and short on open displays of feeling.

Is it any wonder that we, as a nation, are unable to be better judges of our fellow men and actually elected the Watergate automatons? And why? Because we don't actually see men or have a sense of men, of what their movements, too often too deliberate, tell us about their inner states. It is becoming less difficult for citizens to look at public figures and see that they may be terribly uncomfortable in their bodies, that they cannot confide in men or draw close to them openly, that they cannot bend or yield, and that their neuroses, as Reich said, are engraved on their muscles.

Such perceptions, after all, are not beyond our ken. A great many of our problems in perceiving our public men stem from the injuries we have done to relationships between males. We fail to see that these men are awkward, stilted, severe, and unnecessarily hard, because we as a society have been conditioned to accept such types of behavior as correct and proper.

In a society where men relate to each other only on certain well-defined levels but in which they are harshly condemned if they exceed or expand on those levels, there will always be many whose primary concern is to show that they will not, under any circumstances, transgress the taboo. In other words, these men will spend their energies proving they do not have any characteristic that would indicate they might.

This is energy spent in extremely negative channels. Instead of proceeding in a positive way, avowing the aforementioned affection recommended by Jesus and Whitman, with both laying on of hands and touch to add to its powers, these men are concerning themselves with power, size, coolness, and competition. There is in them none of the impetus to affection for other men which would suggest that they cooperate. Cooperation means some degree of yielding. Yielding is considered weakness. Weakness is presumed the trait of a sissy. A sissy is queer. Hence an iron fist is the best posture these men know!

The fear of being considered homosexual, whether conscious or, as is true for most men, unconscious, is a cancer that eats away at our national strengths. Eliminating this fear means not only tolerance for men who are unafraid of taboos and who openly draw close to each other but also *encouragement* of such closeness. It should be left to each individual male to find his own directions on the scale of sexual preference.

If he were not subject to the fears inspired by the taboo, if it really didn't matter whether or not he were thought homosexually inclined, and if his relationships with men did develop into physical expressions, it would be obvious that it is good to be close to men. It is healthy, and it adds to society's well-being, because it allows men to perceive that they are appreciated by one another not because of winning, competition, domination, status, and so forth but because they are kind, loving, thoughtful, and sensitive, *characteristics men must develop if they are to survive.*

Anthropologist Lionel Tiger tries to tell us that men have a biologically transmitted and socially learned pro-

pensity to form bonds with other males which are stronger
and more stable than female affiliations. In a major study
supported by a P.H.S. grant from the National Center for
Health Services Research, Alan Booth, of the University of
Nebraska, examined eight hundred Midwestern adults
whose patterns of social habit had been firmly established.
There was a proper range of backgrounds and tendencies
to allow for a good sampling. The purpose of the study
was to compare "the extent and quality of participation by
men and women in friendship dyads, voluntary associations, and kin relations." The study concluded that there
was *no* evidence to support recent claims such as Tiger's
that male bonds are stronger than women's. The conclusion
reads:

> Extensive friendship ties for males are linked to early
> socialization, primarily competitive team activities
> which are not universal in the male population.
> Female friendships are affectively richer. . . . Seldom
> were men's relations with friends and groups more
> numerous than women's. They did not exceed wom-
> en's in sexually exclusive organizations; nor had they
> more same-sex friendships. Women's kinship ties
> exceed men's clearly. Moreover theirs are stronger
> than men's. Women are more spontaneous with
> friends and kin.[6]

There we have it, the poor estate of friendship, the
shame of a nation that might well hope to

> plant companionship thick as trees along all the
> rivers of America and along the shores of the great
> lakes, and all over the prairies,
> > making
> inseparable cities with their arms about each other's
> necks,
> By the love of comrades.[7]

The objection may be made that the homophobia stressed here is stereotypical or exaggerated and that men do indeed enjoy friendships, which grow in their various clubs, at sports outings, and at bars. The depth of a friendship cannot be measured, and there are some, certainly, who have felt lifelong attachments to others of their own sex. Even so, it is possible to ask almost any American male if he has not at some time repressed affectionate feelings toward another male and to find that he has indeed! This means that literally millions of friendships never really bloom but are nipped in the bud under a demand for strict reserve.

Men who have drawn close as friends have been subjected to vicious gossip, and in one case—that of two Hollywood box-office kings—a friendship was brought to a public halt. A rumor circulated that there had been a "marriage" between Rock Hudson and Jim Nabors. It reached such proportions that Rock Hudson felt obliged to say that it was not so to syndicated columnist Hy Gardner. The columnist reported Hudson as saying:

I first heard about it a year or so ago and laughed my head off. I heard it from a woman who heard it through her hairdresser. It is absolutely preposterous and ridiculous. It has reached such tremendous proportions, there's really nothing to say. Despite our denials, some people will believe whatever they want. They'll say: "BS" or "Aha!" ... I'll tell you one thing that makes me sad about this whole thing. And that's that Jim Nabors and I are no longer friends. We can't be seen together. We used to be close friends, that's what's sad about it.[8]

Even if friendships were not burdened by homophobic taboos, it is still difficult to conceive how they might grow and have meaning in a society where the male's values make him an isolate, difficult to get to know because he wears a kind of psychic shoulder padding to make himself seem bigger than he is. Conceivably, it could be argued that traditional masculinist values militate against friendship every bit as much as does the homosexual taboo and in many cases more.

What the poor estate of friendship between men does to friendships between men and women is also open to conjecture. It could be that a man's inability to draw close as a friend to other men may make it just as difficult for him to draw close to women. Friendship, after all, takes place between people, not between sexes.

Can a status-conscious society, basing its evaluations of its members on their possessions, truly hope for *perception* in relationships? How many men judge one another on the basis of earning power, and how fair a judgment is dollar-making capacity as a means of knowing another man? Can men who build facades around themselves feel free to fulfill what Ralph Waldo Emerson called the basic requirement of friendship: being able to think aloud in front of one's friend?

There may be occasional ties between some men which are not entangled in such drawbacks. Still, conventional values strain these ties, making them the more difficult to preserve. Snell and Gail Putney suggest that there is sometimes a kind of localized self-acceptance in which "the adjusted American" feels that he can be himself in the company of one or two friends or perhaps a mate, dropping his heavy role temporarily in the confidence that his intimates will be accepting of him in spite of role slips. If he is able to lower his defenses, feeling relieved because the self he shows is not cause for his friends' alarm, he may in fact learn to like himself as he really is to some extent, at least when he is in the company of these few understanding souls. What results, say the Putneys, is his satisfaction with what he sees when he presents himself to friends and continues to feel their acceptance of him anyway. "He lets his friends be a mirror—an honest mirror—and discovers that, taken all in all, he likes what he sees." The Putneys describe the process of localized self-acceptance as one that works only within very limited frameworks in this nation, "experienced sporadically under favorable circumstances." It is one that is not therefore sufficient as a means of achieving the self-esteem needed by so many (through mirror-friends), and unfortunately, so few can draw upon it because of friendship's sorry state. "Americans render most of their associations strained, superficial, and unsatisfying," say the Putneys.[9]

There are other reasons too why friendship is so rare; they have been mentioned before. The competitive value finds two men circling about each other in its environs, seemingly happy. As they approach each other with competition in mind, a temporary satisfaction may be sustained, along with the illusion that camaraderie is in full swing. The competitive value is only another kind of measuring, though, to see who is bigger or faster or stronger or richer. It is rationalistic in a negative sense because it introduces measurements into human relations, a practice that can eliminate the naturally good feelings one receives in the midst of any emotionally charged, satisfying relationship. Relationships that take place in the midst of competitive sports generally lack spontaneous effusion except under the most stylized format. Athletes, for example, may hug each other at the end of a game, possibly to sustain the impression that they are OK guys and not just battering rams.

Intellectualized methods of getting to know one's friends

are too often used, thus leading to further complications. As said in an earlier part of this book, it takes *time*, often too long, to get to know a person via questions, tests, and answers. There are other means, more direct, that tell us intuitively what we need to know about someone. Instead of listening only to what they say, for example, we may also listen to the tone of voice used to speak. Dogs and other animals know this trick and are able to use it as a cue for wagging their tails in almost immediate friendly response. If human beings depended less on their intellects and more on their perceptive capabilities, it might be that they could bypass excess verbiage and find themselves intimately aware of their relationships with each other without suffering such hesitancy and fear.

One of the most destructive facets of intellectualized knowledge of others is the coolness men pretend to in order to demonstrate objectivity. When they are among themselves, this coolness often keeps them from drawing close as well. One man mistakes another's indifferent exterior for genuine indifference, which is usually not genuine but is instead calculated. Indifference of this kind is often one of the best telltale signs that men are actually uncomfortable and need rescue from their self-imposed stone-faced mien. Indeed, there is hardly anything more heartbreaking than a man who may feel deeply but is unable to show his feelings—beautiful though they may be —to others.

Dominance—the control factor—must also play its part in male relationships. If it is a man's role to play dominant (according to many), then such dominance must be just as obvious in relationships with men as with women. One must "have it all over" the other, and too often friendship parades under the cover of master-servant bonds. The friends do not find themselves imbued with mutual admiration; one is something of a sidekick for the other, a somewhat less-than-whole sidekick who frequently needs *telling* and who must be rescued from his own folly. Gabby Hayes and Andy Devine often played such sidekicks in Western films. They were always a bit sluggish, unpolished, and silly. Their "friends" (the heroes), by contrast, always moved with lightning speed, were capable in most situations, and were forever rescuing their poor sidekicks from trouble. Not the best sampling of peergroup behavior, one might say.

A final difficulty that men often encounter and that strains their relationships with men as surely as it does with women is the intellectualized tendency to judge others by dexterities. I would call this inclination the tyranny of dexterities. A mechanical dexterity, for example, is highly desirable among many men, and yet a man with such capabilities may believe that he is inferior to a man with intellectual dexterities. Although neither is superior, both feel inadequate for lacking the dexterity they admire, and both tend to judge the other according to which dexterities they think easy and which not. Excellence is in the mind of the beholder, however. Men are too ready to "size up" their fellows by thinking in terms of dexterity instead of in terms of other characteristics. A football player, for example, is early on awarded hosannas, which continue if he is still playing past high school. If he is not playing, the hosannas stop, and he may find himself trying (with some difficulty) to adjust to life without his hero image. At the same time, a person who has capabilities in other fields is not accorded the same degree of acclaim. A pianist, for example, may wander the halls of a high school virtually unknown, his particular abilities considered by some as hardly fitting, especially for a man. And yet no dexterity—mechanical, physical, or intellectual —is either decidely masculine or decidedly feminine.

There are too many who win new "friends" and base their relationships with them on how their dexterities match the social register.

Whitman, who was very enthusiastic about the prospect of comradeship among men, spoke of the men he loved most as people who were capable of "love as I myself am capable of loving." And yet, paradoxically, he saw potential in every person. He believed that the continent could be "made indissoluble" with the love of comrades, and thus refused to cut his Calamus poems from *Leaves of Grass* when urged to do so by those who suspected him of sexual deviation. Even though he had to bear such a charge, he knew that affection between men is essential if a nation is to retain its good health.

Chapter 20 ❄ BODY
The One Thing That Really Shows

Dear Dr. Reuben:
In reference to your statement in a recent column that "no male is one hundred percent male and no female is one hundred percent female," I, being a male, insist on making a protest. I am not a doctor but I am entitled to my thoughts as a human being age 60. Now, I will come to your office for an examination to prove to me and/or to show me whereby I am not one hundred percent male—all charges to be paid by me.

—LETTER TO SYNDICATED COLUMNIST
DR. DAVID REUBEN

A nation of men whose posture is primarily aggressive and which admits only of activity, advance, exertion, and ascendancy is unconsciously and ominously warped. Posture is a principal way in which our culture permits an extreme dramatization of differences between men and women. Mannerisms, stances, and gaits emphasize beyond what is needed that a man is unmistakably different from a woman.

Aggressive value-laden mannerisms are somehow emphasized by almost all American men, although men are beginning to discard them and seek different, more personal balances. Those who cling to strict masculinist deportment suffer the delusion that there are only two types of behavior, interpreted as dominance and submission. They do not realize that it may be better for them personally—and that they may be more honest, direct, and comfortable—if they find their own levels of balance rather than adopting those prescribed by gender roles.

The word "posture" as it is used here does not have reference to limbs only but to every bodily feature through which a man's values are expressed. Posture is generally the self allowing its values to be seen. Since posture is an outward show, it may be here more than anyplace else that men openly reveal themselves.

I often think how important it is that American diplomats should be men whose physical mannerisms are graceful rather than aggressive, domineering, or strictly controlled. No matter how well they have mastered other tongues, it will be carriage rather than skills which will impress their hosts in other lands. They will judge tones of voice and the physical impressions the diplomat makes as he moves. If a man is hulking, tough, and too excessively pointed about it, he will either frighten or amuse the inhabitants of other lands. America must be particularly careful not to add insult to the injury that we are one of the world's taller peoples. It might help us diplomatically if along with our gianthood we were able to exude gentleness.

The various ways in which American men take care to give physical indications to each other, making their "manliness" apparent, would be amusing if only they did not succeed in creating so many uncomfortable men, self-conscious and staid. Since a man's idiosyncrasies, quirks, ticks, and affectations are reflected in his body, this means that if values are askew, so often will be bodies. This is because bodies so easily emit vibrations of those intentions shaped by our values. This perspective may already be gaining some support in the popular usage of the term body language. Serious researchers have been examining body consciousness among Americans for some time now. One of the most conscientious of such men is Professor Seymour Fisher, mentioned earlier, whose concern with masculinity and femininity has produced interesting finds.

Posture, since it is a man's way of showing himself—of being present or of meeting the world—is a mood-indicator. It can also be a mood-producer. If a man believes that he must carry himself aggressively even if he does not feel particularly aggressive, it is altogether possible that he may end by *feeling* the part he is playing and becoming violent as a result.

In the United States posture has come to mean (in the public mind at least) straightening up, puffing out the chest, and squaring the chin militarily. Mention of good posture finds men pulling their shoulders back to an extreme angle, demonstrating rather unconvincingly that they are fit. On more subtle levels it has come to mean such things as sitting down and throwing one leg's ankle over the other leg's knee instead of throwing one knee over the other, which is decidedly more comfortable. In some places it means learning to hold a cigarette in a pointedly "masculine" fashion, one that demonstrates an almost athletic control of the butt and begins when the cigarette is lit, ending only when it is thrown away. As it is lit, the male, hopefully, knows how to cup his hands squarely and masterfully against the wind. Humphrey Bogart was a master of this sort of thing. When a cigarette was thrown away in the fifties, it was characteristic of toughs to flip it some distance. Concerned men have long known that there are "ways" to stand, proper gaits, and "methods" to loll. All of these *ways of being* reveal certain values as surely as does a smile.

The transvestite is perhaps the most vehement rejecter of masculinist postures, but instead of finding his own most comfortable bearing, he imitates feminine mannerisms. The fact that he can do this demonstrates how these various mannerisms are mere histrionics. That a man can be both heterosexually inclined and yet so fetishistically hypnotized by the socialized mannerisms of women that he learns to mimic them indicates that neither his initial set of mannerisms nor his adopted ones are innate, but rather learned.

A predicament facing American men in any discussion of their bodies lies in the general unawareness or lack of body consciousness that is characteristic of our Judeo-Christian society, with its emphasis on the body's corruptibility, an emphasis that has led literally millions to turn away from their bodies in puritanical fright. The body has been thought to be the temple of temptation and was carefully covered in public until the first streakers began to demonstrate the asininity of this practice.

There are still relatively few beaches in America where nudity is common, although they abound in Europe. Streakers, harmless and wholesome though they may be, are arrested by the hundreds under archaic laws. And yet to streak is thought moral and right, or at least innocuous, by a majority of American college youths, young men and women who smile knowingly and sometimes patronizingly about the phenomenon.

As recently as our grandparents' time bathers had to cover themselves much more modestly than is the case today. Men, until not long ago, were carefully covered except in muscle magazines like *Tomorrow's Man*. Even in slick girlie magazines, prior to 1968 airbrushed photographs of top-heavy women were commonplace (although only one breast was allowed to show on magazine covers), but the photos of the men accompanying them (either caressing them or making love to them in bed) showed the men *clothed*, usually wearing pants, undershirts, and often socks. Although photographs of naked men were not what really interested the magazines' purchasers, the bizarre fact remains: No one thought to question that millions of men were buying sex-fantasy photographs in which one of the partners was generally clothed, with no seeming damage done to the fantasy. Until 1968, when

Screw began peddling nudity on newsstands in Manhattan, this condition prevailed. *Screw* was the first street-corner newspaper to carry full-page photos of men and women romping about in the altogether. For a while the newspaper was a hit, particularly among Manhattan intelligentsia. Later came *Playgirl,* the magazine that exploits men and makes them sex objects, emphasizing characteristics of manliness to which only a few men can aspire, in mock imitation of *Playboy,* a magazine that does the same to women.

At last the male is getting to look at himself, at least occasionally. His sense of his own body has been so limited heretofore that only a few "muscle men," who strutted about in their own unique burlesques, or dancers, who were body conscious by profession, were allowed to give themselves the kind of attention needed for self-care. When this happened, they were singled out for their narcissism, the dark Freudian term used by society to keep people from daring to take a peek at themselves.

For several decades, ending perhaps in the early 1960s, men wore clothing that gave very little evidence of body contour. Body shirts and tapered pants legs were virtually unknown. Today some men (particularly those who are younger) are developing a keener self-appreciation, sensing that their own symmetry exists and allowing their clothes to emphasize it. It may be that Americans in the twentieth century still have time to recapture some of the body consciousness that was originally part of our Western heritage but that disappeared with the ancient Greeks.

If this is to happen, there are forces to be overcome, however, forces that are working against self-awareness more powerfully than we know. These are the motivating rhythms of technology, created to follow artificial schedules that are used as external standards for human speeds.

If it were not enough that men are bound by silly affectations to prove themselves "masculine," they must also allow themselves to be dragged along at unnatural mechanical velocities. Men are unable, in many urban areas particularly, to keep stride with the technologies that they have created. Tension, which is the baby of technological pace, grows in each person in subtle ways, building itself into the body's movements over the years and creating men who are automatons of an even more ungainly mien than would be the case if aggression, dominance, coolness, and other masculinist characteristics were all there were to contend with. Posture, carriage, and expression demonstrate the evil grip of machine-world living on men's minds.

In stepping between man and nature, technology shows excesses particularly like those resulting from the methodical, overintellectualized tendencies examined in the early pages of this book. Following values set by a mechanized society, men find themselves chopping daily experience into rigid categories that miss a wider natural life that is in process. Time categories, for example, are not in harmony with time as nature dispenses it. Nature takes its own time, neither hastening nor lagging, free of the push to complete on the exact external schedules that characterize present-day activity. Men following technological rhythms have allowed nature's rhythms, which are their own true ones, to be artificially divided by the clock. It is difficult to say just how taxing to human bodies these artificial divisions have been. Drs. Meyer Friedman and Ray Rosenman, after doing research at Mount Zion Hospital and Medical Center, say that the pace of modern living accounts for many heart attacks even among the young. Those who zealously follow machine schedules ignore the calls of their own bodies, which are, after all, more reliable than clocks as guides to movement.

The man who awakens in the morning to the sound of an alarm experiences the first artificial intrusion of the day on his natural processes. He may still be tired, but he rises anyway. If he sleeps late, he skips breakfast or exerts himself to get to work and punch his time clock. His meals are either skipped or gobbled hurriedly at rigidly scheduled intervals. He frets because he feels that he is falling behind in things he believes he should do, and he tries to do more and more things in less and less time. He finds himself becoming discomfited when he isn't immediately seated in a restaurant or when he is delayed in traffic or must wait for a plane. At work there is seldom an opportunity for him to stop and read a magazine or to chat amiably with co-workers. Even if there is nothing to be done, the work ethic demands that he appear to be busy, and so he shuffles papers on his desk. His body may grow stiff and uncomfortable (nature's calls to exercise), but he cannot take a walk. If he feels suddenly fatigued (nature's calls to siesta), he would never think of allowing his boss to catch him napping. Unless he is self-employed, he has no control over most of his waking hours. He must keep his nose to the grindstone. If he does not, and should he wish to maintain a loose and comfortable relationship with his work, it will be thought that he is a slouch.

Efficiency experts are hired by offices to make slavery to the clock even more demanding. Middle-management and supervisory personnel are sent to seminars to be taught to "handle" their time. Popularizers of efficiency techniques charge handsomely for these seminars. One such popularizer is author Alan Lakein, who boasts that he wears no watch, although it is reported that he

> walks fast, talks fast and gains minutes by such shortcuts as never reading a book in its entirety; he zips through the chapter headings and topic sen-

tenees and extracts the meat of the author's message —a technique which, he says, enabled him to complete the Great Books Course in a month.[1]

Routines and rush deprive a man's work of meaning. He may fool himself by insisting they give some opportunities for self-expression, but generally what he means is that he has found some small satisfactions in the midst of boredom. In the meantime his body is habituated into ignoring natural synchronizations and invites its own breakdowns as a result.

Some theorists reckon that strict regulation of bodily functions may add to the prospects of health. The two functions wherein this reckoning may have some validity involve the intake and output of food. There is some evidence, however, that scheduled intake is not as necessary as was once believed and that some people are better off if they eat when they are hungry. There is even more evidence to prove that the regularity of bowel functions is a myth. Some find that it is natural for their bowels to move once or twice daily, whereas for others it occurs every other day or every third day.

For many bodily functions, however, regulation spells spiritless monotony. In play and relaxation, for example, impetus is pulsating rather than precisely recurrent. The introduction of schedule robs playfulness of its spontaneous core. The same is true of sexual intercourse. The man who performs on schedule (every other evening at 10 P.M.) robs himself and his partner of needed elements: degrees of the unexpected.

What is clear is that paying too strict an attention to schedule can easily reduce and destroy and that such attention is not wholly beneficial. It may help to clock-watch for various purposes of reference and to coordinate varied groups or rites that have no other constructs for

action. At work a schedule can and often does reduce
efforts, but addiction to synchronization has usurped more
than its share of power over human affairs, turning awareness into concentration on clocks and calendars. Such
awareness may be natural to prison inmates who are
counting days, but for the average man it amounts to a
severe improverishment of experience. A society that is
regimented by clocks risks great sacrifices to its health
and happiness.

Thorstein Veblen, Bertrand Russell, Alan Watts, and
others have suggested that so-called technological advances might be illusory. It is true, certainly, that gadgetry
designed to save time has, in some cases, left men running
harder in place. Russell tells us that the person who
walked to work a century ago spent thirty minutes in
transit. Today he still spends thirty minutes, since locomo-
tion has moved him far from centers of activity.

What is even more obvious is that a great many "advances" spurred by commercial interests have given birth
to a plethora of stimuli, all demanding attention from the
average man. Although these stimuli have increased, making us look one way and then another, there is no evidence
that our capacities for absorbing them effectively have
kept pace. Surrounding himself with increasing clamor,
man is in need of tranquility, perhaps more so than ever
before. Suitable arrangements have not been made for it.
And as we have observed, when leisure is granted on
schedule, few know how to enjoy it. TV's, newspapers, and
radios ask men to give their attention to occurrences *outside* of themselves, but there is no way of judging the
relative importance of these occurrences. As men pursue
misplaced values, there is little opportunity for them to
reflect inwardly, something that religion once effectively
encouraged them to do.

What has happened to technology is that its users have

bypassed questions of value in their headlong rush to put it to use. Zealous corporate bigwigs believed, no doubt, that machines could confer only blessings and that these would be reflected in the profits they made as the domain of the machines spread. If there was not to be a fair apportionment of goods, there could at least be great quantities of them so that hopefully, in the long run, more and more people would benefit. Values such as thoughtfulness in the use and creation of the machine could be drowned out by appeals to *quantity*. What became the rule of thumb was a belief that mankind's difficulties do not require care and forethought but that they may be solved by technological multiplications, spreading mechanical "benefits" far and wide. This belief is a variation, no doubt, of the Bigger-Than-Thou Syndrome. What has looked on the surface like great abundance has become excess fat. The nation, in fact, is now not unlike an obese man who, in his frustration and confusion, gobbles more and more, believing that consumption will somehow make him feel better. He fails to understand, taking pride in his size, why he cannot move.

The tragedy is that a man becomes harnessed to forces operating outside himself, forces that do not originate from within, and he allows these to keep him goosestepping in time with chronometers and other mechanisms. Thus instead of getting close to his own individualistic body beats, he hears only the *tick tick tick* of time marching on. Countless citizens do not move, dance, or walk from their body centers but on cue from their extremities. Instead of being in command of themselves, therefore, they seem to be disjointed and frantic. Citizens of other nations who are not bothered by such problems are often aghast at the pace followed by Americans, who pride themselves so in *setting* paces, an illusion.

The man who has learned "the profound lesson of reception" (of passivity, that is) might not rush forward nearly so quickly because he would be taking time to absorb, but American men rush because rushing means getting there first, winning, success, and achievement. In the midst of rushing no man can take needed time to be receptive. The code of masculinist aggression, which flees passivity, aggravates the predicament. The man who enjoys the strengths vouchsafed by occasional passivity would not be likely to exaggerate his posture aggressively. He would realize that puffing out the chest, strutting arrogantly, or holding himself in such poses is actually poor posture. He would see that the man holding himself in this way is making an overstatement, and in an age of nuclear weaponry, the making of overstatements, whether physical or psychical, is a clear danger. Good posture is neither overstatement nor understatement. As Lao-tzu said:

A man of sure fitness, without making a point of his fitness, stays fit. A man of unsure fitness, assuming an appearance of fitness, becomes unfit. A man of sure fitness never makes an act of it.[2]

When I say that those who square their shoulders, harden, become inflexible and rocklike, have missed the essence of good posture, I do not feel in the least dogmatic. Good posture, thank goodness, must be discovered by each individual. It means finding one's own center of gravity. Since it is a process of discovery, it is a natural part of an education that stresses self-regulation. It cannot be mastered in the twinkling of an eye at the command of a militaristic calistenics instructor, though. It is as individualistic as the most rugged American individualist could hope for, an inward feeling about what balance means to the self. It is a private discovery.

Professor Fisher writes that he is "impressed with the

role of violence and aggression in maintaining a sense of distinction between what is masculine and what is feminine." He says that "aggressive acting out" is thought to be the sign of the masculine mode. "When a man has arrived," he writes, "at serious doubts about whether his body 'feels' masculine, he may be driven to an act of violence as a way of dramatically re-establishing his masculinity. The angry, thrusting, attacking use of the musculature gives nice reassuring feedback."[3] In another place he writes: "The male who grossly doubts his masculinity feels compelled to turn his body into a metaphorical missile or torpedo."[4]

I infer from Professor Fisher's statements that if it were possible to remove from men doubts about their masculine identity (perhaps by making "masculine" postures less important than personally achieved ones), we might find one cause of violence gone. It is quite possible, in other words, that strict roles, which not every man feels he can master, may give rise to a man's need to prove masculinity by expressing himself violently. It is a task of men's liberation to spread the word that each man's body expresses itself differently and that the discovery of one's own balance (instead of socially prescribed balance) requires the same freedom for everyone. It is not with prescribed formulas for mannerisms that men find their balance but in the absence of such formulas. Within freedom's unlimited highs and lows, back steps and fore steps, side leans and bends, a man should be free to seek his own equilibrium.

Strict enforcements of standards of posture and movement are what men are suffering from today. Each tries a similar method when it is not similar methods that are needed. Any sort of standardized approach to posture tells a man what he may or may not do—in other words, what is correct bearing. This kind of dictation strangles any sense of liveliness before it has had a chance to grow. Spontaneous movement, free and flowing in mind and body, is crushed in the cradle. This type of standardization does not make us a nation of strong men but a nation of weaklings. It makes of us a people deluding ourselves and creating tensions and apprehensions in the process.

The liberated man will come awake to his own unique resplendence as he gives himself room to develop freely in his own manner, rising from the body torpor in which he has drifted.

The sort of self-appreciation discussed here is frequently attacked as narcissism. Fisher notes that this is the particular cry raised by our society when men take note of themselves with more than cursory attention. Society forgets that awareness of one's own beauty arises automatically in certain situations and adds to a sense of well-being. It keeps one conscious of one's body and of caring enough for it to keep it fit. It has extremely positive implications.

Men are shy about their bodies. They often do not know them well. Perhaps they knew them when they were children, but childlike wonder about the self vanishes too quickly. A child often knows every mark on and curvature of his body, but the puritanical strain in Americans makes them afraid of bodily realities, and so men have not carefully examined their bodies for many years. Men's shyness is intensified because women have often been directed away from their aesthetic appreciation of male contours, a problem we shall discuss in some detail in a moment. There are other reasons, certainly, for the male's insecurities, but since women are socialized into passive behavior, they may allow compliments to flow in only one direction. Thus in his relationships the male is often deprived of the feedback he needs to increase connections between his body and his sense of self-esteem. A man who lacks feeling for his body thumps through life tuned off, in essential ways, to himself.

This is one reason he becomes so hopelessly addicted

to any mannerisms in vogue. Since he has only a modest idea of what he looks like, he feels safer balancing himself as he sees others doing, which of course seldom works. Mimicry makes him uptight, as well as passive in the face of those values he allows to invade and use him as their manifestation. These values create the quirks that make him a cross between a robot and a saddle-sore cowboy, always trying to hold himself, sadly, as though he is half the ape that Darwin said he was—a chimp in a china shop, wearing boots and burning bills to light its cigar.

If you think I jest about men's postures and mannerisms, refer to studies made by test-prone authorities like Professor Fisher. He tells us quite emphatically that a "pool of new information has accumulated" to support generally the view that "the average woman feels more secure about her body than does the average man."[5]

This "new information" pool about the intense bodily insecurities of males is important to the theme of this book. If the experts are right, support increases for the thesis (expressed in the chapter on sexuality) that men are more insecure sexually than is commonly thought. In advancing his findings and those of his colleagues, Professor Fisher knows that he is contradicting commonly held opinions, but his view is based on the evidence of formal psychological studies in a field in which he himself is an innovator. His speculations as to why men are insecure are helpful but not necessarily complete. Culture bears the blame for the male's problems in this area more than does any biological difference. Religion, technology, and homophobic hysteria still impede the progress of the man who is afraid to appreciate himself or to be aware of his body in an intimate way.

Other researchers say that mothers are more open and free about showing their bodies to girls than are fathers, who cover their nudity in front of their sons.[6] This should be no surprise, given the "bigger than thou" fallacies and the homosexual taboo. Junior ends up being afraid to look not only at his father and at other men but also at himself.

The average man is considerably more excited and nervous than is a woman if he feels that some object has "bypassed his body's boundaries and gained access" to his interior. Fisher offers an interpretation: "The average man is reared in the tradition that his body should be like a fort. It should be impregnable and anything that tries to penetrate it is dangerous."[7]

This may be caused in some degree by the resistance men show to being passively absorbent, both mentally and physically. Resistance to penetration is tied to a more generalized resistance. Certainly there must be ways considered socially acceptable to allow receptivity in males to grow at early stages of their development. A sensitive educational program could nurture receptivity in children.

When men feel insecure, they look about for role models, not content to build a body culture that would consist of those mannerisms they find most comfortable and useful to themselves. Dr. Robert E. Gould, professor of psychiatry at New York's Medical College, says:

> Society's masculine ideal is John Wayne or Humphrey Bogart—silent, unemotional and strong. But most men aren't like that and I'm not sure they should be. I can picture John Wayne fighting Indians or brawling in a bar, but I can't picture him talking for three hours with a woman. . . . Unfortunately, most of us want to be John Wayne.[8]

If men are programmed to look outside of themselves for role models, then it is no wonder they fail to look at themselves carefully, to appraise themselves by their own internal standards and not by external ones.

Yukio Mishima said that women are not helping men

gain a physical sense of themselves. In his book *Kinjiki* he complained that women do not see male beauty: "Insensitive almost to the point of being blind, they have a discerning eye for male beauty not greatly different from that of a normal male." This may be a natural outcome of women's inferior status, which has produced manipulative tendencies that trade exclusively on feminine charms. In short, the manipulator knows that she must allow her own fascinations to be emphasized out of proportion to those of the male she manipulates. If she gives evidence of appreciating him too much on the physical level, she will dash his image of her as Virgin Madonna. Esther Vilar charges that women, unlike men, "never judge the opposite sex from an aesthetic point of view."

I do not believe that women are quite so incapacitated that they can never appreciate men aesthetically. Kinsey's figures show that only 15 percent of all women are aroused by pornographic photographs. This need not mean that 85 percent of the female population is incapable of arousal by sight but merely, perhaps, that many have been trained away from it. One must concede that pornography usually offers little in the way of more total involvement of body and feeling, factors many women may miss as they peruse it. It may be true that men are more readily excited by the *sight* alone of a naked body. Often, if not usually, men (regarding women as of an inferior breed) have not looked to women because of their inner qualities. Women, seeing things the other way (often regarding men as superior), have sought contact with men's inner qualities, hoping to determine if those men can be trusted (as providers) over a lifetime.

If it is true that men often bypass women as minds and see them as bodies, it is also true that women often bypass men as bodies and see them as minds. Here is a point at which a battle of the sexes need not take place and with which women can assist men and themselves by showing joy and appreciation for those men, giving them feedback about bodily awareness, particularly if the male's feelings show instead of being hidden. As this happens, men, for their part in this two-way exchange, can seek out women beyond their bodies by getting to know them as people who do not in any way resemble the pedestalistic visions vouchsafed by those who suffer such visions. Equality of the sexes must include equality of the right to aesthetic *and* mental appreciation. If men and women reach for each other in both of these directions, a giant step will be taken toward the equalization of the sexes. Mind and body are both very closely related, if not actually mirrors of each other. They are near the base of role reversal.

On the one hand, men would become aware that a significantly larger proportion of the female population found them attractive in a physical sense, and such a realization might go some way toward eliminating rape. Also, if men took care of their bodies better than they do, they might live longer. At present it just so happens that "the female body is considerably more resistive to various body ailments and disabilities and survives longer than the male."[9]

At the same time, a male with better body sense awareness would not be likely to rush through a sexual experience so quickly. His ability to receive pleasure would keep him lolling longer, without suffering the presently over-focused drive to orgasm, often the curse of the missionary position. With as many women showing aesthetic appreciation of men as men showing appreciation of women as whole beings, there would be fewer opportunities for manipulation. Men would know that women are not Madonnas, and that would be perhaps the first significant step they might take toward finding out precisely what particular women are really like, since women are fully human and therefore as potentially curious and adventuresome and sensual-sexual as men. The woman in this two-way passage would rely more on her personality and knowledge and less on her physical "charms," abandoning a rich source of manipulative potential. There are those old-fashioned women everywhere who would object to this loss, as well as to the necessity that they become individuals instead of remaining dependent but elusive butterflies. The male would discover what he lacks: a sense of his own image and an urge to self-care. When hippies began to introduce unisexual styles into fashions and when males began to let their hair fall to their shoulders, many sought to recapture a more acute sense of self-appreciation. In the era of obligatory short hair fewer men were conscious of their images. Their pants were baggier, and they wore drab, lifeless colors. Only the female was allowed to bloom, to wear colors and feathers. Now the male is returning to himself, however, and promises to be as beautiful a peacock as any. Fashion's varieties are endless and should be. It is here, more than any place else, that I would be tempted to draw upon ethologists for support, letting them, if they would, point to the magnificent coats and plumage in the wilds and report back on the great numbers of extraordinarily beautiful males. Since comparisons of human and nonhuman characteristics are merely speculative, though, they can only be superfluous.

What the male might be expected to react to negatively at first would be the female's initial attempts to express her feelings actively as she gains new dimensions of physical awareness. Many women would bungle their first active steps and would find men recoiling under an aggressive touch, saying that their bodies feel as though they're being picked at, that they're being tickled, and that they prefer the feeling of being dominant, even if dominance is an illusion and is destructive of long, playful sexual relationships. Because of his insecurity in his body, a man may insist that little or no attention be paid to it and that he be the *director* of the sexual moves taking place, but such a man can learn the "profound lesson of reception," the ability to absorb both mentally and physically. As he does, he becomes a better partner because he is more cooperative. He allows the woman in his company to demonstrate the richness of her awareness, and being on the receiving end of her awareness, his self-image expands. What takes place, simply, is an exchange. She actively appreciates. He passively accepts her appreciation. He actively seeks her personality and mind. She yields not her image but her *self* to the scrutiny, an act that requires far greater trust and passivity on her part.

Men cannot conceive of themselves as beautiful as long as they are subject to an aesthetic value that promotes as most beautiful a creature who must always be protected. To assist men in gaining a sense of themselves, therefore, women could assume more varied postures, some that indicate what the manipulative woman doesn't want anybody to know: *that she can claim to be stronger,* that her body is more disease-resistant than a man's, and that she lives longer.

With this fact in front of us, the question of which sex is the stronger is reduced to arbitrary definitions. If males always associate the need for protection (on the part of women) with beauty, they will miss (because of the tendency to dominance) their own beauty. In other words, believing that he is dominant, a male cannot conceive of himself as needing protection, which is as untrue of him (all humans seek nurture) as it is of a woman's phony and exaggerated emphasis on this need. Since he relates to this softness and this "need" of protection as a primary attribute of women, he sees beauty only in the faun, an image he does not fulfill himself. Hence his own beauty, no matter how great it may be, goes unnoticed by him. What happens to men of this kind is this: They do not *feel* themselves, and their female companions do not help them feel. Instead these men insist on one-way passage: They *get to do,* a feeling that may account for the odd belief prevalent among certain men that in sex women are "letting men *do things* to them," an exceedingly circumscribed perspective on any relationship. In any cooperative exchange either partner must be free to be acted upon as well as to act upon. Speaking of women who have given up their dreams of handsome movie stars and who "settle for Harry with a bulging stomach or George without a muscle on his skinny body" because these men offer them a financially secure future, Julius Fast writes that later in life "somehow the woman comes to feel that she has sold her birthright and the right to a sexual esthetic, among other things, for an economic mess of lentils. This is one of the key points of man-woman incompatibility."[10]

The burden for liberating the male's body cannot rest with the opposite sex, however. It remains with men. It may be possible that liberated women are right not to admire men physically as long as values such as domination, control, dependence on intellect, and competitiveness shine through their features. This means that the way to image change conceivably lies in a man's own will to reflect new values. If he is able to become sensitive, perhaps, instead of hard-looking, he may find himself able to register feelings on his face which would make him quite beautiful. If this happened, women might easily see and be awed by male beauty. As it stands now, how can one be expected to react rapturously to the stone-faced ape man?

There are three major avenues along which men can gain a sense of themselves, restore their balances, increase freer expression in their bodies, and appreciate their own beauty. The first is through themselves alone. The second is through exercise and sport. The third is through relationships.

A worse than commercial kind of ugliness originates with a man's inability to see through the social charades he plays and with the consequent reductions, therefore, in his responses to himself. New values in place of old masculinist ones would give his manner freedom for a fuller range of expression and hence a greater chance for beauty. A man may be homely without being ugly. He is homely only by conventional standards but can be attractive because the spirit of his new values shines in him. He remains ugly as a rule if he judges himself by conventional standards, failing to reflect sensitivity and trying to remain tough-looking and hard. Not allowing himself to reflect his feelings on his face, he remains attached to old external standards of self-measurement, and his body becomes unsynchronized. He can correct this imbalance himself, as has been said, by reshuffling values. This reshuffling will reflect itself in his self-care, in his moments of play, and in his relationships with those women who will see his inner beauty reflected physically. When his intimates reflect their joy and appreciation of him back onto him, he will become a new man and will experience a new appreciation of his body.

Whoever you are, how superb and how divine
   is your body,
or any part of it.[11]

Chapter 21 ✳ CONCLUSION
Men's Liberation—
Past, Present, and Future

We are what we think, having become what we thought.
—GAUTAMA BUDDHA

The existence of a men's liberation movement is new, but the philosophies and perspectives it embodies are ancient. Through the centuries only a few have adhered to its principles consciously; others have followed them without characterizing themselves as liberated. Now the tempo of the times, the emancipation of women, and the rise of technological and rationalistic structuring necessitate a more distinct awareness, one in which men become cognizant of what to do to keep from being overwhelmed by the extremes of the era, building fulfilling lives free from worn-out value systems.

The philosophical roots of men's liberation might be said to have started as early as 600 B.C. with the *Tao Teh King*, reputed to have been penned by Lao-tzu. In the West, they have grown in such works as Walt Whitman's *Leaves of Grass*, which added (in 1855) a summons for the equality of the sexes coupled with an intense sense of bodily awareness and a celebration of sexuality that had been missing from the manuscripts of the East.

That Lao-tzu and Whitman, each representing their respective hemispheres, coincide and complement each other on so many fronts should give men hope, since there would seem to be an almost desperate need for cultural crossings in an age of East-West tension. The East, traditionally regarded as absorbent and passive, and the West, seen as

311

penetrative and active, need such basic bridges to pass over heavily guarded borders. Unfortunately, American men flee from poetry (claiming that it is sissified or that they do not understand it), but in doing so, have robbed themselves of spirited sources that buoy the inhabitants of other lands. Consequently, although the United States boasts an enormous publishing output, it lacks what many other countries have developed: an appreciation for certain muses and poets whose significance lies in the fact that their values permeate and affect whole populaces. This is not to say that America has not produced such muses but simply that they have not yet come into vogue in any appreciable way. Scotland's enthusiasm for Robert Burns or Iran's for Hafiz have no equivalent in the United States.

Part of the difficulty lies in the manner in which poetry is explained by twentieth-century critics, dull men and women whose fascination with intellectualized banter has elevated a lifeless preoccupation with fashion and structure, bypassing those life-giving breaths that some poets can impart. Bernice Slote writes:

> If one were asked to draw the face of twentieth-century poetry, he would very likely describe its intellectual complexity, its concentration into cubicles of wit, its wasteland derogation of possibilities, its lack of physical joy. He would, in fact, be describing the New Puritanism—that tradition of rigorously honed intellectualism in which the old worship of the soul has been replaced by the worship of the mind, but in which the same sort of exile is imposed on the body.[1]

The disdain felt by Americans for poetry stems therefore not only from the belief that it is somehow antithetical to masculine deportment but also from the fact that it has been kidnapped by masculinists who twist it within their own narrow bounds. The sensitivity that poetry is purported to impart is feared and misunderstood, since sensitivity itself is quelled by masculinist culture. It is difficult for American men to conceive of a poet who is robust and physical. Instead their professors have presented them with the antithesis of such poetry in the works of "respectables" like T. S. Eliot, who sing drearily of wastelands and who decry life, clinging to acceptable religious traditions. Far from being elevating and inspiring, the New Puritanism in poetry is, according to Slote, "fortified in the pulpit of nearly all contemporary criticism. While many readers have admired the classic excellences of the Eliot tradition, they have also viewed modern poetry (which is considered one and the same thing) with a vague sense of estrangement, of loss. Where is the song, the incantation, the magic, the passion of poetry? These seem to be sacrificed, like the body, to metrical essay, analysis, and exposition." Slote believes that modern poetry (which is the poetry of the New Puritanism) "takes on connotations of harshness, obscurity, dogma; it is colored by an intellectual pride and a wry despair." Hence Americans are left drifting without those fortifications of tone and emphasis that come from an association they might otherwise enjoy were they to lay claim to their own intuitive oracles. The philosophical basis for men's liberation, therefore, remains obscure.

Walt Whitman comes closest in the American tradition to exulting the alternatives advanced in this book, and it is for this reason that he can be designated as a prophet of men's liberation. Mysteriously, he saw himself as a prototype of men, an individual who contained within himself a host of universal qualities needed if men are to obtain their freedom in any meaningful sense. He called himself the poet of sexual equality and of the body and the celebrant of sexuality itself. He regarded himself as America's Muse, a status that many have allowed him without, unfortunately, having even a minimal understanding of what it is he says in his *Leaves of Grass*. D. H. Lawrence called him "the first white aboriginal," indicating that within *Leaves* there are manifestations of primordial urges that leap over artifice and etiquette, making a mockery of those nonessentials we presently associate with "civilized" behavior. A fundamental beat recurring through *Leaves* is that of affirmation. Perhaps no poet ever sang with such gusto about the perfectibility of man, flying in the face of those religionists and "scientific" instinctivists who insist on human depravity and aggression.

Not only is the Whitman tradition in harmony with Lao-tzu and the spirit of Zen Buddhism (Eastern outlooks enjoying rapidly growing attention among Western youths and intellectuals), but it coincides as well with the Vedantic mysticism of India, a fact that has been capably demonstrated by Dr. V. K. Chari in *Whitman in the Light of Vedantic Mysticism: An Interpretation.*[2] I call attention to this to suggest that the mating of East and West—of absorbent Mother Asia and of our own penetrating sphere —hints that the equalization of the sexes and the liberation of men may in fact already have roots that, if they are attended to, will grow stronger as each hemisphere moves positively toward mutual discovery. Whitman is important to Americans because he is their own product, and although his perspectives and values are still far from being widely appreciated, they nevertheless have germinated on native soil.

If Whitman has been little understood, the kind of liberation he represented has even more eluded American journalists. Recently there has been a spate of articles about the men's liberation movement which show the confusion of skeptics who wonder if men truly need their own movement. Some of these writers would have it that men's liberationists are attempting mere apologies to women who have convinced them of their chauvinism; others, more hostile, accuse newly organized males of outright masochism, of allowing themselves to be trampled upon and corralled by feminist argumentation. The earliest meetings of men bent on examining their masculinist upbringings have elicited ridicule from threatened traditionalists.

I was a guest speaker at one of the earliest of such meetings, one that took place under the auspices of Oberlin College in Ohio and that to date has enjoyed the most widespread attention from the press. I was appalled to find *Ms.* magazine represented by a rather disgruntled music critic, whose summary of much of the conference's proceedings was caustic and cruel. He castigated a young Oberlin student (whose first public speech had been delivered on the occasion in the presence of his parents) as "a quiet, nervous senior . . . whose potential is best developed from within a supportive movement." The *Ms.* writer continued: "He seemed so terrified of his audience that he read his entire speech in a stiff monotone."[3]

Another account of the conference appeared in the Roman Catholic magazine *Commonweal*, and its author, Dennis Hale, subtitled the piece "Grappling with Some Bewilderments Spawned by Women's Lib." Hale's approach, which diplomatically could best be described as gimpy, demonstrated that he could not conceive of men's liberation as having its own raison d'être, and hence the meaning of the conference for him was "most eloquently summed up" by a nineteen-year-old youth whose "voice was cracking with anxiety" and who said: "I don't even know what's going on around here." Hale concluded that the very idea of a men's movement is "almost silly."[4]

Half a year later *The New York Times* reported sympathetically on men's liberation as "an unorganized but significant movement," claiming that it is "a force to be reckoned with."[5] These complimentary words appeared, strangely, in a section of the *Times* usually perused by women ("Family, Food, Fashions, and Furnishings"), but the hopeful nature of the article would not go unnoticed. Perhaps the media, eager for a different slant, will be ready to welcome men's liberation after over half a decade of continuous attention lavished on the sufferings of the opposite sex. *U.S. News & World Report* hailed men's lib as the latest trend, concentrating in its Establishmentarian way on the economic ramifications of the movement and exulting in the fact that men are now freer to become telephone operators and airplane stewards, a slant hardly geared to evoke enthusiasm about such a movement from men who have no particular desire to hold such positions.[6]

Misunderstandings and distortions in the media's coverage of a fledgling movement are hardly surprising, although there is hope that on the heels of women's liberation magazine and newspaper writers will see a need for corresponding changes in attitudes among men. It may be that writers, like any citizens, find the call for self-appraisal in the light of nonmasculinist values unsettling, and depending on their age and outlook, either cling to or wander from well-worn paths. Many are beginning to question commonplace assumptions about the inevitability of aggression, domination, and control and are seeing that men's liberation involves a revolution in values.

If solutions to the dilemmas of today's male are to be found, they will not originate with theories and formulas, nor will full-scale fusillades against the capitalist system or against the growth of technology have significant effects. Economics and technology are too abstract to claim the attention of the average citizen. Economic mismanagement and the misuses of technology will undergo increasing public scrutiny, but reformation will not come about because men understand what is transpiring and take steps for corrections. The average worker will probably never understand economic and technological intricacies.

The concerns of today's male must be brought closer to home: to what he wants himself, as opposed to what he wants for the system at large. It is his concern with himself that must be touched. The media will assist, as will consciousness-raising meetings where his troubles and insecurities can be honestly aired and where he will see that his frustrations are not unique to him alone.

Thus the liberation of each man from power complexes begins as a personal liberation. It originates with individuals rather than in the structures around them. It is unlikely that the system will readily crumble before the onslaughts of the disenfranchised and disgruntled. It will not respond to the harangues of political organizers. The system, domineering and exploitative, decays because of these very characteristics at the same time that liberationists are working to change it.

Neither the economic system nor the advance of technology can bear primary blame for social chaos. They add to the chaos, they give it strength, but they are only symptoms of maladies, not causes. The causes are more fundamental. They are rooted in the values to which men subscribe, and since men control most businesses, these values are reflected through the economic and technological structures they create. Today's machine economy is only an echo of traditional male attitudes. It is these attitudes that must change before a dent can be made in the system.

A saner society will flower when men liberate themselves from contrived, socially fabricated prohibitions, cultural straitjackets, and mental stereotypes that control and inhibit behavior through arbitrary definitions of what it means to be a man. When it is clear that the worship of the intellect is destructive, as are the idolization of competition, admiration for what is big, and the resort to violence as remedy, men will react differently to one another, with different expectations, priorities, purposes, and awarenesses. Instead of admiring top dogs, domineering masters and bosses, and instead of supporting power coups, they will regard such persons and their activities as anachronistic and counterproductive.

New alternatives to old ways will bring their own satisfactions and rewards. Men who once derived compensation from power manipulation will be helped to see how foul their exercise of "manliness" has been and may actually enjoy the discovery of who they are through honest feedback from their associates, enhancing their feelings, learning how to relax, to play, and to experience new heights of sensual awareness, finding themselves made newly aware through the immediacy of intuitive insight. As these occurrences take place in ever-widening circles, the system will be forced to adjust itself accordingly in such a way as to supply demands. The demands will be those of producers and consumers alike.

Economic theorists might condemn this perspective as impractical and illusory, believing that men will adopt new values only if the economic system is first changed. They are putting the cart before the horse and taking the long route. It is in the values that men now espouse that exploitation finds its justifications.

Marxists-Leninists, being masculinists as much as the next man, have adopted cooperative plans devised (for the most part) a century ago on what were, for those days, extraordinary intellectual constructs. Like all those who accept strict programming, however, they still follow various principles that conflict with unforeseen developments. Lenin could not have conceived of the unlimited power of nuclear bombs, for example, or it isn't likely he would have recommended (good masculinist that he was) *violence* as a means to overthrow a rotting regime.

A change in any society is not first apparent in its overarching framework. It occurs much nearer the center —in the aspirations and attitudes of those who have created its framework. An economy mirrors the values of those who take part in its erection. The values and the character of a people are much more profoundly ingrained than we assume, and as Mao has shown, one "revolution" only is not enough to bring about desired changes. Social behavior is rooted in values, and these lie deeper in the human psyche than mere theories and beliefs. Though new economic or religious ideas may win a man's allegiance, they may change rapidly, whereas his behavioral patterns do not.

Men often mistake theories, beliefs, articles of faith, creeds, and the like for values, not realizing that these, being outward expressions, are subject to rapid modification or dissolution. When Roman emperors proclaimed that their pagan subjects were Christians, surface beliefs may have changed, but pagan values retained strong holds.

Beliefs in any society are numerous and conflicting. Values are much less specific, are held by whole populations, and seem fewer in number. In contrast to beliefs, values are usually vague feelings about life and what makes it worthwhile. While beliefs are held consciously, values are hardly—if at all—consciously entertained. They have an abiding quality that derives, in part, from the fact that they *are* unconsciously held, the products of cultural conditioning which almost everyone receives but which few question. They are invisible sentinels, directing, guiding, warning, and signaling. They are powerful because they are imperceptible in ways that beliefs could never be. The man who chooses to believe does so consciously. He is aware of his belief. It is out in the open. Few men choose their masculinist values, however. These are hidden products of a culture and are transmitted covertly, without fanfare or election. The fact that they exist without being recognized and exert their influences without ostentation gives them far more power and durability than beliefs could ever claim.

If—at minimum—survival of the species is our concern, it is certain that masculinist values have outlived their usefulness in a nuclear age and are downright dangerous. These values are not particularly numerous, but they have become the foundation stones of "manliness" as interpreted in this culture. Thus no matter what a man's beliefs or political persuasions, he is subject to the influence of the sex-role values prevalent in his environment. Only by becoming conscious of their existence can he hope to circumvent them should he wish to do so.

An example of this is provided by the ideologists of the Right and of the Left. Members of both groups believe their values to be in conflict. Often on a deeper level they are not. The "values" they hold to be in conflict might better be called *ostensible values*—little more than beliefs. In a more fundamental sense, however, the Left and the Right can be seen as closer to each other than they think. Both groups are subject to conditioning that stamps them with badges of masculinist identity they do not question. Their solutions for social problems rise from the midst of this conditioning, without their being aware. Thus, the bomb-throwing leftist is akin to the red-neck rightist. Both use culturally accepted "manly" recourses to power, assuming that they are most effective means. The values moving them have implications that reverberate farther than bomb-throwing alone. One must not forget that they affect not only extremists but also politicians, Presidents, and premiers at the highest levels of the decision-making processes. Who can deny, therefore, that we must be wary of those unconscious motivations shaped by cultural definitions of male roles?

Since the social structure needs changing, let it be changed in response to changed values. Alternative ways of behaving are already manifesting themselves. There are historical accommodations taking place in response to the challenges of a disrupted civilization. These accommodations, having little of what could be referred to as conscious planning or design, seem almost miraculous.

To change values in this age of mass communications is infinitely easier than to assault the economic structuring of nations. These structures are crumbling because of their own masculinist obsessions, and it is certain that the old values are now subject to more than mere modification. Those who doubt this have only to review events of the past decade to confirm it. The media provide powerful vibrations, which are rapidly felt by the public at large. Americans, in response to increased perceptions, are accommodating themselves to a new world faster than academics of the fifties might have dreamed possible.

Anyone who recalls the milieu of the early fifties knows that the common man of that period would judge developments of today harshly. By standards then the young men of today would probably draw (and frequently still do) epithets such as PINKOS! QUEERS!

Today's youths have made heroes out of draft-dodgers.

PINKOS!

Who refuse to fight!

QUEERS!

For their country!

PINKOS!

They have blurred sexual identities by wearing bright-colored clothing and by growing long hair. Women are wearing blue jeans!

QUEERS!

If young people's values concerning war, employment, appearance, and sexuality have indeed changed or are in the midst of changing, these values are still struggling for recognition, development, and dignity. The rapidity with which society has accorded them a degree of all three is quite amazing. It would seem that in many cases the media somehow realize their roles as transformers and validators of new values. Which networks, newspapers, or magazines of the fifties would have called for amnesty for deserters?

Because of quick social evolution men, both young and old, are beginning to realize that the psychological baggage they have been carrying into office and home is far too heavy. They need a rest, and the old values, with their incessant demands for stiff deportment, are tiring. Taboos, restrictions, and constrictions are disappearing like bald eagles, but masculinist rulings die hard. Many people are not willing to admit that by the standards of the fifties they are pinko queers, and most haven't discovered this amusing fact yet. At present American males are experiencing guilts as they abandon old roles. The roles, after all, were once sanctified and revered.

Where do men go now? They stand at new crossroads, unable as yet to see the damage wrought as they strain themselves to be domineering and competitive. To assist in bringing about changes without resorting to old masculinist methods of one-upmanship (even claiming to be "liberated" can be a form of one-upmanship) is a task for all men who are determined to be self-regulating and self-dependent. They must be men confident enough to say no when the society around them insists that they should live by antiquated precepts. The choice facing them requires courage. It is a choice between integrity and appearance. The man who chooses integrity is not afraid that others will run roughshod over him. He has confidence in all dealings with his fellow men because he has confidence in himself. He is not afraid of losing a mere job. He recalls these lines of Burns: "The coward slave, we pass him by; We dare be poor for a'that." The man who chooses appearances, who plays aggressive games and deceives through various exhibitions of status, has little confidence in others and cannot let go and be himself.

It is not necessary to drop out of society, as the early hippies suggested. "Dropping out" was an unfortunate choice of terminology. What is needed is a call to elevation or transcendence. "Dropping out" does not convey this feeling. Those who incorporate in themselves new values will risk "position" in the system by insisting that it provide them with greater satisfactions than it has. Failing to find these satisfactions and finding himself ejected, the new male will know that he has failed only by the standards of those who have ejected him and not by his own. He will enjoy the confidence that is his if he has been true to himself.

Liberationists, certainly, will advise young men to scrutinize a society that alienates its craftsmen from their work, makes friendships difficult, demands organized affectional relationships, and refuses to share its wealth equitably. They will point knowingly at those who do not love playfulness, who encourage scrambled races to "the top." They will denounce all judgments of men made according to title and position. They will postulate *pleasure* in every creative endeavor instead of *power* as the hallmark of a fulfilling existence. Uncovering the gross insecurities of those wedded to inflexible hierarchies and structures, they will give evidence of how these men turn others into rigid, plodding, spiritless serfs. It remains for male liberationists to clarify the roles such men are playing in their own strangulation.

NOTES

Chapter 1: Intellect

1. Alan Watts, *The Book* (New York: Pantheon Books, Inc., 1966), p. 28.
2. P. Himmelstein, "Sex Differences in Spatial Localization of the Self," *Perceptual and Motor Skills,* Vol. XIX, p. 317.
3. "I'm tired of everlastingly being unnatural and never doing anything I want to do. I'm tired of acting like I don't eat more than a bird and walking when I want to run, and saying I feel faint after a waltz, when I could dance for two days and never get tired. I'm tired of saying, 'How wonderful you are,' to fool men who haven't got half the sense I've got, and I'm tired of pretending I don't know anything, so men can tell me things and feel important while they're doing it."—Scarlett O'Hara in *Gone with the Wind,* by Margaret Mitchell.
4. Florida Scott-Maxwell, *Women and Sometimes Men* (New York: Harper & Row, Publishers, 1971), p. 45.
5. Joe Adamson, *Groucho, Harpo, Chico, and Sometimes Zeppo: A Celebration of the Marx Brothers* (New York: Simon & Schuster, Inc., 1973).
6. *The Voice of the Silence,* trans. H. P. B. (Pasadena, Calif.: Theosophical University Press, 1971), p. 1.

Chapter 2: Feeling

1. Florida Scott-Maxwell, *Women and Sometimes Men* (New York: Harper & Row, Publishers, 1971), p. 23.
2. Ingrid Bengis, *Combat in the Erogenous Zone* (New York: Bantam Books, Inc., 1973), p. 36.
3. Drs. Jack O. Balswick and Charles W. Peck, "The Inexpressive Male: A Tragedy of American Society," *Family Coordinator,* Vol. XX (1971), pp. 363–368.
4. San Francisco Redstockings, "Our Politics Begin with Our Feelings," *Masculine/Feminine,* ed. Betty and Theodore Roszak (New York: Harper & Row, Publishers, 1969), p. 285.

Chapter 3: Intuition

1. Andrew Weil, *The Natural Mind* (Boston: Houghton Mifflin Company, 1973), p. 149.
2. Dr. Helene Deutsch, *The Psychology of Women* (New York: Grune & Stratton, Inc., 1944), Vol. I, p. 136.

3. Lankavatara Sutra, quoted in Christmas Humphreys, *Concentration and Meditation* (New York: Penguin Books Inc, 1970), p. 151.

4. *Ibid.*

5. *Ibid.*, p. 153.

Chapter 4: Mind

1. Dr. Margaret Mead, *Male and Female* (Harmondsworth, England: Penguin Books Ltd, 1950), p. 343.

2. Janet Chusmir, "Emotion, Logic Play Key Parts," Miami *Herald*, January 13, 1974.

3. Germaine Greer, *The Female Eunuch* (New York: Bantam Books, Inc., 1972), p. 111.

4. Valerie Solanas, *SCUM Manifesto* (New York: Olympia Press, 1968).

5. Walt Whitman, *Leaves of Grass* (New York: The New American Library, Inc., 1958).

Chapter 5: Roles

1. Myron Brenton, *The American Male* (New York: Fawcett World Library, 1966), pp. 49–50.

2. Robert G. Ingersoll, *The Works of Robert G. Ingersoll* (New York: C. P. Farrell, 1900), Vol. I.

3. George Gilder, *Sexual Suicide* (New York: Quadrangle/The New York Times Book Co., 1973).

4. Margaret Mead, *Sex and Temperament in Three Primitive Societies* (New York: William Morrow & Co., Inc., 1955), p. 190.

5. P. J. O'Rourke, *Screw*, March 20, 1972, p. 4.

6. Dr. Janet McCardel, quoted by Bill Hutchinson in Miami *Herald*.

Chapter 6: Instincts

1. Dr. Judd Marmor (ed.), *Sexual Inversion* (New York: Basic Books, Inc., 1965), p. 10.

2. Desmond Morris, *The Naked Ape* (New York: Dell Publishing Co., Inc., 1969).

3. Konrad Lorenz, *On Aggression*, trans. Marjorie K. Wilson (New York: Bantam Books, Inc., 1970).

4. Robert Ardrey, *The Territorial Imperative: A Personal*

Inquiry into the Animal Origins of Property and Nations (New York: Dell Publishing Co., Inc., 1971).

5. Sigmund Freud, *Civilization and Its Discontents*, ed. and trans. James Strachey (New York: W. W. Norton & Company, Inc., 1962), p. 58.

6. Patricia Sexton, *The Feminized Male* (New York: Random House, Inc., 1969).

7. Walt Whitman, *Camden Conversations*, ed. Walter Teller (New Brunswick, N.J.: Rutgers University Press, 1973).

8. Max Rafferty, speech at Florida State University, January, 1974.

9. John C. Raines, quoted by Robert J. Donovan, Los Angeles *Times* Service, January 18, 1974.

10. Robert Theobald, *The Challenge of Abundance: Free Men and Free Markets and the Guaranteed Income* (New York: Clarkson N. Potter, Inc., 1961).

Chapter 7: Playfulness

1. Robert M. MacIver, *The Pursuit of Happiness* (New York: Simon & Schuster, Inc., 1955).

2. Report issued by Andreson & Co., New York (1973).

3. Sydney J. Harris, Miami *Herald*, April 1, 1974, p. 7-A.

4. Gunther S. Stent, *The Coming of the Golden Age: A View of the End of Progress* (New York: Natural History Press, 1971).

5. Lao-tzu, *The Way of Life According to Lao-tzu*, trans. Witter Bynner (New York: G. P. Putnam's Sons, 1962), p. 37.

Chapter 8: Competition

1. Charles A. Reich, *The Greening of America* (New York: Random House, Inc., 1970), p. 23.

2. Ashley Montagu, *The Humanization of Man* (New York: World Publishing Company, 1962), p. 297.

3. John B. Connally, "A Time for Toughness in America," *Reader's Digest*, October, 1972, p. 88.

4. Richard M. Nixon, address to the nation, Labor Day, 1971.

5. Estes Kefauver, *In a Few Hands: Monopoly Power in America* (New York: Pantheon Books, Inc., 1965).

6. Morton Deutsch, "An Experimental Study of the Effects of Cooperation and Competition upon Group Process," *Human Relations*, Vol. II (1949), pp. 199–231.

7. Martin M. Grossack, "Some Effects of Cooperation and Competition upon Small Group Behavior," *Journal of Abnormal and Social Psychology*, Vol. XLIX (1954), pp. 341–348.

8. Leo K. Hammond and Morton Goldman, "Competition and Non-Competition and Its Relationship to Individual and Group Productivity," *Sociometry*, Vol. XXIV (1961), pp. 46–60.

9. Stephen C. Jones and Victor H. Vroom, "Division of Labor and Performance under Cooperative and Competitive Conditions," *Journal of Abnormal and Social Psychology*, Vol. LXVIII (1964), pp. 313–320.

10. Linden L. Nelson and Spencer Kagan, "Competition: The Star-Spangled Scramble," *Psychology Today*, September, 1972, pp. 53–91.

11. Thomas Boslooper and Marcia Hayes, *The Femininity Game* (New York: Stein & Day Publishers, 1973), p. 102.

12. Sherman Chavoor and Bill Davidson, *The 50-Meter Jungle: How Olympic Gold Medal Swimmers Are Made* (New York: Coward, McCann & Geoghegan, Inc., 1973).

13. George Sauer, quoted in an interview by Jack Scott, *Intellectual Digest*, July, 1972, p. 49.

14. Tim Holland, quoted in *The New Yorker*, January 14, 1974, p. 25.

15. Montagu, p. 297.

16. *Ibid.*, p. 301.

Chapter 9: Violence

1. Sydney J. Harris, "Strictly Personal," Miami *Herald*, April 25, 1974.

2. Robert Ardrey, in a dialogue with Louis S. B. Leakey on man the killer, *Psychology Today*, September, 1972, p. 75.

3. Dr. Erich Fromm, *The Anatomy of Human Destructiveness* (New York: Holt, Rinehart and Winston, Inc., 1973).

4. Hannah Arendt, *On Violence* (New York: Harcourt, Brace & World, Inc., 1970), pp. 6–7.

5. *Ibid.*, p. 80.

Chapter 10: Work

1. *The New York Times*, February 3, 1974, p. 14-E.

2. Associated Press, "Billion Live in Dire Poverty, U.N. Told," Miami *Herald*, February 12, 1974.

Chapter 11: Dominance

1. Drs. John Lewis and Bernard Towers, *Naked Ape or Homo Sapiens?* (New York: The New American Library, Inc., 1973), p. 89.

2. Robert G. Ingersoll, *The Works of Robert G. Ingersoll* (New York: C. P. Farrell, 1900), Vol. I.

3. Rachel Carson, *The Silent Spring* (New York: Fawcett World Library, 1967).

4. Alan Watts, *Nature, Man, and Woman* (New York: Random House, Inc., 1970), p. 61.

5. *Ibid.*

Chapter 12: Politics

1. Walt Whitman, *Leaves of Grass* (New York: The New American Library, Inc., 1958), p. 143.

2. Merle Miller, *Plain Speaking: An Oral Biography of Harry S. Truman* (New York: Berkley Publishing Corporation, 1974), p. 32.

3. I. F. Stone, Miami *Herald*, February 24, 1974, p. 4-N.

4. Dwight D. Eisenhower's farewell address to the nation, January 17, 1961.

5. Richard M. Nixon, in a speech at the Lincoln Memorial, February 12, 1974.

6. Richard M. Nixon, in a speech in Huntsville, Alabama, February 18, 1974.

7. Dr. Eli S. Chesen, *President Nixon's Psychiatric Profile* (New York: Peter H. Wyden/Publisher, 1973), p. 164.

8. Gerald Ford and Harrison Williams, quoted in *New York Post*, November 2, 1973, p. 4.

9. Gerald Ford, quoted in *Newsweek*, February 25, 1974, p. 30.

10. George E. Reedy, *The Twilight of the Presidency* (New York: W. W. Norton & Company, Inc., 1970).

11. Herbert L. Porter, quoted in Miami *Herald*, January 29, 1974, p. 8-A.

12. Gen. Thomas D. White, quoted in *Newsweek*, November 20, 1961, p. 27.

13. Martin Caidin, *When War Comes* (New York: William Morrow & Co., Inc., 1972), p. 50.

14. Marc F. Fasteau, *The Cult of Toughness in American Foreign Policy* (privately printed thesis).

15. Martha Mitchell with Winzola McLendon, "My Life in Washington," *McCall's*, March, 1974, p. 107.

16. Theodore Roszak, "The Hard and the Soft," *Masculine/Feminine,* ed. Betty and Theodore Roszak (New York: Harper & Row, Publishers, 1969), p. 93.

17. *Ibid.*

18. Charles A. Reich, *The Greening of America* (New York: Random House, Inc., 1970).

Chapter 13: Size and Status

1. "Sexitems," *Screw,* August 9, 1971, p. 17.

2. Seymour Fisher, *Body Consciousness (You Are What You Feel)* (Englewood Cliffs, N.J.: Prentice-Hall, Inc., 1973), p. 120.

3. Charles Drekmeier, "Knowledge as Virtue, Knowledge as Power," *Sanctions for Evil: Sources of Social Destructiveness,* ed. Nevitt Sanford and Craig Comstock (Boston: Beacon Press, 1972), p. 218.

4. Lionel Tiger, *Men in Groups* (New York: Random House, Inc., 1969) p. 254.

5. Studs Terkel, *Working* (New York: Pantheon Books, Inc., 1974).

6. "Enjoy Your Work and Take It Easy? You May Live Longer, Study Says," Miami *Herald,* February 17, 1974.

Chapter 14: Women

1. Simone de Beauvoir, *The Second Sex,* ed. and trans. H. M. Parshley (New York: Alfred A. Knopf, Inc., 1953), p. 688.

2. Walt Whitman, *Leaves of Grass* (New York: The New American Library, Inc., 1958), p. 97.

3. Dr. Joseph Katz, "Double Standard in Sex Is Gone," Miami *Herald,* March 2, 1974, p. 12-E.

4. *The New York Times,* November 15, 1973, p. 34.

5. Whitman, p. 105.

6. Lisa Jacobs, *Screw,* May 29, 1972, p. 8.

7. Ashley Montagu, *The Natural Superiority of Women* (New York: Macmillan, Inc., 1970), p. 114.

8. Ingrid Bengis, *Combat in the Erogenous Zone* (New York: Bantam Books, Inc., 1973), p. 108.

Chapter 15: Sexuality

1. Drs. William Simon and John Gagnon (eds.), *Sexual Conduct* (Chicago: Aldine Publishing Company, 1973).

2. Dr. Margaret Mead, *Male and Female* (Harmondsworth, England: Penguin Books Ltd, 1950), p. 86.

3. *Ibid.*, p. 198.

4. Germaine Greer, *The Female Eunuch* (New York: Bantam Books, Inc., 1972), p. 36.

5. *Ibid.*, p. 38.

6. *Screw*, March 13, 1972, p. 15.

7. Associated Press dispatch, October 26, 1973.

8. Dr. J. Dudley Chapman, quoted in Fraser Kent, "Despite the Revolution Sex Stupidity Abounds," Miami *Herald*, March 2, 1974, p. 17-E.

9. Greer, p. 35.

10. Dr. Alexander Lowen, *The Betrayal of the Body* (New York: Macmillan, Inc., 1969).

11. Michael Perkins, *Screw*, November 1, 1971, p. 16.

12. Dr. Eustace Chesser, *Strange Loves: The Human Aspects of Sexual Deviation* (New York: William Morrow & Co., Inc., 1971).

13. Drs. George L. Ginsberg, William A. French, and Theodore Shapiro, "The New Impotence," *Archives of General Psychiatry*, Vol. XXVI (March, 1972), pp. 218–220.

14. Norman Mailer, *The Naked and the Dead* (New York: The New American Library, Inc., 1948), pp. 440–443.

15. Germaine Greer, quoted in *Screw*, August 9, 1971, p. 5.

Chapter 16: Ladies

1. Thomas Boslooper and Marcia Hayes, *The Femininity Game* (New York: Stein & Day Publishers, 1973), p. 185.

2. Esther Vilar, *The Manipulated Man* (New York: Farrar, Straus & Giroux, Inc., 1972), p. 45.

3. Beauty shops are a multibillion-dollar business. The U.S. Department of Commerce predicts receipts will reach $4.7 billion in 1975 and $7.3 billion in 1980 (*Psychology Today*, April, 1974).

4. Vilar, pp. 68–69.

5. Walt Whitman, *Leaves of Grass* (New York: The New American Library, Inc., 1958), p. 258.

6. *Ibid.*

Chapter 17: Coupling

1. Associated Press dispatch, Miami *Herald*, December 4, 1973, p. 3-A.

2. Dr. John Money, "Playboy Panel: New Sexual Lifestyles," *Playboy*, September, 1973, p. 74.

3. Ann Landers, in Miami *Herald*, April 18, 1974, p. 5-F.

4. Walt Whitman, *Leaves of Grass* (New York: The New American Library, Inc., 1958), p. 72.

5. *Ibid.*, p. 184.

6. William J. Lederer and Don D. Jackson, *The Mirages of Marriage* (New York: W. W. Norton & Company, Inc., 1968).

7. *The New York Times*, August 7, 1966, p. 58.

8. Rustum and Della Roy, "Is Monogamy Outdated?," *Family Marriage and the Struggle of the Sexes*, ed. Hans Peter Dreitzel (New York: Macmillan, Inc., 1972), p. 343.

9. *Ibid.*, p. 332.

10. *Ibid.*, p. 334.

11. Wilhelm Reich, *The Mass Psychology of Fascism*, trans. Theodore Wolfe (New York: Orgone Institute, 1946), p. 44.

12. Judge Ben B. Lindsey and Wainwright Evans, *The Revolt of Modern Youth* (New York: Boni & Liveright, 1925), pp. 244–245.

13. Nena O'Neill and George O'Neill, *Open Marriage* (New York: M. Evans & Co., Inc., 1972).

14. *The Dhammapada*, trans. P. Lal (New York: Farrar, Straus & Giroux, Inc., 1967), p. 54.

15. Whitman, p. 193.

Chapter 18: Fatherhood

1. Germaine Greer, *The Female Eunuch* (New York: Bantam Books, Inc., 1972), p. 245.

2. Philip Roth, *Portnoy's Complaint* (New York: Random House, Inc., 1969).

3. Dr. Stanley Milgram, *Obedience to Authority* (New York: Harper & Row, Publishers, 1974).

4. Dr. David Cooper, *The Death of the Family* (New York: Random House, Inc., 1971), pp. 38 and 39.

5. Maria Montessori, *Il Bambino in Famiglia* (Milan, Italy: Garzanti Editore, 1956), p. 36.

6. Kahlil Gibran, *The Prophet* (New York: Alfred A. Knopf, Inc., 1923), p. 17.

7. Walt Whitman, *Leaves of Grass* (New York: The New American Library, Inc., 1958), p. 118.

8. George B. Leonard, *Education and Ecstasy* (New York: Delacorte Press, 1968).

9. Dean Harrison, "The Sensational New Birth Control Pills for Men," *Companion*, March, 1969, p. 52.

10. *Ibid.*
11. *Ibid.,* p. 48.

Chapter 19: Friendship

1. Dr. Margaret Mead, *Male and Female* (Harmondsworth, England: Penguin Books Ltd, 1950), pp. 104–105.

2. Dr. George Weinberg, *The Action Approach* (New York: St. Martin's Press, Inc., 1974).

3. Dr. George Weinberg, *Society and the Healthy Homosexual* (New York: Doubleday & Company, Inc., 1973), p. 1.

4. Walt Whitman, *Leaves of Grass* (New York: The New American Library, Inc., 1958), p. 257.

5. Alan Watts, *Does It Matter?: Essays on Man's Relation to Materiality* (New York: Random House, Inc., 1971), pp. 65–66.

6. Alan Booth, "Sex and Social Participation," *American Sociology Review,* Vol. XXXVII (1972), pp. 183–192.

7. Whitman, p. 115.

8. *The Advocate,* September 15–28, 1971, p. 15.

9. Snell and Gail Putney, *The Adjusted American: Normal Neurosis in the Individual and Society* (New York: Harper & Row, Publishers, 1964).

Chapter 20: Body

1. Edwin Kiester, Jr., "Mr. Efficient," *Human Behavior: The Newsmagazine of the Social Sciences,* May, 1974, p. 48.

2. Lao-tzu, *The Way of Life According to Lao-tzu,* trans. Witter Bynner (New York: G. P. Putnam's Sons, 1962), p. 49.

3. Seymour Fisher, *Body Consciousness (You Are What You Feel)* (Englewood Cliffs, N.J.: Prentice-Hall, Inc., 1973), p. 58.

4. *Ibid.,* p. 59.

5. *Ibid.,* p. 44.

6. A. Kacher, "The Discrimination of Sex Differences by Young Children," *Journal of Genetic Psychology,* Vol. LXXXVII (1955), pp. 131–143.

7. Fisher, p. 45.

8. Dr. Robert E. Gould, quoted in *U.S. News & World Report,* March 18, 1974, p. 49.

9. Fisher, p. 43.

10. Julius Fast, *The Incompatibility of Men and Women and How to Overcome It* (New York: Avon Books, 1971), p. 90.

11. Walt Whitman, *Leaves of Grass* (New York: The New American Library, Inc., 1958), p. 46.

Chapter 21: Conclusion

1. Bernice Slote, James E. Miller, Jr., and Karl Shapiro, *Start with the Sun: Studies in the Whitman Tradition* (Lincoln, Nebr.: University of Nebraska Press, 1960), p. 3.
2. V. K. Chari, *Whitman in the Light of Vedantic Mysticism: An Interpretation* (Lincoln, Nebr.: University of Nebraska Press, 1964).
3. Robert Christgau, "Are You Ready for Men's Liberation?," *Ms.*, February, 1974, p. 12.
4. Dennis Hale, "Do Men Need Their Own Movement?," *Commonweal*, January, 1974, p. 414.
5. *The New York Times*, June 11, 1974, p. 46.
6. *U.S. News & World Report*, March 18, 1974.